A Question of Balance

A QUESTION OF BALANCE

BOOK ONE OF
THE DOCTOR AND THE WITCH

TRISH REYNOLDS

Dedication

For Joan and Frank who never stopped encouraging me to find the magic within myself.

Disclaimer

All characters and places in this book are either fictitious or used fictiously. Any resemblance to actual persons living or dead is purely coincidental.

A Question of Balance
By Trish Reynolds
Cover art by Connie M. Neuber
Published by Pagan World Press,
a division of Dubsar House Publishing
ISBN 1-59405-502-5
Copyright © 2003 by Trish Reynolds
All rights reserved.
This book may not be reproduced, in whole or in part,
in any format whatsoever,
without permission from the author.

Contents

	The Theory	1
1	Conspiracy	3
2	Between the Worlds	7
3	New York	17
4	All Tied Up	33
5	Thanksgiving	45
6	The Institute	61
7	Heaven and Earth	73
8	Home Office	83
9	The Witch Goes South	87
10	Side Tracked	95
11	Reunited	99
12	Dartmoor	107
13	Tintagel	125
14	Troubles	141
15	Avalon	149
16	First Class	167
17	Hedgerows and Cairns	183
18	London	195
19	The Doctor	213
20	The Witch	233
21	The Merry Men	253
22	Bryn Gwddyn	265
23	As Above	279
24	So Below	293
25	Robin Hood	311
26	Tea	324

Bonus Excerpt from Book Two

The Theory

They say that over ninety percent of our Universe is composed of 'dark matter', invisible mass which exerts influence over every bit of matter. It neither reflects not transmits light and so is impossible to perceive with our human senses. This dark matter acts as a net keeping the galaxies in balance. It prevents the stars and their satellites from spinning off into whatever it is that exists outside our own Universe, and counters the pull of the light matter, which we observe as the stars.

The theory is that the planets, our Earth included, are all composed of this dark matter. Particles of it are constantly rushing around, even in and through our own bodies. It is, they say, the dust of exploded stars—the result of the Big Bang. Even we are composed of bits of dark matter, proteins and protoplasm, whose molecules and particles will endure as long as the Universe itself in one form or another; star stuff.

Perhaps it is the dark side of our spirit which keeps us in balance, keeps us from spinning off into some void beyond ether. I don't know. I understand that we need this other side of us. I also understand that when we become unbalanced, or the world we share becomes unbalanced, everything is threatened.

The other kind of matter, the kind that transmits light, is too bright for us to look upon directly. It too exerts its influence over all existing matter, balancing the dark.

I think, perhaps, that it is the balance between the two, ninety percent dark and ten percent light, that maintains the order which permits life to exist.

I am not a scientist. I am a witch.

TarishAnu Dickson

Chapter One
Conspiracy

The screen was filled with a woman's face, blue eyes, blond curly hair tangled around even, freckled features. It was a good face, pretty without being beautiful. Middle thirties, I thought. She looked like someone that might be nice to know.

"English?" I asked the huge man seated behind a desk of proportionate measure.

"American, Doctor, of Scots-Irish descent. Her name is Tarish Dickson and she lives in New Jersey, about fifty miles west of New York City. A former hippie, still highly idealistic, but pretty tough when it comes down to it. The extremely self-sufficient sort. Miss Dickson also has a highly developed sense of justice, if our intelligence is true. She's been married, a bad one, and is now single with a teenage son. No serious relationships in recent years. A car accident has left her right ankle permanently damaged. Occasionally, she uses a walking stick. According to her medical records the surgeons hadn't expected to save it at the time. They were quite surprised to find it healed as well as it did."

He pressed the pause release and the video tape continued. The woman was loading groceries into the back of an old Chevy estate car that had seen better days. She was talking to someone out of camera range. Sir went on.

"She is a Marketing Administrator for a large corporation. It appears that she is well thought of in her industry and has earned a number of awards for her technical writing."

"Her accent isn't New York, or even New Jersey for that matter. Difficult to place exactly." I mused out-loud.

"Educated in London, family in Sheffield, and a maiden aunt in Scotland. There are several dozen cousins in Ireland." His voice was devoid of any emotion. He was simply describing my newest subject.

"That would explain it, sir." I caught a flash from her left hand as she reached up to close the rear gate of car. "There Hold please." The picture froze. "Can I have a close up of that. Focus on her left hand." Now it was a hand with rings of various designs gracing each petite finger. I was only interested in one. "Yes, that's it, Sir. The Crown of Fae." I felt myself getting excited. "Is she..."

"A witch, Doctor. She practices a Celtic version of the neo-pagan Wicca. Her great-grandmother on her father's side was something of an infamous witch in Leitrim back in Ireland at the end of the last century. Apparently, Tarish has inherited her 'sight' and has elected a life-style which will support her use of what they call 'white magic' these days."

"And the ring? Do we know how she got it?"

He shook his head, multiple chins quivering. "No. We know only that it has surfaced and she has somehow acquired it. One of our spotters saw it on her at a recent conclave in Manhattan. It would appear she knows nothing about its history." He nodded again. "However that may be, Doctor, she holds the Crown and she is what we are stuck with."

"Has she any training? Extraordinary PSI potential?" I asked wondering how this pretty woman would hold up.

"Nothing that we know of." The screen went blank. "Report to Rollison in New York. He'll brief you further."

'Yes Sir." I stood and stretched.

"And Doctor..."

I groaned inwardly. I ksnew that tone of voice. I was about to receive the sermon.

"Yes, Sir?"

"Under no circumstances will I accept any breach of policy for any reason. Am I clear? This woman is not being recruited nor is she being sheltered. We merely need her to get the other two items. Secure her co-operation by whatever means necessary. Remember, Doctor, your objective is the Book. The woman is entirely expendable."

"I don't see how you could be any clearer, Sir." As a rule I really don't like using people, but there was too much at stake here to quibble over ethics.

I went to pack my bags.

Chapter Two
Between the Worlds

I'm a witch and so I feel I should have known there was something different about that day. I didn't. Being a practicing witch has its advantages and it's drawbacks. One of the drawbacks is being on every occult mailing list in the English speaking world. Yes, witchcraft is an occult science, but I'm not a crackpot. I don't send money to astrologers who promise to pick winning lottery numbers for me. I don't attend orgies in posh, private nudist camps. I'm a quiet, stay at home kind of person with a steady mundane job, a teenage son, an ex-husband and a car that quits on a regular basis. In other words, I'm just like millions of women in the United States today, except that I'm a witch. It's my religion as well as my way of life. I don't worship the devil.

Like so many of us, I receive junk mail on my PC both at home and in the office. On a Monday in late September I received the one that would change my life. As usual, I went through the e-mail quickly at my desk, relegating most of it to the recycling bin. There was one letter that was different. It just didn't feel like the usual spam. It came from someplace called BITS which apparently stood for British Institute for Technological Studies. Since I have family in England and had attended university there I didn't just junk it.

The letter said that my name had been taken from the mailing list of one of the occult organizations to which I belong. It went on to ask if I would consider being interviewed by one of their researchers, an anthropologist doing a study on practical occultism in today's society. For some reason I didn't toss it. Instead, I sent a reply and promptly forgot about it.

Two weeks later, I received a response. It was signed by a Dr. Arthur Neville Pendargroom MD, PhD, thanking me for responding to the inquiry. There was a telephone number to call in Manhattan to set up an appointment if I was truly interested in assisting in a study of occult practices. This was, the Doctor assured me in his letter, a serious study and my experience would be invaluable. I was intrigued. What kind of research would a technological organization be doing in the field of occult practices? How could I refuse? I phoned and was given an appointment for the following Saturday.

Travelling from north western New Jersey to the Big Apple on a Saturday using mass transit, is an adventure all on it's own. Being a witch gives me no special power when it comes to the foibles of our modern day transportation system. I arrived, somewhat disheveled at my destination, a smallish office building in midtown. From the outside it was an unimposing looking structure, but the security inside made me think I'd accidentally stumbled onto the New York headquarters of U.N.C.L.E. I was stopped at the front desk and had to walk through a metal detector first. Then I was scanned by a woman in an unattractive uniform that reminded me of a prison matron in an old Barbara Stanwyck movie.

Finally, in a small back office, I was asked to present my letter. The man at the desk phoned giving my name to someone on the other end of the line. He asked me to have a seat and wait without even the offer of a cup of coffee. In a few minutes I was introduced to a man who looked like he was in his late forties, but had had a rough time of it getting there. He was exactly what you'd expect an anthropologist to look like. About five feet ten, he was balding. What hair he did have was combed over to one side in an effort to cover the bare scalp which took up most of the poor man's head. He wore half glasses and peered, actually peered at me, over the rim. He smiled and held out his hand. I shook it and found to my delight, his was a firm grip, not one of those wishy-washy limp wristed. His name was

A Question of Balance

Rollison, but I was to call him Rolly, everybody did. He spoke with a soft accent, British, but with overtones of New York indicating he'd been living in the City for some years at least. I smiled back and handed him the letter.

He led me to a bank of elevators and pressed the button for floor five. As we rode, he explained that Dr. Pendargroom was funded through BITS by the British government and had published papers on the practical application of occult sciences for government use. I began to think that perhaps this wasn't such a hot idea. Shades of Ian Fleming crossed my mind as I pictured Her Majesty's Government recruiting entire covens; enlisting them in a secret war against terrorist magicians of the very most evil kind. I have a vivid imagination which is a plus working with magic.

The elevator stopped and we got off. If I thought security was tight below, it was practically non-existent up here. The place was a zoo. People were working frantically at computer stations, inputting data at a speed that defied explanation. There were several interview desks in open cubicles with room for two people to sit across a small writing surface. Several of these were occupied and I could see there were two different kinds of interviews going on. Real, actual interviews, where one person sat and asked another questions taking notes on a form and then there were the demonstrations. I'd seen this type of thing in movies of course. You know, where the researcher sits on one side, shuffling Zeiner cards and the psychic sits on the other rattling them off. Real Uri Geller stuff. To my untrained eye it looked like the psychics were doing well. I hoped that they wouldn't expect anything like that from me.

Then he strode through the chaos and all the confusion seemed to retreat from him. He was dressed in English country tweeds, with a white, open collar shirt that needed to see the business end of an iron. The Doctor looked like he was ready for a fox hunt not a research project. Beneath a mass of curly brown hair, a pair of very clear gray-eyes sparkled, as he introduced himself. I remember clearly what he said, in a rich baritone with just the proper 'public school' inflection.

"Hello, I'm the Doctor."

His grip was warm and cool at the same time, and he smiled at me. For some reason he reminded me of John Lennon when he smiled. He was very tall, about six three or four. He towered over my five feet three inches. I suddenly felt small and insignificant. This man had presence.

After thanking Rolly, he led me into a large private office with a view of the mid-town cityscape, at least, a view of the bricks next door. I wouldn't exactly call it Spartan, but it wasn't an elegantly furnished space. The thing that dominated the room was a computer work station that dwarfed anything I'd ever seen, and I work in a 'high tech' industry. There were two comfortable looking chairs, one of which I was led to. The other one, behind the main console, was his. He asked if a nice cup of Darjeeling would be to my liking. I asked him how he knew that Darjeeling was my favorite. He just tapped his forefinger against his nose, smiled and dialed Rolly to bring in the tea tray. I was fascinated to say the least. Perhaps it might be more accurate to say that I was mesmerized by this man, this doctor.

He had contacts in a coven in England with whom my coven was associated by tradition. I was impressed. The Doctor really seemed to know his stuff. He rattled off the names of several colleagues of his whose work in the field I was very familiar with. I wondered why I'd never heard of him. In fact, I wondered it right out loud.

His response was a smile and a wink. He preferred to remain anonymous, he explained. On that subject, he asked that I call him Doctor. It was a simple enough request, if somewhat affected I thought at the time. But then British academics are known for their eccentricities. Without thinking too much about it I agreed.

We parted that day with an appointment set up for one week away. He told me to come prepared to,

A Question of Balance

"Get down to some serious work." It was my turn to smile. Magic to me, was not, could never be work. He wanted to know if I needed any special kind of environment. I said just some quiet space. The interview was over and I was amazed to find we'd been talking for nearly three hours. Oddly it didn't seem like any more than an hour had passed since I'd first entered the building. He walked me to the door and I went home.

As a witch, I'm used to travelling 'between the worlds' as we call it. That is the altered state in which we meditate, work magic and travel astrally. Each night before I sleep, I meditate and put myself into a between state. Usually I don't cast spells, my life seems to work out for the most part without any intervention. On the whole I tend to worship rather than manipulate. That night I went to sleep as usual. Except that my sleep wasn't usual.

I dreamed vividly that whole week. In fact, I think I was not so much dreaming as projecting myself to a between state and travelling there. I was with the Doctor every night in this way. He seemed very comfortable on this level, and showed me around enthusiastically. After two or three nights of this, I finally decided that if we were going to be travelling companions in the dreaming world, I was going to have to have more control. I consulted a shaman friend, an expert on lucid dream travel, and got some pointers. That night I was ready.

When we met in the dream state, I asked him a few questions. His answers were vague at best. I decided it was time to take control. I visualized my conception of what the dreamscape should look like and it came to be instantly. For a moment he stopped and stared around him as though he didn't know what to do. Then, he laughed and squeezed my hand tight.

"Will you help me?" he asked.

My answer came even before I knew what I was going to say.

"Yes, of course I will. What are we doing?"

He told me a story about balance, specifically the balance of light and dark in the Universe. Well, I was already familiar with the concept. That's part of what we do, we witches. We try to achieve a balance in our lives and in our existence on all levels. We try to keep a balance between the light and dark in ourselves and stay in tune with nature. If we can accomplish that, probably over the course of a number of incarnations in the material realm, we will have achieved something.

The Doctor explained that there are some times when the balance tips too far to one side and someone has to help to tip it back. When this happens, the entire order of the Cosmos is threatened with eternal chaos. Sounds a lot like today's world.

He was very serious, though. The power from which all else sprang, he explained solemnly, would not interfere in the course set into motion by its sentient beings; Free Will and all that. So, he went on, he'd been chosen to try and restore the balance if he could, with whatever help he was able to recruit. I told him I'd help and I wasn't about to back off now. Besides, it was only a dream. He told me to prepare for our next mundane appointment by meditating on the Tarot; Justice, the card of the Major Arcana which represents balance.

I woke up in the morning exhausted, wondering if I was going crazy or what and it only got worse.

In spite of everything that was going on in my head, I managed to get to work. I couldn't concentrate very well, this 'dream' kept dogging me, playing itself over and over again in my mind. Finally, I picked up the phone and called. I was informed politely, that the Doctor wasn't available, but did I want to speak to Rolly? I didn't. Angry now at being blown off, I slammed the phone down and got to work, pushing everything else out of my mind. My conscious mind anyway.

That night, after my meditation, I lay awake in bed. It wasn't that I was afraid to go to sleep. I just preferred not to. About two in the morning, however, my resolve lost out to fatigue and I must have drifted

A Question of Balance

off. Suddenly, he was there, looking as though he'd been waiting for hours.

"What took you so long, eh? This is no time to be suffering from insomnia; we have work to do."

"Look," I began cautiously. "I think I must be going crazy or something. I mean, this is a dream, right?"

"A dream? Well, of course it's a dream, in essence. But that doesn't change anything," he said. "You did promise to help. The balance, remember?" He smiled that John Lennon smile at me.

"Just one thing," I said, placing my hand on his arm. "Before we go, can I ask you a personal question?"

"I don't see how I can stop you asking," he said, staring down at me with large soulful eyes.

"Are you married?" There, I'd said it. I don't know why it mattered. It was only a dream, after all. I had no romantic interest in the Doctor in real life anyway. I hardly knew him. Besides, he was just too weird, even for a witch.

Smiling gently he shook his head. "No. I'm not. Now, can we get on with it?" There was just a touch of impatience in that last phrase. It annoyed me.

"Get on with what? I still don't know what in Hades we're supposed to be doing." I refused to move. Firmly, I stood my ground awaiting an explanation.

"Of course you do, Tarish. We're going to help restore the balance. I explained all that to you." Now, the impatience was clear.

"But how?" I cried, exasperated. " I mean, I know how to balance my own life, at least how to try, but how in the name of Luna do we balance the whole world? Forgive me for saying so, but this sounds like the plot of a Saturday morning cartoon adventure."

"The Universe," he said quietly. "It's not just the world, Tarish. It's the whole thing and we're wasting time." He took my hand, and it gave me chills. "You belong to a community which attempts to do much good for your world. And, you do, you do. But you're going about it in a higgledy-piggledy sort of way. You need to have more focus. The amount of energy that you people waste is unbelievable, practically criminal."

Just what I needed in my life, I thought, a certifiable lunatic. He seemed to read my mind.

"No," he said. "I am not crazy and neither are you. Don't worry, you'll get used to it."

I wasn't so sure.

"There are three things, Tarish. Three symbols, if you will, of the Power that balances all things. They are the Crown of Fae, The Key of Enlightenment, and the most important thing, the Grimoir of Infinity. Without the book the other two are relatively useless. Oh, they have power of their own, to be sure, but to be effective, powerful enough to alter the whole balance, the Key, the Crown and the Grimoir must be held by one person. The Grimoir gives detailed instructions for releasing and using the power." The Doctor gripped my hand and started walking.

"That's the problem, do you see? We have to recover the Key and the Grimoir and take them out of play, that way the balance will right itself and maybe even tip a little in our favor." He grinned at me. "That would buy us some time I think. Maybe even enough for a little holiday."

"Oh, is that all," I said. "But you forgot something."

"Did I?" he exclaimed, stopping. "What was that?" His eyes were sparkling again and that made me nervous.

"This Crown of Fae. Don't we need that too?"

"Oh that." he laughed. "We already have it." He lifted my hand and pointed to my pinkie ring which my sister had discovered for me in a small antiques shop in Ireland. I stared, it did look like a tiny crown. More a coronet, actually. I shrugged.

"So, where do we get the Key?" I asked.

He smiled again and began walking along a road that looked suspiciously like it might wind up at the Emerald City. I followed along.

This yellow brick road didn't lead to anywhere in Oz, though. At least, not that I recognized. No

A Question of Balance

Scarecrow, no Tin Man. Not even a housecat. It did lead to a large room. No building or anything, just a door in the landscape that opened onto a large room.

The room was furnished in early Victorian, very period quite lovely, in fact; a perfect parlor setting. A door on the far side of the room creaked open slowly.

I positioned myself to the best advantage right behind the Doctor. Whatever was coming out of that door, I wanted to be sure it didn't see me first. I'm not a coward or anything in my nightmares, I'm always powerless against the monster behind the door. It was suddenly flung wide and the monster started towards us. Its form was vague and indistinct as it stalked the Doctor and me. Here I was sharing my own nightmare with a man I hardly knew. I could sense the Doctor was scared. I could feel him quaking. This thing was huge and hairy and hungry. I really wanted to get out of there. I really did, but of course the door we'd come in through was gone. There was nothing behind me but blank wall and I had forgotten all my lessons in dream travel completely.

I've read somewhere about how a Native American tribe taught their children to overcome fear. They were taught that in a nightmare, they were to confront the creature of their worst fears. Not only that, but they were to ask for a favor, a talisman of some kind. That was supposed to give the child power over the monster, and thus over his fear.

Well, I'd already run out of places to back up to and was now in danger of being squashed by six feet four inches worth of quivering scientific researcher. I stepped around him and confronted the beast.

"You are a product of my fear," I said, bravely. "You must grant me a favor. Give me a symbol of your friendship."

The monster shape shimmered and seemed to kind of melt, then re-form. Suddenly I found myself staring into the face of my tenth grade geometry teacher. Without a word, he lifted a long chain from around his neck. From the silver chain dangled an old brass key, the kind that somebody's grandma used to lock the jelly cupboard with. He held it out to me. It had worked! As soon as the key touched my fingers, the music started. My clock radio. It was time to get up and start another day.

Chapter Three
New York

It was Saturday again and time for my second appointment at the Institute. Once more I braved the New Jersey Transit System and arrived on time. I had brought with me the tools I would need to do some simple spell casting; my athame, a double edged knife with a black handle used for casting the circle, a small cauldron, consecrated candles and a sea shell.

This time Rolly was waiting for me in the lobby and checked my belongings through without having any security conscious matron pawing them over. We took the elevator to the seventh floor. When the doors slid open, the quiet struck me with the force of a blow. There was absolute silence. I was led to a semi-darkened room and told that the Doctor would be in shortly, but to go ahead and set myself up. He left me alone while I did just that.

By the time I had the altar arranged to my satisfaction on the table provided, the Doctor had arrived. He winked but I couldn't trust myself to say anything. He was wearing a long silver chain around his neck. I couldn't see what was on the end of it, he had it tucked into his waistcoat, but I had a sinking feeling that I knew.

"Shall we have some tea before we start?" he asked, eyes crinkling around the edges.

I managed to nod dumbly. He guided me with a hand under my elbow to a smaller room down the corridor from the one where I'd set up. There was a coffee station and a pot of hot water with some tea bags. I reached for a paper cup and a tea bag. He stopped me.

"You should never drink good tea from a paper cup, Tary, it's bad form." He smiled and handed me a china cup and saucer.

During all this time, I still hadn't managed to utter a single word, which was very out of character for me. Finally, I left the tea to steep and smiled up at him tentatively. I couldn't decide whether or not to mention the dream. As it turned out, I didn't have to.

"You are very clever, you know. You've an instinct for this sort of work, I think." He was stirring his own tea casually.

"I do?" I gulped. I wasn't really sure just what he meant by that.

"Yes, you do. Who was that chap, by the way? You know, the one that the monster morphed into. Someone from your dark and misty past?"

"Uh, you mean the dream?" I stammered, feeling freaked.

"Why, have you been travelling with someone else recently? How many monsters do you usually run into in the course of a week, Tarish?" He lifted my face gently with a finger under my chin. I got lost in those gray-eyes.

"It was an old teacher of mine," I blurted. "Geometry."

"Ah, mathematics. I might have guessed that'd be your weak point. Well, not to worry, we can't all be good at everything." He pointed to my tea, which was getting quite strong by now. "Why don't you fix that and take it with you. If we're to get anything accomplished today, we should get started."

"Oh yeah, sure." My mind was racing a mile a minute, but nothing intelligent or even semi-intelligent would come out of my mouth. I added sugar and cream to my tea and followed him out.

Back in the room where my things were laid out, I got some of my confidence back. "How did you do that?" I asked, looking him straight in the eye.

"What? You mean the dream? Well you did invite me. Very hospitable of you really, considering we've only just been introduced. But Tarish, I'd be more careful if I were you. You can't trust just anybody these days." He grinned at me and pointed to the altar.

"Now, are you ready to start?"

He'd set some instruments about the room, just within the circumference of where I would be casting the circle. "These are for measuring energy. They're very sensitive and will register the slightest change both within and without. I've done this sort of thing before, and they shouldn't effect what you're doing."

"Okay," I replied brightly. "Are you going to stay?"

"Oh no. I don't want to interfere with your concentration. I'll be right next door. When you're done, just pop in and let me know. Are you prepared to cast a spell?

I explained that I would cast a solitary circle and then a spell. Nothing spectacular, just a little weather working. The forecast had been calling for rain. I was going to try to push that front out to the east over the sea and get the sun to shine. That's not as hard as it sounds, and it's very impressive as long as the conditions are all there. He nodded and left me to my task.

When I had finished I opened the circle and gathered my things together into my backpack. I was just done, when the Doctor knocked and entered without waiting for me to reply. He checked his instruments carefully then looked at me.

"You are good. These readings are very high. There was quite a static electrical buildup. We don't usually get readings that high from a solitary ritual. You've raised a respectable amount of energy, young lady." He raised an eyebrow. "But then, I suspected that you would, especially after the other night."

"Can we talk about that, please?" I asked. "I'm still a little nervous about all that stuff you told me about the balance, especially if it wasn't all just a dream. I mean, I can't take on saving the whole world. My own life is tough enough to deal with most times, without taking on that kind of responsibility." Besides, I thought, I can't even balance my checkbook.

"I understand. Listen, why don't you try something for me tonight. When you go between call your guide and ask her—it is a her, isn't it?"

I nodded.

"Yes, I thought it would be. Ask her to explain where you fit in. It will be more effective coming from someone you trust. I won't intrude. If, after you've done that, you still want to call me I'll be there." He patted my shoulder. "The Grimoir won't be so easy as the Key. You work very well in the Invisible Realm, but the Book is in this world, Tary, and it's in the possession of a rather nasty group. I don't want to mislead you in any way; there could very well be some danger associated with getting it back. Real, physical danger."

I didn't know what to say. He had given me a lot to think about here. For one thing, why me? I guess anyone put into the position where they have to do something inexplicable would feel that way. But I was really nobody very special. I knew lots of people better than me, further along on the path. Why not one of them? I supposed I would have to do as he suggested and hope that my guide would explain it in terms I could understand. She often spoke in riddles, but then, that's typical of oracles, spirit guides and the like.

That night as I tranced, I called for the Unicorn to guide me. She has been my friend and confidant in the Invisible Realm since I was a small child. As usual, I waited in the beech grove. She didn't keep me waiting long.

"Sometimes, it is those who need to learn the most who are sent," she told me. "You have not yet fulfilled your vision. Consider this to be your time. You shall experience the Vision of the Universe through this man, and he will gain immeasurably from your trust."

"But what if I blow it?" I cried. "I mean, is this for real? Can what happens on this plane really have such an effect on the material?" I knew it sounded stupid. That's how magic works, after all. We send into the invisible world to have our will manifest in

A Question of Balance

the material world. She just smiled, knowing what passed through my mind even as I did myself.

"Let him lead you this once, child. You can only do what your heart tells you is right. If you do that, you will not fail."

The Unicorn disappeared and I was left by myself in the silver grove. I brought myself out of trance and climbed into bed. In less than ten minutes, I was dreaming and the Doctor was waiting.

"Well, what's your answer?" He was pacing impatiently.

"Like I said before, I'll help you the best I can. I have to tell you though, I'm not entirely sure that this is all real. I mean, even a witch sometimes has doubts, and this is pretty far fetched, you'll have to admit." I don't know what he was expecting, but the relief on his face was clear.

"Here," he said. He took the chain from around his neck and hung it around mine. The brass key dangled against my breast. "Go on, touch it. Feel it in your hand. It's real, Tarish and solid. When you wake up, it'll be there, just as real and as solid as it is now."

"But, I thought you said that in order to be powerful enough to affect the balance, the Key and the Crown had to be held by one person?"

He nodded silently.

"Oh no. Not me. I don't want that kind of power. What makes you think I won't throw everything off? Are you crazy?" I was appalled at the idea of holding so much power in my own inept hands.

The Doctor tapped a finger against his nose and smiled that smile. Once more I lost myself in the depths of those gray eyes and then it was morning, a beautiful and sunny October Sunday morning. I reached down and there was the chain and the key. Suddenly, the sun just didn't seem so bright and I felt chilled.

Monday I contacted my shaman friend Sam again. The big question of the day was have you ever brought anything out of a dream with you. He smiled and told me yes, upon occasion it is possible. I didn't explain why I wanted to know. I still figured that there was a "reasonable" explanation. Maybe the Doctor had slipped it on me before I left the Institute that day. I was beginning to think I was hypnotized or something. Well, whatever the explanation, it was a Monday, and I still had to make a living in the mundane world.

Rolly called me several times that week, to ask questions that he said the Doctor wanted to know. Finally, I told him that if the Doctor wanted to know something, he could jolly well call me himself.

It was Wednesday and I'd just gotten home from work, after spending an hour on a twenty-minute commute because of traffic. My son Jace was nowhere to be found and I was understandably a bit waspish. I hadn't been sleeping well. I was also fasting for the month of October. A small sacrifice, symbolic of preparation for the dark time of the year. The period between Mabon and Samhain is when we prepare ourselves to bid the God farewell on October 31, as the Wheel of the Year journeys into winter.

I'd changed into my workout clothes and was busy peddling the stationary bike when the doorbell rang. I admit, I was cursing, expecting to find one of my son's friends when I opened the door. I stood there, sweat dripping into my eyes, and stared at the Doctor.

"I'm sorry to bother you like this but I was in the neighborhood and... may I come in?"

Well, what was I going to say? I let him in apologizing for the state of the house, as well as myself. "You were in the neighborhood?" I questioned, skeptically. "This neighborhood? I am a little off the beaten track."

"Well, yes. Rolly is a member of a health club west of here, and as we practically have to pass right by to get there, I thought he could drop me and we could have a little chat, you and I." There it was, that smile.

Actually, we had a very nice visit. The Doctor told me stories of home, how he'd been sponsored by his grandfather to Edinburgh, and subsequently had

A Question of Balance

gone on for a Ph.D. at London University. I'd spent two years myself at the in London studying drama, so we had some common ground. He had a house in Yorkshire and a London flat as well. We chatted for a couple of hours over several pots of fresh herb tea. I didn't offer him anything to eat since I was fasting. He said he understood and even offered to take my son out for a hamburger or something. He obviously didn't have any children of his own, at least not teenagers.

Before I knew it, it was ten o'clock, my son was home and it was time for the Doctor to meet Rolly. As he left, I told him to feel free to stop by anytime, and Rolly too. After the door closed behind him, I leaned back and smiled. I had actually enjoyed him. It had been a long time since I'd had a social visit from a man, and I'd really liked it.

We saw quite a bit of each other after that. We went out to dinner, went to the movies, all the sorts of things you do with a friend. I was working hard at keeping it platonic for the moment. We discussed the Grimoir and how he was tracking it and what we would do once he found it. The Doctor was very experienced at this sort of thing, I found. He had made a great deal of progress in tracking down the Book.

In the occult community, there are two paths that we talk about. The one I travel, as are most of the people I know is what we call the "right hand" path. It is the path of light. There are those who, for reasons only they can know, choose the other, the "left hand" path. These are the practitioners of the, so-called, Black Arts, you hear so much about. Some groups worship the Christian concept of the devil, and some, deities of a darkness far older. What they all have in common is evil, in its purest form.

I don't know why someone would deliberately devote their life to such darkness. I suppose some of the current demonic craze is inspired by visions of Power, dominance over the material world. I can see how certain disillusioned people, turned off by the hypocrisy rampant in the modern Judeo-Christian world might be tempted by these powers. They do promise ultimate victory over one's enemies, after all, even if the enemy is oneself, as is inevitably the case.

However this may be, rationally I can understand that light cannot exist without dark and the same for the opposite; but these cults do not believe that. It is their belief that pleasure can only be truly achieved with the total defeat of light, and the total ascendancy of dark. Needless to say, some of these people are utterly ruthless, completely devoid of any kind of conscience you or I would recognize. The Doctor had apparently done much research into organizations of this type, and made some enemies. They don't like their activities exposed to the light of day, except on their own terms. Several well-publicized murders have been linked to these groups in recent years, and many more have not. Personally, I've always avoided any contact.

It was one of these groups, the most powerful and influential in the world, according to the Doctor, which had possession of the Grimoir of Infinity. I was told that they were also actively seeking for the Key and the Crown, both of which I now had in my possession. This meant that the next phase of our adventure had to take place here, in the real world. I was daunted.

Magic itself is like electricity; it's neutral. Electricity can make the lights work, cook dinner, warm a house or kill. It's all in how you use it. The same holds true with magic. There are, of course, certain laws that govern its use, just like with anything else. One of these is called the "Law of Karmic Return" sometimes known as the Threefold Rule in Wicca. It basically states that whatsoever you send out into the cosmos returns ultimately three times strong. If you send out nothing but good, then your lives should be thrice blessed. Now, I'm not exactly sure what kind of a pact those who deal in the Black Arts have made with the Cosmos, but Karmic Return applies every bit as much to them as to anyone. That's one of the things that make it so hard to understand. I guess it's like anything else, the "it only happens to the other guy" syndrome takes over. Of course, there is usually nothing these people will not do to accomplish their goals.

These were the people we had to track down and steal back the Book from. I didn't personally want to add to anybody's Karmic Burden by getting in the way of one of these black magicians. I'm not finished with my journey in this incarnation yet. I'd like a chance to experience my own Crone aspect; I want to live to become a wise old lady.

The time between Samhain, more commonly known as Hallowe'en, and Yule, is the time when Darkness is supreme upon the Earth. The days are short and the God of Sun and Light is dead, waiting to be reborn of the Goddess again at Yule, the Winter Solstice. Beginning with Samhain, the veil is thin between the worlds and there is much transference. This then, is the time when the conditions are right for evil to rear its ugly head. This was also the time when we had to seek this evil and steal from its minions the Grimoir of Infinity.

The Doctor's mundane visits had become more frequent and we often went out for coffee, or sometimes just a stroll in the air. We talked about everything, including what we'd come to refer to as my little adventure. I invited him to attend my Coven's Samhain ritual. He was delighted. It was a wonderful night, the best I can remember. There was love and magic moving on the air so tangibly, that if you put out your hand you could touch it. By the time the evening was over, we were both exhausted. I invited him to spend the night, rather than drive all the way back into the city. He accepted and slept on the couch like a perfect gentleman.

Though most American families count the start of the 'holidays' with Thanksgiving, we start with Samhain, and so the days got busier and busier. Finally the week before Thanksgiving, the Doctor told me it was time. We knew where the Book was and we might never have another opportunity. I took off a few vacations days from work and made arrangements for my son to stay with friends while I went away for a long weekend. The time had come to complete our task.

It was cold and bleak driving upstate New York where this group was planning their rite. Several times in the last month, I was told, they'd performed the same ritual, designed to call the Key and the Crown to them. Now, here we were, delivering the complete package right to their doorstep. I sure hoped he knew what he was doing.

It was late afternoon when we pulled into the motel where we were going to stay. Though just three o'clock, the sky was leaden, throwing gloom into every corner of the world. It was a chain place, like a Super Eight or Holiday Inn or one of those. I honestly don't remember. We checked into two rooms. I didn't bother to unpack anything. I was hoping that we could get in and out and be on our way home by morning.

The Doctor's contact had drawn up a map, showing us how to get to the outdoor temple they would be using. I thought we should get there early, before nightfall while we still had some natural light on our side. He disagreed. So, while we waited for full night to descend, we walked down to the coffee shop and had a light supper. We finished up by five thirty, and by then it was getting really dark. The Doctor had rented a dark blue Caddy for the trip. He handed me the crudely drawn map and we started driving along the highway. It was about twenty miles before the exit we wanted, plenty of time for me to start getting cold feet. I wasn't nervous anymore; I was more than halfway to being terrified. There was a really bad feeling to the night.

As a Priestess in my Tradition, I am privileged to wear a special ring. It is a half moon and a star, wrought in sterling silver set with a tiny diamond. It encircles my right forefinger; a symbol of my status as a priestess. My finger began to itch beneath the ring as we got closer to our destination. Purely psychological, I told myself, as I rubbed at it.

By the time we reached the turn off, I was nauseous. I've never been carsick before, so I ruled that out. I made him pull off the road where I got out and threw up whatever it was I'd had for dinner. That done, I felt a little better. The Doctor filled a glass with water from a thermos he kept in the car and I drank.

"Do you think you could try a little tea?" he asked, concern etched in the lines around his eyes.

"Better stick to plain water for now," I said. "I'm better already, I think. How much further?"

He picked up the map from the floor where I'd dropped it. "Not far, another two, maybe three miles along here, then we turn off onto a gravel road, marked private."

"Well, let's get it over with." I sat back in the seat, breathing deeply through my mouth to try and settle my stomach.

We continued on and found the turn off. It was indeed marked 'PRIVATE' and there was a gate across, blocking the access. He pulled up close and got out, leaving me alone in the car. I don't know what he did, but the gate swung open easily. The Doctor got behind the wheel and pulled the car through, then went back and closed the gate behind us.

Things got weirder. He found a place to pull off the drive and parked the car in some bushes. From here we went on foot. This was difficult for me since I'm a bit lame, the result of an old injury. I manage all right, with the help of a walking stick to keep me steady over the rough spots, but climbing through wet woods on stormy night was not easy for me. The nausea made it worse and it was difficult to keep up with someone whose legs are taller than I am. He kept having to stop and wait for me, showing that damned impatience again. I couldn't help it. I was never meant for this sort of night-time reconnaissance. I was cold and sick and just wanted to rest. I am just not the heroic type. Nevertheless, it was keep going, or be left behind, and I didn't want to be left behind.

It was mid-November and the leaves were pretty much all fallen, leaving the trees stark and barren against the sky. I could see the flickering of a fire through the naked woods, as the Doctor crept forward, keeping himself between me and whatever was going on. The sound of chanting came clearly on the night, and I felt as though I were going to be sick again. I stopped following and turned into some scrub, covering the sounds of my retching the best I could. When I turned back the Doctor had disappeared. I couldn't see him, but I could still hear the chanting, so I figured he hadn't been discovered.

I crept as close to the fire as I could, close enough to see thirteen hooded figures. There were others scattered around the glade, I could feel their presence, observing the ritual taking place at the fire's edge. I willed myself to blend in with the trees, and whispered the words of cloaking, memorized years ago and never until this night used. I strained my eyes in the dark, trying to see where the Doctor had gone. Then I saw. He was lying, dead or unconscious, on the very outermost edge of the Circle. His jacket was gone and his shirt had been torn all the way down to his waist. Obviously, they'd been looking for the Crown and the Key, expecting him to be wearing them around his neck. I reached under my sweater and touched the Key. It felt warm, almost hot to the touch.

The smartest thing would have been to try and find my way back to the car and go for help, but for that moment I was paralyzed. I simply could not move. I knew exactly what a rabbit caught in the headlights of a car feels like. For a few minutes I just crouched in the wet underbrush, trying to blend in with the surroundings, but that couldn't last. I felt another wave of nausea crash over me and I fought for control over my lurching stomach. I lost. By now there was nothing left to come up but bile. When I was done, I looked up, right into a pair of the palest eyes I'd ever seen. They were set in the face of one the most handsome man I'd ever encountered off the big screen. He reached out a hand and helped me to my feet. With a long sword, he cut an entrance in the circle and drew me in close to the fire.

A QUESTION OF BALANCE

I couldn't stop staring at the huddled form on the ground. The man turned me away physically while the Doctor was removed. Then, he held out his hand and I felt my heart pounding so hard I was afraid it would stop altogether. Slowly, without even realizing what I was doing, I pulled the chain out from under my sweater. The man smiled as I began to pull it over my head. It was the smile which stopped me. There was something predatory about it. He reminded me of a shark. I stopped and shoved the Key back under my clothes. The man grabbed my right wrist and held it up close to the flames so I could feel the heat. My Goddess ring felt like it was on fire and suddenly, it fell from my finger in two separate halves. The other ring, the Crown of Fae, was on my left pinky, shoved deep into the pocket of my jeans. For the moment it went unnoticed.

The man pulled a tattered brown leather bound book from his robes and held it up to my face. It had to be the Grimoir. I reached for it, certain that if I could grab it from him, I could get the Doctor and myself away. I never even touched it. He twisted my right wrist painfully, and someone else pulled at my left arm, tearing my hand from my pocket and pulling it around behind my back. I felt something cold clamp hard about my wrists as they handcuffed them together. They were very tight and hurt. I was too frightened to do more than stand there shaking. I was too scared to even cry. After what seemed like hours of staring into the beautiful, evil face of the man, I was led away. My walking stick lay useless on the ground as I limped between two men. They took me into a large old house set on the wooded property. For some reason, they left the chain around my neck alone, and never even noticed the ring on my little finger.

They led me into a closet and uncuffed one of my hands. The chain was passed around a pipe, then refastened. I couldn't sit or even stand up straight chained to the pipe, and I was feeling sick again. I just crouched there and cried, wondering what they'd done to the Doctor, if he was dead or alive. I really don't remember too much about this part at all. How long I was kept like that, I couldn't say. Finally, though, someone did come and unchain me from the pipe. This time my hands were chained in front of me, which was a great relief. For some reason I thought it was a woman who led me out of the closet, but I really don't remember. Somehow, I wound up in a large dining room. The man with the shark's tooth grin sat alone at the head of the table, sipping wine. The remains of a large meal littered the damask tablecloth and I wondered how long it had been since I had last eaten. He motioned me to sit and I did.

Holding out the two pieces of my ring in the palm of his hand, he asked softly, "What tradition?"

"I am dedicated to Cerridwyn and Cernunnos", I replied, my voice trembling.

"Do you follow Druidic Law?" he asked.

"What specifically do you want to know?" I was beginning to think there might still be a way out of this.

He smiled with his mouth, but not his eyes. "I want to know how much of a danger you pose to us. Now, answer me, please. Do you follow the ancient ways?"

I suddenly realized what he was getting at. "Not all of them." I tried to keep my voice guarded, I don't know how well I succeeded. "Every tradition must change with the times in which we practice, don't you think?" I tried to smile sweetly. "I came with a friend. I believe you have him somewhere on the grounds?"

"A friend? I thought perhaps you'd brought us a sacrifice, my dear. I'm sorry if we've misinterpreted your intent."

I must have paled considerably. I know I felt on the verge of fainting. He stopped and thought a moment before he went on. "This friend, is he a policeman?"

I shook my head. "No, he's a doctor. An anthropologist. He's studying occultism in today's society

A Question of Balance

for a University paper." He seemed interested, so I went on.

"I'm his assistant. I heard about your group and thought we could get some candid, first hand experience, that's all. We didn't mean any harm. I'm sorry, I should probably have called and made some arrangement first, it was very rude to just show up. You see, this is all a misunderstanding. We're no threat to you. Why don't you just get the Doctor and I'll take him out of here."

His eyes stared right through me. "Perhaps that could be arranged. Have you something with which to bargain? Some small talisman perhaps, a token of your good faith? A Key?" He got up and stood right over me.

I didn't say anything. I tried not to look at his eyes and he noticed. He lifted my face and brought his close. His breath smelled like some kind of perfume, sort of a sweet, sick smell that reminded me a little of Sen Sen. I turned away, disgusted. He slapped me hard across the face. I wasn't expecting that and I fell off the chair, tasting blood in my mouth. I stared at him. He smiled and reached down to help me up. Ignoring his hand, I got to my feet and just stood there, stupidly. Someone came in and led me away again, this time down a long flight of stairs to the cellar. The handcuffs were removed and I was tied with thick, heavy rope which was fastened to a ceiling beam. I wasn't lifted off my feet or anything like that, but it was still uncomfortable to feel so totally helpless, like a side of beef in a butcher's window.

They left me alone for a long time, hours it seemed. I kept thinking about the Doctor, wondering if he was still alive and if I would be for much longer. It's funny, but I wasn't really afraid of actually dying. I guess my belief in reincarnation is indeed faith. But I was very afraid of pain. If they were going to kill me, I hoped it would be quick. I closed my eyes trying to think of a spell that would loosen the ropes, not exactly the sort of thing I'd been trained for. I wondered, half hysterically, if wiggling my nose or blinking my eyes would help. It didn't, and nothing else came to mind.

CHAPTER FOUR
All Tied Up

Where was Tary? There were voices speaking somewhere in the background, but I couldn't make out the words through the pounding in my head. My eyes felt glued shut and it was some little time before I realized that my wrists were bound tightly behind my back and attached to my ankles; 'hog-tied' I believe is the American expression. I'd been unforgivably careless and that carelessness may just cost more than Tary's life. She was no match for what I'd dragged her into. I was feeling a sort of helpless rage at whatever power it was that had chosen her, but mostly at myself. A word caught my attention and I forced myself to concentrate on the conversation taking place.

"...the election board. You don't really think he can win this on his own do you?" The voice speaking into the cell phone was dry, sibilant, one that I knew well, although we had never come face to face before... Malcolm Dennings. His attention now focused on me. "With the Power of the Key, it might just be possible to decipher some of the simpler rites, enough to gain the sort of political influence that will make me the dominant factor in U.S. politics."

He was already quite powerful enough and my Director was very concerned with the scope of his influence. Besides being a high priced, high profile attorney with political aspirations, he was the Lord High Priest of a cult known simply as The Order. This insidious group had infiltrated the very highest levels in the governments of the most powerful countries in the world and their objective was the complete domination of civilisation. A remarkable and outside of fiction improbable objective. At least up until now. The Grimoir together with the Key and the Crown would give Dennings knowledge enough to release a chaos so virulent that after totally destroying all we know on Earth, it would spread like a plague from this planet to infect the whole of creation. Already, simple possession of the Book had extended his personal power to a very great degree both here in the U.S. and as far abroad as my own country, perhaps further.

"I want to know who he is and what he and the woman think they're doing here. She has brought us the Key. It should be no great effort to get her to release it to me, but the other one...?" I thought perhaps I could detect a small note of concern in his voice as he wondered about me out loud. I quickly dismissed that notion. The man I had studied for the past year would worry about nothing. To him I was no more than a flea. That's the way it is with megalomaniacs. I strained to listen. He hadn't mentioned the Crown of Fae. Perhaps it had been overlooked, at least that is what I told myself.

I tested the ropes surreptitiously, feigning unconsciousness, apprehensive at what he might do to Tary. It was no good. I couldn't move. Suddenly, a bright light was directed into my face, my head lifted by the hair and an ampoule of spirits of ammonia broken under my nose. I coughed, gagging as the fumes invaded my senses, flooding my throbbing head with white-hot pain. My eyes flew open involuntarily, watering copiously as I tried to flinch away.

"Get him up." The order was snapped, and obeyed instantly. The rope between my ankles and wrists was cut and I was hauled up, a chair shoved under me. It was a good thing it had arms, or I would have tumbled off as a wave of vertigo washed over me.

"Secure him in the chair." My host thoughtfully made certain I would not topple from my seat. Another rope was passed under my arms and tied, binding me to the chair with my wrists still pinioned firmly behind my back. My legs were similarly restrained. It was a very uncomfortable position. I squinted in the harsh light, trying to see the face behind that softly menacing whisper.

"Who are you?" he asked quietly.

I said nothing, allowing my head to fall forward on my chest as though I had passed out again.

For a moment there was silence, then a hand tangled in my hair held me immobile as the ammonia was again shoved under my nose. I choked and it was removed, but the hand remained, forcing me to face the inquisitor hidden behind the glare. He reached out, stroking the hair out of my eyes with a long slender finger, wiping superficially at the wet tears with a casual thumb. He was wearing beige gloves with a pinkish cast to them, the softest leather I had ever felt. Bile rose into my throat.

"Let me repeat the question. Who are you?"

When I remained mute, the hand in my hair tightened, pulling back hard exposing my throat. My jacket and shirt were gone, my under-vest filthy and ripped. Gently, Dennings slid a long delicately curved knife from a jewelled sheath bringing the point to rest just under my chin. I felt my flesh crawl as his fingers brushed lightly against my cheek.

"The Doctor. I... I'm the Doctor." I managed to croak the words, though my throat was raw and dry.

The point of the knife was removed, but the blade was not re-sheathed, a gesture not lost on me.

"Your name?"

"Just Doctor, please. I find that it's much easier in my work if I remain anonymous to my subjects for as long as possible."

He raised the knife slightly. "Subjects? What exactly is your work, Doctor?"

I breathed in deeply through my nose to steady myself. "I'm an anthropologist involved in research on occult practises in modern western civilisation. You know the sort of thing I mean? Witches, Neopagan religions, there's even a new trend in modern vampirism becoming popular in the underground youth population of several countries just now." I paused.

"I see. A fascinating occupation, though one fraught with peril I think."

I nodded, smiling my best. "Sometimes more so than others. Take today for example. I woke up this morning never guessing that I'd be mistaken for... it was this morning, wasn't it? Or was it yesterday already? Time does seem to... have..."

His expression stopped me in mid ramble.

"There has been only one mistake, Doctor, and I'm afraid you have made it." The voice was cold and oddly toneless to be so threatening, but there was no misunderstanding the implication. I was in serious trouble.

"I don't think you quite understand..." I burbled on, panic licking at the edges of my mind. "We just heard..."

"Oh I understand, Doctor. You heard of my little group and decided to just drop in, is that what I am expected to believe?" I had to strain to hear him, he spoke so softly.

"What do you mean 'expected to believe?' It's the truth." My words sounded hollow. I was drawn with fatigue, my head ached abominably and I was dreadfully worried about Tary. "My assistant? Pretty, blond about five foot..."

"Yes, Doctor, she is quite safe, this assistant of yours. Tell me, how is it that she wears an old brass key around her neck?"

His words chilled me. "Oh, I don't know, probably has some sentimental value to her. You know women, always collecting little bits of their personal history, wearing them like charms..."

He gripped my throat tightly with one hand, choking off my words. "This Key, Doctor, is much more than that. I think it's time we stopped playing with each other. Who are you?" The grip loosened just enough for me to pant an answer while gulping for air.

"I told you, I'm the Doctor..." His grip tightened again. I was amazed at the strength of those long fingers as they began to crush my oesophagus.

A QUESTION OF BALANCE

"Your name. I want your name and who you work for." The pressure eased slightly.

"Pendargroom." I gasped. "Arthur Pendargroom ... London University." The hand around my throat was withdrawn and I drew in deep shuddering breaths waiting for him to either speak or finish me. He did neither. The silence went on until I couldn't stand it anymore.

"Please tell me, where is she? Tary? How do I know she's safe?"

I could just make out the gleam of white teeth as he smiled from the cover of the white light. "Oh, I think you do know, Doctor Pendargroom. I must keep her safe, mustn't I? Does she know what it is she holds?"

"Don't be silly, it's nothing, just an old key that's all. Probably..."

The back of his gloved hand slammed hard into the side of my face, which was still immobilised by someone's fingers entangled in my hair. Immediately tears sprang to my eyes and I saw stars.

"As you insist in maintaining this charade, I will seek my answers elsewhere, from the woman herself... Tary you say?"

My heart was lead. "No, please. She doesn't know anything. She doesn't..."

"Silence him. We'll find a use for him later." Then he was gone, the bright light extinguished. For the few moments it took my eyes to adjust I was effectively blinded. There were at least two of them in the room with me. One pair of hands gripping my hair tightly, another prying opened my mouth forcing in a vial of some liquid that burned as it trickled down my throat. I tried not to swallow, but my head was yanked back, my jaw held closed and my nose covered until I had no choice. Suddenly the hands were gone. I had just about adjusted to the dim lighting when it too was gone and I was left in utter blackness. It wasn't long before I faded into blackness myself.

It could have been hours or days before I came around again. I had no way of telling in the dark of my prison. Gloved hands slapped lightly at my face as a sibilant voice whispered insistently.

"Doctor... Doctor Pendargroom."

I opened one eye into a bright glare and promptly closed it again, moaning softly. If I thought my head ached before, this new level of intensity made me wish desperately for oblivion. The slapping became a bit less gentle and I forced myself to full wakefulness.

"That's better." I could sense more than see the smile.

"Is all this light really necessary?" I whispered, trying to keep my lids half closed against the stabbing pain in my eyes. My throat was dry, my lips cracked, and I was desperately thirsty.

He chuckled. "I suppose not, really." There was a click and the light was gone. I blinked to clear my vision, trying to focus on the face of Malcolm Dennings, the most dangerous man ever born.

Fair, almost white-blond hair framed a face any local Greek god would have been delighted to claim. Not a wrinkle or blemish marred it's ageless perfection, yet the most striking feature were the eyes, pale, luminous, almost without colour. I couldn't help staring into those haunting, somehow reptilian eyes. They were the eyes of a god... or a demon. He was infinitely more impressive in person than the pictures I had seen.

"Your photographs don't do you justice Mr. Dennings, but I can't say much for your wardrobe." He was theatrically clothed in heavily embroidered scarlet robes.

His smile broadened to reveal a dazzling mouthful of brilliantly white, perfectly shaped teeth. He might have been an advertisement for tooth cream. "Strictly ceremonial, Doctor, but impressive enough in the proper setting."

Dennings drew up a chair and sat facing me. As far as I could tell, he was alone this time. "I had a chat with your assistant. She seems to bear out your story. There is also little doubt that she understands exactly what the Key is. In any event, she is unwilling to exchange it for your safety."

"Why wouldn't she support my story, it's the truth... well mostly the truth anyway."

"Please, Doctor Pendargroom, I know who you are. I insist that you drop this useless pretence." For some reason, it seemed important to him to speak with me. It was fairly obvious that he knew more than I would have hoped.

"All right Mr. Dennings. You know that my assistant, Tarish holds the Key of Enlightenment. You must also know that it cannot be taken from her by force without rendering it useless, and she will never give it up willingly."

His smile gentled. "Not even to save your life, Doctor Pendargroom?"

I shook my head, trying to believe it myself. The truth was, I just didn't know. "No. Not even to save my life."

He sighed. "I really am sorry, I would have liked to have known you better. There are so few people approaching my intellectual level that I often grow bored." To my astonishment, he seemed to genuinely regret whatever it was he had planned for me, not that there was much consolation in that.

I managed to quiet my racing heart and plunge ahead, but I had to know the worst. "Tell me Dennings, how do you plan to retrieve the Crown of Fae. You know, even if Tarish does give up the Key, you need them both to invoke the knowledge in the Book."

"The Crown is being sought even now, Arthur... may I call you Arthur?"

"By all means... Malcolm, isn't it?" I prayed that my relief wasn't written on my face. They hadn't yet discovered that Tarish held that as well; that was something.

"Malcolm, yes, though most call me M... it's not important. As I was saying, the magic which will bring the Crown to me has already been released, and is working, just as the magic brought the Key within my reach."

"Tary and I brought the Key, Malcolm. A bit less than perfectly thought out, perhaps, but not magical."

The expression on his face could only be called smug. "Ah, but therein lies the beauty of the thing. So natural, so simple, that you didn't even realise it yourself. That is how the magic works, Doctor Pendargroom, being able to create a series of seemingly unrelated coincidences to achieve exactly the result I want. The manipulation of synchronicity. That is what makes it so perfect a tool for a man like me. Powerful and subtle. It is all the better since there is no defense against what any intelligent person believes to be superstitious nonsense." He nodded almost to himself. "Fortunately, for me that is, there are very few men like yourself, men of education and intelligence who truly understand the nature of the Universe."

"Understand?" I shrugged as well as my circumstances would allow. "I have no special understanding, Dennings, just an open mind and an insatiable curiosity. And you know what they say about curiosity..." I realized what I'd been about to say and stopped, having no desire to give him any ideas. I needn't have worried. Dennings was deep in his own thoughts, paying scant attention to my ravings.

"Yes, magic truly is the perfect tool", he mused as if I wasn't even there.

"Tool?" His attention was on me again. "No, Dennings, in your hands a weapon. What makes you think you'll be able to hold it all to yourself anyway, eh? What about Mayfair in England or Giogello in Milan, Chasseret in Paris? Then, there's Kendrecznokov and Manovitch in Russia, they've been doing very well lately, haven't they? Oh and your friend the Imam in Persia, not to mention your Taliban sources....."

The reptilian eyes narrowed. "So, you know of my colleagues. You recognise the work of my Brethren in the former Soviet Union and Afghanistan? I believe you are more dangerous to me than I had thought.

A QUESTION OF BALANCE

Yes, we are more than a little involved. Think of it Arthur..." his eyes had grown vague. "...history manipulated to create order from the chaos free will has produced..."

I tested the ropes furtively, thinking that if I could just get loose, it would take me less than a minute to wring his neck. It was no use. "And what of the terroristic plots, the bombings? What of the hundreds of thousands of lives in utter turmoil. Those left to die of famine and violence and disease, yet you say that's not evil? Our governments have simply not yet realised that what will rise to fill the void your Brethren helped to create will not be the democracy and free enterprise they envision, but a hell designed from the demented ravings of a madman once called Gregori Rasputin. A hundred... a thousand times worse than communism. The world is falling into chaos and terror even now..."

He touched his finger to my lips to shush me as one would a child...

"Chaos, perhaps Doctor. But when I have the Three, when I am the sole possessor of all the knowledge held within the pages of the Grimoir, from that chaos will emerge the next step in the evolution of our species. As it was in the beginning so shall it be again. I will lead mankind into..."

"Into a timeless black void, which is the only place your kind can ever lead, Dennings. It has been tried before you know. A new order... peace through domination... the creation of the 'new improved man'. Remember Alexander? Napoleon? Hitler? They all met tragic ends as men and as leaders failed utterly." There was no use telling him that the power he so craved to possess was the kind of power that would use him. He would become it's slave, the possessed not the possessor, and all sentient life with him.

"They had not the same opportunity I do, Arthur. They did not truly understand the nature of darkness. The Great Dark and I will be one and I shall hold dominion over all." He cupped my chin gently in his left hand, trapping my eyes in his. "You could be among His chosen, Arthur. I feel it within you."

For a moment I was paralysed, then my gorge rose again at the feel of the soft, incredibly supple leather against my skin. I recognised it for what it was. In that instant I tore my eyes away and averted my face.

"Nice gloves." I muttered, cringing, feeling defiled by his touch.

"Yes." He rubbed his hands sensuously along his cheek, revelling in the feel of it against his smooth face. "An indulgence, I admit."

"I doubt the donor saw it quite the same way." Once more my stomach turned as I imagined the suffering inflicted on some innocent soul for a madman's indulgence.

"A sacrifice, Doctor. One of my own creatures born only to fulfil whatever purpose I deigned to give it. You too will be sacrificed unless Tarish decides to part with her treasure. Tell me, how much does she know."

I shrank inwardly. "Not enough," I murmured softly. "Not nearly enough."

He seemed satisfied with my answer. "As I thought. It will give me the greatest pleasure to seduce her to the path of Darkness, Doctor." His eyes glazed over. "A child of light is the highest offering of all."

"I don't think so, Dennings. She's a bit naive, but not so innocent as all that. Untrained in the kind of magic and power you draw from she may be, but I would tread softly were I you. There is something... something..." I tried with all my heart to believe myself as my voice cracked and failed.

His smooth brow creased in concern. "Forgive me, Doctor, my neglect has been unconscionable. You must be thirsty. I know the after-effects of the drug, and it has been some hours since your arrival." He stood, patting my cheek in an oddly intimate gesture. "I'll send someone down to see to it."

A Question of Balance

"Thank you." I sagged against the ropes bitterly disheartened at the feeling of gratitude his promise of water had elicited in me. I was both terrified and captivated by the man, even with all I knew. What chance did Tary have?

Though my throat was parched, aching for water, I couldn't help speaking to him once more. "Will we have another opportunity to talk? I find you horribly fascinating."

He smiled, a small sad smile that for the first time touched his eyes. For one brief moment I saw a glimmer of deep blue reflected there, then they faded back to colourlessness.

"Alas, I fear not, Arthur. I discovered at an early age that it is best not to make pets of animals marked for slaughter. It's a betrayal in the end you see, for both." He turned and walked quietly up the stairs leaving me alone.

As soon as he was gone, I began working at the ropes. So long as I was alive and conscious there was hope. Given enough time, I knew I'd be able to free myself.

Dennings had been gone about ten minutes and I was making progress, when another man, dressed in a plain brown robe came bearing a tall glass of tepid water. He held a straw to my lips and I drank deeply, draining the precious liquid gratefully. The brown robed man stood silently, as though he was waiting for something. In my mind I cursed, wishing he would go away, so I could continue working my arms free. Suddenly I understood and damned myself for my own gullibility. I was getting dizzy, the cellar room tilting crazily around me.

"No." I shook my head trying to clear it. "He drugged the water." The realisation hit me with the force of a blow. In the last few minutes, I'd come to see a Malcolm Dennings I'd never known existed. A Dennings that seemed almost human. It had been a serious mistake to underestimate him.

As my consciousness failed I screamed in rage and frustration. *"Dennings you bastard..."*

The man in the brown robe laughed grimly and kicked the legs of the chair, toppling it, and me, to the concrete. The pain of the impact jarred through every part of my body. It was the last thing I remembered for a very long time.

Chapter Five
Thanksgiving

The door opened finally, and two men dressed like monks took me down. By now I was beside myself with worry over the Doctor. My hands were left tied as I was led back upstairs and outside. I wasn't sure if it was still Thursday, or if we'd gone into Friday night already. My sense of time was all screwed up, I guess from fear and lack of sleep. Although I kept asking, neither of the two would tell me anything. Finally, we were back in the fire clearing where I'd first seen the group. The fire was out and a fresh one had been laid. Two rituals in one night was unlikely so I figured we must have gone into Friday. I hadn't let anyone know where we were going or how long we'd be. I hoped he had. Even so, nobody would be looking for us until Sunday at the earliest. Sunday was two days away, assuming this was Friday night. I shivered, and it wasn't just from the cold.

The length of rope was thrown over a tree branch above my head and made secure. Then, they left and I was alone and helpless in the dark night. There was no moon and it was black. A perfect night, I thought, for a ritual sacrifice. But who? Me or the Doctor or both? I struggled to free my hands, the rope burning and scraping the skin of my wrists. It always looks so easy on television. It wasn't. After a while I could feel blood running down my arms. Goddess but it hurt. To this day I still bear the scars from those ropes.

Long before I managed to free myself, the clearing was occupied again. With the fire lit, I could see that an altar had been set up on the eastern edge of the circle. It was really a very nice arrangement, one that any coven would be thrilled to have. There was something on the altar though. It looked like a scarecrow. With a sinking feeling in the pit of my stomach, I recognized that mop of curls. It had to be the Doctor. His flannel shirt was gone, and even from a distance I could see his under-shirt looked ready for the garbage. I shivered, feeling the biting cold through my heavy sweater. He must have been freezing, if he was even still alive. I wasn't sure how long I'd been there, and he'd been there, exposed to the frigid late November air, for even longer. It didn't look as if he was moving.

The nausea was back and I fought unsuccessfully, to keep from retching. By now there was nothing to come up but the heaving got to me and I realized I'd wet my pants. If I was going to die, I would have preferred to do it with dry pants.

Chanting had begun and the High Priest appeared at the head of the altar, complete with a distorted mask, a perverted depiction of the Sabbatic Goat. Great, we'd stumbled right into a nest of the very worst. These people worshipped not a deity so much as a concept; the concept of Evil as an incarnate being! Well, at least I figured the Doctor was still alive. Drugged probably, but alive. A dead sacrifice would do them no good. As I watched, I thought I saw him move as an anonymously shrouded figure slapped liquid from a crucible into his face and over his chest. Naturally they'd want him awake. These people feed off the energy they build, and nothing, no emotion, builds as much energy as terror. As his movements became more animated I realized we were nearly out of time.

I pulled frantically at the ropes using the energy of my own terror as a tool. I visualized the skin of my hands peeling off like gloves, slipping easily through the ropes as the blood made them slick. The thought made me dizzy, but it was working. My hands were beginning to slide through the ropes. The High Priest waved a book over his head. It had to be the Grimoir. He pointed at me and the other twelve turned to stare. He waited for me to give some indication that I would hand over the Key. I didn't give in. Somehow I

A QUESTION OF BALANCE

knew that's what the Doctor would have told me to do, that he would understand. Besides, I still wasn't really convinced that they were actually going to kill him.

In some rational part of my mind I'd managed to convince myself that it was all some kind of Dungeons and Dragons role game being played out, that there would come a point when the Doctor would sit up laughing, and the priest would turn out to be an actor. This was New York on the cusp of the twenty first century, not some Scottish village in the Middle Ages. The Key was just an old key, nothing mystical about it. It had to be! My mind was starting to shut down. I didn't know why they hadn't just taken it from me; I wasn't exactly in any position to stop them. In any case, I was willing to play my part in this crazy game just to get it over with. Once committed, I decided I wasn't about to give up the talisman and be responsible for eternal chaos throughout the whole Universe, whatever that meant.

Somehow I managed to gather enough courage to meet the pale eyes behind the horrific parody of the Horned God, telling myself it was all either a very bad dream or a worse joke. Playing my part, I shook my head negatively, trying hard to seem heroic. I guess he understood, since he turned back to the coven continuing with the ritual. I didn't recognize the language or the cadence, but the stronger the chant, the more nauseated I became. This time my sick stomach worked to my advantage. With the next convulsive heave, I pulled hard and one of my hands slipped free, then the other. The Doctor was struggling weakly on the altar to which he'd been tied. His whole body was shaking, shuddering with cold and fear and pain. No, it was an act, some weird game... it had to be. The problem was, what could I do about it?

Oddly, nobody seemed to notice I had broken loose. I slipped around through the woods, limping, trying to move quietly. I got very close to the altar, close enough to see right into Arthur's eyes. The gray was totally surrounded by white, pupils wide and dilated with drugs, as he stared in horror at the curved dagger brandished over him by the goat headed priest. A robed figure grabbed his hair and pulled back his head, extending his neck to leave his throat completely exposed for the blade. His wrists had been tied above his head to metal rings hammered into the stone slab, and his legs were stretched out, straddling the stone at its narrow end. Thick ropes around each ankle were bound to stakes on either-side. With a jolt I realized that the sacrificial altar had been designed for much smaller bodies than his six feet four inches.

For an instant I was immobilized with disgust at the abominations my wild imagination told me were usually performed here. It was the sound of his feeble voice crying "No! Please no!" over and over again, that released me from my paralysis. The priest was holding the dagger in one hand and the Book in the other. Suddenly I understood it was no game.

I don't know what made me do it, or even how I managed it, I only knew I had to do something. They were really going to kill him, and I had to stop them. I lunged, grabbing hold of the goat headed Priest's dagger arm. Whatever he'd expected, it wasn't that. I hung on with both hands throwing my full weight into dragging down his arm. The knife fell from his hand, and as he grabbed at me the Book slipped to the ground between us. I let go of him and snatched it up, clutching it in my arms across my chest. My bad leg couldn't keep up with my momentum and I went down sprawling in the dirt at his feet. For a moment, nothing moved. I could scarcely draw breath as I pushed myself to my knees and waited to feel the blade enter my back. I risked a glance toward the Doctor.

"The Book, Tarish!" he cried, breaking the profound silence that had grown up around the glade.

"Use the Book!"

Slowly I opened the Grimoir of Infinity and stared blankly at the first page. Then, everything seemed to happen at once.

A Question of Balance

"Read it!" called Arthur before he was silenced by a vicious blow across his face.

I turned to him helplessly. "It isn't in English!"

His eyes were filled with pain as they fastened on me. Blood dripped from both corners of his mouth. His voice was so low I could hardly hear him as he whispered.

"Use the Key, you stupid girl. Do I have to tell you everything?" The priest had retrieved the knife and now raised it to strike at him. Arthur's eyes closed, his lips forming a silent "please".

I had no clear idea what I was supposed to do, but I pulled the Key from under my sweater and gripped it in my right hand while I held the Book opened in my left. Suddenly, the words on the page were clear. It still wasn't English, it was ancient Aramaic. Don't ask me how I knew that, or how I could read it, but I did; and how, I did!

The strange words issued from my mouth almost as if they were alive. They came softly at first, then louder and louder until not even the wind that had swept in could drown out the sound of my voice. An energy I'd never imagined existed coursed through me as I read on. The ancient text came as easily to my mind as if I'd been born to it. It felt like every hair on my body was standing on end as I rose slowly, never loosening the grip on the Key glowing between my fingers with a pale blue light.

A part of me seemed unconnected, watching from a distance with a kind of detached interest. I saw the high priest remove the mask and let it fall, staring as if transfixed at my left hand. Without pausing in my recitation, I followed his gaze, amazed to see that the tiny ring around my pinkie was glowing with the same clear-blue radiance still pulsing from the Key. I could feel my lips curl into a kind of smile or was it a snarl, as a triumphant ecstasy burst over my entire being. My merest thought sent tiny tendrils of light snaking out, arcing the distance between me and the priest in less than a single heartbeat. For a split second he was completely outlined in the ethereal brilliance of an Aurora Borealis. Pleasure such as I had never known exploded in my mind filling my vision with a brilliance so dazzling that I could see nothing through it. I was swept away in rapture.

Through the cloud surrounding my mind came a voice like a beacon, calling me, guiding me gently back into myself. For a moment the glint of a silver horn and flowing mane of purest white caught my mind's eye. I knew she was urging me to return. In that moment I felt a flicker of resentment at my spirit guide for trying to lead me away from my true power. Then suddenly I was tired, very tired. Slowly I allowed myself to be guided back and the brilliant light retreated, leaving me hollow and drained. I opened my eyes to a moonless night in a forest glade, feeling small, lost and broken. Reluctantly, I closed the Grimoir.

The group had scattered like leaves in a storm as I'd begun the first line. By the time I'd reached the last, the only things left in the glade were the smoldering fire, the goat's head mask and the altar, with the Doctor lying unnaturally still upon its cold surface. I didn't know whether they'd fled, or whether the incantation had dissolved them all to dust, and to be perfectly honest, at that moment I didn't much care.

I staggered to the stone and bent over Arthur, relieved beyond measure to feel his breath coming in warm, shallow bursts against my cheek. He moaned softly as I tried to wipe away the blood around his mouth as gently as I could.

The whole left side of his face was bruised and swollen and a small gash over his eye leaked sluggishly. He was nearly blue with cold. Impulsively, I brushed my lips against his mouth. His eyelids fluttered and opened.

"I say, we've got this reversed haven't we? I mean, I always understood that it was the prince who..." I kissed him again, with feeling. When I stopped, he half smiled. "If you're not going to untie me, I may just have to bring charges. Taking advantage of a helpless man who's unable to defend his honor is a criminal offense you know." His teeth had started to chatter, his chilled body shuddering convulsively with cold and reaction. I realized I was crying.

I worked as quickly as I could on the ropes, knowing he had to be suffering from exposure and the gods only knew what kind of abuse. My fingers were cold, stiff and aching, my hands rubbed bloody raw. He was as patient as Job with my fumbling, never uttering one word of reproach or complaint, but I could feel his shivering and felt guilty about making such a slow go of it. Eventually I managed to get him free, and for a long moment we sat together on the stone, huddled in each other's arms. When he'd stopped shaking too badly, he tilted my chin up and bent over, for a very long kiss.

"Better?" I asked standing back and offering him a hand up.

"Oh..." He rubbed at the back of his head. "Nothing too bad I don't think. I'll live." His eyes hardened as he noticed for the first time my disheveled state, the ripped seam at my sweater, a long tear in the knee of my jeans.

"Tarish..." He brushed a lock of hair away from the deepening bruise on my face where the priest had left his palm print "Did... did they... he... did he hurt you?"

"You mean the high priest?" I thought I knew what he meant.

He nodded. "Yes, the high priest, Malcolm Dennings. Did Dennings...?"

I burst out, "Malcolm Dennings?! That was THE Malcolm Dennings, Malcolm Dennings the..."

"Yes that Malcolm Dennings." His arm was around my shoulder. "Did he touch you? hurt you? Did he...?"

I tried grinning. "He hit me in the face, handcuffed me to a pipe, locked me in a closet, hung me up in a cellar, and tied me to a tree." I shrugged, "But he didn't hurt me."

Some of the sparkle seeped back into his eyes. "Are you sure?"

I answered quietly. "I'm sure, but I was scared. Arthur, I've never been so scared in my life. I don't ever... want to... want to... be that scared again." I tried hard, but the tears came anyway in great gulping, nose reddening sobs.

"Shh, Tary. Oh my dear girl, I'm sorry, so very, very sorry." He held me tight as I sniffled, wiping the tears off my dirty cheeks the Book crushed between us. Later I realized that he hadn't reassured me.

Eventually we managed to stumble together through the woods and find the car. We barely paused at the motel long enough for Arthur to pull a sweater over the tatter of his undershirt, not even stopping to wash up or change before heading straight down the New York Thruway to the city.

We spoke very little on the ride, but I caught him glancing occasionally at the Book still clutched in my arms, and a worried frown formed a crease between his eyes as he drove. I think I must have dozed off. The sun was just coming up, sparkling on the river, as we drove over the bridge. We both looked just wonderful, and I'm sure we smelled even better than Molly's sow, but we were alive. Not only that, but we had the Grimoir of Infinity.

We got to Rolly's flat in the East Village and showered. When we were clean and dry, our host treated us to a traditional English breakfast of eggs, tomatoes, bacon, fresh kippers and porridge and gallons of hot tea of course. He tactfully refrained from asking anything about our recent absence, or commenting on our disreputable condition. We were both exhausted, both needed time to sort out what we thought had happened before we'd be ready to talk about it. Finally, after swallowing a couple of aspirins provided by our host, the Doctor and I crashed, me on the couch and he in the guest room. He'd wanted me to have the bed, but I was already half asleep and didn't feel like moving.

It was Saturday night by the time we'd slept ourselves out. I woke up, immediately feeling for the Book, which had been right up next to my pillow beneath my left hand when I fell asleep. It was gone.

A Question of Balance

I sat bolt upright, throwing off the afghan, frantically searching under the sofa cushions. I felt a hand on my shoulder and whirled, striking out with my fists.

"Tary, it's me." Arthur shook me gently by the shoulders. "It's all right, you're safe, remember?"

"The Book, Arthur! The Grimoir, it's gone!" I was close to panic. "I had it before I fell asleep and it's..."

"I know, Tarish. Don't worry, Rolly took It." He glanced at the clock. "By now It's safely on It's way to London by special diplomatic courier."

"Rolly?" I shook my head. "I don't understand. How could he have taken It? I know I would have felt him, I would have woken up..." I felt cheated, betrayed. "Why? I thought I was the one who was supposed to have It. It belongs to me! The Grimoir is mine Arthur, mine!" I was getting hysterical. "I want It back, I need it back now!"

He sat down pulling me down beside him, holding both my hands firmly. "I know, Tarish, I know. I was afraid for you. There is so much you don't understand. There was something in the aspirin, something to make you sleep so we could get It away from you before it was too late."

I stared at him. "You drugged me? You? To steal the Book?" My eyes filled with tears of rage and I struggled to get away from him, but he held tight. "How could you? I trusted you, I thought I was falling in love with you."

There was such pain in his eyes that I had to look away. I didn't want to see it. He'd betrayed me. I had trusted him, risked my own life to save his, and he'd treated me like that. He'd just been using me from the start. It was clear now. Never in my life had I ever felt so stupid, so naive, so... empty.

"I know." He said softly. "I'm sorry."

The tears spilled over and I looked back, glaring at him accusingly. "You did it on purpose, made me love you, just to use me. I thought... I was beginning to think that you... maybe you..." My voice broke and I couldn't go on. He wouldn't release me, though.

Finally, my tears slowed. "Am I your prisoner now?" I spat bitterly, trying to tug my hands from his grip. "Like Dennings?"

He paled, and released me immediately.

"No, no. Of course you're not my prisoner, Tary. I'm not like Dennings."

"Aren't you?" I sniffled and he handed me a hanky.

"No."

For a little while neither of us spoke. Then I looked at him again. "What did you mean, 'before it was too late?'"

"The longer you had the book, Tary, the harder it would have been for you to give it up. It was already too late for you to simply hand it over. That's why I had to steal it from you. Don't blame Rolly, it was my idea to give you the sleeping pill. He wanted to wait until you woke, to try and explain things. I thought it would be easier this way."

I nodded, beginning to understand, a little anyway. He was right. I would never have given It up gracefully. I suppose I was starting to get obsessive about It. Goddess, how did I ever get mixed up in all this?

He gathered me into his arms, and this time I didn't resist as I began to cry again. "You are right about one thing though," he murmured softly into my hair.

"Oh yeah? That's novel for me lately. Don't keep me in suspense, will you, Doctor Pendargroom, tell me."

He trapped my tear streaked face in his two hands so I had to look at him. "I do love you Tarish Dickson. I didn't mean for it to happen, but there it is. Now, what do you suggest we do about it, eh?" His eyes were sparkling.

"I dunno, Doctor." I was wary. Better late than never. "What would you suggest?"

"Oh," he grinned at me. "I'll think of something."

It was somewhere near dawn when I woke again, disoriented and shaky. I sat up, grabbing at the comforter, realizing that I wasn't at home in my own

A Question of Balance

bed, realizing also, that I hadn't a stitch on beneath the covers. My breathing was labored and my heart was pounding so hard I could hear the blood rushing through my ears. A classic anxiety attack.

"Tarish? what is it, are you okay?" A long arm snaked around my waist and pulled me back into the warm darkness of the queen size bed.

"Oh, Doctor. I don't know. I thought it was a dream. I thought I was... I just forgot where I was."

"Arthur..." He murmured as he held my head gently in the curve of his elbow against his chest. The memory of where I was and what had happened slowly seeped back.

"What?" I asked, not sure it I'd heard him correctly. In truth, I was a little uncomfortable with our new found intimacy.

"I just thought you ought to get used to calling me Arthur, Tary. Bit awkward having one's beloved using titles, at least in bed."

"Beloved?" I'm afraid I snorted a little, but really, beloved?

"Well, lover, intimate companion? I know, how do you feel about wife, eh?"

I cringed. Things were moving along awfully fast. First he'd lied to me then used me, then he drugged me after I'd saved his life, and now a marriage proposal? All in two months? I needed time.

"Girl-friend?" I counter-offered.

"Really? I don't know, that has such a juvenile sound to it, don't you think so? Still, it does make me feel young. I don't think I've had a 'girl-friend' since my university days."

"Oh, the olden days, huh?" I snuggled in closer, enjoying the warm feel of him. It had been a long time. "Do you need an answer today?"

"No, Tary, not today. Just think about it."

I drifted back to sleep.

The next time I woke it was to the smell of crispy bacon frying, and coffee. I was alone in the bed, but there was a bathrobe laid out for me. I took ten minutes, well, maybe it was twenty, to put on a face and freshen my hair. When I resembled something human I stumbled through the huge main room of the loft to the table where Rolly and Arthur was sitting.

"You look better this morning. Did you sleep well?" asked Rolly, with a side glance at the Doctor.

"Morning?" I yawned. "Is it Sunday yet?"

"Sunday morning, Tarish." Arthur leaned over and kissed me lightly. "What would you like to do today after we finish debriefing you? It's a lovely day for November."

"Debriefing me?" I blinked.

Arthur sighed. "There's a lot you need to understand, a great deal that I've no business telling, but Rolly and I decided that before we report back to the Institute, we'd..."

"Report back to the Institute?" I kept adding sugar to my coffee distractedly. Gently, Rolly slid the cup away and poured me a fresh one.

"Sugar?" he asked.

"Uh, yes, please. Three and a little cream..." It was just as well he stirred it for me too. My hands had begun to tremble slightly.

Arthur took one hand in his. "You've got to know, that it's not finished yet. Malcolm Dennings will not forgive what we've done to him."

"What we've done to him? What have we done?" I asked.

Rolly chuckled grimly. "Tarish, besides making him look more than a little foolish, you've managed, in one fell swoop, to put a serious halt to his very well laid plans which had been years in the making."

I thought hard to the last time I'd seen him, surrounded by that bright aura of light. Or had that been a figment of my imagination, an illusion born of desperate fear. I couldn't decide what was real and what wasn't any more. "But I thought I destroyed..."

"No." Arthur spoke quickly. "You never did. Stunned him, perhaps weakened him for some time to come, but Dennings' power has most certainly not been destroyed."

I found I was actually relieved. Although I hadn't had any kind of chance to even think about it, somewhere in the back of my mind I'd been storing up guilt already. The vows I'd taken as a priestess were specific. Magic was never, under any circumstances, to be used to harm. Not even in self defense. The Threefold rule. Whatever harm I'd caused Malcolm Dennings, was now bound to rebound on me. Not a pleasant prospect, but at least he wasn't dead. I nodded and let him go on.

"He no longer has the Book, but The Order is still a powerful presence in the world, and they will continue to be. The only saving grace is that he doesn't know just who you are. It'll take him time to recover, and even longer to track you down. We've got some breathing space."

"But.." I tried the coffee. It was strong. "..why don't we just go to the police or something? Expose him. You should be able to discredit him, no?"

"Discredit him how? Tell the authorities that one of the most universally respected men in America is an evil, megalomaniacal, sorcerer? With what proof? There's only your word for most of what happened out there. I don't remember much. I'm certain by now, there's absolutely no tangible evidence left that would link him to any cult at all, much less The Order. Your word Tary? No offense meant, but he'd chew you up into little tiny pieces in any kind of a public forum." He paused, "Besides, even if we did manage to somehow discredit him openly he would go right on, only someone else would be in the public eye... and it might take us years to find out who."

I hated it, but he was right. "So what do I do? Declare war on the son of a bitch? A magical fight to the finish? Challenge him to the duel of the demented magi? Who is he supposed to be anyway, the anti-Christ or something?"

Arthur smiled and squeezed my hand.

"No mage wars Tary, nothing like that. You've done quite enough, more than anyone had any right to ask. The Book will be kept hidden in England, somewhere it will be unlikely to be discovered by him. The rest of this war will be waged by others, professionals. You're out of it... and for the moment, so am I."

I looked at him sideways. "You are? So what will you be doing with your time then, Doctor, if you're not off chasing bad guys?"

"I thought I would finish my paper, naturally, and spend as much time as I can with you. Assuming you can stand the thought of having me underfoot."

I admit knowing that he would be there staying close was comforting. I was beginning to trust him... just a little.

"One more thing I don't understand. Why didn't they just take the damn key and have done with it, eh? The ring too for that matter."

"They couldn't take it from you by force, Tary. You are the holder of the Key and the Crown, though they didn't realize you had them both. That was what saved us. Even evil has to abide by the rules and the law in this case stipulates that the talismans must be either found, inherited, or freely given, otherwise they will be rendered useless. They were forbidden to harm you to get them."

"I guess that's a relief. What would they have done if killing you didn't make me change my mind?"

He frowned. "I don't know, and I don't want to speculate. But be assured, as an unwilling guest of Malcolm Dennings your life would not have been a pleasant one. Nothing you do will ever change what they are."

I shuddered, wondering how long it would have taken me to go completely crazy. "So what now?"

"At least with the Three out of their reach, the world has an even chance again." He sipped at his coffee absently.

"Was that what you meant by restoring the balance?"

He smiled. "Well, sort of. It's a little more complicated than that, but I think that's enough for now."

I began to feel a little better about things. I knew he was still holding something back, but at least nobody was asking me to take on all the evil in the world.

"I feel better, I think." I squeezed his hand back and then pulled away, reaching for the bacon and scrambled eggs Rolly'd just put out. "You know, I'm starving. Care for an egg, Doctor?" He held up his plate, grinning.

"Tary, I do believe you're losing your accent!"

I reddened and changed the subject.

"So, what are you doing next weekend?" I asked.

"Next weekend? Why?" He looked at me, one eyebrow raised.

"It's Thanksgiving. I thought you might like to come to my sister's with me." I shrugged. "It's an American tradition that dates back to..."

"I know," he interrupted. "The pilgrims, right?"

"Right," I said.

"How appropriate, I'd be delighted." He brushed his lips against the top of my head. I smiled, wondering how I would ever explain our matching bruises to my family. Somehow I was sure the Doctor would think of something.

Chapter Six

The Institute

"It's too late now in any event, Doctor. There's nothing you can do about it." Rolly was trying so hard to rationalise it all away for me, but it was no good.

"She's an innocent, Rollison. A very pretty babe in a deadly wood. I'd no right to involve her in something I knew..."

He put a hand to my shoulder. "She was already involved. You know that. It was only a matter of time before Dennings found her on his own and without benefit of your protection. What chance would she have had then, tell me that. At least this way her knowledge may protect her to some small degree. At least now she understands what it is..."

"She understands nothing. Do you hear me, Rolly? Nothing!" I was trying hard to get control of myself. "What kind of a world is it where good people are dragged into this kind of a mess. She doesn't need us, Dennings, or the bloody-god-forsaken-Institute screwing up her life for her. She was happy, contented before all this."

"Arthur, she was a witch before you knew her. For many, many years before."

"Wiccan, Rolly. Don't call her a witch, a Wiccan priestess, practitioner of reconstructionist Celtic religion, bit of a fluffy bunny to be honest. Oh she uses magic, of a sort; good luck charms, some simple divination, perhaps the occasional scrying or healing circle. There is nothing she knows that could ever have prepared her for this." My friend remained silent, sensing that I simply had to vent my frustration. Like the good friend he was, he listened.

"Her people use the natural Earth energies to heal, for pity's sake, to help, and seldom for herself.

Did you know that her coven's sanctioned her, cut her dead, so to speak?"

He shook his head, a picture of mute dejection.

"No? It's true, she can no longer go to them in perfect love and perfect trust. She's meddled in someone else's karma, in the whole world's karma, fooled in matters where she had no right to and all because of me." I turned to him, miserable, hoping that he would be able to find some excuse that would bear weight. The poor sod looked as miserable as I was.

"I'm sorry, Arthur. There's nothing I can do."

I was furious. "You mean you're going to let that fat bastard cut her off like that? Just like that? Without so much as a 'by your leave, thank you and so sorry for the inconvenience.'"

I was more than furious, I was scared to death. Without the kind of protection the Institute could give her, Tary's life wouldn't be worth a farthing if Dennings found her... and eventually he would.

"You know policy, Arthur. Sir's hands are every bit as tied as mine are. Legally we have no jurisdiction here, and the Official Secrets Act specifically prohibits soliciting aid from her government, or even notifying them in a situation such as this. There is nothing I or Sir or anybody can do about it. She isn't the first, you know, and she won't be the last to..."

"Damn it man. She is the first woman I have ever loved and I will not abandon her to The Order without even a backward glance. Even if I didn't love her, she saved my life. I dragged her into an event over which I had no control. My intelligence was faulty and I had no back-up. You tell me what went wrong. A break-down in communication is not a good enough answer, Rollison, and you know it. There's something off beam in London." I got my voice under control with a supreme effort. "I was responsible for what almost happened to her, and... and I still am."

"You are not responsible. London has sent word that..."

I turned to him, desperate. "She still has the Key and the Crown, doesn't that mean anything? Surely that..."

He interrupted me. "I tried that argument, but you know as well as I do that without the Book, the Key and Crown are not dangerous, or even particularly useful to any great degree. Oh, they may give her a bit more access to the Power than she is used to, a special insight perhaps. They may even offer some small measure of protection. I had the devil's own time getting Sir to agree to letting her keep them. It was the best I could do."

"Well it's not the best I can do." I turned and moved to the door of my office.

"Doctor, where are you going?"

I turned. "I've got two years worth of leave coming. I'm taking it now."

"But Doctor... Sir? What shall I tell Sir? He hasn't authourised any..."

I bit my tongue and left without answering.

It had been over a month since our little encounter with The Order. Christmas had come and gone and Dennings had made no effort, or so it seemed, to either track Tary or retaliate against me. Life had seemed very good. It had, at least, until Rolly informed me that I'd been recalled to London.

Although Tarish hadn't yet made a decision to formalise our relationship with a legally binding ceremony, she had agreed to a Wiccan Handfasting Rite, a bonding ritual performed by the High Priestess of her coven. Yes they had sanctioned her, but they hadn't really cut her off completely, and it was by her choice as much as theirs. She was now considered a practising 'solitary', still welcomed at major rites and Sabbats but essentially 'on her own'.

I had sensed the disapproval of Marianu shortly after our adventure. Tary had openly sought comfort and advice from her group after her ordeal, keeping secret only what I had told her about Dennings. She only referred to him as 'an influential figure'. Marianu placed the fault for Tary's current situation on me, a bad influence. I could hardly deny it, after all I blamed myself. Still, she'd supported Tary's petition and presided at our bonding.

Of course, there was a good deal more than a grain of truth in what Rolly had said. Dennings would have found her eventually, and she wouldn't have stood a chance against him. The problem was, I didn't think she stood a chance now, and the next time he wouldn't hesitate to destroy her. Worse than that, he could and would, destroy her soul.

Two years worth of leave gave me twelve weeks, three months which would bring us to nearly the Summer Solstice. I hoped that whatever was going to happen would happen by then while I was still here. Together we might have a chance. I was also banking on the Institute coming to our aid if it became necessary. I thought they would if I were actually at risk. There is rather a dirth of individuals with my somewhat peculiar qualifications after all. I could not be easily replaced. I'd been with the Institute for twenty-seven of my nearly forty-seven years. I felt they owed me something at least, even if they did not.

The weather was good, hinting at an early Spring and still nothing too terribly out of the ordinary had happened. Oh there were some annoyances that I suspected had occult roots, but if that's all Dennings' strength was up to we could handle it. Unfortunately Tary refused to do more than simple warding. She would not even consider anything resembling putting up a real magical defence. She was very careful about releasing any of her personal power and had taken to cutting her own hair at home disposing of the clippings in a special protective ritual. The same with fingernail parings. Whatever she could do, without actually initiating any action, she did. That was her way, I had to be content with that.

Meanwhile, I maintained my own flat in the City, although most of my time was spent in New Jersey, as you may have guessed. There was always something to keep me busy two or three days a week at the Institute. Sir, my Director, had unexpectedly

A Question of Balance

agreed to my taking some of my leave with the stipulation that I over-see the PSI experiments.

It was a Tuesday late in February, and I had just finished going over a report sent up to me by a colleague, an American working on a grant at a very prestigious University in New Jersey. His research involved studying the anomalous behaviour of simple mechanical devices when subjected to direct interference by bio-electric magnetic impulses. In other words, his experiments were designed to show that human mental force, thought waves if you prefer, can actually effect a machine's action. It was a fascinating and well documented study, and I was thoroughly engrossed in the material when Rolly entered, white faced and trembling.

"Rolly? What is it, has someone died?" That's how bad he looked.

He held out a medium sized manila envelope. I stared at it, not understanding. It had been addressed to Mr. Rollison at BITS in care of our New York address. I noticed that it has no postal markings, so I assumed it had been delivered by special messenger.

"So?" I lifted my eyebrows, wondering what could have upset my usually stalwart friend.

He lifted the flap and slid out a piece of black cardboard which had been cut to fit the envelope. Attached to the cardboard were two English half-pennies. There was a legend in blood-red calligraphy: "To be placed upon the eyes of Arthur Pendargroom."

There was nothing more, and naturally, no signature, but then, there was no need. Dennings had managed to track me down at last.

"How was it delivered?" I whispered, dread closing in about my heart.

"I don't know, Arthur. I left my desk for a few moments, and it was there, bold as brass when I got back. Nobody saw anything, and security hasn't passed through any visitors all day."

My thoughts went immediately to Tarish.

"Call Tary for me Rolly, and tell her I'm on my way home. Try not to alarm her and don't tell her about that!" I glanced at the thing. "Send it down to the lab. I want to know everything about it by six o'clock tonight."

I grabbed my jacket. Rolly stopped me, placing his hand on my arm. "Wait Arthur. Are you sure you want to go out there just now?"

I glared at him. "What do you mean am I sure I want to go out there just now. Of course I'm sure you git. If he's found me he must be getting close to her too. I've got to..." Suddenly it struck me. "You mean, that may be exactly what they want me to do right?"

Rolly nodded. "Otherwise why send it here? Why send it at all? If they don't know where to find Tarish, they send something like this to frighten you into bolting right to her." He shrugged, "then all they have to do is follow you."

I sagged into my chair. "Oh god, Rolly. What do we do?"

There was really only one answer and we both knew it. I had to leave Tary and leave her now without even a proper good-bye. I wondered if she'd ever forgive me.

"Do you think you can...?"

Rolly nodded. "Of course, Arthur. I'll find a safe way of contacting her for you. Is there anything specific you want me to tell her?"

"Yes... tell her I..." I laughed sadly to myself. "No, nothing she doesn't already know." I looked up, at him. "Call London for me, will you friend? Let Sir know what's happened and that I'm on my way home. And book my flight out. I'll take charge of this personally." I took the cardboard and the envelope and held them gingerly, touching them as little as possible. Until it was actually time for me to leave, I would work in the lab.

I hadn't really expected to find anything in the way of evidence on the envelope and cardboard, or the pennies themselves, for that matter, nevertheless I went through the motions. When I was finished with the scientific tests, I called in one of our staff

A QUESTION OF BALANCE

para-psychologists, a PhD and a gifted psychometrist himself. "What do you think, Brian? Can you get anything?" I hovered anxiously at his elbow.

"A moment, Doctor. You know how I work; cautiously, especially when we have reason to assume these items have been handled by our dear friends of The Order. It wouldn't be the first time they've laced a 'clue' with a suggestion bad enough to leave a sensitive in shock, suffering psychic trauma for days.

"Although we haven't been able to verify it, there was a nasty rumour going around about a year back, that one of the Kremlin team members was actually killed by just such a device. Sent into shock so deep he couldn't be brought back and died of heart failure." His blue-green eyes were deadly earnest as he lectured me sternly. Brian O'Connell was the best, and I agreed with him.

"I know, I remember. I'm sorry Dr. O'Connell. I'm just worried, that's all. You take your time and do it right. The Institute can't afford to lose a man like you."

He smiled. "I know you're anxious. I would be too if it had my name on it."

"No, it's not that. It's Tary. I..."

"Yes, Doctor. I know it's Tary. For weeks that's all I've heard from you. Got it bad, have you?" He was beginning to go around the edges of the cardboard, carefully feeling his way psychically without actually touching it. I knew what his prattle was doing. He was trying to distract me a little.

I watched him closely, ready to intervene at the first hint of trouble. "Badly, yes. I'm afraid so. At least, I'm not afraid so, I'm really quite pleased so. What I mean is that yes, I love her. I only wish she would let me make it legal."

His eyes twinkled. "Let you make it legal? Why, I would never have suspected that there's a touch of male chauvinist..." his features suddenly went slack, pupils contracting to pinpricks of dark in the calm sea of his face. Perspiration beaded up along the softened line of his jaw, on his upper lip. His long finger had made contact with one of the half-pennies.

"Brian?" I moved in closer.

He blinked once, just to let me know he was okay, then gave himself over to examine in minute detail whatever he was seeing. I gave him three minutes. That should be enough to see whatever there was. Longer than that, and he might have trouble coming back. It was the rule, three minutes, no more.

Gently I moved the card from beneath his hand, and turned him to face me. "Brian, this is the Doctor. Can you hear me?"

"Yes," came the slightly slurred response.

"Tell me what you saw. Tell me, Brian, what did the pennies show you?"

"Fire... light... explosion of bright white-light. Not hell fire, but... something not evil... not benign... nothing. A book... large... book... bound in leather... not leather... skin... His eyes. My god don't let him see me. My god, Arthur those eyes, don't let him see..."

"Brian. You're okay do you hear me? You're okay. You're here in the lab at the Institute. I'm the Doctor, the Doctor. Can you hear me? Brian?"

I shook him. "I hear you... Doctor."

I breathed. "Good. I want you to listen carefully, listen to me, Brian. Only to me. Can you do that?"

"Yes" he whispered almost soundlessly.

"All right Brian. I want you to close your eyes. Close them until all you see is dark. Close your eyes for me now Brian."

His eyes slipped closed. "That's very good. Now, I want you to count to three with me. Have you got that? Count to three and on three you will open your eyes and be back with me here."

His face was oddly featureless as he nodded assent, without any discernible expression at all. I crossed my fingers.

"All right then, with me. One.."

His toneless voice echoed, "one.."

"Stay with me, now Brian. Two... and three."

A Question of Balance

Suddenly, his eyes were opened and he sneezed violently. I pushed him into a chair and got him a glass of water while he collected himself.

"Thanks," he mumbled before downing the contents without pause. "Better." He gave me the empty glass and folded his hands to still the slight tremor that always followed a session like this.

"Was it Dennings?" As if I had to ask.

"Yeah, Dennings. My god he's grown."

I sat down in the chair across from him. "Impossible. How could he have without the Book."

Brian shook his head. "No, not that way. I mean he's grown personally, the amount of energy I could read in those... those eyes was greater than anything I've ever seen in a human being. I could swear he was right here, right in this very room."

A slow chill crept up my spine and I glanced around uncomfortably in spite of myself. Then, I laughed. Nerves. "Well he isn't."

Brian smiled. "No, he isn't, is he?" Then his expression turned serious. "Arthur, if he's grown that much in the last year, his Power with the Three would be incalculable. He'd be completely invulnerable."

I wasn't so certain of that. I'd actually studied the Grimoir, I mean the hard text. I'm not an expert in ancient languages, but what I was able to translate was quite enough to convince me that not just anybody could rule the Grimoir of Infinity, even with the Key and the Crown. According to the little I'd understood, the Book Itself has something to do with the choice of beneficiary. That didn't give me a warm fuzzy feeling at all.

"You could be right, Brian, I just don't know. I only got a quick look at It before Rolly whisked It out of the flat. I didn't want to take any chances with Tary. I'll be going back to London shortly and I'll have a proper look at the Thing, run some tests, do a carbon analysis, the works." I grinned. "You know me, if I can't quantify it, analyse it, qualify it and explain it, it just ain't so."

He grinned back. "Well you just do that then, Doctor. And if you manage to find out anything more than where the bindings came from, or how old the parchment is and what was used for ink, I'll buy you the biggest steak in New York City."

"Done." I cried, just as Rolly entered.

"Everything's set. You're to be at the Consulate at eight tomorrow morning. Mark will have your airline tickets. Your flight will be leaving at seven-thirty tomorrow evening. I asked for a window seat for you."

"Mark? Whatever for, Rolly. Couldn't you just have them sent from the travel agent by messenger or something? I do have an Express card, you know. Never leave home without it."

He was being very mysterious. That was his one major flaw. He could be damnably secretive sometimes. Especially when someone, like the government, told him to. He was nearly the perfect bureaucrat. "Oh very well, I'll pick them up at the consulate if it will satisfy your sense of protocol. Tary?"

"I had Mark call her. He explained that you've been recalled on a matter of some urgency, and will correspond yourself at the first opportunity."

"Oh, I'm glad he was so sensitive about it." I rolled my eyes. "Never-mind, it's no more than she'd expect. Work on a way I can get a letter to her, will you old chum?"

He smiled. "Already working on it, Doctor."

I yawned. "Better get home and pack then. Tell Tary to hang on to my things at her house. With any luck, I'll collect them myself."

I shook hands with Dr. O'Connell. "Thanks, Brian, I'll see you soon. Will you be in England any time in the near future?"

"As near as I can, Arthur. As near as I can. You take care of yourself, and try not to worry too much about Tary. Rolly and I will do what we can to see that no trouble finds her. Count on it."

"Yes Brian, thanks. I will."

A Question of Balance

Rolly walked me out to the waiting taxi. "Will I see you tomorrow?" I asked.

He smiled a strange little smile. "Oh, I'll try and break away, pop over and see you off. Go home and get some sleep. Brian's right, try not to worry so much."

"Yeah, well I'll try. Goodnight."

I didn't. Get much sleep that is. Every time I dozed off, I fell into bad dreams. Not too surprising. It seems to be an occupational hazard. Anyway, I managed to stay in bed until just dawn, at which time I saw no point in lying there. My bags were packed already, so I left them with the doorman along with instructions to have a taxi waiting at precisely seven fifteen; then I went out for breakfast.

At precisely seven fifteen I returned and miracle of miracles, the taxi was waiting. I arrived at the consulate a few minutes early. Most of the staff weren't in yet, but Mark found me and dragged me into a small back office, where a teapot and a plate of muffins were sitting out. Before I could so much as blink, he disappeared again, telling me to wait right there. I helped myself to tea and waited. In a few minutes, there was a light tap at the door.

"Come in?" I said, getting to my feet to see if the door was locked. It wasn't and opened just as I reached it.

"Arthur." Tary flung herself into my arms. She was followed immediately by Rolly, who was doing his finest impression of a Cheshire cat.

"What is this? What's going on around here?" I asked helplessly. "Don't you think this was taking a chance, Rolly?"

He shrugged. "It was either this or she was going to storm the Institute, make a target of herself. I thought this would be preferable. Really not so much of a risk. She came in with the morning staff wearing a dark brown wig, and an absolutely appalling raincoat. She can go out the same way at the end of the day."

Tarish smiled at me. "Don't frown so much, you're getting wrinkles. I learned that cloaking spell... I mean really learned it this time. I even managed to avoid Jason with it."

"Oh?" I raised my eyebrows sceptically. Just at that moment, Mark walked in.

"Good. Are we all ready then? I have the documents here, all ready to be signed. Rollison, will you be the first witness?" He handed Rolly a paper and a pen. "Sign right there. I'll have my secretary sign the other space."

"Witness? Documents?" I was beginning to see what exactly was going on.

"Yeah, we need all that for our wedding." Tary's face wore the biggest smile I'd ever seen. "You still want to, don't you?"

I sighed. "Now that I'm leaving you want to get married?"

"Well you see I've done this before, Arthur, and I think this way we've got a fair shot at making it work." She giggled.

To that I had no answer.

Mark had also thoughtfully provided us with a guest suite for the day, complete with bed and bath; a short, though memorable honeymoon. Leaving her was more difficult than I had imagined possible. She was arranging to have her passport renewed, and hoped to join me in England, for a holiday at least, in a few weeks. Rolly thought it would be a good idea to have her out of the U.S. for a while. While I wanted her to come, I also had some reservations. Well, she seemed to be taking a hand in her own fate just now, and if I knew Tarish, there would be no way to stop her from doing exactly as she pleased. It was going to be a long few weeks.

Chapter Seven
Heaven and Earth

"Tary Dickson, you did what?" Kathy's mouth hung opened and I laughed over my cup of tepid, dishwater coffee, the only kind available from the company cafeteria after ten thirty in the morning. I was taking a rare break to talk to my best friend about my plans and to ask for her help.

"I said I got married M. A. R. ..."

"I know how to spell it, Tary, I just don't believe you did it. After you and Johnny split up you said you'd never, and in all caps NEVER, get married again."

I sighed, not quite believing it myself. "Yeah, well, never say never, right?"

"And you didn't say a word to me, of all people me!"

My best friend in the world glared at me accusingly. "Does anybody know? Did you at least tell Jace? Your Mother?"

I shook my head. "Nobody. You're the only one who knows. It was all so fast. You know Art's been after me since Samhain to make it legal, but when everything started happening... I mean... his being recalled back to London, who knows when he might get back here? I just suddenly realized that I couldn't lose him. Don't ask me why, Kath, because I don't know. This was the one way I could think of to show him that whatever happened, whatever he did, I'd always be there." Of course I couldn't tell her about the threats, or about the Order or the danger my husband was in. How could I? Even to me it sounded like a B-movie.

"So, what now?" she asked, the accusation replaced by the glow of shared secrets in her eyes. "What do you need me to do?"

"I've got to get to England Kathy. I can't tell you everything, not yet, but believe me I have to get there. Can you take Friday off? I have to go into the City to the passport office and I could sure use the company. Then, and here's the biggy, Jason. Would you...?"

"No problem," she blurted happily. "You know how Mickey feels about his big 'cousin' Jace. "I can drop him off at the bus stop in the morning after I take Mick to school. He'll be so excited!"

"Thanks, Kath." That was one big concern taken care of. My son was almost seventeen, but I still couldn't leave him alone for two or three weeks at a time while I was out of the country. Thank the Goddess he and Kathy's eight-year-old got along well. "You'll at least have an instant baby-sitter if you want to go out."

She grinned. "What about work, though? Do you have any vacation time?"

That was the other big problem. Work. "I've got three weeks vacation and four personal days left, not to mention sick time. The problem is we're so busy now I feel kind of guilty just taking off like this."

"And you talk about me! You are entitled to a life you know. They'll just have to get along, that's all. You know as well as I do that there'll never be a good time. Just go."

She was right of course "Yeah, Richie Henderson can fill in for me. I've covered for him enough times." I still couldn't believe it was going to happen, that I was going back to England to be with my new husband.

"Of course he can, Tary. I'll be in my office if he really gets into trouble. I won't let him screw anything up, I promise. Friday sounds fine. Why don't you drive to my house and we can take the train in."

"About ten? I'll bring coffee for the ride in." My beeper went off. It was my son. "I've got to answer this."

"Call me if you can think of anything else I can do." She stood, "I mean that, Tary."

"Thanks Kathy." What else was there to say? A true friend is the best possession.

I gulped the last of the dregs in my cup at my desk as I dialed my home phone number. "You beeped?" I asked when Jace answered the phone.

"Ma, Marie called and wanted to know if she could come over tonight for a reading or something."

"Marie? Your friend Jack's mother?" That was odd.

"Yeah, he said she was upset about something. Is there any spare money in the house? I wanna get something to eat."

"Wait a minute, Jace, what is Marie upset about? She wants me to do a reading?" Marie had never asked me for anything like that before, or even acknowledged that she knew I was a witch. I mean, it's no secret. I'd even had a story with photo and by-line in the Daily Register, but it isn't something everyone's comfortable with.

"I don't know, just call her. C'mon Mom, everyone's waiting in the car. Where's the money?"

"The spare money?" I inquired.

"Any money. Can't you sport me five bucks? Please? I'll do the dishes when I come back, okay?"

"There should be five in the laundry kitty, but those dishes had better be done when I get home." I'm something of a soft touch.

"Thanks, Mom." The line clicked and he was gone.

I hit the release button and checked my address book for Marie's telephone number. It's funny, I'd known her for years, her son and mine had been close friends since third grade, and yet I didn't really know her at all. Still, it is one of those things that, as a priestess in my Tradition, I felt obligated to do. When someone seeks my help, I try to help. I don't advertise or anything like that, and I don't charge money. Sometimes people give me gifts, sometimes small donations of money, but no payment is ever solicited or expected. It's just something I do, Tarot readings mostly, but sometimes Runes and occasionally a personal healing spell or diet spell, you know the kind of thing I mean.

I dialed the number. After three rings, the answering machine came on. I started to leave my name, but Marie picked up.

"Tary? Oh, thank you for calling. Can I come over tonight? I need something, I need you to... to... I don't know what to call it... some kind of a spell? Is that right, a spell?"

I couldn't help smiling. I have one friend who asks me to do one of my 'special prayers'. My mother always calls it 'that witch dance'. "Tell me what it is you want to accomplish, and then I'll know what to call it."

"Okay, I'll try to explain it..." she began. Like me, Marie is a single mother who, upon occasion, tries to manufacture some sort of a social life. It seems that she and a friend had met some creep in a popular small club in Morristown. It's one of those after-work yuppie type meeting places, but it can be fun sometimes for a change of pace. When she'd rebuffed his rather more overt than normal advances, he'd gotten weird.

"I didn't pay too much attention, really. There are some strange characters out there, Tary, you know?" Boy, did I. "Anyway, he was wearing the star, like yours."

"A pentacle?" I suggested.

"That's it, a pentagram. He said he could curse me, my children. Ben is away at school, but I worry so about Jack. I tried to forget about it, but then I started getting these phone calls. My phone is unlisted and I don't know how he got my number, but he's been calling a lot lately."

"Marie, I know how worrying that kind of thing can be, but I really don't think..."

"Wait a minute, I'm not finished. This morning there was a dead rat or mouse or something dropped through the mail slot, and it had that pentagram pinned to its back. When I went outside both front tires were flat and there was a note on my dashboard

A QUESTION OF BALANCE

inside the car. Tary, all the doors were locked and the alarm was still set. "

I cringed. This sounded really nasty. "You've got to call the police, Marie, make a formal complaint of harassment. You've got his number on your caller id haven't you? This kind of kook is capable of almost anything, and I don't mean curses."

"I did call them. They took a report, but I couldn't remember his name, or where he lived or anything. I gave them the number off the caller id box. They said it looked like a public coin phone number, but they would check it out. I'm not even sure I described him accurately. They told me to change my number and my locks as a precaution and to call them if I saw him hanging around. They didn't take it seriously, I could tell. It was like it was my own fault for being out in a bar and what do I expect, you know?"

I did know. "Okay, I'll be home about six. Come over at seven. The moon is waning so that's good. What did you do with the mouse?"

"I picked it up with the snow shovel and put it in the dumpster, why? What was I supposed to do with it?" She sounded terrified.

"Just what you did, Marie. It would help if I had something he had handled recently, that's all."

"The note! I saved the note from the car in case the Police wanted it. They didn't so I tossed it out.... but the garbage hasn't gone out yet. Jack was in a hurry to go someplace, and he said he'd do it..." She started to cry.

"It's okay, Marie, the note's just fine. Don't touch it too much, if you can help it. Pick it up with a towel or something and bring it with you. Try not to worry. I doubt there's anything he can do magically to hurt you or the boys. Tonight I'll do a binding, just to be sure."

"Oh, Tary, it's been such a nightmare. Thank you. I'll be over at seven." We hung up. Great, as if I didn't have enough on my mind. I was pretty sure he was just one of those creeps you get sometimes, who like to bully women. I was much more concerned that he would do something physically than metaphysically. Magic, especially anything powerful, requires skill and training. Chanting the words to a Black Sabbath song backwards at the new moon in a graveyard while swinging a dead cat around your head three times might be dramatic, but it isn't magic. I figured that a binding couldn't hurt though. As Shakespeare wrote, "There are more things in heaven and earth, Horatio, than are dreamt of in your philosophy". At the very least, it would make Marie feel better. I'd also remind her about changing her phone number and locks.

I got home around six. Jace was still out so I opened a can of soup and made a sandwich and a nice cup of tea. At 6:30 I took a ritual bath with protective herbs added to the water. Then I put on my black robes complete with cowl. When Marie rang the bell at seven I was just finishing draping my altar with a purple cloth with a black pentacle. She gasped when I opened the door to let her in.

"Ohmagosh!" She stepped back then flushed bright pink. "Oh Tary I am so sorry. You are the most level-headed, normal person I know. I mean I knew you were a witch...I just never expected you to look so....well....witchy!"

I laughed. "Well this sort of spell requires the full works. Can I make you a cup of tea or something before we start?" I led her into the kitchen.

"No, thanks, Tary. I really just want to get this over with." She held out the barbecue tongs holding the note written on what appeared to be yellow legal pad paper.

I took the tongs from her and carried the note to the living room. I passed it through the smoke of the incense I had burning and laid it on top of the dish of salt. Carefully I unfolded the paper. It looked like some sort of diagram at first glance....but it was somehow familiar too. There was a circle, in a circle, in a circle, quartered with unfamiliar runes at the quadrants. Two opposing triangles formed a hexagram with more runes at each of the points. It looked like something from H.P. Lovecraft, maybe out of the Necronomican, or possibly a talisman from

A QUESTION OF BALANCE

Raphael's 'Ancient Manuscript'. Neither source is a reliable foundation for magic. It was definitely meant to appear ceremonial and would be daunting enough to someone who got their information from popular fiction. I was not impressed.

"I'm going to fold it, Marie, and then I want you to hand me that red cord". I nodded to the cord on the far side of the altar. I poured a teaspoon of flash powder into the center of the paper then folded it in triangles three times so that by the time I was finished it had nine folds in it. I took the cord from Marie and wrapped it around the bundle nine times. And tied it off with nine knots. As I performed each task I chanted: "By three and nine your power I bind, Around and around you shall be bound". As I chanted I fell into trance building with my mind a wall around the talisman that would not be breached. When this was done I held the bundle in the candle flame and dropped it into the cauldron. In a moment there was a satisfying WHOOSH as the flash powder caught and the bundle disintegrated to ash in a burst of blue flame. As the note crumbled I whispered "In no way let this spell reverse or bring upon me any curse. As I do will so mote it be."

I smiled at Marie. "It's done." I stirred the ashes with my wand making sure there were no live embers before carefully pouring them into a small envelope. "Take this and bury it near your front door. He shouldn't bother you again."

For a moment Marie seemed overwhelmed. Awkwardly she took my hand. While we had known each other for years, we had never been close friends. "Thank you so much Tary." She smiled. "Is it appropriate for me to give you a gift in appreciation?"

I laughed. "Not at all necessary, Marie. These days we witches aren't dependent on the kindness of those we aid to survive."

"Even so, "she said. "There is something I want you to have." Marie reached into her purse and took out a silk bag. She opened it and took out an exquisite brass, cuff style bracelet and handed it to me. The detail was quite remarkable, Celtic knots and crossroads. I thought I could see satyrs and green men cunningly worked into the leaf design around the edges.

"Oh Marie I couldn't. It's just lovely though." I handed it back to her.

Marie took the bracelet and put it on my wrist. "Tary I really want you to have it." The tiny clasp caught with an audible click and she smiled. "Now you have to keep it."

I stared at it. "I do? Why?"

"It's locked on now. According to my family legend it can only be removed in a place of great enchantment."

"Oh?" I said. I moved the bracelet around and around my arm trying to figure it out. I couldn't see where the clasp opened. "Well how perfectly cunning," I said with just a touch of ambivalence. It was a pretty piece, but I was sure I wasn't going to want to wear it the rest of my life. I pictured a hacksaw cutting into the delicate filigree as I commented. "I had no idea your family was involved in magic and such."

Marie laughed. "They aren't. It's just a silly old story. My great-grandmother was half Gypsy or something. There actually is a way to get it off," she said quickly as if reading my mind. "I have a little key for it home somewhere. I'll look for it and bring it over when I find it. In the meantime enjoy it. It really looks gorgeous on you."

I had to admit it did look nice.

"Well thank you very much Marie. Thanks. Now go and bury those ashes."

When she had gone I took a hot bath and soaked. By the time I was ready for bed I had forgotten I even had the bracelet on.

Friday Kathy and I went into the City. There was only a short line at the passport office, so we had plenty of time for a long lunch and some shopping for my trip.

"I still can't believe you're married and off to England in a week", said Kathy over a sandwich and a cup of tea.

I giggled. "You can't believe it? I still feel like I am totally zoned out...walking around in a fog. I almost feel sorry for Jace who wonders where in hell his cranky, normal mother got to."

"How do they get along? Jace and this mysterious Doctor of yours?" she asked curiously. I knew she was thinking about what she could expect from her Mick in a similar situation.

"Oh okay I guess. You know Jace, everyone is a geek to him and well the Doctor is sort of a geek, but in the very best way of course." I grinned. "Let's go. I have to stop at the travel agent and pick up my tickets now that I have a valid passport. I also want to start packing!"

She laughed and picked up the check. I left the tip.

Chapter Eight
Home Office

My sudden marriage to Tary had my mind in a spin. It is not surprising I was unable to get a wink of sleep on the flight. This chain of events would surely not please the Director. Sir had a car waiting for me at Heathrow. From the plane I was escorted directly to his office in London, bypassing both airport security and customs. I was exhausted, unshaven and thoroughly depressed by the time the great man made his appearance.

"Doctor, you look tired. You need some rest." He sat in the custom-made-for-his bulk chair and pursed his lips at me disapprovingly.

"Oh, I couldn't agree with you more Sir." No sleep had made me bold and I stood. "So if this isn't important, I'll get settled in somewhere and ring you in the morning?"

"Sit." He ordered.

I sat.

"I want a full report of your activities which lead up to the recovery of the Grimoir of Infinity. Leave nothing out."

I gaped at him. "You can't be serious, Sir. Haven't you read my reports? I thought you wanted to talk about your security problems. You must know there's something wrong here. You've got a leak in the home office. I really don't think..."

"Doctor, perhaps it was a mistake having you brought here directly from the plane. You are not yourself." He rummaged in a drawer and slid a sheaf of papers across the mammoth desk at me. "If we can just take care of the business of your contract, you may go rest. I have reserved the Hays Mews flat for your use until I decide where to put you."

"My contract, Sir?" I was so befuddled I couldn't see straight.

"Yes, Doctor. Your contract with the Institute expires at the end of the month. These are the new papers. Just sign and you may be on your way."

"My contract expires?" I remembered. "I need some time to think about this Sir. Before I left the States I got married, you see, and this might be a good time for me to consider other options in the way of..."

"Married? Preposterous! Inconceivable! Don't worry Arthur, I have a good deal of influence. I'll see that this marriage is annulled. Just get on with it and sign the contract, then get some sleep. I'm thinking of sending you to..."

"Annulled? Preposterous you say? But I don't want to be annulled, Sir." I couldn't believe what I was hearing. I had expected a lecture, possibly some sanctions that would keep me attached to London for a time...but nothing like this.

"Naturally, Doctor, your position with the Institute has given you the highest level of security clearance outside of MI 5. You know you are supposed to have any potential liaison screened carefully." He shook his head, "...and a foreign national...well policy is quite clear when it comes to..."

"Policy Sir?" I felt like I was in a nightmare. "I don't know if you realise it, but that particular foreign nation happens to have saved my life. She was responsible, in no small measure, for the recovery of the Book. You have a complete dossier on her. Is there anything that could possibly prevent..."

"Doctor!"

I was silenced.

"You were warned at the outset that this woman was not being recruited, merely used for our purpose. That purpose now having been fulfilled, she shall fade back into the life from which you plucked her. I granted you several months to ease yourself out of the situation...months which you apparently squandered. I must insist Doctor, that you have no

A Question of Balance

further contact with Tarish Dickson." His jowls quivered at me.

"From which I plucked her... squandered? Look here! You don't seem to understand me. I married Tarish Dickson before I left the United States, Sir, only hours ago. I have every intention of staying married to her for as long as she'll have me. There is nothing in my contract that stipulates I have to remain celibate, is there?"

His lips twitched in something resembling a smile. "Celibate? Certainly not. We have never interfered in your romantic life in the past so long as your usefulness as an operative was not compromised by the relationship. In fact, Doctor, the standard contract does limit any serious affiliation, which could adversely affect the performance of your duty. Although rare, there have been occasions when certain operatives have been taken out of the field and given leave to marry. In those circumstances they were totally in accord with regulations. You, Doctor, have gone completely outside of channels in this affair..."

"Marriage..."

"As you wish. In any event, I am afraid that you must end either your relationship with this American or your affiliation with the Ministry."

"You say it's in my contract? Where, the fine print?" I stood and peered at the papers as if to locate the specific clause. But I knew he was right. It was in there somewhere. "No never mind. I'll show you preposterous. Take your contract, Sir, and your bloody Institute. I think it's long past time I did something else for a living besides jumping at your whim, putting my life in constant jeopardy... and for what, huh? For what? The world's no better off for me being in it that I can see." I pushed the papers off the desk and let them flutter to the floor.

"You are over-wrought, Doctor. Please calm yourself. Of course you must sign. What else can a man like you do?"

"Do? I'll show you what I can do, Sir. I can... I can... well... I can teach, that's what I can do. I had an offer from Professor Bectinson. I'm certain they'll take me on at Leeds. Teaching, now there's somewhere I can make a real difference."

"Doctor, do you realise what you are doing? You are tired, irrational. I was wrong to..."

"Oh you were wrong all right, Sir. But I was wrong too. I should have done this years ago!"

"You are not thinking clearly, Doctor. In your situation you cannot simply walk away from..."

"For probably the first time in more than two decades I am thinking clearly. I'm finished with you, the Institute and the Ministry!" He was saying something, but I paid no attention as I stormed out.

I was confused, feeling as though I'd been cast adrift. London didn't even feel familiar to me anymore as I stood on the street, bags in hand wondering which way to go. Whatever in the world would I tell Tary? That I got the sack because of her?

I walked aimlessly for a while, no particular destination in mind. Even my flat was property of the Ministry. I was tired in desperate need of sleep. I toyed with the idea of checking into a hotel, then realised that what little cash I had would have to last me for some time. Technically I was still on the books until the end of the month, but I knew Sir would make sure there was no comfort to be had from that quarter. For the first time in my life I truly had nowhere to go. I wondered how difficult it would be to get a work permit for the US...and what sort of employment someone with my background could hope to gain. Then I realised that the Ministry would make damned sure I never got a visa. They took a dim view of people leaving the covert community and I would be made an example to others not to try.

Could I teach I wondered? My old professor at Leeds seemed to think so. A taxi pulled up to the curb letting out a passenger. I took advantage and climbed in.

"Where to guv?"

"Victoria, please," I answered, making up my mind. I had a train to catch, a train north to Yorkshire.

Chapter Nine
The Witch Goes South

The train south was late leaving Paddington and when it finally did, I had to scramble on having to drag enough luggage for two weeks worth of almost anything. My bad leg didn't help matters, but a trainman took pity and helped to toss my baggage on just as the train began to pull out.

Breathlessly I made my way to the dining bar and purchased a hot cup of tea before finding a seat. It was the middle of the day so the train was nearly empty and I settled in comfortably enough to begin my watch out the window.

Very soon London disappeared; replaced by rolling countryside so green it would have made a leprechaun jealous. Villages, some tiny, others quite large slipped magically across the screen of my window. Houses still thatched, not yet polluted with roofs of gray slate or asphalt shingle blended softly with the land. In isolated places, seen only by the mostly indifferent passengers of passing trains, stood an occasional ruin. Old stone farmhouses and ancient cisterns looking bleak against the landscape sparked my imagination wildly, as if I needed encouragement to weave my fantasies.

I was actually glad that Arthur had decided not to come to the New Forest with me, for this was a moment too poignant to share with another living soul. I'd fallen quickly, naturally back into the British way of English and couldn't imagine speaking it any other way. No tourist was I, but a lost child found again, and happy to be coming home.

Lady Jessica Trewlane, the High Priestess of the Coven Home of my Tradition, met me at the station. She was my hostess for the night and showed me such kindness I felt as if we had known each other for centuries. She was in her early fifties, plump with blue eyes that had loads of laugh lines and long wavy red hair touched with silver. Lady Jess was quick to laugh and free with her hugs. It felt immediately like a family.

We had a lovely supper and I was introduced as the coven cousin from America to a small group of friends. Together we would attend the dawn Rite marking the Vernal Equinox, the feast of Ostara. I would be formally initiated as spring was welcomed to a winter-weary world. For me, it was a dream come true and the Doctor had made it possible.

Hampshire is a beautiful part of England and the New Forest felt like a fairy tale forest to me. When the dawn broke and the sun rose over the canopy of the trees, I stood skyclad as I made my vows. Though the morning air held a definite chill I was warmed with the touch of grace. Lady Jess fastened a small silver pentacle around my neck as I knelt in circle. A member of the coven placed a warm cloak around my shoulders as I was raised to my feet. Each of my new coven sisters embraced me in welcome. The profundity of the experience was more than my simple words can describe. I continued my journey south by train the next day renewed spiritually and physically.

As Hampshire receded the hills of the West Country spread out before me, tors rising dramatically in the distance. Here, jocund day, did indeed, stand tiptoe on the misty mountaintops. My throat constricted and tears stood in my eyes while I tried to blink them back. Wooly sheep still in their winter coats grazed lazily along churchyards and open fields of early spring. The White Mare carved into the chalk of the hillside just outside of Westbury appeared standing starkly pale against the green. I was coming home to the lands of Epona. I swallowed hard and let the tears roll silently down my cheeks.

The Hotel in Exmouth on the Devon coast was lovely, a picturesque, Georgian style posting house overlooking Lyme Bay. I couldn't have asked for more. This was a holiday, one that the Doctor and I

A QUESTION OF BALANCE

had earned. The world was once more on the brink of peace, an uneasy stasis achieved between the forces for good and for ill. Soon I would be in the arms of my husband.

I'd been completely prepared for the unpredictable English weather, and was pleasantly surprised to find that it had been custom ordered for me. The days were warm and filled with bright sun. The Hotel garden was bursting with spring flowers and bright foliage. Daffodils, iris and crocus spread color like a fine carpet all the way down the cliffs to the sea, where crystal green water licked gently at beige sand. In the distance across the estuary unfolded Torbay, it's lands rolling away inland in great velvet patches like a quilt, tall hedges dividing the multi-hued fields like fancy stitch-work.

Taking the air deeply in through my nose, it was almost as though I had never breathed before. I lost myself for hours wandering the formal gardens like a solitary Alice in search of a grinning cat or door mouse, but all was peaceful. It was Thursday and the Doctor would be arriving tomorrow.

I slept like a trout, as they say, and awakened to the trilling of the phone by my bed. Sunlight spilled into the room through antique lace curtains and I smiled before I answered, remembering where I was. The telephone was quite insistent, though. Refusing to lend credulity to the illusion of a Victorian bed-sitting room it kept ringing.

I lifted the receiver to my ear. "Hello?"

Arthur's deep voice came clearly. "Yes, hello? Tary, is that you?"

"Yes. Where are you?" As I glanced at my watch, I realized that where he should have been, on the Intercity enroute from Yorkshire, didn't match the background noise filtering through his cell phone

"Look, I've been delayed. I'm in London. Are you all right? How was your flight? Did you get to the New Forest for the sabbat? I'm sorry I couldn't meet you at Gatwick, but I explained all that. Tary? Tarish are you still there?"

The lump in my throat was back and I had to talk around it, trying hard to disguise my disappointment. "I'm here. When are you coming then?"

"Oh, I expect I should be there sometime tonight. I can make the connections into Exeter, and as long as I don't miss the last train to Exmouth I should be in time for dinner."

I didn't say anything.

"Tary, I'm sorry, really. I'll explain everything when I see you tonight." The deep voice softened. "I love you."

I found myself smiling in spite of my disappointment. "I know, I love you too. I'll just walk through the village today then, and get familiar with the place. I'll see you tonight."

"Yes, do that. I've got to go..."

I don't know, but there was something in the way he said it that made me feel strange. "Art? Art, is everything okay? Are you in any trouble?"

"No, no, I'm fine. Everything's all right. Look Tary, I've really got to go. I'll see you later. Don't worry." He hung up.

Don't worry? I called him Art, and he didn't correct me. He hates it when I call him Art. For a long time I stared at the phone still in my hand. I finally hung it back on the cradle when it began making rude sounds. There was a soft knock on the door and I remembered that I'd ordered breakfast in.

As I nibbled at my toast I was thinking. Arthur and I had become very close; in fact, we'd been made Hand Fast before he left for England. Hand Fasting is a ritual bonding between two people similar to a marriage. At the time, it had seemed like a good idea. Of course at the time we didn't know that he was going to be out of work, his funding cut by the current world monetary situation. The point is, that we were bonded, and that made us connected. I ought to have no trouble establishing a psychic link, especially since a mere hundred and fifty miles or so separated us.

A Question of Balance

Having made up my mind to do a little psychic spying, I finished up my breakfast and took a quick bath. I set up my things, lit the candles and incense and drew the heavy drape across the window to shut out the light. I felt especially sensitive, in total harmony with the cosmos. In seconds I had sunk into a light trance. I stretched reaching out for the familiar feeling of the Doctor's mind. Nothing. Absolutely nothing at all. I reached out further and touched on my own unconscious, my higher self. Gradually I let myself slip, into a deep meditative state.

From this perspective I felt totally connected with all creation. I called out for Arthur and felt a distinct mental barrier, as though there was a wall set between him and me. It's difficult to explain the sensation, but it was a very real, nearly physical barrier. He was shielded. That's not an easy technique to learn, I know. Arthur had never shielded himself from me before, why now? I probed a little, testing the fabric. Almost instantly a repulsive image appeared in my mind's eye and I pulled back sharply. This was not of his doing. He may have been able to master a shield of some sort, but it took an expert to produce that kind of psychic retaliation, and he was no expert. For that matter, I wasn't sure even my own talent was up for this. I heaved a mental sigh and drew back, allowing myself to drift into normal consciousness.

I opened my eyes and uttered an invocation of protection for the one I loved. At least I could do that much. It struck me just how alone I really was over here, in a strange country with no real friends. I debated with myself whether or not to call Lady Jess. I finally decided not to just yet. I remembered the disapproval of my own Coven back home, of my involvement with the Doctor's quest.

Most witches today are reluctant to become involved in the eternal battle between good and evil, at least on any kind of a personal level. Mostly, they leave those who follow the left hand, or dark path to do what they will. We all have our part to play in the balance, and who, after all, are we to interfere in someone else's Karma, to determine what is good and what is evil? Live and let live. I'm certain it's a good point, but be that as it may, I had become involved on a personal level, and it looked as though I still was.

I dressed and set out to do exactly what I'd told Arthur I was going to do. As I wandered through the Market Square, fingering trinkets and knick-knacks, I tried not to worry. The trouble was, I knew him, and I knew the sort of people who were likely to call him enemy, some of them very powerful. Even with his association with the Institute severed his enemies and now therefore mine persisted, only now, we were on our own.

I stopped and phoned the hotel to see if there were any messages. There weren't. It was getting on toward late afternoon and I'd missed lunch. That was no problem. Packing up the purchases I'd made into my small duffel bag, I headed toward a lovely looking Victorian teashop for a world famous Devon cream tea. The most wonderful scones with clotted cream and fresh strawberry jam were served on delicate china along with a pot of tea. I determined that the reputation of this County was amply justified. As I sat in the crowded tea-room, I noticed another single lady enter the shop and look around. She was dressed in brown corduroys and a sweater. A floppy brimmed hat was pulled over close-cropped salt and pepper hair. A small backpack similar to my own was slung over one shoulder. The hostess walked over and apologized that there was no seating at the moment. The lady smiled, gray eyes lighting up.

"Mind very much if I wait?"

It was another American, travelling alone.

Without a thought, I waved the hostess over and asked her if the lady would care to join me. She did, introducing herself as Marge Kelly as she sat.

"You're an American, aren't you?" I asked, "So am I. From New Jersey."

Marge smiled. "Staten Island." We shook hands.

A Question of Balance

"What a pretty bracelet," admired my tea companion. "Did you find that here?" She traced the design on the cuff gently with her finger.

"Actually no. I got it as a gift from a friend back home in New Jersey. I understand it was from Ireland though." Just then the waitress appeared with another pot of tea and some more scones.

It turned out that Marge Kelly from Staten Island was an avid traveler and hiker. She was a retired widow who worked as an international courier, accompanying cargo and packages in return for very cheap airfare to different parts of the world. I was shocked to hear her say she was nearly sixty with three grandchildren. She certainly didn't look it.

We had quite a pleasant tea, chatting about her travels around the Southwest of England. I told her I was interested in horseback riding the moors and she was kind enough to recommend a riding stable where the Doctor and I could hire horses and a guide out on Dartmoor. When we had finished up, I must admit I was reluctant to see her go. In truth, I was feeling more than a little lonely.

"Well, you take care now, okay?" Marge smiled. "And don't forget to call me back in the States if you're coming to New York"

"Yes," I said. "I'll do that." She waved as she caught her bus, and I was left standing alone in the Village Market. I looked around. It was after six now and most of the shops were closing or closed already. Soon it would be dark. I made my way back to the hotel. There were still no messages. Well, I though philosophically, dinner was served from seven to nine thirty. It was quite nearly seven now, which should mean that Arthur was almost here. It was nearly eight thirty when the phone rang. I jumped and grabbed the receiver.

"Arthur?"

"This is reception, Miss. A Doctor Pendargroom rang and left a message late this afternoon. I'm sorry for the delay, but I'd swear it wasn't in your box when you inquired. Then just now, I turned and saw it there, practically staring me in the face. I thought I'd better ring and give it to y..."

"Yes." I snapped. "Well what is it?"

"Just that you're to dine on your own, Miss. The gentleman said to tell you he'll be in late this evening."

"Nothing else? Are you sure?"

"I'm certain Miss. There was nothing else." The voice on the line paused a moment, then asked tactfully, "Will you be wanting supper in the dining room then?"

I answered yes, and said I'd be right down.

In a few minutes I managed to repair my eye make-up enough to be presentable, and I entered the dining room. The matre'd, William, seated me with a flourish of napkins, calling me Madam with the accent on the dam. I was hard pressed not to burst into giggles, but I managed some dignity and said simply, "Thank you William", as he handed me the menu.

The distraction of dinner was good for me and by the time desert and coffee came, I was feeling confident that an apologetic Arthur would be phoning from the rail station any time now. At 9:30 I tried his cell phone but got no answer. By then I figured I wouldn't see him until morning. I must have fallen deeply asleep very quickly because when the phone rang it jolted me awake.

"Hello?" I practically screamed.

"Hello Tary. It's me." He sounded very tired.

"Art. Artie, where are you?"

"Arthur", he corrected gently. "Or Doctor. But please Tarish, never Artie."

I breathed slowly in relief. I hadn't even realized I'd been holding my breath.

"Well, Doctor," I said, trying to force my words to drip with ice. The best I got though, was tepid tap water, I'm afraid "...where are you?"

"I'm at the Exeter Central station. Oh, the train is here; I've got to run. I'll be on the ten thirty into Exmouth... be there at eleven oh five. Bye bye."

Once again I sat staring at a dead telephone receiver until it started beeping at me.

"Bloody great." I mumbled, stumbling into the bathroom.

Chapter Ten
Side Tracked

Things were going well at Leeds. Professor Bectinson had recommended me to take his post as chair of the Anthropology department. My credentials were in good order, and I thought I would settle in nicely before it was time to leave for Devon. But to quote Robert Burns, "The best-laid schemes o' mice an' men Gang aft agley." I was still on the Institute's books and Sir wasn't about to make my life easy.

"You heard me Doctor. I want you at the British Museum in the morning." I could practically hear his jowls quivering through the phone line. "Must I send Max to fetch you in?"

"That won't be necessary, Sir. I'll be there." I sighed as I hung up the phone. The British Museum where the Grimoir was being housed had been broken into. The vault where it was normally kept had been torn apart...literally. Fortunately, Professor Bectinson had taken the Book to a conference in Edinburgh where he was presenting a paper. Sir had decided that my expertise was required on the official investigation. It would make me late to meet Tary. I decided to see how it would go before ringing her and spoiling her day.

The trip to London was uneventful. Max was there to meet me as I alighted from the train.

"Good to see you, Doc. I hear this is the end for you!" He took hold of my duffel bag and carried it to the waiting car.

"You make it sound so ominous, Max!" I chuckled. "I would rather like to think of it as a beginning personally."

"What you at Leeds? A teacher?" He laughed. "Come on, how long before you get the itch. There just isn't anything exciting going on up at Leeds now is there. Not like you're used to."

"Now what is all this anyway? I am an ordinary man, a doctor of anthropology, why shouldn't I make a decent teacher?" I watched out the window as he pulled into traffic.

Max winked "Wasn't Indiana Jones a university professor?"

I laughed. "I hardly think I qualify as the swash buckling type, Max!"

He grinned at me…"Aww now I always thought you had a little Errol Flynn in you! What does the missus think?" he asked slyly.

"Tary? Well I don't think she sees much Errol Flynn in me either since she seems to do most of the rescuing." I said smiling at the thought.

"So it's true then. You went and done it. Got married an' all right under Sir David's nose!" He grinned. "I won 10 quid offa Fletcher. He said it wasn't so. Thanks Doc!"

"I had no idea my private life was such a topic of discussion not to mention wagering." I said pointedly, wondering what else was being said about me.

We arrived at the Museum.

Sir hadn't exaggerated the damage. The vault was littered with debris much of it no larger than a matchstick. Bits of paper were strewn along the floor and on the shelves that were left. Most of them seemed to have been torn apart.

"What coulda done all this?" mused Max as we surveyed the ruin.

"I don't know," I said under my breath. This amount of damage would have taken five burly men hours to accomplish. The perpetrators, however, had had only minutes before the alarm was sounded. At least that is how it appeared.

"Max," I started grimly, "see if you can reach Professor Bectinson at the conference in Edinburgh. We've got to warn him. If they did all this to get the Book, god only knows what they will do to him if they find out he's got it."

"Right," he said. "I'm on it."

A Question of Balance

I rummaged through the wreckage trying to piece together anything that seemed to fit. It was like attempting to do a jigsaw puzzle in the dark with half the pieces missing. As I got to the bottom of a pile of debris my breath caught in my throat. A long piece of shelving survived nearly intact. Nearly, but not quite. There was a long track of what looked like claw marks gouged deeply into the hardwood plank. I removed the piece and marked it to go to the lab for a complete forensic work-over. I held out little hope that they would discover what manner of creature made those marks.

I realised this was going to take me some time, so I went upstairs to the Museum café to get a cup of tea and to ring Tary at the hotel in Exmouth. I attempted to keep the conversation light, not to worry her. As I was speaking to her, Sir David appeared at my elbow, forcing me to cut the conversation short.

"No, no, I'm fine. Everything's all right. Look Tary, I've really got to go. I'll see you later. Don't worry." I rang off.

'Well Doctor?" he asked, taking the chair across from me.

"I don't know, Sir. There is little doubt who is responsible. I read Mayfair's hand in this. I will have to wait until I get the analysis back to make a judgement as to exactly what it was that did the damage...but we can be fairly sure who the conjuror was." I finished my tea and glanced at my watch.

"Have you another appointment Doctor?" my director asked.

"I was supposed to be on the 10:40 train into Exeter this morning, Sir, to meet Tary. I am hoping I can still make the evening train."

"Well I shan't keep you then. Carry on with the investigation. I will expect a report before you leave," he said, pouring a cup of tea and helping himself to a scone.

"Yes Sir. Of course Sir." I said before I turned and walked away.

Maxwell joined me down in the vault. "No go, Doc. I couldn't get the professor. I left a message with the event organiser's secretary."

"Well, that will do I suppose, thanks Max." I finished marking what pieces I wanted further analysis on, then went to find an office with some privacy to type in my preliminary report. It was nearly half three, so I rang the hotel in Exmouth to let Tary know I would me on the late train. I left a message with reception and turned my attention to the task at hand.

I barely made the 19:30 train from Waterloo to Exeter. Luckily I managed to get a seat. After going nearly 20 hours straight, I was exhausted and dozed most of the trip. I rang Tary when I reached Exeter. It would be another thirty minutes on a local train to Exmouth...plenty of time for her to organise a taxi to come fetch me.

I must have woken her and she did not sound altogether pleased. I missed her so much I would have been glad to see her even if she bit my head off....which she sounded nearly ready to do. In spite of my good intentions I was beginning to realise there was more to being a husband than just the ring. I hoped that Tary would be patient with me as I learned to navigate a whole new way of life, in effect a new culture in which I was a virtual stranger. In many ways this was the most difficult assignment I had ever faced.

Chapter Eleven
Reunited

I had reception call me a taxi and met the train at eleven oh five. He was one of the last to stumble off, unshaven and rumpled, weighted down with a large duffel bag and a brief-case. Even from a distance I could see the shadows under his eyes and the tiny wrinkles which hadn't been so evident the last time I'd seen him just a few short weeks ago. His hair was clipped short now, gray-shot brown curls tamed into a semblance of business-man-style order. I waved as he looked up. He smiled. At least that hadn't changed.

Dropping his bags on the platform he rushed to meet me. By all the gods of Earth it was wonderful to be crushed in those long arms again and feel his breath warm on my cheek in the evening chill. It was also embarrassing. I let him kiss me for a minute then I motioned to the driver to take the bags and led the Doctor to the waiting taxi.

"So", I said as the car wound it's way through the village toward the Beacon Hill. "What was it this time? Possessed Pygmies? Linda Blair's Birthday? A Satanic Ode to spring, perhaps?" I turned my face as he tried to kiss me.

"Tary, don't be like this."

"Be like what?" I shrugged, staring out the window, trying to keep my voice steady.

"Oh come on, Tarish," he quipped, "You know I often get..."

"Yes, tied up in your job." I finished for him. I was trying hard to be angry. "I was worried to death. I do know just how often you get tied up in your job, that's what frightens me." Tears spilled over and he pulled me close, not saying anything at all. He just stroked my hair and let me cry myself out. Finally, I looked up. He grinned at me and brushed my lips lightly with his.

"I did tell you not to worry," he whispered, tapping my nose with a forefinger.

"Yes, I know, but the..."

The taxi stopped.

"We're here, Tary. This is it, isn't it? Why, it's lovely." He leaned over to see the taximeter. "Here, mate... keep the change, I'll manage the bags."

In a few minutes, we were up in our room. I turned to confront him.

"Now, do you mind telling me..."

"I don't mind at all telling you how wonderful you look, Tarish. But I am tired and hungry. I haven't had a bite since tea. Let me just wash up and ring room service. After I've eaten something we can talk."

I opened the duffel bag and started unpacking mostly to keep my hands occupied.

"I could do with a shave and a full bath too, but not until I've eaten." He stared at his reflection in the bathroom mirror. "I do wish it wasn't so late. We could have gone into the pub."

"What is going on, Arthur?" I wouldn't be put off.

"Tary, I think we ought to be seen in public, together. Once we've established we're here with plenty of witnesses I'll feel better. It'll be harder to make us disappear you see." He smiled that John Lennon smile and winked.

I was beginning to get angry as the resentment built up. This was supposed to be a holiday, our honeymoon in fact. Why couldn't they just leave us alone, even for a little while? I wondered bitterly, and not for the last time, how I'd ever gotten mixed up in all this. Why was it me who'd 'inherited' the Crown of Fae. It wasn't fair. I sometimes felt like a puppet, with no more control over my life than Kermit the Frog. There was a knock on the door and a tray of sandwiches was delivered.

"I want to talk." I said hotly, passing him a plate.

He kissed me hard on the mouth and I melted.

"Okay", I said. "Okay, that too."

"Good," he beamed. "Now, let me eat."

A Question of Balance

Much later he looked at me, eyes bright spots centered in dark circles, hair curling damply around his ears, and sighed. "I thought you understood what working with the Institute was about. They may have cut me loose, but not for another two weeks."

"I still don't see what a burglary at some museum in London has to do with anything...unless..."

He frowned. "Never-mind Tary... it isn't important. I'm here now, let's just enjoy the time."

The first stirrings of panic had started closing in around my stomach. It had been more than four months, with nothing more extraordinary than a slight mishap with a bicycle, the sort of thing that can happen to anybody. The human mind is a complex thing, and time has a way of making the lines around memory fuzzy and indistinct. I mean, I know what happened, the job I helped the Doctor do for... Whoever. I was there, after all. Wasn't I? But that was over. Life had settled down into more or less normal grooves. Now, I was afraid that all that peace and calm, if you could ever call life with the Doctor calm, would be shattered again.

"I don't know." I was pouting.

"Tary?" He was exhausted, I could see it, but he wouldn't quit. I gave in a little.

"All right, but I still don't understand. We retrieved the three talismans, right? See I still have the Crown and the Key and the Book is safely buried in some deep vault at the Institute somewhere isn't it? Isn't it?" I moved to the bed and sat down close to him. "What else can anyone expect of you? Of us? I was there, and I still have my doubts as to what really happened." I shuddered, and he pulled me down beside him. "It almost seems like a nightmare that was over a long time ago. I can't even remember it clearly anymore."

"I know, Tary. I know. I'm sorry. I'm afraid we've made some rather terrible enemies, and I'm afraid that they haven't quite given up yet." He kissed me, and for a while we just got lost in each other, leaving the Cosmos to get along without us for a brief time.

The next morning I let him sleep in while I walked again in the gardens. It was so peaceful and quiet it seemed almost impossible to imagine anything dark or evil existing in such a beautiful place and on such a glorious day. But, I have a pretty good imagination.

I closed the little gate behind me and as I turned, I caught a fleeting glimpse of a bicyclist riding along the lane below the cliff. I thought I recognized the sweater and the floppy brimmed hat, and a small backpack slung over one shoulder. I waved and called. "Marge. Marge, up here."

For a moment the bike slowed and I thought I saw it's rider turn toward my voice, but then she was around the bend and out of sight. How odd since I thought Marge Kelly was on her way to other parts yesterday. I'd seen her myself getting on the bus to Salisbury. Shrugging I turned back to the Hotel. Maybe it wasn't her, or maybe she changed her mind. A cloud passed in front of the sun and I shivered. Suddenly chilly, I hurried up the steps to the Hotel.

I was reluctant to wake Arthur. We hadn't really gotten much sleep the night before and I knew he was all done in. I'd skipped breakfast, and was hungry, so I stopped in the Hotel bar to get a light lunch and a Pepsi. Robbie, the bartender kidded me that since I arrived he had to carry up a whole case of diet Pepsi from the cellar.

He was an appealing young man, about twenty two with a longing for adventure. An aspiring photo-journalist, he'd been planning a trip around the world for next year, ending up in Cambodia to do a photo spread on the troubles still brewing in that little corner of the world.

We chatted pleasantly while I ate a ham and cheddar sandwich on a wonderful crusty brown roll. The day seemed suddenly more normal. Maybe Arthur was wrong. Maybe it was just his imagination working over-time and there really wasn't anybody looking to make us disappear at all. Maybe... and maybe not.

A Question of Balance

Well, it was two o'clock and Robbie was closing the bar until dinner, so I climbed the stairs back to our room and entered quietly. Arthur was awake, sitting up reading the newspaper.

"Out for a walk?" he smiled, putting the paper down on the floor beside the bed.

"Yes. It's perfectly gorgeous out today. You really must come down and see the gardens."

"Maybe later. I thought that perhaps tomorrow we'd have a little ride. I've called the local horse school and arranged a short lesson for you and a ride along the beach. How does that sound?"

I grinned. "Sounds like a perfectly normal type of thing to do on holiday."

He grinned right back at me. "Oh, it is, it is. That way, you'll be more prepared when we go out on Dartmoor."

"Prepared? Prepared for what? Just a nice little jaunt, I thought, you know, walk and trot?" I was thinking about my hemorrhoids.

"Walk and trot? On Dartmoor? You can't be serious, Tary. I called the stable number you left and arranged for a full half-day excursion. Dartmoor's a very big place, and you want to see at least some of it, don't you?"

"Oh. Well, yes, I guess so."

"Well there are great hedges and wide parcels of open plain and huge rock formations and tors and you can't think a simple walk and trot would get you very far." He made it sound so logical.

"I guess not," I answered. "But hedges? We can go around them, right?"

Arthur shook his head sadly. "If you think the rest of us are going to stand and wait while you try and find a way 'round, you're daft. That's why I thought a quick lesson was in order." He stood up and put his arms around me. "Don't worry, they'll have you jumping in no time at all."

Yeah, right, I thought to myself.

We enjoyed a lovely dinner in the dining room and a few drinks in the bar before settling in for a quiet, intimate evening. We had a lot of catching up to do. I was so preoccupied I completely forgot about seeing Marge.

Much to my surprise, and Arthur's delight, I did quite well in the ring the next day. My riding skills, ingrained in me as a teenager, were rusty, but still there, and in spite of my trepidation, I had no difficulty managing the small jumps.

"Good, Tarish. Excellent," he called by way of encouragement.

I pushed the hair trapped beneath the riding hat out of my eyes and laughed out loud. "I can just imagine how I'm going to feel by tomorrow morning, though. Maybe we should postpone Dartmoor for a day or two?"

"Nonsense," he grinned, as he helped me down. "A good hot soak and a massage... you'll be fine, I promise." He winked at the instructor. "Listen to me, Tary, I am the Doctor, after all. Besides, it's all arranged."

The brass cuff around my wrist felt suddenly tight. I rubbed at it.

"What's that?" asked the Doctor, holding my arm still at the elbow so he could have a good look.

"Oh, nothing. It was a gift. It apparently doesn't come off until it wants to, and then only in a place of great enchantment." I pulled back my arm.

"Magic?" He raised one eyebrow.

"Yes, sort of. I'm not all that certain of what its power is, but it is pretty, and it was a gift."

"Gift? A gift from whom?" he asked quietly.

"Oh, just a friend that I did a favor for, that's all."

I'd had it on for weeks and had almost forgotten it until now. For some reason, the skin underneath was irritated and itchy, and I rubbed my finger along the tiny bumps to ease it.

"Here, let me see." Arthur lifted my arm in front of his face and peered at the small ring of red bumps, which had formed underneath the brass ornament.

"I have some hydrocortisone cream in my shaving kit. That ought to ease the rash." He looked it over carefully. It was funny but in the daylight my wrist looked almost black and blue. I hadn't noticed that before.

"Does it hurt?"

I shook my head and pulled my hand away.

"No it's fine. I've been wearing it for weeks, ever since you left in fact. I don't even notice it anymore. Come on. I'm getting hungry."

The taxi had pulled up to take us back to the village. I had the car drop us off at the Victorian tea-shop where I'd had tea the other day.

"This is very nice. How are the scones?" Arthur asked before alighting from the taxi. The driver indicated that they were very acceptable and Arthur paid him off.

Inside, there was a different hostess than the one from the other day. We sat down and ordered the cream tea.

"I was very impressed," I began, licking the clotted cream from my fingers. "So was Marge, when we were here the other day."

"Yes, I can see why," he said, spreading his scone liberally with strawberry jam. "Delicious. Who is Marge?"

I told him the story.

"You know what's odd? I could have sworn I saw her cycling down along the sea yesterday morning. I called, but I must have been mistaken. She was on her way to Salisbury Friday. It must have been someone else."

"Yes," he mused. "You must have been mistaken. A place like Exmouth On-Sea is bound to have more than it's fair share of active older retired ladies, and they do all seem to favor those floppy brimmed hats, too."

"Remind me never to buy a floppy brimmed hat when I retire." I said teasingly.

"Don't worry," he said with feeling. "I wouldn't let you near one."

I laughed and finished up my tea. We spent the rest of the day shopping for souvenirs to bring home for my family. I wanted something special for Jace, but nothing seemed quite right. I wasted a lot of time looking before the Doctor made a suggestion.

"Oh look, one of those will be perfect for your Jason." He laughed, nodding in the direction of a gaggle of teenaged girls. "Pick one out and I'll tell them to wrap it to go."

I punched him in the arm as I giggled. We walked back up the hill to the hotel arm in arm like any couple on their honeymoon.

After dinner we visited one of the recommended local pubs. Rob was there with his girl friend and we had a really fun evening. Rob and Sissy were so cute together. I wondered if I had ever been that young. He and the Doctor played a game of darts and I was pleased to note that Arthur was not particularly good at everything. We laughed a lot. On the way back to the hotel we walked along the beach. All in all a nearly perfect day.

Chapter Twelve
Dartmoor

I rolled onto my side, snuggling into the curve of Arthur's back. Just the merest twinge of stiffness in the back of my calves reminded me that I was jumping horses yesterday. I woke him up with a nibble on the ear.

"Wakey, wakey! Dartmoor awaits!" I was really looking forward to our excursion.

In Exeter we hired a car and driver who knew the moor well to take us around. Our ride was scheduled to go out at two, so we had plenty of time for a little sight seeing by auto first.

So far, in spite of my early misgivings and Arthur's intimations, nothing in the least unusual had happened to spoil our holiday. I had almost forgotten that there was even a slight possibility of any danger. Especially out here in the bright sunshine, it seemed as far-fetched as the sky falling.

"So, you're interested in the moor then, are you?" asked the driver making conversation. "Would you like me to take you to see a pisky ring?"

I looked over to Arthur.

"A stone circle, Tary. The moor is dotted with them, some of them quite old, I understand. Is that so?" he directed to the driver.

"Oh aye. Some very old, but none older than the one I be knowing about." He glanced around at us.

"Then take us, please", I said, squeezing The Doctor's hand. "Is it far?"

"No, not far. That's what put me in mind of it. It's right around here a ways. I'll find it, Miss."

True to his word, he turned off onto a pony track and found the stone circle. The standing menhirs averaged about knee high on Arthur. There were thirteen.

We got out and walked the few yards to the circumference. Closing my eyes, I let my mind drift, and was immediately rewarded with the feeling of old magic which permeated the fairy ring. I felt comfortable here, as familiar as if I was standing in my own garden.

Slowly I walked around the circle deosil and entered at its eastern edge. I made my obeisance at the four directions and reached out my arm to remove the cuff. It just seemed natural to leave it here as an offering to the old gods. But the bracelet had other ideas. It felt tight and any attempt I made to loosen it, irritated the already red and puffy skin underneath. Well, I thought, I guess this isn't the right place.

I exited the circle and walked back to the waiting taxi with Arthur.

"What was that all about?" he whispered.

"What? Oh, nothing. I'll tell you later."

We found the riding stable in the village of Widecomb-in-the-Moor, a charming place, all cobbles and thatch. Our driver had agreed to wait for us in the local cafe. We had hired him for the day and at least doubled what he would otherwise have earned for the time with half the work and the afternoon to himself. He seemed happy enough with the arrangement, and the cafe.

There were two other couples and a single lady riding out with us. One couple was German, with very limited English and the other, young honeymooners from the North of England, near Arthur's home in Yorkshire. The single lady said she was simply playing hooky for the day from her office, which was local. Her name was Patricia and she'd ridden the moor often.

Soon we were all mounted and making our way in single file along the narrow cobbled lanes of Widecomb, sharing the way with an occasional auto. It wasn't long, though, before the Village was behind us, with open moor spreading out as far as we could see for miles on either side. We left the pavement

A QUESTION OF BALANCE

and headed straight out, following a pony track toward the distant rocks.

Now that we no longer shared the road with more modern conveyances, we were able to spread out. Arthur pulled his horse alongside me so we could talk as we rode. Everyone had told me that the weather on Dartmoor was a law unto itself. Well, the law ruled in my favor that day. It was cool, about fifty-five degrees Fahrenheit, and very sunny, perfect for horseback riding. From the top of a small rise we could see for miles around us. Our guide called for a canter to make better time toward the distant rock formations, among which prehistoric stone huts huddled, monument to the ancient Britons who once roamed the land.

Patricia joined Arthur and I, the three of us cantering smoothly several lengths behind the rest of the group. I reined in, wanting to take some pictures from a distance, to show perspective when we got closer. The Doctor and Patricia stopped too. I took several snaps, not trusting to luck and a restless horse that refused to stand perfectly still. The rest of our group had gotten quite a distance ahead by the time I was satisfied, but it was no problem keeping them is sight. Arthur suggested that a short gallop would have us caught up in no time.

A gallop is a lot faster than a steady canter. I gulped, turned the chestnut mare's head and kicked my heels, keeping Arthur and Patricia's retreating backs directly in front of me as I tried to catch up. I held the reins short, a little wary of stones and holes into and over which my horse could stumble. The last thing I wanted to do was break my neck in a fall. Apparently, though, Arthur and Patricia held more confidence in the surefootedness of their mounts and were moving at quite a good clip. In fact, it almost looked as though they were racing each other. I reined up short and stared. They were racing each other, and not even a backward glance for me. I fumed and held the mare to a fast trot, determined not to lose either my dignity or my seat.

When they reached the rest of our group, Arthur finally turned to see what had become of me. I waved, and began to canter. He waved back and pointed, indicating that they were going around the other side of the huge rock tor. Then, they turned and were gone. No problem. Even though they were out of sight, once I got around those rocks, it should be easy enough to spot them. After all the day was crystal clear, and the visibility on the moor seemed endless. I was slightly annoyed, but not in the least frightened, it was too beautiful a day for that. Along the track, I stopped again to take a photo of one of Dartmoor's famous ponies, and then several snaps of the longhaired wild sheep that grazed here and there. Finally, I reached the rocks and went around. They were gone.

I didn't panic. Standing up in my stirrups to get a better view, I scanned the area in all directions. In the distance, I could see a solitary car or two cruising slowly along one of the small narrow lanes that dissected the open moorland. There also seemed to be a small encampment of some sort over toward the eastern horizon. It was very difficult to gauge distance, in fact, it was impossible for me, being a complete amateur at this sort of thing. It looked like my best bet would be east, at least it looked as if I might find people. That's what I made my target.

As I turned the mare's head my right wrist suddenly began to ache. I stared at it. Beneath the bracelet, the skin was a mottled purple and bluish, with angry red blisters along the outer rim. It was definitely quite bruised. Well, there was nothing I could to about it now. The bracelet wouldn't come off, and fiddling with it hurt, so I ignored the discomfort and rode on.

The sun had sunk very low in the sky by the time I'd reached the encampment. There were two land Rovers and an ancient looking old covered wagon painted red and gold with a green canvas covering and two smallish ponies grazing tethered alongside. The motor bike and ten speed leaning casually up against the side of the gypsy wagon made an incon-

A QUESTION OF BALANCE

gruous picture, blending the old with the new. I couldn't resist taking a shot with my camera. A young teenaged girl came around the side and waved as she walked over.

"Hello? You lost or something?"

I blinked. Blond haired and blue-eyed, this pretty little thing dressed in jeans and a sweatshirt was not what I'd pictured as a gypsy.

"Yes. I got separated from my horse caravan. Have you seen them?"

"No, not anybody on horses today, Miss. Where'd you ride out from?" Her freckled nose wrinkled as she squinted up at me.

"Widecomb," I answered, once more scanning the horizon. the sun was even lower now. "Can you point me in the right direction?"

The girl laughed. "Oh, I expect your horse'll see you back safe. They always find their way to the stables when dark starts coming onto the moor."

She rubbed the white patch between the mare's eyes and whispered. The horse blew warm air from her nostrils, and the girl looked back up at me again.

"You just let her have her head, and you'll be fine."

Then she frowned, slightly. "Widecomb, eh? You come quite a ways. It'll take you some time to get back. Just trust your pony there and she'll see you through safe though. They won't cross the bogs. More sense than most people."

"Yeah, more sense than this one anyway." I smiled and tossed the girl a fifty pence piece. "Thank you." I called, turning the mare's head, back in the direction I thought I'd come from.

An hour later I was closer to being ready to panic. It was nearly dusk and my horse seemed perfectly content to wander aimlessly, grazing on the tall moor grass whenever I let the reins loose. She certainly seemed in no hurry to find her way back to the stable, in spite of the coming dark. My arm ached now all the way to the elbow and I wondered if the damn bracelet was cutting off the circulation. As soon as we got back, I was going to have Arthur cut the cuff off, if he had to.

I stopped a minute to let the horse drink. Over the lapping of water, I thought I could hear something else. It sounded a lot like someone calling my name from very far away. In my everyday life, I seem to manage just fine without relying on working magic, and I do so rarely, so I forget, sometimes, that in instances of need, I do have a viable option. Closing my eyes, I let my mind wander as aimlessly as my horse until it settled on something. I let the visualization clear in my mind, and whispered.

"Arthur, Arthur, come find me." The wind took my whispers with a subtle gesture and I smiled, knowing that I should have thought of this hours ago.

In a few minutes, the shouts became louder, more distinct.

"T A R Y... Where are Y O U..." The Doctor's voice echoed from the rocks that had been thrown into weird relief by the setting sun, and stood menacingly all around me. Somehow, I had managed to get back to exactly the place where I'd last seen them.

"Here," I called as the mare whickered softly, and side-stepped.

Suddenly he was beside me, holding onto the reins of my horse with one hand and speaking into a two-way radio held in the other.

"She's here, I've found her. She's okay."

A burst of static, then a voice came weakly through the tiny speaker. "Good, where are you? Stay put. It's dangerous out here in the dark. We'll come for you."

Arthur grinned at me. "Well believe it or not, we're..."

A chunk of stone about the size of a fist clattered down from the rocks above and landed with a sharp crack between the two horses. My mare side-stepped, pulling up her head and rearing slightly. The reins were yanked from Arthur's hands and his own horse moved back skittishly. The radio fell and landed on the stones, breaking up as it hit.

A QUESTION OF BALANCE

Another rock fell, and I was having a hard time keeping the mare quiet.

"What the devil's going on." cried Arthur, battling for control over his own mount. "Is the sky falling?" He looked up.

No more stones fell. It was completely silent. I looked at him. "Why did you say that?"

He blinked back at me. "Say what?"

"About the sky falling?" My voice shook.

"About the what...?" Seeing I was near panic he moved his horse, calm now, in closer to mine.

"It's an expression, Tary. Just a silly expression. Look, the sky's not really falling. Just a few loose stones from the top of the tor, that's all. Perfectly natural." Gently he patted my hand. Looking ruefully down at the shattered remains of the walkie-talkie he sighed.

"There's a bit of hard luck, though. We're cut off now. They're right you know, about the moor being no place for strangers at night." He looked around in the gloom.

"We need something to signal them with. A light or something. Did you bring your torch?"

I giggled hysterically. "Of course I brought my torch. I always have my torch, a screwdriver, pliers and my pocket-knife, you know that. Be prepared, I always say. Never know what you're going to run into..." I started to cry.

"What's the matter? If you brought the torch, hand it over. They can see the light for miles on a clear night."

I sniffled. "It's in my purse back at the stable. I didn't want to ride with my pockets stuffed with junk."

"Oh."

"All I've got is about three pounds sixty pence a two shilling piece... and my knife." I was rummaging around in my pockets.

"Well..." He didn't say anything else.

"I don't even have my cigarettes.." Now I was really ready to panic. Then I remembered the girl.

"The gypsy girl said the horses would find their own way back to the stables when it started getting dark," I said hopefully.

"Tary," he said gently, "there haven't been any gypsies on Dartmoor in this century. Besides, do these animals look like they're going anywhere at the moment?"

He was right. We must have got the only two horses in Great Britain who couldn't find their way home.

The Doctor dismounted and walked around, then came and stood at my knee.

I looked down at him.

"Well, come on," he said, a bit impatiently. "I'll help you down."

"Down?" I asked dimly.

"Yes, down," he reiterated. "Down, as-in-off-the-horse." He pronounced each word clearly and distinctly, as though he was addressing a rather stupid and willful child.

"But I thought..."

"Are you planning on sitting on that mare all night? Not very comfortable sleeping, I shouldn't think."

"Sleep?"

He sighed, his voice gentling. "Look Tary, I take the blame myself. I shouldn't have left you on your own like that. I just didn't think you'd have any trouble catching us up. You shouldn't have. I can't see how we missed each other."

"Pixie led. I was pixie led..." My arm was throbbing and my head hurt. I just sat there shaking, wishing for numbness. He reached up and lifted me from the saddle. As he set me on my feet, my legs gave out... both of them. My walking stick was the other thing left at the stable. The day had been warm and pleasant, but with the sun gone, it was turning very cold, very fast. My fingers felt stiff inside my gloves, and there was no way I could keep to my feet without his arm to support me. From wrist to neck and down my back, my whole right side felt as if it was on fire. Suddenly, I was nauseous, about to be sick. I don't usually get ill like that, but I remembered one other time... in the woods of New York State... I leaned over and heaved.

I sat up against a large outcropping huddled in my jacket, with Arthur's coat wrapped around me. He'd been trying to start a fire, but my matches and my lighter were with my cigarettes, and he'd never been a Boy Scout.

"I wish you could just call the fire to this kindling, like they do in those grown-up fairy stories you're so fond of," he puffed, working a reasonable facsimile of a bow drill onto a piece of softwood. "You know, close your eyes, say the magic words and poof. Instant barbecue." I knew he was trying to joke, to keep things light, but I wasn't in the mood.

Slowly, I stood facing him. His coat slipped off my shoulders and lay like a dead thing at my feet. I couldn't have been more than half-conscious, the memory's dim at best. Anyway, I remember closing my eyes and visualizing a burst of flame leaping to the kindling as I called on the salamanders, elemental guardians of fire. He says I pointed right at the pile of twigs and suddenly, the softwood caught and poof, we had fire.

Then I fainted.

When I came to, Arthur had wrapped me up again and was sitting beside me, holding me close. His face looked worried in the flickering firelight. My right arm was laying in my lap, throbbing as though it was alive in its own right.

He smiled. "How exactly did you do that?" He inclined his head toward the fire.

"Magic. It's what you wanted, right?" I was feeling very sleepy and warm and perhaps a little smug.

"Hmm. That arm is looking bad, Tary."

I winced as he touched it. It didn't feel as bad as it had before though. Even the bracelet felt a little looser.

"Leave it, it's okay. I just want to sleep."

"All right. I'll leave it for now, but tomorrow I want to have a very good look at it, and a very good explanation of where it came from."

I nodded, yawned and fell asleep.

It seemed like days, but of course it couldn't have been more than a couple of hours before Patricia, Bonnie the guide from the stable, and our hired driver found us.

Apparently, I'd been sleeping deeply, and was still groggy as the Doctor helped me to my feet. For a split second I stared into the faces of our rescuers. Lit by the flickering light from the dying flames, it seemed as though the two women weren't human at all. For the merest fraction of an instant, I imagined I saw skeletal features superimposed over the faces of Patricia and Bonnie. I blinked, and everything was normal again. Just three normal people watching in concern as I got my feet under me.

Bonnie looked at Arthur.

"Doctor, can she ride?"

I answered, a little miffed at being spoken about as if I wasn't even present. "I am perfectly able to ride," I said, as I brushed the dead grass from my trousers and handed Arthur back his coat.

He peered into my face. "Are you sure, Tary? Before it almost seemed you were..."

"That was before," I snapped, waspishly. Then, I realized how I must have sounded.

"I'm sorry. The nap did the trick. I'm fine now."

He was still looking at me strangely and seemed about to say something, but Patricia spoke first.

"Well then, if you're fit enough, I suggest we get going. I for one am freezing out here."

After Arthur had helped me onto my mount, he turned to the man sitting a huge roan gelding, our hired driver. "Thank you. It was awfully decent of you to wait and come out and hunt for us, Will. I appreciate it."

The big man smiled. "No trouble, sir. I couldn't very well go off home to my wife and tell her I lost my two fares on the moor, could I?"

He grinned. "Besides, I'll charge you the full regular fare into Exeter. I'm afraid there's not a train to Exmouth until the morning though."

A Question of Balance

Arthur also grinned, and shook Will's hand firmly. "Agreed then." He mounted up and we were on our way moving slowly across the dark face of the moor.

My wrist had settled into a dull ache, and the bruising seemed to have abated some as well. Still, I felt a little queasy as an occasional slight nausea unsettled my stomach. Bonnie rode ahead, picking her way carefully while Arthur and Will rode on either side of me and Patricia followed close behind. The moon was in it's fourth quarter, but a slight mist seemed to cast a haze across it's light.

Bonnie stopped suddenly, her horse acting skittishly. She turned to the rest of us as we pulled up behind her.

"The horses won't cross the bog. We'll have to go around."

"Around?" Arthur groaned. "What bog? I don't remember a bog when we rode out."

"We must have come from the other direction," suggested Patricia, nudging her horse up so she was alongside Arthur.

I turned to Will. "You know the moor, can't you point us right?"

The huge man half smiled and shrugged his massive shoulders sheepishly. "Nobody can know all the moor, Miss. She's right, though. There's no horse what'll cross the bog, especially at night. Got more sense than most people."

Almost reflexively, I began to answer, "..more sense than..." I stared, my mouth gaping open.

"Tary, what's the matter?" The Doctor was looking me with alarm.

"The girl," I muttered. "That's exactly what the girl said. She said the horses wouldn't cross the bog... that they'd got more sense than most people."

"Well," he said comfortably. "That's a common enough expression in these parts."

Suddenly, Bonnie's horse whirled and plunged directly into us, screaming like a charging stallion. Arthur's horse backed and reared, while my mare seemed to stumble, pulling sharply at her bit. We were separated now by some yards. From behind, I could hear another horse, probably Patricia's, rearing and coming down hard, again and again. I wanted to turn and look, but it was all I could do stay in the saddle, clinging to huge fistfuls of mane.

"This way." Will shouted, grabbing for the reins which I'd managed to drop.

Arthur turned his horse's head, and in the dim light, I could see his normally pale features go dead white. He nodded to Will. "Get her out of here. I'll come behind."

Will didn't waste any time for explanations. He pulled the reins over the mare's head like a lead and turned sharply, my horse with him. I had no idea what was going on, only that I was feeling as ill as I ever had. There was no time to wonder, either. Trying to stay on a panicky horse when my stomach seemed to have acquired a will of it's own required all my concentration.

Vaguely, I could hear other noises, sounds of cursing and wild laughter which seemed to follow us close for a while on that wild ride. Then it faded away on the wind. Arthur's horse pounded behind Will and I. Over the thunder of hoof beats and the wind, he shouted, "Make for the Ring, Will. The fairy ring."

I thought Will chuckled softly. "Aye, and that's right where I'm heading. Put the Piskies to the magic."

I remember thinking, in a moment of clarity, that this whole episode was crazy. Here we were, three perfectly sane, normal adults in the year 2002, fleeing on horseback across Dartmoor from... from... I realized I had no idea what we were running from. The Hounds of Hell? Baskerville Hall was probably somewhere in the area....I squeezed my eyes shut tight and concentrated on hanging on.

It seemed we'd been galloping for hours when Will finally gave a gruff shout and pulled the roan to a stop. My mare, sweating and panting in the chill air, halted right behind him. Arthur reined up alongside and swung down in one fluid motion.

A QUESTION OF BALANCE

"Quick," he yelled, as he lifted me from the saddle and handed me over to the man he called Will. "Get her into the circle."

Will nodded and began to pull me along. I resisted.

"What about you?" I called, with absolutely no idea why getting into the circle was so important I only knew that I was suddenly terrified for him. Terrified of what might happen if Patricia and Bonnie, or at least what we knew as Patricia and Bonnie, caught him outside.

"You just go on. I'll be there in a minute." He turned and disappeared into a stand of conifers near the edge of the pony track.

"The eastern edge," I gasped as Will once more started toward the circle. "We must always enter at the eastern edge."

He nodded once and we walked around to the east, then stepped into the stone ring.

Immediately, the nausea abated and my wrist ceased to throb. I was actually able to think again. Making a short courtesy to the quarters, I began an invocation inviting the four elemental Guardians to join us and aid in our protection. A white mist crept in, seeming to come from a depression in the Earth at the circle's center. It didn't feel at all damp or uncomfortable, but rather warm and enveloping, like a blanket.

I heard the sound of horses moving in the darkness outside the ring. There were ours, of course, but I could also hear others moving in toward us in the distance.

"Arthur." I had meant to shout, but only a whisper escaped from my throat. It was enough.

The mist parted eerily and the tall lanky form of the Doctor seemed to appear out of the air.

"It's okay Tary. I'm here." He smiled. He was carrying a long, stout oak branch, brown leaves and acorn clusters still clinging.

"The sacred Oak from the Wystwood." grinned Will. "Aye, that were a smart move. We may yet need protection this night."

"Protection?" I stared from one to the other. "Protection from what?"

For some reason, the whole scene suddenly appeared ludicrous. Arthur standing there, peeling bark from what I assumed would be a quarter staff, with big Will looking on, making suggestions, was like something out of a B movie. A very bad one. I started to laugh.

"Tarish, instead of laughing, why don't you help?"

I put my hand over my mouth and mumbled, "How?"

Arthur put out his hand. "Knife."

I smiled to myself, and with the precision of a surgical nurse, I pulled it from my pocket, opened it and slapped it handle first neatly into his palm.

"Knife, Doctor."

He threw me a look from under his eyebrows, but said nothing as he continued to peel away the bark and small branches in great strips.

I shrugged. "If you could only see how silly we all must look..." I began.

"Shhh. Shh, listen." He stopped, head cocked to one side.

"It's only the horses wandering off." I huffed, the words tumbling from my mouth as steam rising into the night air. "I bet they have no trouble finding their way home now."

"No, not them. Listen. There are other horses."

He was right. It sounded like a lot of other horses. There were voices too. Dry, sibilant voices that sounded only vaguely human. I recognized Patricia's.

"Drive the ponies through the ring," it spat. "Drive them through."

Will started. "They mean to stampede the wild ponies into us." He moved in front of me protectively.

I'd seen the little ponies that run wild on the moor, and they hardly struck me as dangerous. None of them was any taller that ten or eleven hands at most and they didn't normally travel in large herds. Not much of a threat, to my mind.

A Question of Balance

He looked at me as though reading my thoughts. "I promise you, Miss, that fifteen or so of them little ponies can do a lot of damage if we're in the way and they're frightened. It's a way of getting us to break the circle."

I suppose he had a point. Fifteen or so of anything could be dangerous, and those cute shaggy little ponies did have sharp, pointy little hooves.

Fortunately, it didn't come to that. Without giving it a second thought, I took the staff from Arthur and walked the circumference of the circle deosil, reinforcing the magic that was there inherently. Piskies, fairies or whatever, had made the job easy. The circle held tight, I was certain that nothing driven by any of the dark arts would be able to pass through. I was right. The terrified ponies broke and passed around the ring, disappearing into the woods beyond.

I let out a sigh. "Is it over?"

Arthur listened. We could sense, more that see through the mist, that the two creatures who'd chased us were still there, though unable to pass the barrier.

"What time is it?" he whispered.

I looked at my watch and gasped. "It's nearly one," I cried. How could it have gotten so late?

Will smiled. "We're all right then. At one, they'll have to leave."

"Why?" I didn't understand.

"Why, it's only the darkest hour, the first, when the black arts hold sway." He looked puzzled. "You being a priestess, I thought you'd know these things."

Now it was my turn to be puzzled. "Magic doesn't work like that back home. The time is always taken into consideration, of course, but we generally work almost any type of magic whenever it's needed." I suddenly realized the importance of what he'd just said.

"How did you know I was a witch? A priestess in fact?"

"You wear the sign, of course, girl. Do you think I'm blind. We know the old ways, here. Not many of us, but some. I can recognize the symbol of power."

I gulped. "Oh," I said, wondering which one of my pendants was the one he was referring to.

"I would like to know one thing," he asked quietly.

"And what is that?" said Arthur, sitting on the ground tailor style.

"I'd like to know, since I helped and all, just what makes you two so special anyway? The kind of magic loosed upon the moor this night's not usual around here; not in my lifetime anyway. You must be something special, all right. Either you, or the girl."

I plopped down next to the Doctor. "It's a very long story."

Will grinned and sat down in front of us. "I don't think you want to be leaving the circle just yet, m'Lady, so, why don't we pass the time with a tale." His eyes twinkled in the misty starlight.

Arthur began...

...by the time we were finished Will's eyes were opened wide.

"Is all that true?." he exclaimed, looking at me.

I shrugged. "As nearly as I can remember it, yes." I let my smile broaden. "Of course, we only have the Doctor's word for his end of it."

Arthur stood. "Only the Doctor's word." he huffed. "As if you didn't know by now, my dear, exactly what the Doctor's word is worth.." He was pacing.

"Why, my word is good on almost any plane of existence you'd care to imagine. I've been known to even..." he stopped glaring and frowned as the laughter I'd been trying to hold in burst loose.

"You were teasing me." He sounded almost hurt.

"Yeah," I said smugly, enjoying myself. "Makes for a nice change, don't you think?"

He looked at his watch and reached out a hand to me. "Come on, it's nearly three and still a long way back to the hotel." Turning to Will, who stood, he asked, "Where's the car?"

A Question of Balance

The huge driver grinned and pointed. "Right the other side of the trees. Just a feeling is all, but I somehow knew it'd be more convenient to leave her there and not at the village." He winked, "and I took the liberty of seeing that your bag and your stick were safely in the boot." Grinning, he led the way.

By the time we reached the Exeter St. Davids station, we had only about a half-hour to wait for the first early morning train to Exmouth. We stopped in the buffet and had strong tea and buttered rolls. Neither of us had eaten since lunch the previous day, and we were ravenous. We knew though, that breakfast would be served at the hotel and after a bath, we intended to enjoy it before napping.

It was early afternoon when we emerged into the sunlight, none the worse for our excursion. The nausea hadn't returned and my wrist underneath the brass bracelet was nearly normal, not painful at all. Arthur had examined it closely while I tried to recall everything Marie had told me about it when she gave it to me. It wasn't very much. There was still no way of getting it. Since it wasn't doing any more harm, and I still wasn't certain of its power, I decided to let it alone for now.

Together, we spent the day quietly, walking through the Village Market and buying presents for people. I was trying to figure out just how I would get two china teapots home without breaking them when I spotted a familiar floppy brimmed hat disappearing into Woolworth's.

"Come on," I said, dragging Arthur away from a tobacconist's counter. "I want to follow that hat."

We practically ran up the steps to the store, my walking stick clattering angrily against the pavement at being so roughly treated. In my haste to find the hat, I almost tripped over a folding baby stroller, earning a black look from the mother. I paused to apologize while the Doctor went into the store to try and spot our quarry.

Mother appeased and child sleeping peacefully, I entered the store, looking around. There was Arthur speaking to a lady in a floppy brimmed hat. He was turned facing me, so I couldn't see her face, but the sweater looked about right, and that was definitely *the* hat.

"Arthur, Marge," I called, moving to greet them.

The lady turned and I was looking at a complete stranger.

"I'm sorry my dear, but as I was just telling this gentleman, my name isn't Miss Kelly, or Marge. I'm afraid you have me confused with someone else."

I stammered, embarrassed. "Oh yes, of course. I'm terribly sorry to bother you, it's just that you were wearing the hat, and that sweater. Forgive me, but a friend of mine has one just like it." I tried what I hoped was a disarming smile. It must have worked, because she smiled back kindly.

"That's quite all right, dear. No harm done. Goodbye."

As she started to go, I stopped her. "Excuse me, but you don't happen to ride a bicycle occasionally, do you? Along the Sea Lane perhaps?"

The old woman chuckled. "Goodness no. I haven't ridden a bicycle in years."

I heard her still chuckling, "..fancy me on a bicycle," as she left the store.

I looked up at Arthur. "Sorry. Same hat, though."

He laughed and grabbed me by the arm to lead me from the store. I resisted a little, suspicious.

"Hey," I asked. "Why the rush?"

He smiled. "I want to get you out of here before you spot the candy counter."

An idea leaped into my mind. "Jelly Babies." I cried, triumphantly.

"Not Jelly Babies" he groaned.

"Jelly Babies." I affirmed, tugging him to the candy aisle. "I can pack them all around the teapots to cushion them. And to think, it never would have occurred to me except for that hat."

He merely rolled his eyes and followed me grudgingly.

CHAPTER THIRTEEN
TINTAGEL

"It's not finished you know." Arthur spoke softly, not wanting to be overheard by the staff. We were between courses at dinner and I was making notes copiously in my journal, recording everything that had happened. I felt compelled to get it all down before these memories faded away like the others.

I stopped to nod at him. "I know. They know where we are, don't they?"

"Yes."

"Marge?"

He frowned. "Got to be, hasn't it? She was the one who recommended that stable, right?"

"But she seemed so nice," I protested.

He didn't say anything, but his look spoke volumes.

"Why?" I paused. "Belay that, I know why. What I don't know is how."

The Doctor touched the brass cuff lightly. "It's got to be the bracelet. Somehow, they can track you through it."

I shook my head. "Impossible, the bracelet was given to me weeks ago by someone not even remotely connected to any of this. Marie's not involved with the occult."

He patted my hand. "No? Think about it, Tary. How did she meet this evil fellow who threatened her children? If she's not affiliated with the occult community, then they went out of their way to find her; someone who wouldn't raise your suspicions. I mean, where would she get a magical bracelet? And how did she know to come to you for protection, eh? And another thing, how is it that once you had it on you completely forgot about it?"

"Okay, okay, I get the point. I just find it hard to believe she would do anything deliberately to cause me harm. I've known her for years, Arthur. Her boys and Jason grew up together." I sighed.

"Tarish, it's got to come off." He traced his finger along the interlocking designs, just as Marge Kelly had done. "Somehow, we've got to get it off... and the sooner the better."

Suddenly, it felt tight again. I pulled my hand away, wincing. "I think it's got other ideas."

"Yes, I rather thought it might." Arthur sipped thoughtfully at his wine.

"We'll leave it go tonight. Tomorrow..." he smiled a little, "...well, I'll think of something."

Our waiter appeared with the entree.

"Good, I'm starved." Gently, he squeezed my hand and whispered, "Don't worry."

Sure, easy for him. But my wrist was throbbing and my appetite was ruined.

After dinner we stopped in the bar to socialize before turning in. Neither of us was ready yet, to be alone with our dilemma.

Arthur swirled sherry absently around in his glass and I sipped at my usual diet Pepsi. Robbie was behind the bar.

"So," he said cheerfully, "how was Dartmoor? You didn't come out of the saddle, did you?"

"No," I smiled. "In spite of a rather wild ride, I managed to keep my seat."

"We got lost, actually," interjected Arthur, winking at me. "Even our guide didn't know where we were."

Rob smiled. "Oh well, at least the horses always manage to find their way back to the stables, don't they. And they won't cross..."

"The bogs," said the two of us together.

"We know, they've got more sense than most people," I laughed. It felt good to laugh.

"So it's the same in America then?"

I sighed, scratching absently at my wrist.

Robbie looked. "What's that? Allergic?"

"Something like that," I replied, trying to ignore the persistent itching.

The bar was quiet, empty except for an older couple enjoying an after dinner cordials in the lounge.

"You should take it off, give the skin a chance to breath, " he added, helpfully.

"Yeah, I know. Thank you Dr. Rob." I returned peevishly.

Arthur winked at him. "It won't come off. It's magic." He was using a stage whisper. Gesturing conspiratorially, he leaned over the bar. "You do believe in magic, don't you Rob?"

His eyes lit up. "Gaw. It isn't, is it? What kind?"

The Doctor and I exchanged looks. He'd said it jokingly, and Rob's reaction was totally unexpected.

"Uh," I stammered. "We're not really sure, actually."

"She means she's not really sure. I am sure. I believe it was designed to keep track of her."

"Of her? And her a priestess? Why?" Robbie was staring.

"Am I wearing a sign or something?" I asked. "How is it everyone seems to know I'm a priestess?"

"You're wearing it, Tary. The wee symbol of the Fae, isn't it?"

"I admit, I must be", I acknowledged. "Do you think you could point it out to me?"

The barman blinked at Arthur. "Doesn't she know?"

"No," he whispered back, "and neither do I. Will you please tell us?"

Rob pointed to my left hand, wrapped around my glass. "It's the ring. She is wearing the little crown, isn't she? The Faery Queen's coronet?"

"You recognize it?" I gasped, glancing at Arthur.

"Do you follow the old ways too?" he asked the youth.

"What me? Nah, but my Gran used to. I've seen pictures, drawings of that little crown in some of her books and stuff. That's a real fine one, might almost be the real thing," he added admiringly.

Arthur and I exchanged looks. "Yes, it might be, mightn't it," he agreed. "Listen, Robbie, tomorrow's your day off, isn't it?"

He nodded.

"Doctor," I nudged him, none to gently, with my walking stick. "I don't think..."

"Now Tary, I get a good feeling from Rob here, don't you?"

"But it could be danger..."

"Yes, I know, but we do need help. I wouldn't do anything to endanger the lad" Now, where had I heard that one before I thought to myself.

"Just being with us would endanger him, Art."

"Arthur."

I ignored him and went on. "We've no right. Besides, how can we be sure he's not on the other side?"

"Other side of what?" asked Rob, intrigued. "If there's anything I can do..."

We spoke simultaneously.

"Yes."

"No."

Rob blinked behind his glasses. "Don't I get a say?"

"No!" Again, we spoke together, glaring at each other.

"Well," smiled the barman. "At least that's something."

"What is?" said Arthur.

Robbie grinned. "I was beginning to think you two couldn't agree on anything."

Nobody spoke. Arthur just sat there looking bemused. It was an expression I'd never seen on him before, and was so alien to the man I'd come to know and love that I couldn't help myself. I started to giggle.

Now, anyone who knows me will tell you that once I get started, I'm almost impossible to stop... and it's contagious. Soon, I was laughing so hard that tears streamed down my cheeks and I was gasping for breath. The older couple had retired for the evening so only the three of us remained. Arthur

A Question of Balance

and Rob tried asking me what was so funny, but the more they asked, the harder I laughed. It was nothing in particular, you see, just the whole crazy situation.

It didn't take long before they caught the giggles, exchanging puzzled glances and shrugging their shoulders as I dissolved helplessly.

I'd just about gotten myself back under control when Julian, the Inn Keeper and William, the matre'd, strolled in and asked innocently what was so funny. That set me off again. Arthur eased me off the barstool and guided me firmly to the door.

"I'll talk to you tomorrow, Rob. Good night all."

I turned to add my own farewells but couldn't. Red-faced, William replaced my half-finished glass of Pepsi on the bar... he'd been sniffing it. I almost collapsed as I gasped and choked on my laughter. As the Doctor and I headed for the stairs, I heard Julian say to Rob, "What was in that?"

It wasn't until much later that I realized the brass cuff had become considerably looser and less irritating than it had been in days. It was later yet before I realized the significance of that.

I was deep underground, a cavern or a crypt, I couldn't be sure in the flickering dimness of the single candle. Walking hunched over in front of me, so he wouldn't scrape his head against the low roof, was Arthur. At least, it was and it wasn't. He seemed older, ancient, with long white hair and a beard to match. Dressed in flowing robes, he looked more like a wizard, Gandalf or Merlyn... but his eyes belonged to the Doctor.

I cried out, hearing the echo of my voice reverberate against the walls and ceiling. "Where are we going?"

Smiling wisely, he opened his mouth to speak. I knew he was about to tell me the secret, the way to rid myself of this horrible curse.

"Hello? Yes, this is the Doctor, who's here?"

I sat up rubbing my eyes and staring, as the last remnants of the dream faded. Arthur was speaking into the phone.

"Yes, Rob. What time is it?" He was fumbling on the nightstand for his watch. I reached over and turned on the lamp.

"That's brilliant, Rob, brilliant. Yes, we can be ready. Six eighteen? No, no, we can do it. Yes, we'll meet you out back in, twenty-five minutes. Bye."

The receiver was replaced.

"What was that all about?" I asked, noting that the sun hadn't yet made its appearance.

"Come on, we've got to hurry. Rob's had a brilliant idea." He swung his feet over the edge of the bed.

"Yes, I gathered as much. What exactly is this brilliant idea?"

"I haven't got time to explain," he said over his shoulder moving into the bathroom. "I'll tell you on the way. Get dressed, we've got to catch the six eighteen train to Exeter. Tintagel, Tary. We're going to Tintagel."

Knowing better than to argue, I quietly got up and plugged in the teapot.

By the time we met our young friend in the courtyard around back, the sun had started to rise, early fog retreating back into the sea in stages. I shivered. It would be a nice day, but right now I was freezing.

"I remember my Gran had these friends of hers, others that followed the old ways there. They run a shop and a kind of museum in the village not far from the ruins. If you can't lose that thing in Merlin's cave beneath the castle..."

The dream came back to me in a flash with a clarity that was startling. "Did you say Merlin's cave?"

Rob smiled as he led the way down into the village toward the rail station.

"Aye. The caverns beneath the old castle. The legend says it's where he hid the dragon. The one whose breath made the bridge Uther used when he sneaked in to lie with Ygrain." He looked at me. "It's supposed to be a place of great enchantment."

"And that's what we're looking for, Tary, isn't it? A place of great enchantment?" Arthur held my hand as we walked, helping me to keep up with their brisk pace. I was beginning to warm up.

"I was having a dream, just when the phone rang. I was dreaming that we were underground, in a cave or a crypt. It must mean something, Arthur." I was actually beginning to be hopeful that I could lose the cuff in Merlin's cave.

"If these friends of my gran are still there, they can tell us the best way to get into the caves." Robbie was speaking animatedly, filled with the thoughts of a glorious adventure.

"I hope you're right." Under my breath I added for Arthur's ears, "...and I hope we're not bringing down more trouble on other innocent people."

When we were finally settled on the bus to Tintagel, Arthur and I started our story for Rob. It was early Saturday morning and the coach was virtually empty but for us. By the time we reached Cornwall, he knew the whole story. At least as much of it as we did.

"That's a pretty weird tale," he said. "I'm not really very much into all the occult, but I know there must be something to it. Even if there's nothing to all this black magic stuff, the Ord..."

I thought Arthur was going to have heart failure. He leaned across the seat and clapped his large hand over poor Robbie's mouth, nearly scaring him to death.

"Don't say it. Don't even think it, if that's possible. I know enough about the way magic works, Robbie, and even mentioning a name of power could be enough to put them onto us." His eyes were deadly serious, his face pale and stern. Slowly, he removed his hand and Robbie gulped.

"Yeah, sorry Doc. All I meant was that these blokes are nasty just in every day terms. Even without all the mumbo-jumbo, they're a dangerous lot."

"Yes, they are, and it'll do you well to remember that." He softened his voice and smiled.

As we approached the village of Tintagel the driver turned and asked where we'd like to be let out. "There used to be a small shop, near the High Street I think, with a museum attached. It was called Merlin's Cave," said Robbie.

The bus driver knew it, and let us off right in front.

"Is this it?" I asked, staring at the garish, cartoonish mural decorating the white concrete building, bold letters proclaiming, "Merlin's Cave—Shop and Museum."

A yellow and red sign on the door said they were open.

"Must be," said Arthur moving toward the door. "Let's see."

Rob and I followed him in. We browsed while a young woman waited on some customers, their clothing and cameras glaring 'tourists' in neon. They left, and we three were alone with the shopgirl.

"Hello", boomed Arthur. "We're looking for..." he turned to Rob, "...what was the name?"

"Pratcher, Nigel Pratcher, I think. He used to know my Gran, Miriam Codswyth?"

"Oh yes, that's my granddad. He's in the back. Just a minute." She disappeared through a door marked "To The Museum".

In a moment, she returned, smiling. "He does remember her. He'll be right out."

"You have some interesting things," I said, looking over a case filled with sterling silver rings of every description.

"Yes, we do have a unique collection." She walked over. "Hi, I'm Gloria."

"Tary," I answered. "Do you mind if I look at some of them?"

Gloria brought out the tray and put it on the counter. I was looking specifically for a man's Celtic cross ring, for my son, but there wasn't one there.

"You've some interesting pieces yourself", said the shop girl, eyeing my fingers.

A QUESTION OF BALANCE

I smiled at her warm and open face. "Thank you. Each one of them means something."

"Oh, I know. What Tradition are you?"

"I'm a Priestess of Cerridwyn," I answered.

"Ah," she smiled.

"Yes," I said. "In fact I was down for the Spring Sabbat at the New Forest."

"With Lady Trewlane, how exciting."

I was gratified, to say the least. "Yes, it was actually."

"Here to see the ruins?"

Smiling, I said, "More the caves."

Before we could continue, an old man shuffled in. He looked really old, but seemed quite spry. He was quite a large man, dressed in loose trousers and a sweater with a traditional wool cap perched at a jaunty angle. His eyes were startlingly blue, like Paul Newman's, with lots of laugh lines.

"I'm Nigel Pratcher. Where's Miri's grandson?" He was eyeing the Doctor.

"Here, Sir. Rob Sayer. She was my mum's gran, really, but the only one I ever knew."

Nigel turned to stare critically at our young friend.

"Not much of the look of her, have ye boy. Still, there is something around the eyes, I think." He turned to his granddaughter. "Gloria, put the closed sign out and we'll have some tea while we hear all about what's brought these folks such a long way."

Rob smiled. "And how do you know we've come so far?"

The old man smiled knowingly. "Devon," he proclaimed, pointing to Rob, "Yorkshire", he added, indicating the Doctor, "And.. Now you're a puzzle Miss. American, right?"

I nodded dumbly.

"Ye don't sound like one, nor dress neither. Maybe there is some civilization acrost the pond after all."

"How did you...?" I started.

He chuckled and tapped a forefinger on the side of his nose. "Come on through, Gloria's got the kettle on."

We were led through the small museum and into a tidy little kitchen in the back.

As we sipped the tea, Arthur explained my problem. The old man examined the bracelet minutely and sighed.

"Now that's what comes of meddling, my dears. But, there's no sense in talking to the younglings. They do as they will, even those what follows the old ways."

"Granddad," said Gloria softly. "Will she be able to lose it in the caves do you reckon?"

"I think not, girl. I think she'll not get near the caves. The last land slip blocked the path and it were tricky enough afore." He eyed Arthur and Rob critically.

"Even them two might not get down there, and the guard's pretty much closed it off anywise."

"The guard?" Asked Arthur.

"At the ruins. They charge a pound, isn't it, for the privilege of climbing about what was there long before the National Trust."

My disappointment must have been obvious for the old man patted my hand in a comforting gesture.

"But in the dream I was so sure."

"I'm sorry lass, but you'll have to look elsewhere I'm thinking. Still, you are here, and the day's lovely, bright and warm." Nigel Pratcher winked at us.

"Go and have a look at the ruins. Enjoy yourselves. You'll be safe up at the castle. I can promise ye that nothing ill can pass those tumbled walls, even now after all these centuries."

We had to be satisfied with that.

The three of us said good-bye to Gloria and her granddad with a promise to stop back before we left.

Nigel was certainly right about one thing, the day was glorious. It had warmed up and bright sunshine flooded the village. I loved all the little shops and took my time browsing in one called Dragon's Breath. I found a lovely brooch of Celtic Silver to use as a cloak pin, and bought a handful of leather bookmarks to bring home as souvenirs. We found the castle ruins with no trouble at the end of the High Street.

Luckily for me there was a Land Rover ferrying passengers up the steep track to where the ruins sat high up on the cliffs overlooking the Cornish coast. The earliest foundations uncovered so far had been dated to the fifth century, the actual time period of King Arthur. We alighted from the Rover and took the turning down to the coastline. After climbing down the steep and rocky trail to the caves as far as we easily could, I was convinced that there was no way I'd be able to manage it, even if the guard posted had let us by. In fact, I doubted that Arthur could have done it. Maybe Rob, but the rockslide had put quite a pile of boulders in the path, and there was the constant danger of another fall.

"Well, we wanted to see Tintagel, didn't we?" The Doctor said, putting a cheerful face on things. "Here we are, the sun is warm. I know, let's pay our pound and explore the ruins."

I agreed, anxious now to gaze at the very same scene that would have greeted Ygrain fifteen centuries ago. I felt like we were literally stepping back in time.

We paid our admittance and began the climb up the ancient stone stairs that wound around the cliff to the tower and battlements above. Rob was way ahead of us while Arthur stayed behind keeping pace with me. I find climbing even normal stairs arduous, and these were definitely not your normal average stairs. Finally, we were at the top.

Even without the ruins, the climb would have been worth it; the view from the cliffs was spectacular. Fortunately, I had remembered to bring my camera, and got a series of photos that turned out breathtakingly well. The weather was absolutely perfect, bright sunshine and very warm for March. We explored the ruins and sunned ourselves like basking dragons on the warmth of the great plates of rock that jutted out over the sea below. Almost before we knew it, the day fled by, and we found we were starving.

Climbing back down wasn't nearly as bad as the climb up, but it still took me some considerable time. We managed to get to a small teashop before they stopped serving, so I could indulge myself with a cream tea. I wasn't disappointed, it was delicious, and I wondered how anyone in Britain ever managed to keep his or her cholesterol under control.

I was letting myself idle, listening with half a brain to the conversation between the Doctor and Rob, when a small movement near the door caught my eye. A floppy brimmed hat disappeared around the corner as I watched.

"I'll be right back," I said. They barely paused in their conversation, assuming I suppose, that I was going to find a toilet. I wasn't. This time, I was determined to find Marge Kelly.

She was moving quickly along the narrow lane when I emerged from the shop. I picked up my own pace to try and catch up. When I was closer, I called out.

"Marge, wait. Miss Kelly, it's me, Tary." The figure stopped and turned. I was only forty-five or fifty feet away, so I could see her face clearly. It was definitely the woman I knew as Marge Kelly. A tiny smile seemed to play around the corners of her mouth before she turned. I began walking toward her again, but she disappeared down a side alleyway. By the time I reached the spot, she was nowhere to be seen.

I was about a half a block from the old Post Office. The teashop where Arthur and Robbie were still presumably sitting enjoying their afternoon tea, was another block beyond that. Should I go back and tell them? After the other day in Woolworth's, would Arthur even believe me? No, I decided. Not without proof. Although it was getting late in the day, the sun was still bright, so I decided it would be safe enough for a little look around.

I turned in at the alley and walked down slowly, looking for a door or side passageway to explain Marge's disappearance. I got all the way to the end,

A Question of Balance

where a large stone wall rose up blocking any further progress. There was no sign of anyone. I stood there, scratching my head in confusion. Maybe this wasn't the way she'd come. It was, I was certain of it. But if so, then where was she? There wasn't any door that I could see. Oh well. I guess this was that proverbial 'blind alley' you hear so much about. Standing there wasn't accomplishing anything, and the Doctor and Rob would be starting to wonder where I'd got off to, so I turned back.

As I moved toward the street, I thought I heard something behind me. I turned too quickly and lost my balance landing hard on my seat, the walking stick clattering from my grip. My wrist had begun to ache. I looked to see what had caused the noise, but there was nothing at all, just the solid stone wall. I got shakily to my feet, dusted myself off, and bent to retrieve my stick. It wasn't there.

Okay, I told myself, don't panic. Just move slowly and carefully to the street. I tried. I couldn't have been more than a few feet from the mouth of the alley when I felt something grab at my ankle. I didn't have my walking stick, so I went down easily, like a sack of grain. I had no opportunity to look to see who had hold of me. My only thought was to get out of the secluded alley and onto the High Street where there were people. I tried to scramble forward on my hands and knees, something scrabbling for a hold on my right leg. I was filthy and panting for breath, and desperately afraid to look behind me, so I just kept going, one inch at a time.

Suddenly, my other leg was seized, and I began losing ground slowly. "NO!" I screamed as I pushed hard with my elbows, trying to gain back those precious few inches. I was very glad I was wearing a heavy long sleeved shirt or my arms would have been really scraped up.

A large hand came down over my mouth as the grip on my legs relaxed. I tried to bite, but couldn't get a purchase as I was dragged to my feet. Whoever it was, was tall and powerfully built. I brought up my left leg and swung it back, aiming for where I thought the assailant's crotch would be. I hit nothing, but was thrown all off balance again as my right ankle buckled under me. Instead of steadying me, my attacker suddenly let go and I went sprawling face first in the dust.

Immediately, I curled up and tucked my head under my arms in the accepted public school method intended to protect you from nuclear attack. I felt a pair of strong arms pry my hands away and slide under my arms to lift me to my feet. I began to struggle again and prepared to scream.

"Tary, Tary, it's me. Stop it, it's me."

I recognized that voice. I stop struggling and slumped into an inert ball of jelly. Relief and terror and a touch of embarrassment, combined to render me totally incapable of any sounds even vaguely human. I'm afraid the resultant grunts and burbling were more bovine than anything else.

"Tary, what happened? Shh, it's all right now you're safe. Come on, look at me." He turned my chin so I could see it was really him. Rob was standing right behind, my walking stick in his hand.

I still couldn't say anything, as the two of them helped me to my feet. I sagged against Arthur as we made our way to Mr. Pratcher's shop. The sign on the door read closed, and there was no answer to our ring.

"No one home," said the Doctor, stating the obvious. He checked his watch. "Well, the coach ought to be here soon anyway. Come on Rob, help me get her to that bench over there."

When I was sitting, he took a moist towelette from his pocket and wiped the worst of the grime from my face.

"Can you tell us what happened?"

I took a deep breath. "I saw Marge again. While we were having tea I saw her go by. You and Robbie were involved, so I...so I..."

"So you thought you'd just follow and see what she was up to, eh?"

I nodded. "I didn't think you'd believe me again, if I told you I saw her."

A Question of Balance

He put his arms around me. "Of course I'd believe you. I think it was her that we followed into Woolworth's the other day. Somehow, she made a switch in the store with an accomplice or something." He rubbed a hand through his hair. "For all I know maybe it was magic. There's no doubt in my mind, Tary, that this Marge Kelly's been with us even more than you've seen her."

I nodded again.

"There's our coach," said Rob, as subdued as I'd ever seen him.

It pulled up, and we got on. I dozed off and on all the way to Exeter, my head on Arthur's shoulder. It was very late by the time we got back to Exmouth, and I was never so grateful to see a taxi waiting outside the station. It was only a half-mile walk to the hotel, but it was uphill and I was spent. Having missed supper, we'd made do with a cold sandwich at the station in Exeter while we were waiting.

Rob bade us goodnight and went around the courtyard to the cottage where the staff lived. Arthur and I made our way to the room. I took a quick bath and tumbled into bed, but it was some time before Arthur and I actually got around to sleep.

Chapter Fourteen
Troubles

I was amazed at the resilience Tarish had shown time and time again. No matter what happened, she seemed to bounce back with the agility of a small child. Even after being nearly frightened to death, or worse, she lay beside me sleeping peacefully, her face an expression of serenity. I touched her forehead gently, tempted to follow and share in her dreams since my own kept me from closing my eyes. I was afraid though, that instead of partaking in the peace she had managed to find I would merely infect her with my own apprehension. Tary didn't know everything I did. She didn't know that Malcolm Dennings had his counterpart right here in England. Indeed, there was nowhere on the Earth we could have gone where The Order had not already established a foothold... at least, nowhere worth going.

I gently extricated myself from her embrace. She smiled and turned over, sighing in her sleep. When I was certain my movements would not awaken her I rose from the bed and padded barefoot to where the electric teapot stood empty. I took it into the bathroom and warmed some water for cocoa. When it was ready, I took my cup and made myself as comfortable as I could in the armchair next to the window. There were some sweet biscuits as well, left for an afternoon tea we hadn't had.

It's funny how such ordinary noises like the ripping of cello-wrap, sound over-loud in the absolute stillness of the hours between midnight and dawn. My wife never stirred. My wife...I still couldn't get used to that. After badgering her for weeks, I'd been positively bowled over at our rushed wedding at the consulate in New York, and absolutely devastated at having to leave her on the very day of our marriage. The confusion of resigning from the Institute and subsequently obtaining a position, which had been recently vacated by an old professor of mine at University, had served to keep me distracted for a time. Still, I'd missed her terribly. Those months we'd been together in the States were very precious to me.

As I watched her sleeping, I couldn't help but wonder what would happen. I half wished I had her gift for divination...then again, maybe not. I wasn't sure I wanted to see what our future held. The moment was all that mattered. Perhaps it was my way of life with the Institute that had taught me that.

After Sir had got over his shock at my emotional out-burst in his office he'd wasted no time at all in having my credentials rescinded...and more. I'd been placed in the category of a risk to national security, which effectively cut me off from perfectly legitimate venues to which, as a University professor, I would otherwise have been entitled. For example, despite my long-standing friendship with the curator of antiquities at the British Museum, I found my station no longer permitted me access to any of the archives. I was on 'The List', she'd explained to me, apologetically. Even so, as a purely personal favour, she'd arranged to permit my dearest friend and mentor, Professor Bectinson, to take the Book with him to a conference on pre-biblical middle-eastern cultures. It had also been she who'd convinced Sir to telephone me at Leeds, catching me just before I left to meet Tary. It was that event which had made me late for my own honeymoon.

Now that I was no longer a member of Sir's little family my access to knowledge of what was going on in the field was limited to what I could read into newspaper stories. Believe me, that was substantial enough to convince me that The Order was moving quickly toward the day when the fate of all humanity would be in the hands of their Lord and his High Priest; with or without the Book.

A Question of Balance

In every major political hot spot in the world, tensions were growing, fed by the practised deceptions and subtle magical influences of my enemies. Natural disasters added to the general chaos, which was creeping over the Earth, covering it like a burial shroud, so slowly and with such subtlety, that almost no one noticed. Mud slides in Eastern Europe, earthquakes in California, volcanic eruptions and freak storms abounded. There was snow in Tel Aviv, deep frost in Florida, while it was warm and sunny in Alaska. The polar caps were melting. Tary on her own in a short solitary ritual had been able to shift a weak storm front enough to bring a cloudless sky to New Jersey in spite of scientific predictions to the contrary. The power Dennings had at his disposal, power fed to him by every member of The Order around the world as well as his own well honed abilities, made Tarish's simple Earth magic pale by comparison. Even without the Book, they were coming perilously close to achieving their ends. The global economy was in tatters and to my mind Eastern European civilisation had collapsed. The Middle East was a volcano about to spew forth. The western way of life was not far behind, and under constant threat. I suspected that at the heart of it all was Dennings at the head of The Order.

Brian had been more right than he knew when he'd said that with the Power of Infinity in his hands, Dennings would be invincible. With such Power and knowledge and the strength to wield it, Malcolm Dennings would be able to set himself above the gods, for a time at least. Time enough to destroy what it had taken millennia to create.

Those poor souls who did notice what the world was coming to were, for the most part, considered disturbed, eccentric, or just plain crazy. Even Sir didn't seem to realise that the Book was not the only weapon Dennings had. He had the cunning of a jackal, and the savvy of a street fighter, combined with almost limitless charm and the charisma of a Hollywood actor. He also had the kind of wealth and mundane power usually found only between the pages of a Sidney Sheldon bestseller. He fed the causes of fundamentalism wherever it would cause the most harm.

Malcolm Dennings was the epitome of the American system. Born the only child of a North Carolina small farmer, he'd shown no particular abilities in grammar school. It wasn't until his first year of secondary school, high school, that a teacher of English Literature saw something in the teenage Malcolm. He took complete charge of the boy, and the making of Dennings as we know him today was begun. Perhaps it was this early teacher who introduced him to the magical arts. All the facts gathered from my research merely show that by the time he was a senior, ready to complete his education, eighteen year old Malcolm Dennings had competed and taken first honours in nearly every national scholarship awards examination. He chose Harvard, where he was accepted on a full scholarship.

He completed his education brilliantly, in record time, taking a mere six years to achieve a full degree in Law. He had the distinction of passing the New York Bar examination at the first sitting, a notable accomplishment. From there, he might have been expected to go into one of the prestigious law firms who clamoured to make him a junior partner immediately, an unheard of prospect. Dennings had other ideas. Instead he opened his own offices, using money invested by fellow Harvard graduates. Their money was well turned as the young attorney made a name for himself immediately. If he had ever lost a case, it was well out of any one's memory.

His rise to fortune was legendary in a country that places great emphasis on the individual's right to succeed through hard work, intelligence and luck, regardless of his beginnings. A legend among legends by the time he was thirty, Dennings was in his late fifties now, and still looked not much different. His political power was subtle but not to be underestimated. It was acknowledged in the United States' capital that leaders of both political parties came to Dennings for advice and service, although he public-

A Question of Balance

ly supported neither. He was an infrequent, though oft invited guest at the White House.

Perhaps tellingly, he was never married, yet never ever was there a hint of scandal, a breath of impropriety spoken. The women in his life adored him, apparently remaining loyal even after his interest waned. He had very few enemies. Anyone who might have been a threat suffered extreme misfortune. I was one of the very few who hadn't yet died tragically of natural causes or in an accident or simply vanished. Of course in his mind I was not terribly important to such a great man. I was a mere annoyance, less than a stinging fly on a summer day, a nobody. Especially now that I had been cut off from the Institute I was virtually powerless against such a man.

My god! I realized suddenly that I was possibly the only human being in the world who recognised the danger, and without the Institute I was hopelessly out-matched. I was far less than even a fly...and I was alone. I shook myself. Maybe I was insane, paranoid, suffering from too many years of living from one covert operation to another. Could I be seeing evil occult plots in perfectly normal, natural events? Perhaps I'd become so obsessed with Dennings, that I'd created an arch-sorcerer, a personal nemesis in my own mind. I was no doubt suffering delusions, a combination martyr complex and saviour syndrome. I'd probably be hearing 'voices' soon. The idea had appeal; at least it was better than believing the world was about to be destroyed by some self-styled Lord of Darkness. I yawned, resolved to look up a good psychiatrist as soon I returned to Leeds. I'd almost managed to convince myself as I drifted into an uneasy doze in the chair.

I woke suddenly. The sun was shining and a warm breeze stirred the lace curtains at the window. There was nothing to explain why I was suddenly over-come with dread. Tary still slept peacefully, and there was nothing at all out of order. Impulsively I brushed my lips across her forehead. She stirred a little, then turned over. I smiled.

It was nearly eight-thirty by the travel alarm on the bedstead. I decided to dress and telephone London University. After the burglary at the museum, I had contacted Walter Bectinson to warn him of the danger I'd unwittingly placed him in. Although he'd scoffed at the idea, he had agreed to send the Book by registered post to the University. I wanted to check to see if it had arrived safely. Tary was still deep in sleep, and I didn't want to alarm her. She'd had enough of a fright already. There was a call box outside the dining room that offered a good deal of privacy. I could order up some breakfast and telephone while I waited.

"Good morning, William." I stuck my head into the empty dining room.

William emerged from the kitchen wearing a spotless white pinnie.

"Good morning Doctor. How is madam this morning? Will she be joining you for breakfast?" He was a fawning, funny little Irishman. I liked him.

"Not this morning, William. We had a late night, so I thought I'd bring up a tray, let madam sleep in, if it's not too much trouble, that is."

William smiled. "Oh no, Doctor, no trouble at all. What would you like?"

I thought about it for a moment, my stomach grumbling. "Oh, how about a bit of everything, scrambled eggs, sausages, crispy bacon, tomatoes and mushrooms. I had better take some porridge as well, kippers too if they're fresh, and plenty of coffee."

"Very good. Shall I have Terri bring it up?"

"No. I have to make a call. I'll take it up when I'm finished on the phone. No need to interrupt everybody's schedule, eh?"

"Thank you, sir. I'll go and see to it."

I left grinning, my spirits picking up.

They were not to stay up for long.

"Professor Bectinson's office," It was Susan, his secretary. She sounded as if she had a cold.

A Question of Balance

"Susan, good morning. This is Doctor Pendargroom."

"Oh, Doctor..." she was sniffling.

"Listen Susan, I'm in a call box, so listen carefully. Walter was sending me a package from Edinburgh. Has it arrived yet?"

Her voice was tiny as she answered. "Yes, Doctor. It was in this morning's post."

"Good. See that it's locked up somewhere for me will you? I'll have someone from the museum pick it up." She didn't answer.

"Susan? Are you still there? You really ought to take care of yourself, you sound..."

She sounded awful. "Oh, Doctor Pendargroom..."

I listened mutely.

I was still standing, holding the receiver in my hand, long after the connection had been broken. I wasn't crazy after all. Tary and I had big troubles.

"Oh, Tary. What have I got you into?" I moaned to myself, shaken to the very core of my being as I dialled the telephone number of the Museum.

Terri was knocking at the door of the coin box.

"Doctor? The tray for madam's breakfast is ready."

I nodded and completed my call, replacing the receiver on the hook. As I stepped from the call box, Terri placed a large tray into my hands. "Oh, yes, thank you. I'll take it up now."

I felt numb as I climbed the stairs to our room. For a few minutes I stood outside the door, the key in the lock, reluctant to go in and face Tary with the news. Finally, I steeled myself, turned the key and entered. She was still asleep, but she stirred as I set the tray down, looking sleepy and mussed and very, very vulnerable. I turned, fussing with the drapes at the window so she wouldn't see the tears in my eyes as I fought to regain some composure. I wasn't quite alone. I had dragged Tary into this mess with me, and I was responsible for whatever was going to happen to us both.

I forced my lips into a smile and turned to face her.

Chapter Fifteen
Avalon

"Good morning," said the Doctor. His cheerfulness seemed forced as he set the breakfast tray down and pulled the drapes away from the window. "It's a bright day out there again. Feeling up to a bit of travelling?"

I groaned and sat up. "What time is it?"

"Nearly half-nine. I brought you some breakfast."

I could smell it and my stomach grumbled.

He handed me a steaming cup of coffee with a little cream and three sugars. It was exactly right.

"Are you human yet?" he asked, eyes crinkling.

"As opposed to what?" I answered. The coffee hadn't yet reached my brain, and I'm afraid I was a bit grouchy.

"I thought we could spend the day at Glastonbury. It's quite lovely out, and it's not that much of a trip."

"To see the Chalice Well?"

"And the Tor..." he agreed. "And the Abby, Tary. I've a feeling about the Abby Well."

"What well?" I looked around him to the tray. "What else have you brought me, I'm starved."

"Toast, eggs, porridge, some sausages. The Abby Well."

"Porridge?" I wrinkled my nose. "I'll have some eggs. Any relation to The Chalice Well? Cerridwyn's Cauldron? Avalon? Yummy, mushrooms too."

"Yes and tomatoes. Or the Holy Grail, depending on your particular mythological preference. Yes, there is a relationship. "

I laughed, "Between the Holy Grail and tomatoes?"

He didn't laugh, he just babbled on. "Common legend has the grail being hidden in the Chalice Well.

But the name Chalice Well doesn't refer to the Holy Grail, it refers to the iron content of the water, a Chalybeate Spring. It was, in all likelihood, sacred to the local indigenous peoples probably with Druidic associations. In 1210 it was officially named Chalicwelle like Chilkwell Road. If Joseph of Aramathia had brought the Holy Grail to Glastonbury, it would make more sense for it to have been concealed on the grounds where he established the first Christian Church in England than at a Druid Enclave. In any event, it's all there, at Glastonbury." He handed me a piece of buttered toast. "There's something else... something I ought to tell you about." His face was grim.

"What?"

"When I was delayed in London..."

"You said you had some loose ends to take care of at the British Museum."

He nodded. "Yes, that's true, more or less."

I stopped chewing and set down my toast. "More or less?"

"There was a burglary, Tary. Person or persons unknown vandalized the contents of one of the storage vaults. According to the official police report, there was nothing missing, but..."

"The Grimoir. Did they...?" I practically jumped off the bed.

"No, no. They didn't get it."

I sagged back against the pillows, breathing deeply. "What then?"

"As I said, according to the official report, the room was merely vandalized. I was there, Tary, it was in a shambles. The place had been literally torn apart. My guess is that when they didn't find what they were looking for, they just destroyed everything in a fit of pique." He rubbed his eyes wearily.

"What about the Book?" I asked impatiently.

"Oh, the Book is safe, I think. I had arranged to have it loaned out to my old Professor, Dr. Bectinson head of the Anthropology Department at London University. He had it with him at Edinburgh for a conference. After the incident at the museum, I telephoned to let him know that I thought he might be in considerable danger because of the Book."

"And?"

"I rang up the London University this morning. They'd only just got word, Professor Bectinson is dead, a heart attack while he was at Edinburgh. It's listed as a 'death by natural cause'. He was getting on, and not in the best of health. Nobody had any reason to look beyond the obvious." His eyes glittered.

"Oh Arthur, I'm sorry." I reached out, but he stood up and moved away, staring pensively out the window.

"Yes, I know," he said softly. "So am I."

He turned back to me. "They didn't get the Book. At least, I don't think they did." He just stood silently for a moment.

"Then you don't think it was them...?"

He turned on me, eyes flashing. "Oh, it was them, all right. It was them. I don't think they got the Book because I told him to send it on ahead to the University, that I would pick it up this week and return it to the Museum." He paused. "I thought that if he didn't actually have it in his possession, he'd be safe." He blinked rapidly to clear his eyes. "How could I have been so stupid?"

I wanted to get his mind off that track. "Then it's at the University?"

"Well, there's a package addressed to me. I'm sure that's what it is. I telephoned to the Curator of Antiquities. She's having it removed secretly, under guard." He breathed deeply.

"In any event, there's nothing we can do until we get that damned bracelet off you. Until then, they can find us anytime they like."

"Why Glastonbury?" I asked quietly.

"Because of the Abby Well." He sat back down on the edge of the bed.

"I know there are probably hundreds of places in England that fit the description of the place in your dream, but as it happens, so does the Well. It's located in a crypt beneath the Lady Chapel. It also has mythological significance in both the Celtic Tradition as well as Christianity. When you stop and think about it, it adds up."

"Don't you think we should go to London? I mean, don't you want to make certain of the Book?"

"If we were to show up in London now, Tary, it would be a dead give-away. They know where we are, remember? They can track us. No, we've got to stay as far away as we can, from the Grimoir of Infinity."

He lifted my arm gently. "And, we've got to get rid of that thing."

I nodded. "I'll get dressed."

It was difficult to think about evil when the day was so beautiful. Where was all the rain and fog England was famous for? Since I'd been here, there'd been only one day that was overcast, and I'd spent that day travelling. I sent up a silent "thank you".

Glastonbury turned out to be quite easy to get to. We arrived at the gates of the Abbey ruins just before noon.

"Do you want to stop for lunch? There's a tea shop across the street that looks all right."

I shook my head. "I'm not very hungry. Let's just go in. We can stop for tea before we leave."

"That's a good idea," he said. "You'll probably want to do some shopping as well. Glastonbury's famous for their sheepskin and leather goods."

I studied his face. All the way on the train I'd prattled on about trivial things, stuff and nonsense about my job and different friends. He was distant, preoccupied, barely speaking a word. I had meticulously avoided any mention of what was on both our minds. A man he'd cared very much for was dead, and in all probability, at the hands of the same people who were dogging us. Soon, he would have to begin dealing with that. The guilt I knew he was feeling would consume him otherwise. Soon, but not just now. For the moment it was enough to be here doing what we thought we should. Maybe Glastonbury wasn't the right place, and the bracelet wouldn't come off. If that was so, I was determined to send Arthur to London alone, while I headed for

A Question of Balance

Land's End in the opposite direction to try and draw them off. I suddenly realized he was talking.

"I know a little outlet shop where you can get hand stitched gloves for your mother, and your sisters." He blinked wide sad eyes at me.

"Let's find the Lady Chapel first, Art. Then we'll see."

"Okay," was all he said as he followed me through the turnstile.

I stopped and picked up a copy of a pamphlet being handed out to a group of school children touring the ruins. It was a simplified layout of the Abbey and it's outbuildings, with features of interest marked along with a bit of history. I found what I was looking for.

"It's this way Doctor. The Lady Chapel is on the other side of the old cloisters. Come on."

He followed behind, holding my hand like an obedient child, all the life gone from his step.

There were a few pictures left in my camera, and I took them. One of the Lady Chapel walls and another of King Arthur's purported grave. The last one, I wanted to save for the crypt.

As we entered the remains of the Chapel, we could look down from the boardwalk which had been built around the upper floor, into the under chapel itself. The space, which would have held floor and ceiling, was open to the sky and a shaft of sunlight fell upon the small altar below. I snapped my last picture and looked around for the way down. There it was.

Together we made our way down around the uneven spiral stairs until we stood in the shadow of the altar's cross. In my mind, I could see the cross as the hilt of a broad sword rising from the blessed stone awaiting the hand of he who would be king to pluck it out. Of course this wasn't the place where the original Excaliber had stood encased in its stony sheath, but that didn't stop my imagination.

"There it is, Tary." He was pointing to a small round arch in the stone wall that looked as though it led to an underground passageway of some kind. A small white sign with an arrow underneath proclaimed it the way to 'THE WELL.'

His voice held just a hint of his usual animation, but at least it was something. I tried a little reverse psychology to bolster his enthusiasm.

"Looks dark and damp, Art. Do you think it's safe?"

"Arthur please, and of course it's safe. You don't think they'd have a signpost pointing the way if it wasn't, do you?"

"No, I suppose not." I smiled.

"Come on then. There's nothing to be frightened of. I'll be right behind you."

I stared at him. "Why don't you be right in front of me?"

"All right, if that'll make you feel better, I'll lead. You follow me." He turned on his heel and bent to enter the small opening. I was right behind him.

It was a very short passageway with a set of very steep and uneven stairs at the end, around a sharp curve. A large white candle in a sconce was the only illumination. Right where the stone wall began to turn was an ornately carved archway between floor and ceiling. It was covered with old iron grillwork. In spite of the damp chill down here, I felt warmth seeping through my entire being, radiating outward from the grill. Slowly, I moved around Arthur to kneel next to the well.

The stone floor was uneven and hard, but I didn't feel anything. I could see the water sparkling dark and clear just beyond my reach. I ran my hand along the ironwork, tracing an ancient pattern and the grating seemed to expand to allow my arm entry to its depths. As my fingers broke the surface of the still water, I felt a tingle run up my arm. There was a soft click and the two ends of the brass cuff popped open. The bracelet came off slipping deep into the silent water as I watched. It made barely a ripple as the Well claimed it. I withdrew my arm.

Arthur, kneeling behind me, touched my cheek and I collapsed into his arms. It was over. The bracelet was gone. I was free of it. I reached up to feel his face and my fingers came away wet.

"Professor Bectinson was my mentor and my friend," he said. "The only other person I was closer to was my grandfather."

"It wasn't your fault, Arthur."

"No," he answered, coming to his feet. "It wasn't my fault, but it is my responsibility."

"Mine too," I said quietly as he helped me up.

"Yes." he mused, "yours too."

"Why?"

He sighed, "I don't know."

"I'm hungry."

"So am I."

We stumbled from the crypt holding hands, feeling like children. I don't ever remember seeing the sky quite so blue, or breathing air so clean or flowers and grass and trees quite so bright as they seemed in that moment.

"I want to buy more film." We stopped in the Abbey gift shop, then went to have our tea.

The Town, of Glastonbury, caught me rather by surprise. With all of its ties to Arthurian legend, I somehow expected it to be smaller, less busy and more quaint. What I found was a bustling touristy town. Mystic shops burning incense and charging exorbitant prices sat side by side next to clothing and leather goods stores announcing in window after window 'EASTER SALE' or 'HUGE SAVINGS'. The sidewalks were clogged with all sorts of people. In one courtyard we turned into, the sign proclaiming it 'THE Glastonbury Experience', I thought we'd time-warped back to 1965. It was too much for me. I longed for the quiet peace back in the Abbey grounds.

"Let's find the Tor," said Arthur gripping my hand tightly lest we lose each other in all the bustle.

"It shouldn't be too hard to find; it is the largest thing in the area."

I agreed, quoting my tourist guide statistics. "It rises high above the Town of Glastonbury some 560 feet..."

"Yes," he said dryly, making toward a bench. "Why don't we sit here a minute and get our bearings."

I pulled out my pocket Fodor's and located it on the map.

"I see it on here, but you've a better sense of direction than I have", I said, handing it over.

He looked and stood up, pointing. "That way."

In ten minutes we had left the noise and people behind us. As the town disappeared, the land opened up on either side and I could see the Tor standing majestically, crowned by the Tower of St. Michael's at its summit. At my first good look, I realized that I'd never be able to make the climb.

"I'm waiting here."

"You're not climbing? Tary, you've got to. Look, it's not that bad. I'll help you along. You can..."

I shook my head and put my hand on his arm. "Arthur, look at it. It's all slope and grass. No, you go up. Stop in the Tower for a while and make your peace. You can use the time. It's been a rough twenty-four hours for you."

"It's been rough for both of us." He took another long look at the huge hill, and turned back to me. "Are you certain. Will you be okay down here?"

I nodded, and said. "Yes, of course I'm certain. I want to visit the Well Gardens. Besides, the exercise'll do you good."

As Arthur went ahead to make the climb I turned off into the Chalice Well Gardens. For awhile I wandered the paths stopping here and there to meditate and reflect. I found myself drawn to the wellhead, staring down into the depths of the Spring itself. Finally I glanced at my watch shocked to see how much time had passed as I wandered lost in thought. It was starting to get dark and Arthur had been gone a little over two hours. Well, that was about right. Nothing to worry about. In fact, if I squinted and stared really hard, I could just about make out a couple of people coming down the side of the Tor. The Doctor would be one of them no doubt. It was a gift he had, the ability to talk to people he

A QUESTION OF BALANCE

met and make friends, one that I admired since I was so different. As I watched the figures moving carefully, I wondered who these new friends might be and secretly, hoped we weren't going to be stuck having dinner with them. I left the Garden through the back gate and walked to the foot of the Tor to meet him.

The three had reached the bottom, the Doctor's tall lanky form standing out clearly. He was talking animatedly to the woman walking beside him, her companion, a stocky man, just behind. I stood as they approached. For some reason my stomach gave a lurch. I remember thinking that I must be hungry. It was fast approaching dinnertime.

"Doctor," I called, waving. "I was just beginning to worry." I began to walk toward them. He looked up at me and waved. I thought he was about to shout something when the man stumbled into him. For a second, I thought Arthur was going to fall, but he caught his balance and with a sharp glance behind continued toward me quietly. Suddenly, I realized there was something wrong. As the trio approached I felt the contents of my stomach rise into my throat. I recognized the woman.

"Tary, look who I found skulking about St. Michael's," said Arthur, "I believe you know Miss Kelly?"

I nodded, not trusting myself to speak.

"And this oaf is her..." he shot a glance at the man, "friend, Mr. Thornhill."

Mr. Thornhill pushed him again, and this time he went down, landing hard on his shoulder.

"Doctor." Immediately, I went down beside him.

"It's okay Tary. I'm not hurt." He looked at Marge. "No thanks to your pet. Can't you keep him under control?"

The stocky man growled and pulled back his leg, ready to aim a kick at Arthur's mid-section, but Miss Kelly put out her hand.

"No, Dick. Leave him alone. Just get them on their feet and keep them moving. I don't want to attract any attention." She smiled at me. "It is nice to see you again, Tary. I'm sorry it couldn't have been under other circumstances."

I stood slowly, grasping my walking stick and transferring it to my right hand with some half-formed plan about using it as a club running through my mind. She must have realized.

"I'm sorry, dear, but you'll have to limp along without this."

As she went to grab it, I pulled back a step. Arthur grabbed Mr. Thornhill's ankle while he was distracted watching me, and pulled him down. For a moment, Marge let her attention wander to what was happening, and I pulled the stick back like a baseball bat. I never made the swing. In truth, I don't know if I even could have. Never in my life have I ever deliberately hurt anyone. It didn't matter though, because Arthur grunted in pain and rolled, clutching at his side. Mr. Thornhill stood, a wicked looking knife reflecting the last rays of the sun glinting in his right hand.

I stared for a long moment as blood began to seep through Arthur's fingers. He didn't scream, or cry out, or even moan. He just rocked back and forth on his heels, holding his hand pressed to his side, breath hissing raggedly between his clenched teeth.

The stick fell from my fingers as I dropped to my knees beside him.

"Oh goddess! Arthur, Arthur..." He looked at me and winked, then put his head down. I bent closer and he whispered softly.

"It's not as bad as it looks, but play along." He let out a low groan and fell over onto his side, eyes closed tightly as he gritted his teeth against the pain.

"You killed him." I screamed glaring at the man Marge had called Dick. I turned back and put my arms around the Doctor, praying that they were just words.

"You stupid imbecile." said Marge, stepping closer. She shoved the man out of the way and bent over.

I looked at her, tears running freely down my face. "He's hurt badly, maybe dying."

A Question of Balance

Pushing me roughly aside, she snapped, "Hold her."

Thornhill grabbed my shoulders and yanked me to my feet.

"Leave him alone." I shouted, mostly for affect, as she bent over Arthur's still form.

I thought, in the gloom, that her mouth twisted up into a tiny smile as she reached over and slammed her fist cruelly against the wound.

The Doctor groaned, loudly this time, and I knew it was no act. She pulled his head back and stared into his face.

"You have a minute to get to your feet or I'll let my pet play with your pet."

He closed his eyes, took a deep shuddering breath, then opened them again. He grunted a little, but got up and stood on rubbery legs, his hand still pressed tightly against his side. Thornhill let me go at a gesture from his mistress and I moved in to help support Arthur.

"I'm sorry, Arthur," I murmured as I took some of his weight.

He was white as a sheet, but I thought that the blood was beginning to slow. Somehow he managed a sickly smile. "No, Tary, I'm sorry. I shouldn't have got you into this."

The reality suddenly hit me. This wasn't a game, or a movie; this was real life; he was bleeding real blood. If the Doctor was right, and I had no reason to think he wasn't, one man had already been killed. All the same terror that I'd experienced that night in New York came flooding back, striking like a physical blow. How could I have forgotten? I staggered under the realization that this time, without the Grimoir, my magic was probably out-matched; and on the physical level, we were already beaten.

Thornhill moved behind us, his knife pointed in my general direction. "Move."

We began to move slowly, following Miss Kelly.

It was nearly full dark, but I could see the outline of a Dodge Ram pulled off the lane ahead. I knew our chances for escape would be zero once we were locked into that van. I looked around for someone, anyone at all who might be able to come to our assistance, but the area was deserted.

Arthur stumbled, nearly taking me down with him. He hadn't spoken a word. It seemed all he could do to keep one foot moving in front of the other. His face looked like pale wax in the light of the nearly full moon. Beads of perspiration dotted his forehead. As I steadied him, he half smiled, looking ghastly. I knew enough first aid to recognize that he was going into shock from the trauma. My heart sank as I realized he would be very little use in any sort of escape attempt. Again, as in New York, it was all up to me.

Thornhill grunted, poking at me impatiently to keep us moving.

"He's hurt, can't you see that?" I said, turning.

"He'll be dead if you don't keep moving." He pointed the knife.

"He needs to rest." I was trying to stall for time.

Whether Arthur understood or not I didn't know, but he suddenly slumped against me. There was no way I could support his whole weight, I had no choice but to ease him to the ground as gently as I could. His eyes were half closed and going glassy, but I thought he tried to wink.

I turned to the thug. "If you want him to get to the van then you'll have to help me get him there. He's lost a lot of blood."

I wiped Arthur's face with the sleeve of my jacket and he licked his lips. Marge had taken my walking stick and my purse, but I was not entirely weaponless. I still had my little knife tucked into the webbing of my boot. They hadn't thought to search me that far. The problem was, I was not an experienced fighter and my little three-inch pocketknife would be no contest against Thornhill's long sharp blade. The other part was that neither Arthur nor I were in any shape to run very far. Me with my bad leg and Arthur in his current condition would be no match for a determined Brownie, and these two, I feared, were much more experienced than that. Still,

A Question of Balance

I thought, it might come in useful if they tied us up or something.

Marge walked back and looked down at us. "If you can't keep him moving, we'll have to leave him here."

"Fine," I answered, "leave us both, why don't you."

Thornhill grabbed my arm and pulled me to my feet. I know Marge smiled as she drew back her hand and belted me across the face.

Tears sprang to my eyes, but I didn't fall down, or cry out. I simply stood and stared at her, feeling the sting of her palm hot on my cheek. This was the second time in my life I'd been struck by one of these people. In my mind I vowed it would be the last.

Slowly, I bent and whispered into the Doctor's ear. "Can you do it?"

He nodded. "If you'll help me."

He was burning up, his body trying to fight the intrusion into his flesh by generating heat. I was afraid that he would be unconscious soon, or delirious. As gently as I could, I placed my arm under him and helped him to stand.

A pair of headlights appeared around the curve of the lane as we approached the van. They were travelling slowly. Thornhill moved in very close and I could feel the pressure of the flat of his knife through my jacket.

"Just get in quietly," said Marge. "I would rather have you both, but remember, Tary, the Doctor is expendable if need be."

I nodded. Arthur was gasping for air, every breath drawn an effort. I could see the taxi light now, on the top of the approaching car, and I started thinking crazy things. As it drew level with the van, it stopped and pulled over right in front of the Ram. Someone looking for directions, I thought to myself, wracking my brain to calculate my chances of dragging the two of us into the cab before Thornhill got his feet under him. Thornhill must have read my mind because he took hold of my arm and held it tightly as Marge started to approach the vehicle.

The window rolled down and a voice called out, "Is that you? Tary? Doctor?"

By the goddess, I thought, it's Robbie!

Thornhill released his hold on my arm and started to back away, prepared to disappear into the shadows if there was any sign of trouble.

Suddenly, Marge moved quickly, turning toward us. She lifted my walking stick and threw it like a javelin, screaming as she ran to intercept us. Thornhill was no longer behind us, so I moved Arthur as fast as I could toward the waiting taxi as Rob opened the door. For a few seconds, everything seemed to be moving in slow motion, like the last scene from Bonnie and Clyde.

Rob moved toward us as we were moving toward him, with Miss Kelly between. I saw her drop my purse after she threw the stick, and pull something from her waistband. It was too dark to see clearly, even in slo-mo, but I'd seen enough movies to assume it was a gun. I guess the taxi driver had too.

The cab lurched forward and I made a quick directional change, shoving Arthur with all my strength into Rob, and following on top. All three of us went down as a small, somewhat disappointing crack sounded. I'd expected a gunshot to be much louder. Then, time speeded up again.

I grabbed my purse and my stick and Rob grabbed Arthur under the arms, flinging him into the back seat of the taxi. I was right behind. The driver didn't give Marge another chance to aim before he stomped down on the accelerator, taxi doors slamming shut as he took off.

For a minute, our young friend stared at the blood on his fingers. I didn't have time to explain. The wound was bleeding with a vengeance now, and the Doctor was making little grunting noises as I probed with my hanky. Robbie took out his own handkerchief and started to wipe his hands, but I grabbed it and added it to my own, trying to stem the flow of blood. Arthur made a move to sit up straight between us. His face turned ashen with the effort.

A QUESTION OF BALANCE

The driver turned and looked from me to Rob. "Where to?"

The Doctor made a noise that was half laugh and half cough. "The local constabulary, I think," he said. Then, he groaned as the car hit a bump. "Or the hospi...hospi..."

"The nearest hospital, quickly," I finished for him, as Arthur finally passed out. "Have the local constable meet us there."

Robbie looked at me while we waited in the corridor for the surgical resident to come out.

"After I got that call from Mr. Pratcher, I really didn't know what to do. He was so insistent, though. Said he scryed the two of you were in trouble. He actually used that word, scryed, like in a crystal ball or something."

I nodded, "It's amazing," I said, agreeing completely.

"I never was so glad to see anybody as I was you two, though," he went on, the words spilling from his mouth like a flood.

I smiled. "You mean we were never so glad to see anybody as you."

"No, I mean, I took the train, and that used up all my cash. If I hadn't found you, I couldn't have paid off the taxi."

I laughed out loud as I realized that had been a major concern of his, too. How to pay off the taxi. I sobered quickly enough as the young man in a white lab coat approached.

"How is he?" Rob and I both asked at once.

"Are you his family?" said the surgeon.

"I'm his wife," I said. "Is he all right?"

"It took twenty-six stitches to close the wound. He was lucky, amazingly there were no organs involved." He narrowed his eyes.

"Perhaps you could talk to him, Missus. He's insisting that he won't stay for observation. I've given him an anti-tetanus, and an antibiotic, but he's lost quite a bit of blood. I'd really rather he stayed here the night." He glanced over at Robbie.

"I'm sure the police will have some questions for you two as well," he added. "Naturally, I've made a report. We had the local PC in, but they want to bring in a detective in the morning." He raised his eyebrows. "A domestic, was it? Kitchen knife?"

I didn't like his tone and was about to say so when Arthur appeared, jacket folded neatly over his arm.

"It was nothing like that, I assure you. Just a couple of hooligans looking for an easy wallet to lift, that's all." He smiled weakly. "I suppose I should have just let them have it, really."

The surgeon looked skeptical. "Perhaps, if that's what happened."

"Oh, it is," insisted my husband. "And when the police constable asks for me, you can tell them I'll make a full report in the morning."

"You can't leave..."

"Can't I?" He took my hand and walked to the door with Rob following like a puppy.

"Good night, doctor," called Arthur over his shoulder as we left the building.

We got into the taxi which I had paid to wait.

"Take us to the rail station, please." He squeezed my hand as the car moved off. "We can stop at the chemist in Exeter to fill this," he held up a prescription form. "It's for more antibiotics."

He grimaced as we went over a bump in the rough street.

"Did he give you anything for pain?" I asked, concerned.

"No. I can't afford to be muddled just now. We have much to do." He turned to Rob, patting him affectionately on the knee. "And how did you ever manage to track us down, eh? It was a fine bit of luck for us that you did, though." Although he was trying to be casual as he took the younger man's hand, I could hear his voice shake with emotion. "I'm very grateful, to you Rob. You may not have realized it, but I believe you saved our lives back there." He looked at me. "Well, mine anyway."

A Question of Balance

When Rob had finished his story about Nigel Pratcher's call, the Doctor smiled. "I'll never disbelieve anything again."

I laughed. "As long as it's proven to your complete satisfaction, qualified and quantified into nice neat little packages." I grinned, "Or unless it happens to have saved your life."

"Yes. Like tonight." He yawned. "I think we'll take the Intercity back, first class."

On the first class coach back to Exeter, Robbie and I talked while the Doctor dozed. "So, do you think this Professor Bectinson was really killed because of the book?" he asked, his eyes very bright and wide behind his glasses.

I nodded. "There's no doubt in my mind, Rob. One of the first things we learn is, 'there is no such thing as coincidence'. We're going to have to go to London. Not tomorrow, Arthur needs at least a day to rest, but as soon as he's able to travel."

"I wish I could go with you two." He smiled eagerly.

"No, you've already done quite enough. I only hope you haven't put yourself in double Dutch." I patted his hand. "Besides, you still have your bit to do, haven't you? Cambodia next year, remember?"

"Yeah, but..."

"But nothing, Rob. There are still things going on all over this planet of which the general population of the free world isn't aware. I think trying to bring some of them to light it a quest worthy of Percival himself."

He grinned at me. "Do you think so? Really?"

"We all have our part to play. Don't underestimate the value of yours. Stick to your original plan, Rob. They'll be with you."

"Who?" he asked.

I raised my eyes, "Whoever They are who look after fools like us."

Arthur stirred as the train pulled to a stop. Between us, Rob and I managed to get him off the platform and into a taxi. He felt warm and was very stiff, but at least he wasn't burning up, and his eyes were clear. We found a pharmacy and stopped to fill the prescription, then took the taxi all the way back to Exmouth.

"Blasted thing's pulling," he complained as we climbed the stairs slowly to our room.

"Well, what do you expect? Perhaps you should have taken the doctor's advice and stayed in hospital over night."

He flashed me that grin of his; "I'm the Doctor, Tary. Besides, I didn't fancy having to answer an interminable number of questions put by the local constable. It's not as if we'd be dealing with the Metropolitan Force. At least in London I have some contacts. No, it's better this way. I'll get a good night's sleep and tomorrow we'll make an early start to London."

I got Arthur settled into bed and switched on the TV in our room. I was just dozing off when the Doctor rolled over in his sleep and groaned loudly waking himself and me up.

"Have you got any aspirin?" he whimpered.

Chapter Sixteen
First Class

It was a full two days before Arthur was fit enough to travel. In those two days he rested, with Robbie and I looking after him. The knife wound while serious, enough, seemed to be mending and I thanked the goddess that it didn't fester. Even so, it was painful and made movement awkward. The Doctor made a lousy patient.

"Tary, did you find out why they didn't deliver the Sunday Independent?" He took a sip of tea and made a face at me. "It's cold!"

I plugged in the kettle. "I'll make you a fresh cup."

"No, never mind that. I want the paper! Would you just nip down and see if they've got it at reception?" He moved to set down his cup and yelped. "And could you bring me another aspirin or three... oh, and a glass of water?"

I looked at my watch. "It's about time for another antibiotic too. I'll run down and see about some lunch. You shouldn't take them on an empty stomach."

The kettle began to boil.

"I know how to take medication, Tary. I am a doctor! Could I have those aspirin now please?" He scattered the remnants of Saturday's paper onto the floor impatiently.

Everyday, he'd gone over the news with a fine tooth comb, the Independent, the Tribune, and the Mirror, searching for anything that might indicate what our enemies were up to. His imagination and mine worked overtime to find a tie in between every murder, assault, rape and robbery and our own situation. In the London papers, as in any metropolitan newspaper, there was more than enough to keep us occupied at that little game. But, it wasn't getting us anywhere. Arthur wouldn't even trust the telephone lines, and so we'd had no contact at all with anyone from either the Institute, Museum or the University. There was a short piece about the death of Professor Bectinson and his contributions to academia. We missed the funeral. I know that bothered Arthur, but there was no way he was up to it.

There was a soft knock at the door. It was Terri coming from the kitchen bearing a tray.

"From Rob, the tray of luncheon." He came in and set it on the desk, removing the cover with a small flourish, his eyes crinkled with the effort translating to English in his head. . "Cheese, ham and biscuits. Some, oh, some sweet? A cake, three levels?"

Arthur was already reaching for the paper rolled neatly on a corner of the tray.

"Good, the Independent! Thanks Terri!"

Terri smiled. "The Doctor is feeling some better, yes?"

"What?" said Arthur, as he opened the paper, searching the headlines first.

"He's feeling better, yes, thank you Terri," I said. "Thank Rob for me, will you?"

"I will. He will come and see for himself the Doctor when he closes the bar."

It sounded as though he'd rehearsed that line, and I giggled. "Tell him..." I looked over at Arthur who was going through the paper "Never mind. I'll come down and tell him myself,"

When Terri was gone, I brought Arthur the aspirin and antibiotic. "I'm going down to the bar for lunch, if you'll be all right for a bit?

He looked at me distractedly, fine, fine. Go on, go on."

"Don't forget to eat something!" I warned. "I don't want to hear about your stomach later."

He never acknowledged me, so I left.

There was a couple having lunch at a table near the corner, but the bar was unoccupied so I moved to sit at my usual place. There was a small bag, a kind of a backpack hanging from the back of the stool.

"Someone here, Rob?" I asked.

He looked at the pack. "No. A woman just stopped in for a pint, but I'm sure she left. Can't imagine how she left that there, though."

"Oh," I said. "Did you recognize her?"

"No. She's not a resident at the hotel. An older lady, maybe a yank, or Canadian, I'm not very good with American accents." He reached over the bar to retrieve the bag. I stopped him.

"Wait." He looked at me curiously. Gingerly, I undid the straps that held the bag closed. I had a queasy feeling in the pit of my gut... Inside was what appeared to be a clump of feathers.

"Could it have been Miss Kelly?" I said softly, not taking my eyes away from the contents of the bag. "You got a look at her, didn't you, that night at the Tor?"

"Not a very good one, no," he breathed. "But she wouldn't have come here. She wouldn't have had the cheek!" He paused, uncertainly. "Would she?"

Gently, I lifted the dead morning dove from the pack. Its neck had been wrung, nearly twisted off its body, in fact. Fortunately, my back was to the tables, so there was no one whose appetite I ruined before I shoved it back in the bag.

Robbie stared. "'What's it mean?"

"Nothing good, that's for sure," I replied. "Do me a favor Rob, and don't mention this to Arthur, will you?" I closed up the bag and put it on the floor. "He has enough things to worry about just now."

"Yeah, right, Missus, I won't." He poured himself a quick shot and downed it before he looked at me again. "But, if it's something bad, don't you think he ought to know?"

I smiled a little "A diet cola please...and we don't know yet that it's something bad. I'll do a little spell of my own, to find out." I took a large swallow of soda. "I am a witch, after all. I should be able to counter this..." I nudged the parcel with my stick, "...whatever it is, without too much trouble."

"Gaw, can I watch?"

I frowned. "I don't think so, Rob This kind of thing is best done solitary."

"Oh," he said, disappointed. "I suppose so."

"I came down to thank you for sending up lunch. That was sweet of you."

"All part of the service madam," he joked, with a mocking bow. "How is the Doc anyway? Think he'll mind a bit of company after I close the bar?"

"He's grouchy as a bear! You come up, at your own risk! In fact, I came down for a spot of lunch just to get away from him for a while. Have you got any cheese and biscuits I can nibble on?"

At a little after two, Rob closed the bar. Picking up the satchel t carried it up the stairs, our young friend in tow. I knocked at the door, calling out, "It's just me, I've brought company," before I went in.

Arthur came out of the bathroom, rubbing a towel across his hair. He had on a pair of unzipped jeans and an opened shirt.

"Oh, Rob. Come on in." He gestured to one of the chairs. "Sit. Cup of tea?"

"No, thanks. I just popped in to see how you were feeling. The Missus said you were feeling better today."

Arthur laughed, wincing a little. "The Missus told you I'm grouchy, didn't she?"

"Well," I said to defend myself. "You were when I left." I looked at him. "Why are you dressed? You've got to be careful you don't open that again!"

"I know what I'm doing. In fact, I was just about to change the dressing. I could use some help.."

In a few minutes he had a clean bandage. He even managed to zipper up his jeans with a minimum of fussing.

"What's that?" asked the Doctor, pointing to the satchel lying where I'd dropped it, near the window.

"Nothing." I changed the subject. "Are you sure you want to try a walk? Maybe one more day in bed would..."

"...drive me mad, Tary!" He interrupted. "Really, I'll be fine. Just a little walk in the garden. Besides, we've got to leave tomorrow. I won't wait another day. There's too much going on."

"What?" asked Rob excitedly.

"In London? There's lots going on."

"Oh, you mean in general," he said.

"Yes, there's a lot going on in general Besides, I can't sit around a hotel room in Exmouth-on-Sea forever, now can I?" He winked at me. "I've got things to do, people to see.."

"So, tomorrow you'll be off then?"

The Doctor looked into our young friend's Eyes. "Yes, Rob. Tomorrow we'll be off for London."

Rob and I helped Arthur down the stairs and into the peaceful garden. We sat on a cozy little bench and Robbie withdrew tactfully.

"We'll see you tonight!" called the Doctor.

"Will you be up to it?" I asked.

He breathed deeply, color entering his cheeks as the salt air entered his lungs. "Oh, I think so. I feel worlds better today, Tary. Worlds better."

"As long as you're determined, I'll walk down to the rail station and pick up our tickets while you have a nap."

"A nap? I don't need a nap, matron! I'm perfectly fine."

I glared. "You are not perfectly fine. You were stabbed and suffered a serious wound! It took twenty five stitches..."

"Six..," he interrupted.

"What?"

"It was twenty six.

"You are incorrigible! It was a nasty cut, nothing to play around with."

"'tis not so deep as a well, nor so wide as a church door, but, 'tis enough, t'will do..." he quoted dramatically.

"Okay Mercutio," I muttered. "And a plague on your house too,"

He smiled and stood up. "Let's walk down to the sea."

After walking to the sea-lane and back, Arthur relinquished his position on a nap. I lifted the canvas satchel and stole from the room silently as he snored. When I was on the beach, I breathed easier. There was no one to be seen along the shore this late on a day so early in the spring. I was alone. I lay the pathetic little bundle down carefully and drew a circle in the sand around myself with my walking stick.

I had no implements or tools of any kind with me, but that didn't matter. Tools, like candles and incense are merely props, aids to focus the attention and sharpen concentration. Magic itself requires nothing more than a human mind, a need and the desire. I had all I needed to perform this spell.

I sat cross-legged on the sand and opened my mind to the cosmos. Having touched infinity and returned, I was able to visualize clearly. Visualization, is the key to working magic. In my mind's eye I saw the gentle bird as it had been in life. It's brown-gray breast rose and fell drawing in the breath of life. One black eye cocked toward me and I entered the pupil falling deep, ever deeper into the well of darkness I found therein.

Images came quickly, clearly. A small fire, a clearing in a grove; a High Priestess in dark raiment raising hands in supplication to a god born of the evil in the mind of Man. It is only there that such a god can exist; but it is a suitable place from which to wield power. A tiny thing fluttered helpless wings in the hands of the sorceress as she held the sacrifice up to the darkened moon. In a strange tongue, one never used by mortal man in ordinary speech, she issued a vile incantation. The words were unknown to me, but the meaning was clear, The Doctor and I had removed the only hold they had on us. This curse was to take the place of the bracelet.

The dove struggled, it 's efforts growing feeble as life was slowly strangled away. On the wings of her captive soul would fly the ill to find Arthur and me, wherever we were. I knew without a doubt that if necessary, they wouldn't hesitate to murder the Doc-

A Question of Balance

tor in order to control me. I concentrated. First, they had to have us. I willed my mind to enter the soul of that frightened morning dove as she fled to the bidding of her dark mistress. With a gentle whisper, I released it to whatever fate awaits those simple creatures of the Mother beyond this life. For a moment I hesitated, sorely tempted to turn the spell back against it's sender. Then, I remembered my vows, the primary tenet of Wicca: "'an it harm none, do what thou will." The words sounded softly in my mind. There would be no difference separating me from my enemies if I misused my own magic, even in what I judged to be a high cause. Slowly I let the energy disperse, then grounded myself with the living Earth.

A long screech reverberated along the seashore, carrying across the estuary echoing off the hills of Torbay. A strange sea bird's call, perhaps, to any who might have heard. I knew that it was Marge Kelly's wail of frustration as my magic countered hers.

When I opened my eyes, the tide had risen and the tiny, limp body, along with the backpack, was gone. Another wave brought the ancient sea to wash over my feet and the water was cold. I picked up my shoes and retreated, standing awhile to watch as the relentless tides erased all traces of my circle.

Arthur was up and dressing for dinner by the time I returned with our railway tickets to London. He shot me a look as I stood disheveled, hair wild from the windy beach, my shoes tracking sand along the carpet.

"I was hoping to get down early tonight, but I see you need a bath. Did you have a nice walk on the beach?"

"Yes. I want to remember it forever." I removed my shoes and headed for the
    tub. "I won't be long, I promise!"
"Did you get the tickets?" he called over the running water. "First class?"

"Yes, first class. It really is an extravagance, though. It's so expensive. I don't see what's so terrible about travelling standard,"

"Oh," he muttered. "You don't do you? Well never mind. I just prefer the quiet of a first class coach, that's all."

"If you say so," I answered, toweling myself off.

Leaving Robbie and Julian and even William...leaving Exmouth, was a wrench. I'd only been there for a fortnight, but I felt as if I belonged. I've never really been totally comfortable anywhere I've lived, not until Devon. Rob and Julian carried our luggage to the waiting taxi. I wondered how we could have become so close in so short a time. Of course, thinking logically, it would have been odder if we hadn't. The Doctor and I owed our lives to the young bartender cum photo-journalist who stood forlornly at the foot of the steps.

"You had better call me in February if you make it to New York," I warned, trying to keep my voice light. "Remember, I'm only about fifty miles from the City and there's a train station three quarters of a mile from my front door."

Arthur placed his arm around my shoulder and winked, "And I can recommend the sofa. It's very comfortable," He grinned and held out his hand. "Thank you, Rob, for everything."

I gave him a hug and a kiss on the lips, but I couldn't bring myself to form the words 'good bye'.

"If you ever get to the North Country, you have my number, right?" said Arthur warmly. Rob nodded, and I knew how he felt. There were tears standing in my eyes too.

The taxi driver helped us onto the platform with our luggage. I got a trolley for my two large bags, which made it a little easier, but I was afraid to let Arthur carry even the moderate weight of his own duffel. The wound was mending but it was still pretty bad. He really, should have been in bed. Well, we were on our way at last to London where I hoped he would seek medical attention.

A Question of Balance

A porter wrestled our baggage into the Intercity first class coach at the Exeter Station. As the train pulled out, we were finally able to relax and enjoy the ride.

"I need to stretch my legs" said Arthur, standing. "Want anything from the dining bar?"

"Why don't you just sit and wait for the steward. I mean we are in first class after all. Shouldn't we enjoy the amenities?"

"I need to walk a bit, have a reccy. What can I bring you?"

"All right then freshen my tea and get me a sticky bun." I said, watching out the window.

He smiled at me. "Are you sure that's all? We may not get to lunch, you know."

"I'm sure. I'm not that hungry

"I'll be right back." He disappeared to the rear of the coach.

I leaned back enjoying the luxury and the quiet of the first class compartment. He was right, it was worth it , especially since he was paying. I think I started to doze off, because he startled me when he slid into the seat carrying the little shopping bag with our goodies.

"Tary?" he whispered, a note of urgency tinting his voice. "Tary, wake up! They're here, on the train!"

"What?" I opened my eyes and stared groggily at him, not understanding for a moment what he meant. "Who's here?"

"We've got to get off!"

"Get off? But won't they just follow us?"

"Not if we leave our things and hop off just as the train pulls out at the next stop! Even if they do spot us, it'll be too late. They'll have to wait until the train stops again and back-track us We'll at least have a good start."

I was now fully awake. "Leave our things? You mean all my luggage? Arthur, I've got some of my best stuff in there!"

"Give me the cell phone"

"Why?"

"Must you question everything? Just give me the phone. I'll ring ahead. Someone can meet the train and take our luggage to the hotel, or someplace safe."

"But, what about the phones? I thought you said we couldn't trust that ...."

"We're on a train. Even they couldn't have gotten to every cell tower on the Intercity line, could they?" He began rummaging through my purse impatiently. "We'll just have to chance it, that's all!"

"Okay!" I said, taking my purse from him. I put in my hand and grabbed the phone. He snatched it and headed off.

"While I'm doing that, get some things out of your bag. Take just what you'll need overnight, some underwear, an extra pair of boots and your toothbrush. We can stick them in my duffel bag and leave the rest."

"What about clothes? Where are we going? How can..."

Arthur shook me by the shoulders. "Will you listen to me please. I don't know yet, do you hear? We have to get off this train first, then worry about everything else. Forget about clothes. Just take your heavy jacket and put on your black boots, the ones with the elastic web around the outside."

"But.....

"And bring your knife, Tary. Tuck it into your boot. Now, go do as I say while I go and phone." He disappeared between the cars.

I spent exactly three seconds in shock, then rose to do as he said. By the time he returned to the seat I had his one duffel bag at the seat. He smiled. "Good girl." He looked at his watch. "We've about twenty minutes 'til the next stop, Castle Park, I think. Drink your tea."

"Drink my.... Arthur, what are we going to do?"

"We're going to pretend we don't know they're here. Then just as the train starts
up to leave the station, we'll jump off. From there... well.. I'll think of something."

A Question of Balance

His eyes were sparkling and that always makes me nervous. "You want to jump off a moving train? Are you nuts? Neither one of us is in any shape to pull a stunt like that!"

His smile turned grim. "We'll have to be, I'm afraid, or neither one of us will be in any shape to do much of anything ever again. You don't think they intend to let us reach London, do you? The only thing that troubles me is I would have thought they'd try more occult means. I know we threw them off when you lost the bracelet, but I really expected that they'd make another magical attempt, rather than all this James Bond stuff. I mean, watching the station? It's not like them!"

"They did." My voice came out very soft and low, almost a whisper.

"Did what?" His pale eyes held mine so deeply I couldn't look away or even blink. I told him about the dead morning dove and my spell.

"Why didn't you tell me, eh? What were you thinking of. We could have used that, Tary."

I was beginning to get annoyed. "I did use it, Arthur. Remember I'm the witch, I take full responsibility for the magic. Any decision about when, how and why it is used, is my decision, not yours." It felt good to exert some control for a change.

"Oh, I see" he said, putting his arm around me, wincing a little as the motion pulled at his stitches. Then he sighed. "I suppose I haven't always been completely honest with you either have I. Well, what's done is done, and very nicely too." He smiled. "We'll have to make the most of the situation while you've got them off balance."

He chucked me under the chin. "Come on, cheer up! It'll be fun! You said you wanted to see more of the countryside anyway." There was that sparkle again.

"Not as a fugitive!" I argued. "How can you call this fun? People are ready to murder us, torture you to get to me? Don't you realize you were almost killed once already?" I stopped and looked into his eyes. "And Professor Bectinson, they did kill him, remember? Arthur, this isn't a game. I don't want to have this kind of fun; I want to stay alive and keep you that way. I want to be normal again!"

"Poor Tary," he murmured, "I haven't forgotten any of those things. But Tary, they've been thwarted at every turn. Don't you see, we're meant to win this one!"

For a moment we were both silent. Then, he spoke quietly. "If Walter's death is to have any meaning at all, we've got to. We will."

A tinny voice came over the public address system announcing the next stop would be Castle Park in five minutes. Arthur looked at me. "Whatever happens know I love you."

I blinked.

"Now, get ready. Take the bag and stand at the back near the toilet, as though you're waiting for someone to vacate. As soon as the train starts to move, open the door and get out. Don't wait too long."

"What do you mean, don't wait too long. I'll go when you go."

He shook his head, "I'm going to the rear of the train, back to standard where I can keep my eyes on them, hopefully without their noticing. You'll have to jump on your own. I'll wait until I'm at the end of the platform before I go."

"No Arthur! I won't leave this train without you! I don't want to leave this train at all! It was your crazy idea, not mine. What if something goes wrong? Tell me, what am I supposed to do if you don't make it off the train?" Panic was starting to close in on me.

He smiled that smile. "Oh, I'll be all right, Tary. If for any reason at all I'm not able to join you, just make for the way out as soon as your feet touch the ground. Call Lady Jess when you're clear of the station and tell her everything. Do you understand me? Tell her everything. Then, make for the New Forest by the fastest means you can. If we do get separated, I'll meet you in Burley."

"But..."

A Question of Balance

"Tary, there's no time to argue, just go!" He turned and left me standing there, his duffel bag looped over my shoulder. For a minute, I thought I might just follow him. Then I felt the train begin to slow. He was right about one thing, there was no time to argue. He must have a reason for doing it this way. I had to trust him.

I stood as he'd told me, right outside the toilet, with one eye out the window watching the platform. No one was moving to enter the train at this door. Very few people traveled the first class coaches, especially in the middle of the day. Finally, I felt a jerk as the train made ready to pull out. I moved to the window and opened it, preparing to reach out and unlatch the door. First class is in the front of the train, so I wouldn't have much time before we got to the end of the platform. I had to get it right on the first try. There would be no retakes on this scene.

The last train guard climbed back in two doors down from me. I heaved a sigh of relief. How do you explain what you're doing jumping off a moving train when you're booked through to London? Fortunately, I wouldn't have to try. It began moving slowly. I reached out and put my fingers on the latch. As the train started to pick up a little speed, I could see the end of the platform rushing toward me. This was it. I released the latch, the door swung open and I.. well, jumped is really too kind a word. Actually, I sort of took a giant step and tumbled. The duffel bag took the brunt of the shock as I hit and rolled on my shoulder.

That wasn't too bad, I thought, looking to see if anyone had noticed my acrobatics I stood up and dusted myself off, watching the rest of the cars rushing by me. It was moving faster now I couldn't imagine how Arthur would make the jump without breaking his fool neck. He did, though, from the next to last car. He says he never even saw me, but from my perspective it was as if he had aimed. He leaped, eyes closed tightly, and landed on his feet, for a second, then he stumbled headlong into me. I went down all over again with the Doctor on top.

"Are you all right?" We said simultaneously.

With an effort, he pushed himself up and held out his arm to help me up. I brushed my hand down the front of my coat. It was sticky. I stared at him. The whole of his shirtfront was stained with a spreading red blotch.

"Oh goddess Arthur, you're bleeding again."

"Am I?" he asked distractedly. "Some of the stitches must've pulled loose." He grabbed my hand and tugged me to my feet. "Come on, we'll worry about that when we have a minute. Right now, we don't.... look!"

He pointed down the track after the retreating train. I stared too. Way down, almost beyond our line of sight, someone was just standing up alongside the track bed.

"Come on Tary! Come on!" We stumbled up the stairs and out onto the street of the village of Castle Park. There wasn't a taxi in sight.

"Look, a Taxi office," I said pointing,

"We haven't got the time to wait. They're on to us. Didn't you see?"

"Arthur, you're bleeding badly again. We've got to find a doctor."

"Yes, later. Let's get out of sight first so I can get my breath." We moved along the quiet street, looking for a likely spot to take cover. It would take our pursuit some little time to get oriented and climb up away from the tracks. We needed every second.

"What about the pub?" I asked, spotting a swinging sign outside a little inn.

"Too public. It's the first place they'll look. We need to get out of the village altogether. Let's head for the wood. There ought to be cover there."

"No doctors," I said.

He sighed. "I know, but we've got to get out of sight." He felt the side where the knife had cut him. "I think it's nearly stopped again. I'll be okay. Come on."

I hitched the duffel higher on my shoulder and trudged after him. We weren't moving very quickly, but we managed to get a fair way into the woods before he stopped. Slowly he sank down onto a tree stump looking gray and tired. I put down the bag. "How are you doing?" Kneeling, I pulled the shirt away from the cut. It stuck and he bit his lower lip as I tugged it clear as gently as I could.

"Smarts a bit," he admitted, closing his eyes. "How does it look?"

Trying not to reopen the wound, I pulled the adhesive away and peeled back the gauze dressing. Some of the stitches in the center had come apart and the wound gaped a little, but the blood has slowed to an ooze that was already clotting over.

"Not too bad, I don't think, but what do I know? I'm a witch, not a doctor."

He half smiled. "Well, I can't see it very well from this angle, describe it to me."

I did. "Get out a fresh dressing and some antibiotic cream from my kit in the bag. I think it should be all right, as long as it doesn't abscess. Let's just get it covered."

After I had the clean bandage in place I looked at my watch "You're overdue for

Medication."

He looked at me. "You didn't happen to bring a thermos of something to drink, did you?"

I stared at him.

"No? Well, I suppose I'll have to take them dry, and on an empty stomach too."

"That should be the least of our troubles," I growled. I rummaged around in the bag and came up with a clean sweater.

"Here, change into that . We're bound to attract attention if you go walking around looking like a refugee from a Friday the 13th movie."

He didn't waste energy arguing. When he was presentable, he got up and started walking again.

"I almost hate to ask, but do you have a particular destination in mind?" I asked as I caught up. It was no great feat since he was moving with all the speed and grace of a galloping turtle.

"When, for tonight, or ultimately?"

I rolled my eyes. "Let's just start with tonight. Later on we can worry about ultimately."

"Well, for tonight I thought we would stop at a little Bed and Breakfast just the other side of these woods. You know, a little farmhouse, quaint and picturesque. Nothing fancy, mind, just dinner with the family and a small bed sit, bath down the hall arrangement. Will that suit you?"

I was relieved. "Absolutely. How far is this place? Do you know exactly where it is from here?"

"Not exactly..."

I glared and stopped moving.

"Well, there's bound to be one, isn't there? The countryside's dotted with those charming little bits of English hospitality."

"So in other words, you have no idea where we're going."

"Well, if I knew, there'd be a chance that they knew." He smiled. "Don't worry, I'll think..."

"...of something," I finished.

"Yes." He grinned.

Chapter Seventeen
Hedgerows and Cairns

Tary wasn't happy. We trudged all afternoon with no clear idea of where we were heading other than to put distance between our pursuers and us. Eventually it started getting dark. The woods had thinned out, and we were in open farmland dotted with sheep and divided by thick hedgerows when I realised I couldn't go on. This seemed as good a place as any to stop.

"I can't move another step, Tary. We'll have to stay here There's a cairn, see over there. It will give us a little shelter as long as it doesn't rain. We can have a small fire and try and get some sleep. In the morning I'll be able to figure our location better."

"You don't have a clue where we are do you?" she accused, dropping the bag and sitting in a patch of grass reasonably free of Sheep dung.

"Well, I wouldn't say I have no idea. I mean, we got off the train at Castle Park. The sun was over our right shoulder when we entered the wood.... or was it to our back? No, no, I'm sure it was to the left as we entered the wood. If you figure that we travelled fifty kilometres, resting every..." I stopped and scratched my head staring into the sky. "If it wasn't so overcast, I could see the stars." I looked at her. "Then I might have a better idea."

Tary couldn't help laughing. "Is there someone we can call for help?" she pulled out the cell phone and turned it on. The battery let out one bleep and went silent. "Damn!"

I shrugged. "So much for technology."

"Listen, we're in the middle of farm country right? So, there must be a farmhouse fairly close. We should keep going until we come to it." She was ever the optimist.

"Tary, it could be miles. It's dark and we don't know the area. We could pass a house within half a mile, and never even realise it." I pressed my hands over my eyes. "I just can't do it tonight, Tary. I'm all done in. Let's try and get some sleep. In the morning I'll be able to get my bearings."

There was a fast moving stream near the cairn where we settled in for the night. She reached into her enormous purse and pulled out a sticky bun offering me half.

"Have you got anything else to eat in there?" I asked hopefully.

"Sure." She pulled out a white bag and proffered it. "Would you like a Jelly Baby?"

I said nothing.

We shared the duffel bag as a pillow, and managed to get a couple of hours sleep. It was cold and damp, but we had a small fire and each other. It was enough. In the morning Tary tried to stretch, but she was stiff. Groaning out loud, she pulled herself to her feet and glared down at me.

"Do you know how long it's been since 1 had to sleep in a hedgerow for the night? A couple of centuries at least, and I was much younger then!" She said peevishly.

"It wasn't a hedgerow, it was a cairn. Hedgerows are much more comfortable. I was saving that for tonight." I grinned at her, then tried to roll over and moaned louder than she had.

"See?" she said smugly.

"Just give me a few minutes. I'll be able to manage it." I tried again. "Have you brought the aspirin?"

I was finally on my feet, but for how long I wondered? The laceration was developing an abscess where the stitches had torn loose. There was still no sign of septicaemia though, and for that I was grateful.

"We're bound to come to a road or lane of some sort soon. England is a too small a country to get really lost in. Once we find a phone, I can ring London and get someone down to fetch us."

"Once you figure out where we are, you mean." She was tired, hungry, filthy, and getting snappish. "So much for first class travel," she sulked.

I knew her leg must be aching and her back protesting from carrying the bag, though she struggled not to let me see. There was no way I could've handled it. We stopped to rest and she made me eat a couple of Jelly Babies.

"They're not that bad. High carbohydrate, high-energy calories and no fats at all. It's what we need, eat them."

"All sugar!" I complained taking a handful. How many of these things did you bring?"

"Four bags."

"You brought four bags?" I chuckled. "Well, I suppose I can't complain. You're right, they will keep us going."

"Just think of it as travel rations," she said, munching.

Now that there was nobody trying to kill us, at least not for the moment, she was able to relax a little and enjoy the experience, physical discomfort notwithstanding. Unfortunately, the strain was beginning to tell on me. By mid-morning, I was perspiring, and it wasn't all that warm. I felt the first symptoms that my wound was going septic and was afraid that if we didn't reach some kind of civilisation soon I would be in serious trouble.

So far as we could tell there had been no sign of pursuit. Naturally, who would have thought we'd be fools enough to take off into the woods when there was a perfectly good village to hand? We finally came to a road. I rested in the shade of a large tree while Tary stood waiting for a car to pass by. It seemed like a very long time, but finally a lorry pulled around the bend in the road. She waved her arms at him and he stopped.

"Could you give us a lift?" she called, pointing back to where I was dragging our bag over to the side of the road.

"Where to?" asked the driver. He was a smallish man, with dark eyes that darted every which way. Romany I thought to myself.

"That depends," I said, dropping the duffel and standing beside Tary breathing heavily.

"On what?" asked the man. He was looking at us strangely; no doubt with good reason. I can only imagine what we looked like having spent the night stranded in the middle of a sheep meadow.

"On where we are currently. We seem to have got ourselves lost somehow. We started out walking from Castle Park yesterday afternoon."

The driver snickered. "Ya come about three quarters of a mile then if ya come from Castle Park. What'd ya do, circle the wood?"

We looked at each other. "Circle the wood? You mean it runs in a ring around the village?"

The man nodded, a gap-tooth smile splitting his face. "That it does, and just runs into the grazing commons. Where do ya want to be?"

"How far are you going?" asked Arthur, putting up a hand to shield his eyes from the morning sun.

"Salisbury. Hop in if you've a mind."

"Great, we can get a train from there to London!" I struggle to lift the bag.

"I'll get it Arthur, just get in the truck." She tossed it behind the bench seat and climbed in awkwardly.

"No wonder they couldn't find us" she said "We never got to anywhere."

I laughed, "I think it was a good plan."

"Plan!?" she exclaimed.

The driver pulled away, and she shut up. It would be a long haul tracking north-east through the countryside to Salisbury along the roads our driver had chosen. He was going back empty and in no rush. We were both famished having gone more than twenty hours with nothing more substantial than a shared sticky bun and some Jelly Babies. Our new friend Kevin, was more than happy to stop at the next pub we came to. More than happy since I had graciously offered to pay for his meals in return for the lift.

The pub, a sign creaking out front proclaiming it the Cock's Roost, was an ancient building all stone with a newly thatched roof. Inside, it was cool and dark, with a log fire burning in a huge hearth at one end of a long common room. The three of us took a table in a back corner and ordered the local special.

Tary said she was famished, but barely touched more than the topping of her shepherds pie. Not surprisingly, they didn't stock any diet cola, but they had regular, so she made do. Kev seemed perfectly delighted with the cuisine, however, and I can attest to the excellence of the local brew. Tary was sitting in the corner of the bench, I was on the outside and Kev directly across, facing us. From his vantage-point, Kev had a good view of the door and bar area.

"Now, I wonder what that's all about", he said, raising his eyebrows. I turned to look as Tary picked at her pie. I slumped down in my seat as I recognised Thornhill.

"Tary, it's Thornhill! He's talking to the barkeeper showing him a picture...of us most probably."

"You got the cops out for ya?" asked Kev, breathlessly. "That bloke don't look nothing like an inspector to me, even if he did flash a badge to the innkeeper."

"He did?" said the Doctor.

"That's what got me attention. It's not the kind of thing what ya see everyday, at least not out here." I got the distinct impression that we'd suddenly gone up a notch in his eyes. "So what're they after ya for?"

"Believe me," said Tary, as softly as she could. "If that is the man we think it is, he's no policeman."

"No," I confirmed. "He's trying to kill us. He's the one gave me this." He pointed to his side, wincing as the motion pulled. "Dirk...nasty... twenty six stitches."

I looked at Tary, squeezing her hand under the table. "We've got to get out of here now. There's probably a way out through the kitchen. Kev, is the door to the lorry locked? We'll just grab our bag on the way."

"No," he answered, eyes popping. "But where ya going to go from here? There's not another village within five miles. We're still a good ways from Salisbury, fifty, sixty miles at least."

"Yes, well, there's no help for it." I started to slide out of the seat. "Let me know if he's looking this way, Kev."

"You're okay, Doc, if you go right now. He's stopping for a pint it looks like."

"Good. That means there's probably nobody waiting outside. C'mon, Tary."

As we started out, Kev looked at me. "I'll meet you in the lorry missus, you and Doc, don't worry, I'll get ya to Salisbury okay."

She smiled. "No, Kev, but thank you. You're not involved in this. One man's been killed already. Just stay here like you're waiting for us to come back and give us a good start, will you?"

I pushed a twenty-pound note into his hand. "Take care, and thank you." I added, "Oh, and if you can think of a way to do a little misdirecting, that could be a help. We've had a change of plan, we're not going on to Salisbury."

Kevin looked at the note in his hand, then grinned. "For twenty quid ya got yourself an expert! Where are ya going?"

"Forgive me, friend, but it's better that you don't know." I grabbed Tary's hand tightly and we walked quietly through the door to the kitchen and on out the back.

We stopped to grab the duffel bag from the lorry. Obviously, we couldn't stay to the road. To avoid being spotted if Thornhill drove by, we forced our way through the hedge and stayed close on the inside as we paralleled the roadway.

"How could they have found us so quickly?" she asked, managing somehow to keep stride with me.

"They didn't did they?" I answered, stopping. "Sit down a minute, Tary."

"But Thornhill... What if he.."

A QUESTION OF BALANCE

"He can't see us through the hedgerow even if drives by within inches. Besides, he had no idea we were anywhere within a hundred miles of that place." I smiled my best, sitting down next her. "And if I'm any judge, Kevin will be busy entertaining him awhile yet. With luck, he'll send him off on a snipe hunt." I felt a twinge of pain and put my head down a minute. "They'll be

looking for us at Salisbury by evening, I hope."

"I don't understand." She shook her head. If they didn't know we were there, why did he...

"Think of it this way, Tarish. If they did know we were there, they never would've sent Thornhill in. They know we'd recognise him instantly." I shifted to a more comfortable position, then looked at her. "You don't ever forget someone who's tried to kill you. Never, ever."

"So you think they just sent him to show our picture in pubs on the off chance that someone would recognise us?"

"Probably being sent to the least likely places. Don't forget, we're now a day behind them." I grinned. "They think we're ahead and we're really behind!" I couldn't resist a bit of a chuckle .

"You're enjoying this!" she accused.

"Aren't you?" I leaned over and kissed her lightly on the lips. "Aren't you really? Just a little?"

She must have stared at me for a full minute before she answered. "You're completely nuts, Art. This kind of thing sounds very glamorous when it's between the covers of a nice leather bound edition in front of a roaring fire, with a cup of tea at my elbow. It's all well and fine when you know the good guys have to win, that the boy will get the girl and that they all get to live happily forever after. But Arthur, this isn't a good book for a rainy weekend! This is you and me crouching behind a hedge in the middle of nowhere! There are people after us, trying to... to... You know, I'm not even sure of exactly what they are trying to do!"

I stood up. "" Come on, that's enough rest. We've still got a long way to go before it gets dark."

"Oh we do?" she stayed put. "Where are we going?"

"Do you mean for tonight, or ultimately?" I winked trying to jolly her along. "Tonight, I promised you a hedgerow, and a hedgerow it shall be!" I went to pick up the duffel, but she held on.

"And what about tomorrow night, and the next, and the next one after that? How much money do you have and how long will it hold out? I've got a return flight booked from London, you know, and the price doubles after the first of the month! I've got a family at home waiting to hear from me, and a job...." she had to stop to avoid the cracking in her voice.

"I thought you enjoyed this sort of adventure story.." I said with a grin.

"Arthur, we don't have someone writing the story for us. All we have is ourselves."

"Is that what you really believe?" I asked to try and make her think.

I could see she suddenly realised what I was saying. She remembered what she'd told Robbie on the train; about Those who look after fools like us. She remembered her faith in reincarnation and Karma and magic. She remembered that there are no coincidences. She blinked at me through the tears that did not fall.

"Shall we go now?" I said, offering her my hand

"So, where are we headed?" she asked grabbing the duffel bag.

I suddenly thought of something and smiled. "Have you got your passport with you?"

She nodded.

"Good, good. Come on, we're going to Plymouth!"

"But that's further South, isn't it? I thought we were trying to get to London! Besides, Plymouth is still in England so why do I need a passport?"

"Yes but they know that, so all the normal ways will be watched. We've frustrated them, Tarish. You've thwarted them with your spell, so they have no alternative but to expend a great deal of manpower and effort in the ordinary way. I dare say

A QUESTION OF BALANCE

most every rail station between here and London will be watched. Not every one, but a great many will. The trouble is, we have no way of knowing which ones. You can be certain they'll be keeping around the clock surveillance on Paddington and Waterloo."

I began walking slowly. I was beginning to feel distinctly unwell.

"You don't plan to walk all the way to Plymouth, do you?" she was concerned, I could hear it in her voice and I struggled to stand straight and brush off the pain.

"Don't be foolish, girl! I plan on getting to the nearest rail station and booking through to Plymouth."

"But you said..."

"Yes, the stations between here and London, but they've no reason to think we'll be heading south, do they?" I turned and lifted an eyebrow at her "So, we head south, to Plymouth."

"And from there?"

"Brittany, Tarish! We take the ferry service to France. I doubt very much if they'll have thought to post sentries on the French rail lines. We shouldn't have any trouble. Then we can take another Ferry service across the Channel further on up the coast, you see? We'll bypass Paddington and Waterloo completely!

"You need a doctor." She didn't ask, she merely stated a fact. "You have no more antibiotic and I didn't like the look of it when I changed the dressing this morning. You're colour is terrible, Arthur."

"Now let's not get into that again." I stopped and sat for a minute. "We can't see another doctor without having to answer an awful lot of questions, right?"

"Yes, but..."

"No, no, hear me out, first."

"I'll listen, but you know I'm right."

"We haven't got the time. I am a doctor, Tary. It's not great, but it's not so bad it can't wait until London. Trust me, I wouldn't do anything to endanger myself further." I smiled at her. "Are you tired of lugging that bag all over creation, is that it?"

"It's not that, I just worry about you!" She lifted the bag to her shoulder. "It's not that heavy."

"Well, come on then, we're wasting time. Let's go find a train station. We can make London by tomorrow, if we're lucky."

She hesitated a minute, but decided to just barge right in. "What do we do when we get to London?"

I frowned. I had been hoping she wouldn't ask that question. "Well, to be perfectly honest that's been a sticking point, hasn't it. Actually, I thought we'd go and see the Director. Officially, I'm off the payroll as of the last of the month, of course, but unofficially..." I shrugged. "It's not as if I was in pure research, you know. I'm hoping Sir will see this as a continuation of my last assignment and help us. The Grimoir was recovered by us in the name of Her Majesty's Government, after all."

"And if he doesn't see it that way?"

"Don't worry so much, Tary. I'll think of..."

"Don't say it!"

It turned out that Kev had been right. The nearest village was five miles distant, but there wasn't a rail station there. It soon became apparent though, that we had to do something about our general appearance if we ever hoped to get a taxi! One night and two days on the road without even a proper wash hadn't done anything to improve our looks. We looked like a pair of middle-aged hippies in our travel stained jeans and wild hair. In truth, I must have looked dreadful, so it was easy to understand why people kept shying away from us. Tary looked a little better, after a quick make up in the public toilet, so she checked us into the nearest bed and breakfast. Maybe a good night's sleep would help. At the least there would be a hot shower and a hot meal.

She rinsed out her blouse and my shirt and hung them over the heater to dry. We looked bad enough and the weather had been good. Imagine what it would have been if it had run true to season and

A Question of Balance

poured rain! Once again, Whoever, had been on our side. It certainly wasn't Tary's doing, which was just as well. I was never one of those who believed that magic, individual spells at least, cause a traceable disturbance in the Ether, but there was no sense taking chances

I was asleep in seconds and slept through the night. Apparently I had been feverish off and on and poor Tarish had been up all night wringing out cool cloths, whispering every arcane fever spell she knew. Finally the sun rose, and I woke feeling better for the rest.

"Good morning. Did you sleep well?"

She shook her head. "No. Let's get some breakfast."

We finally wound up on the train bound for Plymouth. From there, taking the boat to Brittany posed no special problem. Indeed, after recent events, the entire journey along the coast of France was blissfully uneventful. Tary was able to sleep almost the whole of the way while I kept watch over her. It was early evening by the time we arrived at Victoria Station in the heart of London.

"Now, here's the sticky part... They may have someone watching just in case, Tary. We'll wait in the train until the other passengers have all disembarked I think. Go have a look on the other side and see if you can spot anything out of the ordinary."

She did as I asked, moving across the aisle and peering through the window at the crowds milling on the platform. I supposed it all seemed ludicrous, and she said so as she returned to her seat I thought it was the better part of valour not to say anything. When the platform was nearly empty and the train guard was coming down the row toward I was satisfied.

"It looks all clear. We're not going on the main concourse. There's a side exit where the taxi queue should be shorter."

"You lead." She said shouldering the bag again and following me up a flight of long stairs and down a nearly deserted side corridor. There was absolutely nothing suspicious that I could see, but I was uneasy all the same. Once on the street we took our place in the queue for the next taxi. When we were safely inside I finally breathed a sigh of relief. We'd made it to London.

CHAPTER EIGHTEEN
LONDON

"Here's the address," my husband handed the driver a business card. "Can you find the rear entrance please?"

"Sure, Guv," said the driver pulling out into the traffic. It wasn't far and in a few minutes I was being hustled through a side alley into a delivery entrance. Inside at a security desk, Arthur showed his identification and the uniformed guard telephoned someone. We were shown to a seat to wait. It reminded me of the first time we'd met in New York and I smiled to myself, half expecting Rollison to come down to fetch us. It wasn't Rolly though, who came through the door. It was a very attractive woman in her mid-thirties dressed in a beautifully tailored and to my eye expensive business suit.

"Jenny, how good to see you again!" cried Arthur, jumping to his feet. He gave her a perfunctory peck on the cheek and she smiled.

"I didn't expect to see you back here so soon," she said, glancing over his shoulder at me. "You look awful." She turned her attention back to him. "What in heaven' s name have you been up to at Leeds? Student riots?"

Smiling grimly he shook his head. "I'm afraid not, Jen. We have to get in to see him, can you arrange it?"

"It's already arranged." She smiled at him sadly. "We heard about Walter. I'm sorry. You two were very close, weren't you?"

"Yes."

"Well," she said, "he was getting on you know. A heart attack is the way I'd want to go."

"Jenny, can we see him now please?" I could see Arthur was getting impatient.

"You may see him. I'm afraid your friend doesn't have the proper clearance."

I didn't much like the way she said 'friend' but I kept my mouth shut.

"She's not my friend, she's my wife!" he snapped. "Now you go run along and tell him that we both have to see him. Tell him it's vital, do you understand? Vital! We have to talk to him today."

I had the satisfaction of watching her jaw hit the floor at the word 'wife.' I only wished I'd had a chance to wash my hair and change into some decent clothes. She gave me another more searching glance, but I could read nothing behind her eyes.

"Wait here."

We didn't wait long. In a few minutes Jen was back.

"Follow me." Now she was all business.

We took a private, key-operated lift. There were no numbers, but from the length of time it took I'd say we were pretty high up. There were no windows in sight when we got off, just a thickly carpeted hallway leading to a tastefully appointed office. Jen showed us in.

"The Doctor, Sir, and his wife."

I smiled sweetly at her back and squeezed Arthur's hand.

The man seated behind the enormous desk didn't stand. I wasn't surprised. He was, kindly put, corpulent. I looked at Arthur. This was the first time I had ever seen him so subdued, nearly humble.

"Good evening Sir," he said as Jen left. "Thank you for seeing us."

"I don't believe I've had the pleasure?" said the huge man, nodding in my direction.

"Oh, yes, Sir. This is Tary. She helped me recover the Grimoir, it was in my report."

I was becoming alarmed, Arthur's color was getting worse; I couldn't imagine where he was finding the strength to go on. I did know he couldn't go on much longer.

"She saved my life, Sir, and without her..."

A Question of Balance

"Yes, yes, Doctor, I've read the report. Introduce me!"

I stepped forward and stretched out my arm. "I'm Tarish Pendargroom, Sir, but please call me Tary. It's nice to make your acquaintance. "

"So," he said barely touching the tips of my fingers before pulling back his hand, as though afraid sustained contact might give him something contagious. "I am Sir David Marshall, call me Sir. We never expected him to marry, you know. It's unusual in this line of work."

I was about to question exactly what 'this line of work was' but Arthur spoke up before I had a chance.

"We're in rather a tight spot at the moment, Sir. I realize that it's not customary for the Institute to assist once one's association has been broken so to speak, but in this situation..." He licked his lips. By the Goddess, he was nervous! "Well, frankly, Sir, we're about at the end of our run. It all ties in, you see with the Book. There is a leak in your organization somewhere and..."

"I understand all that, Doctor, but I'm sorry, You knew the risks. I have your signed waiver in your file, somewhere."

He rang a buzzer and Jen's voice answered, "Yes, Sir?"

Arthur interrupted, "I know all that, Sir. I'm not questioning the validity of your position or the wisdom of operating procedure. All I'm doing is asking for... begging for your help." His eyes were glassy, with a look of desperation I'd never seen in him before.

"Never mind Jenny." Sir David turned his back, looking out the window for a long moment. He didn't face us as he spoke. "Mrs. Pendargroom, would you step outside, please. Have Jenny fix you a cup of tea."

"Well, I think since I am invol..."

"Do as he says, Tary," whispered the Doctor. "Go on, have a cup of tea. I won't be long." He gave me a distracted hug.

This wasn't the time to start a fight, so I left, closing the door quietly behind me. I didn't have Jenny fix me a cup of tea. Instead, I sat down and asked for an ashtray. After a few minutes, I could hear Arthur's voice raised beyond the door. I couldn't make out any of the words, though I strained. The cigarette burned down to my fingers and I dropped it on the floor. Jenny came around her desk and bent to retrieve it.

"I'm sorry," I said, embarrassed "I'm just very tired. It's been a long week."

"It's all right, I know how it can be travelling with the Doctor." She went and poured a cup of coffee. "Black or white?"

I wondered how she knew about travelling with the Doctor. "White, please, with two sugars."

She set the mug down on the table in front of me, patted my hand and said, "I gave you three lumps. You look like you could use it."

I wasn't at all sure of how to take her.

"Been rough has it? He looks all done in."

"Yeah, it's been rough. He needs a doctor. He was injured " Her eyes showed a little emotion at that.

"I thought there was something. How badly?" She sat down next to me, seeming genuinely concerned. I told her about Marge Kelly and about Glastonbury. I didn't tell her about how we'd managed to outwit them and get to London. When I was done she rolled her eyes.

"He's going to get himself killed one of these days. There's a doctor who works for us sometimes. He won't ask a lot of questions. I'll ring him up for you."

She wrote on a piece of paper and handed it to me. "You just get him to this address this evening. I'll see to the arrangements."

"Thanks." I folded the paper and stuck it in my purse.

The heavy door swung opened, slamming against the wall as Arthur strode out. I had never seen him out of control before. He was red in the race,

A QUESTION OF BALANCE

trembling and breathing heavily. I could almost imagine I saw steam rising from his nostrils.

"Come on, Tary. We're getting out of here!" He took hold of my arm and practically dragged me to the door, Jen following behind.

"What happened in there?" I asked Arthur as Jen inserted her key to call the lift.

"We're on our own," he spat angrily. "I'll tell you outside."

Jen caught my eye around his back. "Do you have the address?" she mouthed.

I nodded. She half smiled and winked. The lift doors opened and in a few minutes we were standing in the street alone.

Suddenly, all the fire seemed to go out of him. He sagged against the bricks, blood draining from his face. Dropping the duffel on the sidewalk, I rushed to his side. "What happened in there?" I slid my arm under his bracing him with my shoulder.

He stared into space for a few seconds, then looked at me, eyes flashing. "That great, bloody, fat..... made it very clear that he won't lift a bloody finger to help us!" His pallor alarmed me.

"Come on, let's get you to a doctor. Jen gave the name of a safe one. You look terrible. We can sort this all out after."

He nodded, and half-smiled. "Okay, but I want to change first. Our things are at the Peerage Hotel in Bayswater. A bit near to Paddington for my liking, but I doubt they've staked out the hotels."

We were already registered as Mr. and Mrs. Brunson and all my luggage seemed to be intact in a small but clean room on the first floor. Arthur insisted on a bath and a shave. When he was done, he looked nearly human again, although deathly pale. I washed my hair and changed into clean dark trousers and a sweater. I gave him my last two aspirin and called for a taxi.

Arthur and I sat quietly on the couch in the lobby waiting for the cab. He seemed to be getting feverish in spite of the aspirin. He still hadn't explained anything more about the Institute or Sir

David Marshall, and I hadn't pressed him. First, he needed medical attention. Explanations could wait.

When the taxi arrived the Doctor didn't protest as I took his arm to steady him down the stairs, a sure sign of just how ill he was feeling. As we got in, I handed the folded paper to the driver. "Can you take us here, please, as quick as you can?"

He glanced at the paper and said, "Right, then," as we eased into traffic. It had been more than twenty years since I'd lived in London as a student and cities change a lot in twenty years. I recognized the general direction we were heading in.

London's East End had been enjoying a gentrification in recent years, but entering that section of the city at night made me nervous nonetheless. I rationalized that if we wanted a doctor to treat a suspicious knife wound with no questions asked, we would hardly find him on Harley Street. Even so I felt a brief stirring of unease in the pit of my stomach. You would think that by this time I would have learned trust my gut.

We pulled in front of a respectable enough looking building with lights showing on parts of two floors. The street itself was well lit and several very ordinary seeming pedestrians were out and about. It was still early, not even ten o'clock, so I ignored my stomach.

"Can you wait?" I asked, leaning over to pay off the driver.

"Sorry Luv, I gotta theater fare on the West End."

"Oh," I said, disappointed.

" 'ere, Luv, just call when you're ready to leave. Dispatch'll send someone. You're not likely to find a cruiser around 'ere after ten." He handed me a card.

"Thanks, keep the change," I said gratefully. It was an enormous tip by British standards, but I really appreciated the advice.

I helped Arthur from the taxi and watched as it pulled around the corner. Just my imagination, I chided myself as the street appeared suddenly more sinister. The pedestrians were gone and a light fog made gray-green halos around the street lamps, dimming their brightness. The weather so far had been on our side, so I figured we were bound for a change.

The Doctor swayed on his feet, and I was suddenly reminded of the urgency of our business. "Hang on. Just a few stairs and we'll be in the doctor's office."

He nodded, leaning heavily on me. The street door to the building wasn't locked so we pushed on through into the vestibule. I stopped and let Arthur lean against the wall while I looked at the paper to see what floor we wanted. The light was bad and I had to squint to read. My concentration was on that, so the first warning I had was Arthur's grunt of pain as he doubled over and slumped to the floor clutching at his side. Two very handsome young men materialized from the shadows, one holding the silver tipped walking stick that he'd just used on Arthur, the other a wicked looking knife. Before I could so much as open my mouth, the second of two moved to me and pressed the very sharp point of the thin blade to my throat.

"Not a sound, Missy, or I'll disembowel your boyfriend right here. Got it?"

He used the stiletto to gesture and I nodded mutely, fighting the familiar nausea.

Just outside a dark panel truck had pulled up. Number One moved me into the back and made sure I was securely tied to one of the inside support struts before going to help his colleague. I couldn't see up front at all.

In a few minutes, the back doors opened and Number One got in yanking Arthur under the arms like a sack of beans while Number Two wrestled his legs in from the outside. I could see bright blood beginning to stain his shirt as he made a feeble attempt to resist. I watched helplessly as Number Two took the silver tipped cane and rammed it brutally into Arthur's side again.

The Doctor let out an agonized cry, trying desperately to curl in on himself. Calmly Number One kicked him in the head. He shuddered once, then went very limp as they finished jostling him into the van. They worked silently, methodically, rolling him over onto his stomach and tying his arms and legs. Number one held Arthur's knees bent, while Number Two ran a short length of rope between ankles and wrists. That position would have been uncomfortable enough for anyone, but in Arthur's condition, it would be excruciating when he regained consciousness

"Please," I begged. "Please, he's hurt, he's bleeding. Loosen his legs. He's no threat to you in the shape he's in."

As if on cue, Arthur groaned weakly.

Number One brought his face close to mine as Number Two got out, slamming the doors behind him. I heard him walk around and get in the front on the passenger side.

"Worries you, does it, to see him hurting?" He smiled and patted my cheek, "That's good. That's very good."

As the van lurched forward, he settled himself on the floor. Casually, he stretched out his foot and pushed Arthur so he rolled over hard onto his injured side. The Doctor gasped in pain, eyes rolling back in his head as he whimpered pitifully.

I bit my tongue realizing that any further protest on my part would only bring more of the same. There was only one way I might be able to help, one way to ease his pain. I closed my eyes and concentrated on going into trance. He slapped me hard, breaking my concentration. I cried out, more in frustration than in pain. An agonized whisper escaped Arthur's throat.

"Tary, don't worry, I'll think of something..." his voice trailed off into a groan. It was all he could manage, just those few words.

I felt my heart pounding against my ribs as I fought back tears, not willing to give this animal the satisfaction of seeing me cry. It was the third time I'd been struck...the third time... and the third's the charm.

A Question of Balance

Without realizing what was happening I relinquished my will to instinct. My mind burned hotter than my cheek with a hatred that was palpable. It overrode everything I had ever learned everything I'd ever believed in. A red haze came down over my senses and the power coursed through me wild and uncontrollable as a tempest. I could taste it, coppery and sweet, like blood on my tongue. The smell of ozone filled my nostrils as the magic built up to an overload within me. The ropes binding my wrists fell apart. I turned my attention toward my captor. He was cringing now; his own face a mask of fear as he blubbered.

There was very little left of me, very little that was even human as I snarled like a crazed beast and prepared to spring on him. The van had stopped, but I never noticed. The only thought burning madly through my brain was to rip the living heart from living flesh. In my mindless fury I could feel it already throbbing wetly in my hands. Through the roaring in my head, a small persistent buzzing began, like an insect. I tried to push it aside, but it kept on, droning louder and louder, growing more distinct. Finally, it was Arthur's voice I heard crying out to me, begging, sobbing.

"Tarish stop! Remember harm none, Tary. If you give yourself over they've won. Please, Tary. Please stop. Listen to me. Listen! Don't let them do this to you. Don't let them.. . please... don't Tarish. Please..." The voice broke giving way to sobs of anguish and despair.

Slowly my mind cleared. I rubbed my hands across my eyes and ran my tongue over dry lips. I was burning with thirst. The only sounds in the van were the Doctor's broken sobbing and the ragged breathing coming from Number One. I let him go and he fell back staring at me, white-faced and trembling, his lips blooded, throat scratched and torn. I tasted blood in my mouth and stared at the gore beneath my fingernails.

Moving stiffly I went to Arthur and turned him gently onto his side. He looked up at me, tears running down his cheeks and I took his head into my lap. I was reaching to untie his hands when a dark cloth was pressed down over my face. For a few seconds I fought, striking out with my hands. Soon though, a black lethargy stole over me and I began drifting away. The last thing I remembered was hearing Arthur crying out my name as I was dragged away from him.

I was consumed with thirst and my head pounded. Slowly I opened my eyes. I saw tile floors, walls; white and sterile; a bed against a wall. I was sitting upright in a chair. A sudden, wracking cough came from the bed.

"Arthur?" My voice came out a hoarse whisper.

He lifted his head off the pillow, eyes bright and focused, and smiled.

"Welcome back. How do you feel?"

I wanted to put my hands up, to hold my aching head, but I couldn't seem to lift my arms. "Thirsty," I croaked

He looked much better. Not great, but definitely much better. My mind was foggy, but I realized that somehow, we must have gotten to a hospital.

"Yes, I imagine you are. A side effect, I think. They've been keeping you drugged since they brought us here." The effort of holding up his head was too great, so he let it fall back on the pillow and stared at the ceiling.

"Drugged?" I was confused. "Why would they drug me? You're the one who's sick." I tried to push myself up, to go to him, but I couldn't move.

"Be still, Tary. If they come in pretend you're still unconscious." Arthur whispered urgently. "This isn't a normal hospital. I'm afraid we're the guests of Miss Kelly and friends."

He tugged at his arms and I realized he'd been tied into the bed with hospital restraints. I saw now, that my own position in the chair was similar. Memory came flooding back. "How long...?" I managed, my tongue and throat swollen.

"I'm not sure. Maybe twenty-four, possibly thirty six hours. They've fed me three or four times I

A Question of Balance

think." He lifted his head again, and stared at me, concern etched in every line of his face "They just kept pumping you full of something, barbiturates, at a guess. I was getting frantic, wondering if you'd ever come around."

"Oh god, Arthur. What are we going to do?"

He sort of smiled. "I'll just have to think of something." For a moment I saw the old familiar sparkle, then he collapsed again in a fit of coughing.

The door behind me opened. I closed my eyes and let my head loll to the side as if I was still unconscious.

"Good morning, sister," I heard Arthur say. "Or is it evening? So hard to tell without a window or a clock."

I could hear the rattle of a tray being set down, water being poured. My thirst grew nearly unbearable.

"Do be careful, will you. I find it's impossible to look one's best with sticking plaster all over one's face!"

I cracked my eyes and watched in amazement as a woman began shaving his

face quickly and efficiently. When she was finished, she folded down the blankets. I could clearly see the restraints as well as a neat surgical dressing that covered his wound. It was the only thing covered. The nurse, I assumed, sponged him down thoroughly and impersonally from a basin, then pulled the covers back up and tucked them in tightly all around.

"I'm honored to be the recipient of all this attention, sister," he said as she worked. "What's the occasion? Are we expecting visitors?"

Suddenly his eyes jerked to a point behind me. Marge Kelly had entered soundlessly. I could feel her hands brush my hair lightly as she leaned on the back of the chair.

"I'm told that you're sufficiently recovered to be of use to us."

His eyes hardened as he met her's. "I will make it perfectly plain, Miss Kelly, that I have no intention of doing anything that could be of use to you."

I could practically feel her smile as she reached down and grabbed a handful of my hair yanking my head upright. Before I could stop myself, I gasped involuntarily, surprise and pain vying with my thirst.

"You are with us, aren't you Tary dear?" she purred.

The Doctor struggled briefly, uselessly against his bonds, then went perfectly still. "Leave her alone. She is still the holder of the Key and the Crown, or have you forgotten? You may not harm her, or take them by force." He spoke softly, almost gently, as though trying to reason with a child.

"Well," she said smugly, "that rather depends on your definition of harm, does it not?"

She let go of my hair and I winced, cringing from a blow that never came. Slowly, she sauntered into my field of vision and stood looking down at the bed. Turning deliberately, Marge poured a glass of water from the pitcher on the tray. She bent and lifted Arthur's head in the crook of her arm, holding the glass so he could drink. I was mesmerized at the sight of the water. My throat burned for just a taste, a tiny sip. A whimper escaped my lips. Arthur turned his head sharply at the sound, pure clear water slopping over his chin, soaking his bedcovers. For a second, his eyes met mine. I looked away, ashamed to let him see the fear I knew was there. Furiously, he turned back to Marge.

"You callous bitch! Give her some water!"

Miss Kelly refilled the glass and set it down on a table near my right hand, smiling, then turned her attention back to the Doctor. My fingers twitched convulsively, although I knew there was no chance I could reach it. I couldn't tear my eyes away from the glass, beads of condensation forming on the outside and slipping down to puddle on the white plastic tabletop. Even when Thornhill came in, my eyes never wandered.

A Question of Balance

"You see, we've no intention of harming her, have we Richard."

He grunted and picked up the glass absently, draining it. Again, she raised Arthur's head gently in the crook of arm so he was able to see me clearly.

"In fact, we plan to do her a great honor. In two days time the moon will be dark." She smiled, smoothing the hair from his eyes. "Since we do not have the Grimoir, we shall have to improvise." She let his head fall back against the pillows and walked toward me. Gently, almost lovingly, she ran her fingers along my cheek and under my chin. "A new initiate, I think, one seduced from the Path of Light would do much to appease the wrath of He who rules the Dark, especially the guardian of the talismans."

I was frustrated that I couldn't work up the moisture to spit in her face, "Oh, don't worry, Tary, willingness is not mandatory. In fact, many of our initiates come to His altar in fear and loathing. They all come around eventually."

She smiled again, and perched back down on the edge of the bed, lifting Arthur's head. She made a gesture to Thornhill.

The thug stepped in front of me, placing the sharp blade of his knife to the neck of my sweater. A quick flick and it was cut through. He grinned lasciviously as he took hold and ripped it opened to my waist. Behind him I could hear Arthur thrashing helplessly as he shouted. "Keep your filthy hands off her!"

Thornhill moved to the side affording my husband a clear view. Then, he stuck the point of the knife between my breasts, under my bra and waited expectantly.

"You see," said Marge, stroking her hand along face. "We will love her, not harm her." Her words dripped venom. "Every single member of the Coven will love her, Dr. Pendargroom. Oh, a bit more brutally than she is used to, perhaps, but she will come to no real harm. You see, we truly do believe that a certain amount of brutality and debasement is necessary for personal growth." She smiled.

I was trembling convulsively. Never before had I ever been so frightened, frightened for my very soul. Arthur had stopped thrashing. "What is it you want of me?" His eyes never left mine.

"I want you to bring me the Grimoir of Infinity, Doctor." It was said so matter of factly, it might have the most reasonable request in the world.

Thornhill moved the blade a fraction, stretching the elastic of my bra. Arthur's eyes closed and he whispered through clenched teeth, "All right. I'll try."

Marge nodded and Thornhill removed the knife. "You will do more than try Dr. Pendargroom. You will succeed, or never see the pretty Tary again. Don't worry, we shall see to it that she is loved, in your absence."

His voice was agonized. "I don't know if I can. I've been cut off; my credentials are no good! He was even going to have me barred from the museum."

Marge's eyes glinted. "Oh, I have the utmost confidence in you, Doctor. I'm sure you'll think of something."

He glared at her. "At least give her some water. You don't intend to let her die of thirst, do you?"

Marge gestured and Thornhill disappeared and returned with a cup. He stuck two dirty fingers into the water and held them to my parched lips. I stared at the precious, glistening droplets. "Suck!" he ordered gruffly.

Tentatively, I moved my tongue along his filthy fingers, questing desperately for the water. He moved suddenly, shoving them deep into my mouth, down my throat. "I said, suck, you bitch!"

I gagged and choked, fighting for air.

"*Stop it!* Make him stop, he's killing her!" I could hear the desperation in Arthur's voice as I struggled for breath.

"Dick," said Miss Kelly, sounding amused. Give her the water and stop fooling around." She looked back at my husband. "He's very playful today."

Thornhill grunted and removed his fingers. He held the cup so I had to lap at the water with my tongue. Finally it was tilted and my mouth filled. I managed three swallows before he took it away. That small taste of water only seemed to make my thirst worse.

"I'll bring your clothes when I come back." She patted my husband's cheek and turned. "Come on Dick, let's leave the lovers to talk things over."

The door closed, key clicking in the lock. For a moment neither of us spoke. Then Arthur tried.

"Tary, I..." He struggled to raise himself up as much as the restraints would permit. "Are you okay?"

I nodded, not trusting myself to speak yet.

"I'll get the Book, Tary. I promise. I won't leave you to that... that... woman..."

"No!" It was my voice coming from my throat.

"What? Of course I will, Tarish. No matter what it takes. If I have to put a crack in the foundations of Whitehall I will..."

"No," I repeated hoarsely.

"But..."

"You can't let them get the Book, Arthur. They have the Key and the Crown. The Book is the only thing standing between life and Armageddon. You mustn't let them have It. It doesn't matter about me."

"Of course it matters! No, Tary, you're wrong. They don't have the Crown and the Key, you do! Only you can..."

My throat ached with the effort but I went on. "How long do you think it will take, Arthur? They have me, and so long as they have you too, they can force me to..." My voice caught in my throat and failed.

"But they can't take them by force. They are can't harm you to get them." I think he was trying to convince himself.

"They don't have to lay a finger on me if they have you, can't you see that?" I rasped. "I want you to go, Arthur. Tell them anything, but get away from here, from me as fast and as far as you can. Whatever you do, you mustn't come back with the Book. If you do, then everything's been wasted.

Everything, Arthur, do you understand? I can hold out as long as you're safe but..." I was starting to feel strange, dizzy and giddy. My eyes refused to focus properly.

"Please, Arthur, I..." I suddenly felt an overwhelming urge to giggle.

"Tary? Tarish, what's wrong? What's the matter with you?"

I forced myself to tune in to his voice. "Artie? S'okay, Artie. Go and play with Jenny." For a second, my mind cleared. "It was Jenny, Arthur. Jenny! She set us up." I was going again. "She said... going to let... we were..."

"Jenny, Tarish? It was Jenny? Stay with me Tary. Come on, stay with me. They must've drugged the water, damn their eyes."

"Not really a doctor..." I was trying hard, but the thoughts kept slipping away from me.

"Come on, Tary, fight it. Fight it! You can do it. How do you know it was Jenny, huh? How do you know she set us up?"

I giggled. "Jenny travels with the Doctor too. She said...she said... I'm thirsty, Arthur. Thirsty, so thirsty."

The nurse entered, followed by Number One and Number Two. They undid the straps holding me to the chair and Number One carried me to the bed. He tossed me on my back, my head dangling over the side. Arthur's legs writhed beneath me as I was roughly stripped of everything.

"Stop that!" I could hear Arthur shouting. "Leave her alone. What are you doing to her?"

All my clothes and belongings were taken, all except two. They left the tiny ring on my left pinky and the old brass key around my neck on a chain. Finally, I was dressed in a loose black robe. Strong arms lifted me. I could still hear Arthur's voice, fading as if from a great distance.

"Please, where are you taking her? Tell me please, where are you..." I heard the sound of a blow and a grunt of pain, then silence.

A Question of Balance

I struggled, feebly, "Please don't take me away. Let me stay with the Doctor." I had no chance. Eventually my struggles ceased as I gradually drifted away. Slowly reality slipped from my grasp replaced by despair and darkness and I knew that I was lost.

Chapter Nineteen
The Doctor

It seemed I lay for hours, after they took Tary away, listening to my own heart beating rhythmically, staring at the ceiling. For the first time in my life I felt truly and completely helpless, and with good reason. Tary was right, you see, when she said that if they had me, they had everything. She is a rare soul, I suppose that's what made me love her. I knew she could withstand anything, any kind of treatment to maintain her own values. I also knew that she could never sit idly by and watch another suffer on her account, not if there was something she could do.

Those of the Order don't understand those kinds of peculiarly human feelings that most of us are plagued with; feelings like guilt and integrity or love. They do recognise them in others though, and will not hesitate to use those feelings, which they perceive as weaknesses, to their own ends. Indeed, they are expert.

In a while, Marge Kelly would come back with my clothes, and I would be released. Released to recover the Book, the Grimoir of Infinity, and deliver it into the dominion of evil. I held no illusion that we would all live happily forever after once they had what they wanted. I knew that with the Book in their possession they would use me, the torment of my body, to convince Tary to release the power of the other two talismans into their hands, I also knew, as did Tarish herself, that in this they would succeed . I had to choose then, between my love for a woman, and my love of all things human. There was no doubt what the stakes were. Eternal, Universal chaos, versus a fleeting moment on the scale of human time in which to love and be loved.

I am a man of science. As a scientist, the choice was clear cut, and linear. I must recover the Book and remove it somewhere safe, if such a place existed, where it could remain hidden, out of reach. At all costs, I could not afford to permit myself to fall again into their hands to be used against Tary. As a man, however, the only logical choice was unacceptable. I couldn't bring myself to leave Tary to the fate I was certain awaited her in the hands of these people. As I said, they are expert not only in the physical aspects of torture, but in the metaphysical aspects as well. Their skills are unsurpassed. I knew Tarish had no chance against the kind of pressure she would be made to endure In a solitary battle, she would lose, and the price would be her soul.

Still, reasoned the rational side of me, was it too great a price to pay, one single soul in return for the millions who lived and would live and had lived?

The man said yes. Even a single flawed soul was too great a price and a gentle soul such as hers, was priceless. The obvious solution was... I would have to think of something.

The door opened, and the nursing sister came in carrying the aluminium pan that was concession to my very human needs. As she positioned it, I talked to her, in part to avoid thinking of the humiliation I was enduring, and in part to see if this time, I might get some kind of a response. Well, it was worth a try.

"Tell me sister, what have you done with my wife? I do hope you're looking after her as well as you're looking after me." No reaction. I wasn't even a person, I don't think, not in her eyes. Just a job, a body to be taken care of efficiently but impersonally.

"She's very important to me. If there's anyway at all you could just let her know..."

Her job done, she ignored me completely and simply left the room. Once more I was left alone with myself and I was in very bad company. In an attempt to escape the reality of the situation I closed my eyes and forced my breathing into the regular, deep pattern of relaxed sleep. I used a technique I learned

A Question of Balance

from a monk I'd once studied with in a Tibetan Monastery. It worked. The only trouble was, I still hadn't quite mastered the necessary control over my subconscious. Although I did manage to sink into sleep, it was a troubled state.

She was sitting, still tied to the chair. The Neanderthal known as Thornhill was pawing at her, tormenting her while Miss Kelly laughed. I tried to stop them, but my cries went unheard. Suddenly, I realised that my perspective was off. I was viewing the scene from above. Looking down, I could see the bed clearly, blood spattered across the white of the bed linen. It was me, my body laying unnaturally still, chest torn opened, eyes staring. Thornhill moved now, and I could see Tary clearly. She seemed to look straight at me, her mouth still dripping my blood. Then, she laughed insanely. Blue flames burned the straps on her arms to nothing and she stood, pointing at me. She was dressed as I had last seen her, but now the robe fell opened. A bolt of pure energy sprang from her finger-tip rushing toward me. There was nowhere for me to hide, no refuge to run to. My body was dead, a useless husk doomed to rot. I was caught, trapped between life and death.
"*Tary NO!*" *I cried out voicelessly.*

Blessedly, I woke then. Miss Kelly was standing over my bed with a strange man. No, not strange I recognised him from a forest glade in New York State, where once before he'd stood over me. Then, he had worn the robes of a sorcerer, the mask of the Goat. Miss Kelly clucked her tongue at me, in a parody of sympathy.

"Nightmare, Dr. Pendargroom?"

I gathered myself and tried a smile, "Oh, nothing too out of the ordinary, thank you."

"Good," she said. "I understand that you have met my colleague before?"

"Have I? Dennings, is that you? It's so hard to tell. It was fancy dress last time, wasn't it?" He smiled down at me, and I understood why Tary had been reminded of a shark.

"Something of the sort, yes."

He patted me on the shoulder and I wanted to cringe from his touch, I didn't. Instead, I forced myself to lay perfectly still, meeting his cold colourless eyes. I suspected that in the glare of an oncoming car, they would reflect back the light like a cat's.

"I can't tell you how pleased I am, Arthur, to have an opportunity to renew our too short acquaintance. You ran away last time before I could really explore your remarkable mind. I am sure your co-operation this time will be to our mutual advantage. He held out his hand to me.

"Oh, you will forgive me, I'm sure, but I am rather tied up just at the moment." I grinned. Suddenly, my right arm was free of restraint. Neither one of them had made a move, nevertheless, it had come loose. It was difficult for me to maintain that smile as I slowly extended my hand.

His grip was icy cold and very firm. I could almost imagine my fingers shrivelling in his grasp. Then, he released me. Marge leaned over and unfastened my left arm in the ordinary way as Dennings watched.

"Don't even think of betraying me again Arthur, or I promise you, your wife will pay the price of your folly."

"If there was any other way, Dennings... if you harm her I'll kill you, I swear it." I whispered. He merely smiled indulgently.

"You'll find everything you need in the bathroom, Arthur. Please, get dressed as quickly as you can. If, as you say, your credentials have been rescinded, you will need every bit of time you have left." His eyes glinted dangerously. "If you want to spare your wife, that is, from our ritual,"

"Yes, of course." There seemed little else to say. They left me alone and I undid the leg restraints myself. I have to say, that I was a little wobbly, quite weak in the knees in fact, as I stumbled my way into the bathroom. It had been possibly as long as four days since our capture, and I hadn't been permitted so much as a stretch in all that time. My wound and the abscess had been expertly treated, though, and was quite improved. I was certainly fit enough to leave hospital.

They came back for me accompanied by the two young toughs from the van. A black velvet bag was fitted over my head, and my hands tied behind my back, then I was led out to a waiting car.

"How do you expect me to bring the Book back here if I don't know where here is?" I asked.

"Oh, you just get the Book, Doctor. There is a folded parchment in your left hand pocket. In it, you will find instructions. When the Grimoir is in your possession, follow them." It was the dry, slightly rasping voice of Malcolm Dennings.

"I see." I was ushered into the back of a car, quite a large one, by the feel of it. Probably, a Daimler Limo.

"Well, I can tell that you are a man of style, at least," I remarked, settling myself. "Tell me, how do you plan to let me out without my seeing the license tag?"

"It has been arranged." The way he said it left me no doubt that it had indeed been arranged. We drove for about twenty minutes in silence. I did what I could to try and recognise any sound that might come in useful for the purpose of identifying where we were, but either the auto was soundproofed, or we were out in the country someplace. Either way, I could discern nothing helpful. Finally, my companion spoke.

"Do hurry back to us, Doctor I am truly looking forward to spending time with you. I haven't yet had the opportunity to repay you properly. And then there is the Lady Tarish. Having your lovely wife in such close proximity tempts me, as I am certain you can appreciate. I am a man who takes his indulgences."

I lurched forward, struggling against the ropes around my wrists. Dennings merely laughed, laying a hand on my head.

"You will sleep now, Doctor. When you awaken, you will be in familiar territory."

"I don't think so, you bastard. Once bitten, twice shy. I don't feel in the least tired, and I'm certainly not going to trust anything you might offer me to eat...or...drink...how are you..."

Whatever he did, it worked as intended. I woke up on a bench in Hyde Park. By the sun, it was nearly noon, but noon of what day? My hands were free and I found I had some money in my wallet and plenty of loose change in my pocket. There was also the folded parchment. I took it out and unfolded it gingerly. It was completely blank. Somehow I was certain that when I looked at it next, after I retrieved the Book, my instructions would be there, as promised. I put it back into my pocket and walked up to the High Street to find a news agent. If Marge was telling me the truth, I had less than two days to recover the Grimoir and come up with a way to stop them. Less than two days. I sighed. I had better think of something!

I took the tube to Bayswater, and went to the hotel first. I needed a base My movements, although probably watched carefully, were unrestricted. Tarish had said Jenny had set us up. Was that the product of a drug induced paranoia, I wondered, or was she right? Even knowing that there was something amiss in the home office, it seemed almost impossible to believe that the number two person in the Institute could have been suborned. Still, I trusted Tary's instinct. To paraphrase one of my fictional heroes, 'when all other possibilities have been eliminated, whatever is left, no matter how improbable, must be the truth.' From what I recalled, Jenny was the only person who knew where we were going to be that night; indeed she had planned for us to be there. I already knew that the leak had to be someone in Sir's confidence. As

A QUESTION OF BALANCE

difficult as it was, I concluded Tarish was probably right.

Well, at least it was a starting point. I could use that information. I opened the drawer to the desk to find my diary and put my hand smack onto one of Tary's bags of Jelly Babies. Jelly Babies. I'm not usually prone to over sentimentalism, but that silly bag of sweets suddenly made the breath catch in my throat. I was sure she wasn't getting any Jelly Babies where she was now.

I had to function, so I couldn't let my emotions get in the way. Absently I stuck the bag into my pocket. I found my book and dialled the special number. It was the number only Jen could answer. It rang four times, then a recorded message. "Please enter your personal code now."

I pressed my personal identification number into the key pad and waited. In a moment, Jen's voice came on the line. She sounded breathless.

"Doctor, is that you?"

"Yes, Jen. It's me. Are you out of Sir's hearing?"

"I am. I've been worried. Tarish never called to let me know what the doctor said. When I got in touch with his office I found out you'd never made it there at all. Where have you been for three days?"

"Listen to me Jen, it's a long, complicated story. I can't go into the whole thing now, this line's not secure. Can you meet me? I'll need to have my credentials, at least my association with the museum, intact. Do you think you can manage that for me? Jenny, it's important. Tary's life is in the balance."

For a minute there was silence. Then she came back. "I've reactivated your security clearance with the University and Museum. The new cards are printing up now. Where shall I meet you?"

"At the same place where we had breakfast last time. You do remember, don't you?"

She laughed. "Of course I remember." Then, she sobered. "I'm sorry about Tary, Doctor. Is there anything I can do?"

I took a deep breath, suspecting that it was she who'd betrayed Tary and me. "You're doing it. Thanks Jen. A half hour then?"

"Right I'll be there." She rang off.

On impulse I grabbed Tary's toiletry kit and tossed some fresh clothes into a small bag. She would need them when I found her.

It was a short walk to Notting Hill Gate at the bottom of Portobello Road that was our code for breakfast. I made it in fifteen minutes and sat down to wait. She was early. There was no way she could have accomplished everything I'd asked and made it here in the time she did. That supported Tary's theory, that she was in league with them. She must've had everything ready and waiting before I phoned. I stood up and waved, forcing myself to smile.

"Over here, Jen." She handed over an envelope with the documents, and gave me a short kiss on the lips. There had been a time when Jen and I had been close, at least I'd thought so.

"Well you do seem better", she said, stepping back a pace and looking me over critically.

"Yes, I've been well looked after, thank you. You do realise you're not to mention this to Sir David? I'm afraid he was very clear the other day."

She smiled a little and placed her hand on my arm. "He was very put out when he got your resignation, you know. I believe he always thought of you as his successor, sort of heir apparent."

"Yes, well I decided what I wanted to do in my dotage was be a University Professor." I went over the credentials. They were perfect. Of course they would be, they weren't exactly forgeries, merely misappropriated originals.

"You realise I've put you on quite a spot with this if Sir discovers what you've done."

"I understand, Doctor. What exactly are you going to do with those?" She nodded at the cards in my hands.

"It's better that you don't know. Something I'm afraid Sir David will never forgive me for." I grinned.

A Question of Balance

"Whatever it is, I wish you luck, Doctor. Keep in touch, will you?"

I nodded. Jen hailed a taxi and was gone. If she was involved with the Order, she would report back to them. That was good. So far I'd done everything just as though I was co-operating to my fullest. The next bit was going to be more difficult. Somehow, I had to get in touch with Sir David, without letting Jen find out about it. Then I had to convince the arrogant bastard that I was right. But first, I had to get into the museum vault and steal the Grimoir! All in all, a busy day and night ahead.

I contacted Marion Walden, the Curator of Antiquities from a call box and told her to expect me. She sounded surprised, and a little suspicious. I assured her that rumours of my disgrace had been greatly exaggerated, and I had perfectly good, newly drawn up credentials to prove it. She sounded pleased to hear it. When I arrived, I was shown immediately to her office.

"Any trouble transferring the Grimoir, Marion? I know I've been a little under the weather lately, out of touch."

She smiled. "No trouble at all Dr. Pendargroom. It was just where you said it would be."

"Good, good. May I see it please?"

Her smile faded to a look of puzzlement. "Why? Whatever for? I thought you had made a complete study at the Institute before it was turned over to us?"

"Oh, well, yes, of course I did, naturally. But there was something I wanted to check. One of the carbon tests came back with anomalous results. I thought if I could just have it for a day or two...?" I smiled.

She hesitated a moment, but I could see I had won her over. She smiled. "Of course, Dr. Pendargroom. I'll just ring downstairs and let them know I'm coming for it then."

This was going better than I'd hoped! She dialled a number and spoke. "Yes, this is Dr. Walden. Dr. Pendargroom is here for the Book, the one known as the Grimoir of Infinity. If you get it from the archival vault, I'll just pop down and fetch it for him." She hung up and glanced at the clock on the wall. "I didn't realise the time, Doctor, nearly four already. You sit here and wait while I get the Book for you. I'll have tea sent in, how's that?"

Tea sounded wonderful. It seemed like ages since I'd eaten. In a few minutes, a secretary brought in a tea cart and poured out for me. There were several muffins, and a pot of jam. Marion had been gone a little while and I saw no reason to wait. I was just reaching to help myself when the door opened. A large and very heavy hand came down on my shoulder. I looked up.

"Fletcher! You're looking well. Oh and Maxwell too I see, how nice." Well, so much for my way with the ladies, I thought ruefully.

"What are you doing here, Doctor?" asked Fletcher, clutching my shoulder quite painfully.

"Well, I was just about to have some tea and muffins. If you gentlemen would care to join me, I'm sure Dr. Walden could arrange for some more cups...and I...

He sighed. "Come on. Sir David wants to see you."

I threw one last longing look at the tea tray. "But, I haven't had my muffin yet."

Fletcher and Maxwell didn't seem to care much about my tea, though, and made quite a show about removing me from the museum through a side door, with my arms handcuffed behind my back. For the second time in one day, I was hustled into the back seat of a car. This time I sat between two former colleagues who knew me well. They were the best, and totally familiar with my methods. No hope at all of slipping by them. As the car headed across London, I counted the hours, the minutes, the seconds, I had remaining. Tary was running out of time.

I closed my eyes and pictured her face. Untidy, blond, Harpo Marx hair, blowing about a freckled pug nose; blue eyes that glinted and changed colour

A Question of Balance

in the sun or the moon. What was she doing now? Would they feed her? Would they give her water? I knew they would do nothing to overtly harm her, but neglecting her, continuing to withhold food and water would be just as deadly as slitting her throat, especially in the state she was in the last time I'd seen her. I tried not to think too much about what she was enduring. I needed my mental faculties to be sharp. I had to convince Sir David that his entire organisational structure was in jeopardy and I didn't know who I could trust.

Inside the building which houses the Institute's public offices, there is a whole series of halls, corridors and rooms, that most of the staff is not even aware of. You can reach them only by riding the key operated security lifts, and even they are difficult to locate unless you knew exactly where to look. It was part of the more covert organisation that BITS represented. I will go no further with my description than that, other than to say, every government has a certain number of these agencies, even the good guys. The way our modern world runs, they are a necessary evil. It was here that I was taken and confined in a detention room.

"Fletcher, Maxwell, please! You don't understand. There is very little time left. Tell him I have to talk to him, please!!" They bolted the door on the outside and left me bellowing after them. They hadn't even posted a guard. Of course, they hadn't removed the handcuffs either. I sat down on the small cot and leaned my head against the wall. My nose itched. My nose always itches when my hands are tied up. I had nothing to do to keep my mind off Tarish. Every minute I was stuck here was another minute she was in their hands. I couldn't stand the thought of Thornhill and those two young hooligans and god only knew who else, touching her in a brutal parody of love that... That line of thought was doing me no good at all. I had to do something.

Absently, I began to knock my head against the wall, trying to jar loose an idea. I had started out with some vaguely formed notion of getting the

Grimoir, convincing Sir that he had a turncoat in the family and having him ride to the rescue like the cavalry in the last frame of an American Western. I figured that once I had the Book and my instructions, they could follow me. All right, so it had some flaws. It was something, wasn't it? Except that I hadn't counted on Marion Walden actually checking with Sir himself. I wondered why she had.

"You'll give yourself a headache if you keep that up." I had been so lost in my own misery, I hadn't even noticed the door open. I couldn't believe my eyes. It was Sir David Marshall himself looming as large as life, larger, in the doorway of the detention room.

"Sir David, I..." It was too much for me. I tried to spring to my feet, but without my arms to steady me, I'm afraid I tripped myself up. Down I went giving myself a really good knock on the head. I saw stars. He stood aside to let someone past him. "Get those things off him. The anonymous someone did, and my hands were free. Of course, my nose had stopped itching. I tried again.

"Sir, I know how this must look, but if you'll give me a chance to explain... I know I can..."

"Yes."

"Oh, but please Sir. You don't understand. If I don't get back there with the... did you say yes?"

The big man nodded curtly, absently toying with handcuffs. "Tell me, Arthur. Explain your actions and why I shouldn't invoke article thirty and have you terminated as an embarrassment to the Ministry and a risk to national security."

I suddenly recognised just how much trouble I was in. "Excuse me, Sir, but I didn't realise that being an embarrassment to the Ministry was a capital offence."

"Doctor!" He glared at me.

I sighed "It's a long story, Sir," I began.

"Come with me." He turned and I followed him out and down the corridor.

He stared at me long and hard after I'd finished my explanation. "You cannot be certain it was

A Question of Balance

Jenny. They could have had you followed from here. Perhaps they picked you up at your hotel. There is no proof."

I shook my head. "That's true, Sir. I have no proof it was Jen, but I know I'm right. She was the one who was supposed to have arranged for the doctor. Tary's feelings are always..."

"You would ask me to condemn a member of my staff... a very close member, based on the 'feeling' of a self professed witch?" He closed his eyes, pursing his lips. "You ask too much, Doctor. This time, you ask too much."

"Just give me a chance, Sir, please. I know she'll trip herself up if you'll help me. I know I can prove it, but not without your co-operation. You know you've had a traitor in your midst for months now. I think it's Jen, and I'm offering you a chance to clear house." I lowered my voice to a whisper, "Tary is lost, otherwise."

It seemed like a very long time before he answered me. I sat quietly, desperately hoping for a miracle. The story sounded thin, even in my own ears. It was true; there was no real evidence at all to implicate Jenny of any culpability except that of helping me.

He spoke. "You truly love her, this witch."

I nodded. "I do Sir, with all my heart, Sir."

He grunted. "You are right about one thing, Doctor, there is a traitor, but Jenny..." He shook his head. "She has betrayed my trust by giving you access to restricted credentials against my direct order, but to say that she is actively working with The Order... I cannot. move without proof. Part of what I had hoped you would accomplish, was bringing me that proof, hard evidence. Only someone working outside the Institute, someone who'd been publicly discredited, might have had a chance. You've failed me, Arthur. You've brought me nothing but conjecture."

I met his eyes, suddenly everything made sense. I was too tired, too heart weary to be angry with Sir.

He'd done what he thought would work, had placed all his eggs in one basket, me, and I had failed.

"Yes, Sir. What will you do now, Sir? If you don't release me they'll... Well eventually they will kill her, when they realise she won't give up. But before they do she will be used, Sir David, used in ways that will make even my most explicit reports pale by comparison. You must realise that I will do everything within my power to prevent that."

He knew what I meant. He knew that in order to keep me from doing what I had to do, he'd have to lock me up for years, perhaps for the rest of my life. Or he could simply have me eliminated.

"What will you do if I release you?"

Yes, what indeed would I do? "Try to find them somehow. Without the Book, I have no instructions to follow. Even so, I'm sure they are, or at least, were, having me watched. If you release me, please make certain that Jen knows. If I'm right, she'll report back to them, and they'll find me. If I'm wrong... well, I don't know."

"And what happens if you are right about Jenny and they do find you? You will not have the Grimoir. What do you suppose they will do then, Doctor? Have you thought about that?"

I shrugged, but didn't say anything. I had thought about that a little. I couldn't afford to think about it too much. If they got their hands on me, if I failed, I could still be of some use. Tary was the holder of the Key and the Crown. Both have a power of their own, even without the Grimoir. I wondered how long it would take before she broke down and gave in to them. Chances are, I wouldn't be much use after that, if I lived, but maybe she would be spared. It was all I had and I clung to it.

Sir David smiled mirthlessly. "Yes, I can see by your expression that you have. It is such a waste."

I stood. "Am I free to go?"

"Sit down, you fool. I haven't said that I wouldn't help you, have I?"

A Question of Balance

I sat, practically falling through the chair. "Yes, Sir, I...I mean, no Sir, you haven't said you wouldn't help."

"No, I haven't. I would never have suspected Jenny, but then, I would not have expected her to betray me, even to you, Doctor. I know there was something between the two of you once, but I trusted her implicitly." He paused for a moment, closing his eyes. "I will take a chance on your instinct. Perhaps she is capable of other, more formidable acts of treason. Until I know one way or another I can no longer count on her." He looked at me.

I stared, not believing my ears, afraid to speak lest I say something to make him change his mind.

"Stop ogling me, Doctor; we have work to do. First, I have to plant a believable story. Then, we have to think of a way to get you the Grimoir without making it look like we gave it to you...and I need a way to track you." He slammed his fist down on the table. "Well, Doctor? Do you think you can manage to escape?"

I smiled at him. "With all respect, Sir, do you have those handcuffs?"

"Are you certain you're all right, Sir? I'm really terribly sorry about all this, but, I think it's the best way really." I had just finished taping Sir David's mouth after handcuffing him to the chair. He was a little red in the face, and I worried that he might suffocate or have a heart attack... but he nodded, breathing evenly through his nose.

Just as I reached the end of the corridor, I heard the alarm klaxon go off. He must've had a foot control under the table that I hadn't noticed. At any rate, he wasn't making it easy for me. That was good. It would make the escape all the more convincing. If I did manage to escape.

Feet pounded along the hallway. I'm no stranger to these kinds of situations. I ducked into a utility closet and pulled on a coverall and a cap. It was late evening by now, so a cleaning man wouldn't draw too much unwarranted attention, especially one who'd just been attacked by a fleeing prisoner!

Stepping from my concealment, I swung an aluminium bucket against the wall, making a racket. Then, I half reclined against the wall, most of my face hidden by the head of a mop and I started yelling!

" 'ere, mates! 'e went into the lift shaft. 'oy you men, 'e went into the shaft, 'oy! Near knocked me bleeding nob off, too!" I got shakily to my feet, and leaned heavily on the mop, keeping it close to my face. I pointed down the hall.

One of the men paused, giving me a cursory glance and a tap on the shoulder "You okay mate?"

"Aye," I answered, thanking my stars it wasn't someone I knew. "You just get after 'im, yeah? Almost took me bleeding 'ead off, 'e done! Bloody dangerous bloke!"

"Don't worry, we'll get him." The security man took off.

That was one near miss, but I was still stuck. They were certain to seal off the building. I decided to push my luck and made my way to Sir David's office. It was the last place anyone would have expected me to head, so it was a perfect spot to pause and take a breath. Besides, if I was lucky, Jen would be there.

I was lucky. "Hello Jen."

She jumped, "Oh Doctor. I thought you were... I mean all that noise. Is it you they're looking for?"

"Yes, Jen, it is me. It should be some time before they get around to looking here, though. We ought to be alone for a while yet" After the way I'd totally misjudged Dr. Walden at the museum, I was a little leery about trying to charm my way around Jen. But, I had to try something. She turned and made a half-hearted grab for the phone. It was easy enough to counter.

"Stop it, you're hurting me," she cried, trying to twist her wrist free of my grip. She's a tiny thing, though well schooled in several variations of Aikido and karate. I had to be careful, or she could wind up breaking my neck. I was counting on her wanting me to succeed.

"Oh, come now Jen. You don't really want to call someone, do you? I just had a nice interview with Sir, in a small interrogation room on two C." I smiled. "He was very interested in finding out. where I'd gotten my new credentials, Jenny.

She stopped struggling and looked at me. "Did you tell him?"

"What! Me rat on you? And after all you've done for Tary and me? Really, Jen, what kind of a person do you think I am?"

"I used to know, once," she cooed, moving into my grip instead of away from it.

I pushed a lock of her hair behind one ear with my free hand.

"If you were to call someone and I was caught now..." I shrugged. "He had only just asked politely, Jen, I don't know how I'll react under more...ah.. strenuous questioning? I mean, I would try, of course, to keep you out of it, but, you know they are professionals. They might use drugs. And I don't think Sir will be too pleased with me after I handcuffed him to his own chair and gagged him with packing tape." I shook my head. "I do hope I haven't killed him. He was getting very red in the face last time I saw him, and I am really quite fond of the old boy, in my own way."

Jen had gone very pale. "You did that? To Sir David?"

I nodded. "I did, which tells you just how desperate I am. Now, I need you to help me get out of here."

She moved in closer. I released my hold on her wrist and gathered her into my arms.

"You and me, Jen, like it used to be, remember? Before you got bumped upstairs?"

For just a second she made a show of resistance, then acquiesced, turning her face to mine. "Yes. I remember."

I kissed her hard until she was breathless.

"Let me call a friend. I think I can get you out of here, but you're going to need help leaving the area. I can arrange it." Slowly, she pulled away and moved toward the telephone.

"How do I know I can trust you?" I said, grabbing her arm and turning her to face me.

Jen just smiled. "You don't have any other options, do you?" She leaned in and kissed me again, then made her call.

"You are a wonder at arranging things, aren't you Jenny dear," I said, embracing her. "I'm sorry it couldn't have worked out between us."

"Well, Arthur, it still may, someday." She stopped and appeared to look embarrassed. "Oh, I'm sorry. I realise how that must've sounded with Tary missing and all. I'm sorry. I didn't mean to sound so calculating."

I hadn't told her Tary was missing, only that we were in trouble. "No. I'm sure you didn't. Come on, let's get of here."

With Jenny leading the way, we actually had little trouble. I held a rag to my head and she explained how I'd been injured by the escaping Doctor. Security confirmed the story, and was actually able to get Sir David's okay to pass us through. Of course, I figured that Sir knew exactly who it was. I hoped he had men he could trust ready to pick up my trail at the museum.

Outside, there was a non-metered taxi waiting at the walk; Jen's contact. I got in. "Take me to the British Museum."

He dropped me around back. I'd worked for many years with the British Museum and was thoroughly familiar with every nook and cranny. Getting in through the side delivery entrance was no great feat. I still had my master key. Getting into the archives, though was going to be more difficult. They were locked by cipher, each vault different. At one time I'd been privy to all of them, but in light of my recent resignation and subsequent disgrace, I presumed they would all have been changed, well, I only needed one.

A Question of Balance

I found the most likely vault and, just on a whim, tried the old code. It didn't work, but it didn't set off the alarm either. That was a built in precaution. Recent changes wouldn't raise the alarm, otherwise it'd be going off all the time, until everyone got used to the new code, and stopped punching in the old one out of habit. That still left me only one more chance. If I blew it the alarms would bring the guards *running*. The code would be a four digit number. Usually, they weren't too hard to crack, since it had to be something easy to remember. Most times it was a famous date. I tried to think, then I tapped in the year that Hamlet was first performed. No good. Just as I tried my second guess, year of the Magna Carta, I heard the alarm sounding. The door clicked, and I went in. It took me about three minutes to locate the Grimoir and get back up to the side door.

There were security guards all over the place and I could hear the police coming.

I reached into my pocket and pulled out the parchment. The following words appeared: "Walk out the front door."

That was it!? Those were my instructions!? I didn't even think I had a chance of getting out the side door, never mind the front. By now, there would be men swarming all over the place. Still, there were men swarming all over the place here too. I walked slowly, inconspicuously slipping the Book under my arm, trying to look as if I belonged. I spotted an inventory clerk that I knew.

"Hey, Dan?" I called, taking a chance that not everyone on staff knew I was off. "What happened? What's going on?"

He stopped, surprised to see me. "Oh, Dr. Pendargroom. You working tonight?"

"Well, not with all this racket, I'm not. What's the fuss about?"

"Don't know yet. I've got to get down and check the vaults." He turned as a police inspector came up behind him.

"Oh, Inspector Ralens, Dr. Pendargroom was down here, maybe he saw something."

The Inspector looked at me wearily, his eyebrows raised in a question.

"Actually, no, I didn't" I said.

"I suppose you didn't hear anything either?" he asked chewing on his pencil.

I shook my head, smiling. "No, I'm sorry, nothing at all."

Ralens grunted. "Okay, go on then, we can reach you here tomorrow if we have any more questions,"

"Oh, absolutely!" I couldn't help grinning as I walked out the front door.

For a few minutes I stood and waited. I had followed the instructions, and walked out the front door. What next? I walked down to the street and stood barely a moment before I found out. A stunning blow to the back of my head, that's what.

I remember thinking, just before everything went black, that they hadn't been very original. I believe I was somehow disappointed.

Chapter Twenty
The Witch

I didn't so much regain consciousness as float upward out of a dreamy drugged state, closer to some kind of reality. There was water. I could hear it splashing all around me. My throat was dry and raw, swollen with the need to drink. I tried to lick my lips, but no longer had any control over my tongue. The water sounds continued and I gradually realized I was partially immersed in it. When I tried to move my hands, to scoop some of the warm liquid into my parched mouth, I found I couldn't. Hands, at the same time gentle and firm, were moving over me everywhere. Slowly, I forced my eyes open.

I was half sitting, half lying in a large stainless steel tub. Warm water rose nearly to my breasts. The woman I thought of as the nurse was running soapy hands over me, washing me as if I was a squalid infant. Under my arms, between my legs, she worked thoroughly. There was nothing sensual or even vaguely erotic in the experience. I was simply an object.

Seeing that I was conscious again, she pushed me forward with a strong hand behind my neck and began soaping my back. I saw that my wrists had been clamped into metal cuffs set into either side of the tub. My humiliation at being handled so dispassionately was profound. It wasn't modesty, exactly. Generally I don't view my body as something to be ashamed of. Although my particular tradition practices robed, not sky clad, there are a few rites, such as initiatory ablution, where ritual nudity is perfectly accepted This however, was nothing less than an intrusion on my person. Nothing, no part of me was spared the ministrations of those probing, impersonal hands.

The worst thing, even worse than the humiliation, was the knowledge that I was slowly dying of thirst, sitting in a tub of sudsy water I tried to speak. "Drink...Please."

The Nurse ignored my pleas and continued with her work. She picked up a pitcher from the floor and filled it with running water from the taps near my feet. I begged, pleaded for a sip, but all she did was pour it over my head to wet down my hair. The water was icy cold and the shock as I was doused paralyzed me. I didn't even have the presence to open my mouth, to try and catch a drop or two as water sluiced over my face. In frustration I began to sob as she washed my hair, but no tears would come. My body hadn't the moisture to spare, not even for tears.

Again she filled the pitcher. This time I was able to catch a few drops of soapy water. It did nothing, except perhaps to make my craving more acute. For a moment, Nurse left the room and I was alone. The water was turning cold now, and I began to shiver. She came back carrying a large towel, Number One and Number Two right behind her. By this time, I was beyond embarrassment. They stood on either side of the tub and each took hold of an arm as Nurse unlocked the manacles. Neither spoke a word, though Number One leered and grinned lewdly as they dragged me from the water. I was held up, shaking and dripping between the two men as Nurse toweled me off with cold efficiency. I squeezed my eyes shut so I wouldn't have to look at them as my hair was rubbed damp and combed.

When I was dry I was taken and restrained as Arthur had been, in a bed made up with silk sheets. There was no pillow. I was so weak, dizzy and ill from thirst and whatever drugs I'd been given, the restraints seemed hardly necessary. I kept drifting in and out of a dream. It was becoming increasingly more difficult for me to discern one reality from another.

There were voices. One I recognized as Miss Kelly's, although it seemed to hold an unfamiliar note of fear. The other voice was masculine, low and sibilant. I thought I'd heard that voice too, somewhere, sometime ago.

"You stupid fool. She's half-dead! Look at her, she's no good to me this way!"

"I had to reduce her power, Malcolm, get her subdued. I know it wasn't what you ordered, but in my opinion..."

The masculine voice hissed at her, "Opinion? You have no right to an opinion. You are my hand, a projection of my will, no more. Margaret Kelly as a person no longer exists outside of me.

The sheets were drawn down, and I shivered a little as cold hands prodded at my flesh. My eyelids were lifted by the gentle touch of a thumb, and pale, colorless eyes gazed deeply into mine.

"Lady Tarish? Can you hear me?"

He was well dressed in a business suit, impeccably tailored and obviously very expensive He looked every inch the prosperous lawyer now, but I knew those eyes. Once before I had stared into their luminous, inhuman depths. I tried to flinch away, but I hadn't even the strength for that.

Marge was whispering into his ear. "Remember, my Lord, she is dangerous. She beat you once before. I suggest it would be wise to keep her..."

He stood and backhanded Miss Kelly across the face.

She fell cringing on the floor at his feet, whimpering excuses. "You weren't there, I tell you. You didn't see her! It was necessary. We couldn't control her power! If it hadn't been for the damned Doctor, she would have killed us all!" Her voice held a note of frightened desperation. It gave me a small measure of satisfaction.

"I am here now. There is no power she holds that I cannot counter!" The barely contained fury in those words chilled me to my soul.

"You couldn't hold her when you had her before. She was nearly the death of you then. I beg you, do not underestimate her." Marge's voice low and shaky.

Malcolm Dennings, the man I knew to be the High Priest of the New York Coven laid his hands on my face. He glanced over his shoulder and whispered.

"Bring me a tray with tea and fresh water and fruit, melon."

The door closed quietly, so I knew she had gone. His attention was all on me again. His eyes were glassy and unfocused as he murmured over me, chanting strange words softly. I began to feel a kind of heat rising all around, and then I was drifting off again. When I awoke, there was water.

"Try to sip a little, Lady Tarish." His eyes seemed to show real concern as I struggled to get the tepid water to flow down my swollen throat. It was difficult. The passage seemed almost swollen shut. How many days had it been? Three, four? A week? I had no idea how long it had been since I'd had anything to drink save those three desperate swallows, but it had been too long. Now, the water was here and I couldn't get it down.

He muttered an incantation of some kind and offered the cup again. This time I was able to take a little. I realized then, that he was holding my head gently, almost lovingly against his chest.

"I'm very sorry, my Lady. This was not what I had intended." Setting the water aside, he brought a different cup to my lips. It was some kind of a warm herb tea that soothed the angry rawness of my throat as it eased down. I took it all, then let my head fall back onto his chest, breathing deeply.

"Can you take some food?" He brought a small piece of some kind of melon, and held it to my mouth.

I accepted the food from his fingers and managed to swallow. He offered another. Soon, I was able to eat and drink easily. When I could take no more, he stopped, and lay my head back down on the bed. He sat back and looked at me, cupping my chin tenderly in soft white hands. "You will be better very soon, Lady Tarish. "Soon enough to take your role in the Rite."

A Question of Balance

I was able to find my voice at last, a tiny cracked whisper. "I will not co-operate with your ritual."

His smile widened and again I saw the gaping jaws of a shark about to close around me. "That is not necessary, my dear. Co-operation only tends to make these things dull anyway. I much prefer a lively ritual, myself." He pushed himself up. "I'll send in the nurse to take care of your more physical needs. Now that you have ingested something, I'm certain you will require her services." He bent down and pressed his lips over mine; a cold and passionless kiss. Then, he left.

When Nurse came in with the bedpan, I found that he was right. She refused to speak to me, or even listen, as she tended to my physical requirements with detachment. I wondered if maybe she was deaf. After she'd gone, I was left alone, and that was the most frightening part of all. Each time I closed my eyes, I relived the nightmare of that night in the van. I felt the surging of the raw Power coursing through me, the savage joy that had filled me as I realized the force of my will. The images came swiftly, vividly. Every time, I would drag myself awake, trembling and drenched in the sweat of my own fear. To think that I could be capable of such devastating power was the most terrible thing of all. That kind of power was more than any mortal had any right to.

Awake finally, afraid to close my eyes again, I wondered where such power came from. The tiny ring on my pinky grew tight for an instant and the key at my breast felt warm. I suddenly realized that somehow, without meaning to, I had somehow invoked the power of the talismans that night; invoked them in a fit of uncontrollable, animal rage. If the two alone were capable of giving so much power to an inept such as myself, what would be the power bestowed upon an adept, one who held also the Grimoir of Infinity? The thought rushed coldly through me. I prayed that the Doctor would not be fool enough to return with the Book. I prayed that he would use his common sense and logic and take the

Book as far away as he could travel, and hide it forever. Better than that, I hoped he would destroy it. Whatever the cost to me, Dennings must never be allowed the use of that Power.

My eyes closed again and I slept. This time, I dreamed of Arthur.

When I woke, Nurse was there. She poured water into a basin and sponged me as I had seen her do to Arthur. I didn't try to speak to her this time. After running the towel over my body, she applied some fragrant oil to my Chakra points. It was the same scent I had recognized on Dennings. I squirmed, against my bonds, uncomfortable having that smell rubbed into my flesh. She ignored me and finished her task. That done, she held a cup of herb tea to my lips, watching carefully as I drank it down. Finally, I was fed small pieces of bread dipped in milk. She wiped my mouth clean with a linen napkin and gathered her things on the tray. Silently, she left, closing the door behind her.

I was alone only a few minutes this time, before Dennings entered. He had exchanged his suit for an ornately embroidered black silk kimono. A gold and silver dragon, outlined in metallic red threads with turquoise scales embroidered deeply along its back, decorated the exquisite robe. A red braided satin rope knotted loosely around his waist held it closed. He sat on the edge of the bed and lifted my head.

"You are looking much better Lady Tarish. How are you feeling?" His words betrayed nothing more than concern, but his eyes...his eyes were glowing.

"You seem to know me well enough. What am I supposed to call you?" My voice was still little more than a strong whisper, but it was sufficient.

His lips turned up into a small smile. "You are indeed better, my Lady. I see the spark of life has returned." With a smooth finger, he stroked the hair from my eyes. "As to what you are to call me..." He stopped and seemed to consider, letting his smile widen. "I think, dear Tarish, that you will call me Master."

A Question of Balance

I turned my face away, refusing to meet those eyes. He turned it back with gentle pressure. "My mortal name is Malcolm Dennings, but you will find that Master suits me well."

I thought of all I had read about the man since Arthur had first told me who he was. He was enormously wealthy, of course, and his legal practice boasted popular authors, movie stars, and various other fabulously wealthy luminaries on his client list, along with the odd politician or two.

"You have heard of me?" He smiled again, removing his hand from my face and pushing the silk sheets lower as he began to explore.

I tried desperately not to let him see the stark terror that was building in my eyes as his hands moved lower, probing gently, insistently down the length of my body.

"Tarish? Have you nothing to say?" His voice was taunting, teasing. I sensed he wanted me to beg, to plead with him. I wouldn't give him the satisfaction.

"I read the papers. I know who you are, Mr. Dennings." I tried to ignore his touch. "I also know what you are."

"Do you also know that tomorrow night, you will be taken in love by the coven? Initiated and dedicated to the Dark?"

I answered him with far more bravado than I felt. "I understand that will be raped by a group of half hysterical idiots led by a lunatic with a god complex. You don't scare me, Mr. Dennings. You can violate me, my body, but my soul is beyond your reach. I will follow the Light from this incarnation to my next until my own Karma is fulfilled and there is nothing you can do about that."

I had spoken softly, quietly, but with a conviction I felt in my heart that I'd never known was there. The understanding finally sank in. Though my mortal body in this incarnation could be desecrated, I was still the master of my own soul. Nobody could take that from me. Like the talismans, it had to be freely given, or be useless.

For a moment he said nothing, then, "They have chosen well, my Lady. You may be correct. However, when the Doctor returns with the Grimoir of Infinity..."

"He will not!" This time I spoke with more conviction than I actually felt. "He "understands what is necessary and he knows I understand. He will not deliver the Book to you, or anyone like you. Not in this life or any other."

He seemed to reflect on that a moment. "If that is true, it still leaves me you. Perhaps not your soul yet. Perhaps never. But for now I do have you, and I will be your Master." The sheet was discarded as he pressed his body down on me.

There is a place each of has, a private place in our minds where we can retreat when reality becomes too much to cope with. I went to that place and was safe, as Malcolm Dennings practiced his mastery.

When he was done with me, he stood over the bed gloating, adjusting his robe, "I was gentle with you tonight, my Lady. Tomorrow I will have to set an example." He smiled again and I shuddered, looking away. "I am not a brutal man, Tarish, but I am capable of brutality."

A tear found its way beneath my closed eyelids and he brushed it away.

"By the end of the Rite you will call me Master. Whether or not you give up the Key and the Crown..." he sighed, "...is something only you can decide. But ponder this, Tary. Is it fair that you should suffer? Why should the responsibility rest solely on your slender shoulders? There is far more that is dark in the cosmos than is light. Inevitably, dark shall win dominion. Why should you sacrifice yourself to merely postpone that eventuality? By whose will is it that you offer yourself?"

I made him no answer. I had none.

Nurse came in to clean me up when he had gone. It may have been my imagination, but I thought she was less gentle with me. As she began to clean me up, she gasped, "His mark!" So, she wasn't a mute

A Question of Balance

anyway. There was a small tender spot just above my left breast. In all the time I had been in Nurse's care, she had never uttered a single word. But now as she moved her hands expertly along my torso she had spoken those two shocked words, "His mark".

I strained to lift my head, to see that sore spot above my breast, but I couldn't. "What mark? Whose?"

Nurse had regained her detachment, however, and simply went on with her work she used something astringent, slightly acidic to cleanse me of Malcolm Dennings intrusion. It burned a little. I thought I saw a look of satisfaction flit across her placid features as I winced, sucking in air through clenched teeth. In helpless frustration I began to pull at the restraints. Nurse responded by treating me with uncustomary roughness as she changed the linen. She fed me indifferently, then left, closing the door behind her.

In a few minutes, I had another visitor, Marge Kelly.

"So," she breathed, running her fingers along the periphery of the tender area.

"So what?" I asked, I had really begun to hate Marge Kelly. I'm ashamed to admit it, but a part of me was pleased to see the bruised and swollen lip.

She stared at me for a moment, her gray-eyes cold as the North Sea. "He has marked you."

I'd begun feeling physically much better since my treatment had improved, That was good, and bad. I was getting tired of being treated like an object, a non-person, and I wanted to strike back. My tongue has always been prone to getting me into trouble.

I smiled, "Jealous?"

I don't know why I said it, except that sometimes my mouth runs faster than my brain. In spite of or maybe because of being raped by Malcolm Dennings, I found I was itching for a fight. For a second her swollen lip curled up into a snarl and I thought she was going to hit me, but I blundered on, unable to stop myself.

"You can't harm me, Marge, remember? I hold the Key and the Crown."

That stopped her in mid swing and I went on. "You saw that night, didn't you? You know what Power I am capable of. Beware, Marge, I am almost up to par again. The Power comes easily to me."

I'm not sure what I was trying to achieve, other than maybe plant a small seed of doubt. Perhaps it was nothing more than wanting her to feel a little of the fear I had been subjected to. At any event, whatever brinkmanship I accomplished was very short lived. I saw the doubt slip from her mind as she regained her composure.

"You are quite right, Tary. I believe Mr. Dennings is being far too careless with you." Her eyes narrowed. "He is my Master, that is so, however I am charged with your safety for the moment. I would be remise in my duty if I were to permit you to escape."

Her finger traced a design along my cheek, but I met her gaze steadily, refusing to be further intimidated. Marge's smile broadened.

"I like you, Tary. You have so much to offer. Your skill is raw and untried, but you have a great talent for magic nonetheless. That talent should be nurtured."

"Not by you!" I spat.

She went on as if I hadn't spoken. "But magic requires concentration. I may not harm you, that is clear. There are however, measures which will insure you cannot call the Power to you. Indeed, I think I must take such measures."

The sheet was blown off the bed by a gust of wind which chilled be, causing gooseflesh to rise along my skin. It died as quickly as it had been born.

"Oh very impressive, Marge," I said, tensing my jaw to keep my teeth from chattering. "That'll show me!"

Her smile remained fixed as she began at my feet drawing her nails very lightly up over the insides of my legs. They left pale white lines behind as she drew them around in circles on my stomach, then up and across my breasts to my neck. As the lines

A QUESTION OF BALANCE

faded, the itching began. It started slowly at my feet, following the lines she had traced to my neck. Soon, my discomfort was acute. There was no rash, just an incessant itching. I began to squirm.

"There now, I haven't harmed you" Marge chuckled, leaning over me. She brought her face inches from mine and whispered softly. "There are a hundred such ways to torment you, a thousand, without causing you harm."

I could hear her cackling all the way out.

Nurse returned momentarily. She picked the sheet up off the floor and covered me, tucking it tightly all around the bed. She extinguished the lights and left. In the absolute dark, the itching became worse. It felt as though thousands of ants were swarming over me, and it went on for hours. Marge was right, I couldn't concentrate enough to either trance or retreat and sleep was out of the question. I thought I would surely go insane as I twisted and struggled against my bonds.

Relief came gradually in stages as the itching slowly faded. The experience left me tense and jumpy, totally unable to relax. I lay there and listened. It felt like late night. Of course there was really no way for me to tell the time, but there was that stillness to the air.

I was vaguely aware that there were hallways and corridors beyond my room. Occasionally I could hear snippets of conversation, footsteps, as people went about whatever business they had here. I had begun to suspect that it was an institution of some kind, an asylum or private sanitarium, a handy place to keep people out of the way for extended periods of time.

I heard voices. There was a conversation going on now. It sounded like it was right outside my door. I strained to listen.

"Mr. Dennings, Miss Kelly asked me to find you. They have him, milord. Took him just as you said, right outside the Museum. A dozen coppers swarming all over, and nobody noticed a thing!"

I recognized the voice that answered; Dennings.

"The Book? Did he have it?"

"He did!" came the triumphant reply. "They're taking him direct to the Temple. He had a knock on the head, and then they gave him some of that phenobarber stuff to keep him quiet, just like you told them, but he's all right."

"Splendid! Tell your master I'll bring the woman as soon as she's prepared."

"Right."

My heart began palpitating, as the last of the itching faded. The door opened and the lights came on. I pretended to be asleep. He was silent, and even though I knew he was there, I still jumped, startled at his cold touch.

"I'm sorry to disturb your rest, dear one, but you must be prepared. I will oversee the ablution and perform the anointing myself. I assure you that resistance will only increase your own discomfort and my pleasure."

I opened my eyes and stared at him. He was dressed in an ankle length tunic, crimson and sleeveless. "My preparation?"

Yes my dear. It is a little past midnight now, and we have some business to attend to before the ritual of your dedication tomorrow or rather, tonight. Surely you haven't forgotten?"

"No, of course not. I just didn't expect you so soon."

"As I said, there is some other business to be handled first, and the rite will not be held here. The preparation takes some little time."

He leaned over and I could feel his breath on my face, smell that sick sweetness. "The other matter is one in which you may be key. You are to be reunited with your lover. The Doctor has been good enough to recover the Grimoir of Infinity and deliver it to us. I want you to witness how we demonstrate our appreciation."

I took a deep breath. "You are a stinking, evil abomination! If I believed in a devil, you would be it."

"Oh no my dear, I am but a humble servant. The English branch of our Order is hosting the ritual. You are most fortunate, there will be many hands to

A Question of Balance

welcome you." He perched himself on the edge of my bed, and held my head against his chest as he stroked my hair.

"Let me tell you what pleasure awaits you. My counterpart and I will begin by sharing you before the entire congregation, welcoming you to the Temple."

I jerked my head, but he held it firmly. "Oh I do understand your trepidation, my dear, but I assure you it is quite possible, and not at all harmful, with the proper positioning. When we have completed our part the entire congregation will be invited to add their love." He continued stroking my hair. "I have been to several such dedications, my dear, each of them memorable in it's own way."

He continued describing in graphic detail what would happen to me, had happened to others before me. Nurse brought in a tray of food, but I couldn't eat a thing. I was nauseated, thoroughly sickened by his monologue. He coerced me into taking a little camomile tea, and that settled my stomach a bit.

Finally, Marge Kelly and Nurse appeared dressed in ritual garb, to perform the ablution. I was anointed with oils, Dennings chanting, as I stood perfectly still, neither hindering nor helping. There was little point in resistance. Number One and Number Two were hovering in the background. Besides, now I knew they had Arthur.

While they were about the business of preparing me, so was I, in my mind preparing myself for the ordeal to come. Not my part in the Rite, that was of little consequence in the over all perspective. I was concerned with having to face, to witness, what they were planning to do to my husband, knowing that it was all for my benefit. There was no doubting what was in store for him. It galled me that Dennings was so sure of himself, so certain that I would hand over the talismans to save Arthur.

He might have been right once. Except, I had felt the power of the Key and the Crown for myself. The effect they had on me was terrible. The raw devastating power that ran unchecked was too terrifying to imagine. If the effect had been such on me, what would the power bestow on one well schooled and well prepared? If such a person held also the Grimoir of Infinity, the capability for destruction would be limitless, literally destruction on a cosmic scale. I knew that whatever they did to Arthur, I could not let the talismans fall into those blood stained hands. I prayed he would understand. Why had he recovered the Book? For a moment, I felt a flash of anger at him for putting me into this position. Then, a deep unbearable sorrow crept over my heart. He was a man, fallible and weak and he loved me.

I was clothed in black silk, my own velvet sabbat cloak arranged over my shoulders. My eyes were bound tightly, the hood drawn down over my face. Dennings led me out, barefoot and blind, to a waiting car. I was left untied. He knew he had me now.

In the car, he kept a tight hold on my hand, as if we were lovers. He made conversation, small talk about the New York social scene and world events. I was pretty much able to ignore him and concentrate, keeping my mind focused on Justice, the card of Balance. The image of the blindfolded lady, sword perfectly balanced across her knees as she held aloft the scales was fixed in my mind. I was that lady now, and the Balance rested with me alone.

The car stopped. There was a fine rain falling and I lifted my face, welcoming nature's subtle kiss. Too swiftly I was hustled inside. My cloak was taken, my eyes uncovered. It was a small parlor in which I found myself, so similar to the one in my first encounter with the Doctor that I had to blink to be sure it was still there. The walls were paneled in dark wood and a lovely camel backed sofa dominated the room flanked by delicately carved Queen Ann chairs and occasional tables. I'm no expert, but somehow I knew that these were the real things.

Another man rose from a wing chair, setting down a brandy snifter. He came and took my hand as Malcolm offered it to him.

"Our host, Lady Tarish, Dr. Quentin Mayfair."

A Question of Balance

Mayfair enveloped my hand in his and covered it with the other. I felt like Maid Marian being given to Sir Guy by the sheriff of Nottingham, all the time knowing that Robin Hood was languishing in the dungeons below.

"Welcome, Lady Tarish, to our Temple. Come and sit for a few moments. May I offer you a sherry?" Mayfair was being effortlessly charming.

"No, I don't drink. You wouldn't happen to have a diet cola would you? And a cigarette if you've got one."

He lifted a wooden cigarette box and offered it to me. "I am afraid that my cellar doesn't stock American style soft drinks." He said, looking amused. "May I offer you some tea?"

"No, thank you." I took a cigarette. I desperately needed the nicotine. I lit it from the flame Mayfair held for me and inhaled deeply, then sat down on the sofa. The two men spoke together casually as I finished my cigarette. Neither had any further direct conversation with me. When I had stubbed out the filter, they stood.

"There is no point in delaying further," said Quentin. "The Doctor has been conscious for some time and I understand he is most anxious to see you." I took a deep breath to steady myself and stood on shaky legs. Each one took an arm as the blood drained from my face. I felt suddenly dizzy and hot.

"Are you unwell, my Lady?" asked Dennings, solicitously dabbing at my forehead with his handkerchief. Concern mocked me from Mayfair's dark eyes as I shook my head.

"You put on quite a show, the two of you. All the trappings of civilized behavior. But the veneer is thin. I see you for the butchers you are."

Malcolm coughed, or perhaps snickered behind his hand. Quentin looked at me solemnly. "You are quite wrong, Lady. We, as you, merely serve a higher purpose. It is plainly a question of balance you see."

"No," I said quietly. "You serve no purpose but your own perverted cruelty. There is no such god as you claim to serve, only the evil that exists in your own hearts. Name him for me if you can, this god who terrorizes all that is born in innocence."

Malcolm smiled. "We do not name Him my dear, though for ages others have. In ancient times, the Egyptians called Him Sutek the Destroyer. The Christian Church conferred upon Him the title of Satan, adversary, and named Him Lucifer the fallen son of Light. The names bestowed upon Him throughout history are legion yet still He remains nameless. How can mortal beings presume to name that which cannot be known? We call upon Him, as He is, Dark. Perhaps one day He shall reveal Himself to us fully. Perhaps tonight when I hold all three symbols, I shall..."

"You never will, Dennings." I felt the color rise into my face. "You will never hold the Key of Enlightenment and the Crown of Fae, not as long as I draw breath. I have touched upon that Power. I understand it a little. There is nothing you can do, to Arthur or to me, which will make me give them up to such as you."

He took me under the arm, squeezing tightly as he shrugged. "We are merely His mortal servants, Tarish. We will try."

Mayfair took my other arm, his grip like iron. "Your beloved husband will long for the release of death, Lady Tarish, and only you can save him."

I tried not to let them feel my quaking as we left the civilized parlor and I began my descent into hell.

It was a huge, cavernous room with high vaulted ceilings. At one end stood four marble columns placed to mark each of the quarters. They were immense, rising from floor to ceiling, carved ornately in some neo-classical design. Centered perfectly stood a huge stone slab ancient and stained. At each corner an iron bracket was set solidly into the stone. Chains with leather straps at the ends were fixed to the brackets. Long deep furrows ran down the center, with a trough at each end to catch whatever was spilled upon that unholy altar.

Arthur was hung suspended from one pillar, his back to the front column on the left side of the stone.

A Question of Balance

His arms had been crossed behind the support and tied, ropes fastened to metal hooks. His legs had been tied together and fastened behind the column too so his full weight pulled at his arms with the force of gravity and the soles of his bare feet were turned up.

I stopped, unwilling to advance further. A deeply hooded figure was holding a sponge to his face.

"Come, my Lady. Are you not as anxious as he for this reunion?" Mayfair pulled me forward.

"No." I whispered.

Malcolm spoke to the robed figure that was attending the Doctor. "How is our guest? Have you made him comfortable?"

"He is secure, my Lord, but still groggy." It was Jen's voice!

I tore free of their grip and ran to him, pushing her roughly out of my way. "Leave him alone!" I stared at him. His shirt was torn raggedly, coming apart at the shoulder seams. All the buttons were gone, and it hung limply on his frame like a white flag. He still wore his faded jeans, but they gaped opened, all the buttons missing. Like me he was barefoot. I touched his face. He opened one gray eye, then the other.

"Hello Tary. Not too late, am I?" He smiled and I felt my heart breaking.

"Oh Arthur, Arthur, why did you come back? Why did you get the Book for them?"

"Well," he said a little of his old sparkle showing in his eyes. "I thought I had a plan." He blinked sadly at me. "Someone seems to have messed up, though. It's all gone wrong. I'm sorry, so sorry..." His head drooped and his eyes closed.

"It's the Phenobarbital, Lord. He's still groggy." Jen was talking to Quentin. "It could be another hour before he's fully awake."

"Oh, we won't have to wait that long," smiled Mayfair, lifting a syringe and stepping toward Arthur.

I grabbed at his arm. "Don't!" Malcolm stepped in and held my arms pinioned behind me as Mayfair ripped the remains of the sleeve off Arthur's shirt, and plunged the needle calmly into the vein just on the inside of his elbow. In a moment, the syringe was empty and he withdrew it, smiling at me.

"A few minutes and he will be ready. He won't lose consciousness again for some time. Enough to reap the full benefit of our little session."

Malcolm had handed me over to two acolytes who bound me to the column opposite my husband with manacles and chains.

"He will not be too damaged? You promised him to me, Lord, if I delivered him to you. You promised I could have him once the talismans were in your possession." It was Jen, speaking to Mayfair.

He cupped her chin in his hand affectionately. "You shall have him, Jenny dear. Whatever is left shall be yours, if you still want it." He sighed and gestured to me. "I am afraid she may be more stubborn than we had expected. If he lives there probably will not be much left of him."

"But I was told... given every assurance...."

"We must all abide by His will, Jen. Do not question." Dennings had come and stood at her elbow. She made a small reverent bow.

"As you say, my Lords. I will go now. There is still much to be seen to." Jenny left.

Arthur suddenly jerked his head up as the drug invaded his brain. I could hear the thunk as it hit the marble. The muscles in his chest and arms tensed and bulged, standing out in sharp relief.

"What have you given me?" he demanded.

"A fairly large dose of methamphetamine, administered intravenously, Doctor. I have used it before and been very pleased with the results." Mayfair patted his cheek, as Arthur strained at his bonds. "There is still time, dear lady."

I shook my head.

"Then we will begin." Malcolm stood next to me, holding my head steady so I could miss nothing.

"We will start with an updated version of what the Inquisition called 'pricking'. They used it to determine if there were devil's marks, places impervious to pain, upon the body of the accused. In those days, of course, they used special pins, or thin blades. We have more modern techniques."

I recognized the thing held loosely in the hooded acolyte's hand. It was advertised as a self defense weapon called a stun gun and would deliver a non-lethal, though excruciating electrical shock. He nodded, and the device was used. Time and time again I was forced to watch as Arthur's body jerked and went into spasm at the touch of the device. He bore it bravely, not once crying out or screaming. I could see the tenseness in his jaw-line, the sweat pouring off his face as he clenched his teeth, refusing to give in to what they wanted. The breath hissed through his nose as it was touched to his face, once, and then again. Still he uttered not a sound. Finally, Malcolm took out a switchblade and stood in front of him, blocking my view. I heard fabric ripping, and knew what was coming next.

I squeezed my eyes closed tightly as the stun gun was used again. This time, a choked sob was wrung from Arthur's lips. Then a strangled moan was torn from his throat. Mayfair turned to Dennings and joked. "It is as well Jen is not here. I fear this would upset her." They laughed at a third prolonged, agonized cry.

I could close my eyes, but not my ears. I sobbed, "Oh, Arthur. I'm sorry, I'm sorry," over and over. Suddenly there was silence except for the Doctor's ragged breathing. Dennings stroked the hair from my eyes.

"We will leave you for now. The Doctor needs to rest a while before we move on to the next phase." He glanced at his watch, "A quarter of an hour, I think will suffice." He looked back at me. "There are no listening devices. You may talk freely."

When they were gone, Arthur took a deep breath and looked at me. "Are you all right?"

It was such an incongruous thing to say and so very like him. I almost smiled.

"Oh, I'm fine." I managed. "And you?"

"Can't complain. At least, not yet. No serious damage done so far."

Arthur, what were you thinking, letting yourself be caught with the Book like that! You knew what would happen!" I could feel hot tears welling up in my eyes.

"Well, I didn't exactly know. You see, I had actually thought of something." He grinned sheepishly at me. "But apparently something got missed in the red tape, I suppose, and here I am. I'm sorry. Typical bureaucratic cock-up. I was expecting the cavalry long before now, Tary, but it looks like they aren't going to make the party. We're on our own."

The tears were streaming down my face. I tried to swallow the lump in my throat, to form a reply, but I couldn't speak. How long would it be before he finally died under the torture? Would he hate me at the end?

"Say, can you go on with this?" he asked, his face filled with concern for me. "You're not going to give in are you? Please, Tary, no matter what happens, no matter what I say, what they make me say, don't let them... don't ever let..."

"I know. I won't." I smiled a little. "You know, lately I've been feeling rather like Maid Marian. How's your Errol Flynn?"

He just shook his head forlornly. "Not very good I'm afraid. What we need now, are some Merry Men!"

I nodded. "I'm going to try to induce a coma... I love you, Arthur."

I closed my eyes, then opened them again, willing myself into a deep trance. If I could maintain a catatonic state they would have no reason to hurt Arthur. At least it might buy us some time, maybe enough for the cavalry to arrive after all. Slowly, I drifted away. They would be back soon.

Chapter Twenty One
The Merry Men

What Tary and I didn't know, while we were having our little session with Dennings and Mayfair, was that my disappearance had put the cat amongst the pigeons as not a single incident since the inception of the Institute had ever done. Sir David's two watchdogs, Fletcher and Maxwell, had let me slip away without a trace, and that was unforgivable!

The visual surveillance had not been really intense, since I'd been equipped with an electronic device, which would send a continuous signal, easy enough to follow. Fletcher was therefore not overly concerned when I disappeared completely from the front walk of the British Museum. Maxwell, after all, had my signal strong and clear on the scope. It appeared that I was just around the corner, waiting perhaps for further instructions. It took them nearly an hour before they realized that I couldn't have been crouching in wet shrubbery all that time, and it took them another ten minutes before they had a back-up check.

What they found was everything that might have concealed any sort of homing device, thrust into the hedge along the iron railing. All my personal effects, boots, belt, wallet, money clip, even the buttons off my clothing, had been left behind when they took me. Naturally, the device was among them. There hadn't been time to have one surgically implanted subdermally, much the best way. The alternative had been the top button of my five button jeans. Unfortunately, we weren't dealing with street thugs or fools.

I can easily imagine sir's wrath, when after an hour and a half, they finally had to report that they'd lost me. He'd really gone out on a limb, and now his organisation had blown what could ultimately be the single most important operation in the history of the human species. Indeed, as he was well aware, he may just have put the whole of sentient creation in jeopardy. I wonder to this day what it was that made him help me. I'd like to think it was a certain fondness for me personally, or perhaps he felt some responsibility for my involvement. More likely, he had seen an opportunity to thwart the Order at the head.

For several years, my work had brought me into close proximity to the street level practitioners, members of the Order who were expendable, but useful for any number of little jobs, murder frequently among them. This was the first time though, that we had a crack at the top, and I believe that is what he wanted. To cut off the head of the serpent!

I can only guess at what he did next to mobilise the small army of operatives and psychics he sent out to try and pick up my trail. In fact it wouldn't surprise me to find out that he'd gone all the way to Number 10. Whatever he did though was simply not enough. The only solid link he had to the group was Jen, and she'd quietly disappeared in all the melee. Of course, I knew where she'd got to, but that information wasn't very useful to me, or to Tary and there was certainly no way of getting a message out. In a way I was flattered that Jen had thought so much of our relationship that she would go to such lengths to have me all to herself. That thought didn't comfort me much however, when the pig-faced, hooded jackal was putting the stun gun to me.

I did not take the torture stoically. I kept myself from crying out, screaming in pain, by reminding myself how gentle this little set would seem once they got going on the really good stuff. They were not only consummate craftsmen in the art of physical abuse; they were also following the original handbook. Written by self-righteous medieval dogmatists, Heinrich Kramer and Jakob Sprenger around 1485 under the auspices of Pope Innocent

A Question of Balance

VIII, and supported by his Papal Bull, the Malleus Maleficarum was the inquisitors chief manual and Mayfair was taking it page by page.

In the church's frenzy to rout out heresy, torture was developed to the level of a high art. Inquisitors prided themselves on the quality of their craft, boasting of their ability to keep the accused alive under their ministrations. Indeed the whole idea behind it was to keep the victim alive for as long as it took to elicit not only confessions, but also indictments against additional victims to add to the growing number of witches and heretics whose lands and properties could then be confiscated. Torture could go on for days sometimes weeks providing employment for an entire cadre of workers related to the keeping and torturing of prisoners. It was a flourishing trade all the way around. Good business for everyone, except of course those unfortunates who happened to stand accused. It will suffice to say that I was viewing the next session with something very akin to terror.

Even if I had known that Sir David Marshall had rallied every available operative in Britain and recalled several from the continent, that knowledge wouldn't have been much comfort. If they did manage to find us eventually, it would be far too late to do me much good. Tary was slipping into a catatonic state, which was all well and good, for her. Unfortunately I had no such ability and they were coming back to begin round two.

I felt the point of a knife nick my fingers. As blood began to well up in the tiny wound, I heard Jen gasp. I tried to turn my head to see behind me, but in my position it was impossible.

"Jen? Is that you? What are you doing?" I asked stupidly

"Shh. I'm cutting you loose. You've got to get out of here. They lied to me Doctor. He told me you wouldn't be hurt. He said that they were going to use you to scare Tary...

"Listen Jen, never mind all that now. For pity's sake don't start with my arms! You'll send me splat on my face. Be a good girl and get my legs. Better yet, cut Tary loose first." I was whispering urgently. Our time was running out. Dennings had said a quarter of an hour and it was nearly that already.

"I can't. There's nothing I can do for her. Dennings has put his mark on her. The best I can do is get you out of here before they come back."

She was kneeling now, sawing at the rope that bound my legs. The knife was dull, the ropes were thick and she was distracted. It was taking too long.

"He's put his mark on her? For God's sake Jen, he's marked her?" The effects of the speed had sent my metabolism racing. It was virtually impossible for me to remain still and she nicked me a little in the heel.

For a moment she stopped and stared around the column up into my face. "Yes, Doctor. She'll never be anything more than his whore, his toy. Dennings has no intention of letting her be touched by the congregation. Oh, he'll share her with Mayfair, for appearances, but then they're going to switch her. There's another girl already prepared to take her place. I'm sorry, Doctor, but she's beyond you now. Best try to forget her."

My heart felt like someone had just poured acid on it. That bastard had marked her. Tradition said she would be bound to him now for as long as he lived. I was sick with the idea of Tary at the mercy of that perverted, twisted mind. "No Jen. I won't forget her. I can't leave without Tary. There has to be something, something somewhere that will break his hold."

She shook her head. "Only he can remove the mark, when he's grown tired of her and only by cutting it from her flesh. I am truly sorry Doctor. I had no idea what was going to happen, what they wanted. I only thought that you would... you would..."

She was sniffling! The wretched girl was crying! Of all the self-centred, spoiled, little bitches. Here my whole world was falling apart, not to mention little bits of my person being at serious risk, and she was feeling sorry for herself! We'd just run out of time. I could hear them returning.

"Jenny, listen to me, listen. Can you get to a telephone?" I didn't wait for her to answer. "Just get to a phone, Jen. Call Sir. He was in on it. He arranged for me to escape, to get the Book. He even knows about you. Just go. Tell him where we are. He'll do the rest. For pity's sake, Jenny, if you have ever loved me you will do this."

"But they'll kill you. They'll torture you to death to get what they want."

"You're wasting time. Get out of here now, before they find you! *Go!*"

She went. Now all I had to do was hang on and pray that she would do as I'd told her. And pray also that Sir David would believe her. I stared at Tarish and felt a tear form in the corner of my eye. I knew what that animal had done to her. I also knew that the only way she could be free of him was if she died or he did. I don't believe in killing people. I don't even like hurting them in self-defence. As far as I knew I'd never been personally responsible for anyone's death. Well, there was a first time for everything.

Mayfair examined Tarish carefully, minutely. She had slumped to the floor against the pillar, though her eyes remained opened, wide and staring. I understood what she'd done. So did he.

"A self induced catatonia," he marvelled peering into her blue eyes, "You didn't tell me she was so well trained."

Dennings smiled, teeth gleaming, "Oh, she's very talented my friend. Not to worry, I can manage this easily enough." He bent and touched her just above her left breast. Tary's eyelids fluttered and she looked up, confused.

"Now, now my dear, we wouldn't want you to miss anything." He raised her to her feet and pushed her back against the pillar, adjusting her chains so she would not be able to slump to the floor again.

Even from where I was I could see the tears of frustration welling up in her eyes as she looked helplessly to me. I winked at her and grinned. She must have thought I was mad. Come to think of it, she probably wasn't too far wrong. Mayfair touched her cheek and she flinched away from him.

"Tonight you will have nowhere to turn my Lady. The altar is prepared for you." He sighed. "But now we have other business."

Two husky young toughs dressed in brown robes entered and were moving to cut me down. One severed the ropes holding my arms and the other caught me as I pitched face forward. They stripped off my shirt, wrestled my arms behind my back and re-tied them before cutting my legs free. I could hear Mayfair lecturing again in the background.

"The art of strappado is an insidiously clever means of exerting extreme pain without actually causing too much damage to the accused. Still a very preliminary form of interrogation, but a very effective one, as I think you will agree. You are familiar with the method?" He was talking to Tary as calmly as if he was lecturing a college student on the finer points of Elizabethan etiquette.

I didn't know if her education had included the finer points of torture popular in the Middle Ages. She made no reply, but her eyes widened as a thick rope was threaded through the bindings around my wrists. I didn't have to see to know that the rope was attached to a pulley mounted somewhere a good deal above my head. I tried to keep silent as they hoisted me to my feet, then kept going. The strain on my arms and shoulders was intolerable. When I was a few feet off the floor, the rags of my jeans were ripped off none too gently. The resultant jerk sent excruciating pain shooting through my arms and back. I'm afraid that I lost my self-control. I choked back my cry as quickly as I could, but I could see that Tary was in torment for me. I was in torment for myself. I was pulled to a height of about six feet, just high enough for my tormentors to be able to walk underneath and grab hold of an ankle.

The bastard Dennings yanked first, smiling the whole time as my wife begged and pleaded on my behalf. I couldn't really hear what was being said over the sound of my own groaning which became louder in my ears as he tugged with more and more vigour. My arms felt at the breaking point, though I knew they weren't yet. Mayfair had a tray brought in and the two of them sat over tea as I swung back and forth above their heads.

After awhile my arms were beginning to bear the intolerable strain and I was going numb. Then the two muscle bound monks came in. Each carried a twenty-kilo weight and a roll of wire.

The wire was wrapped around my upper thighs, at my knees and ankles. Short metal rods were inserted and turned causing the wire to tighten. Then the weights were strapped around my knees and ankles. I tried, but I couldn't keep the cry from my lips as I felt every muscle in my body stretched like an elastic string. Tary went as pale as rice paper as the two young toughs began turning the rods, tightening the wire so that it dug cruelly into my bare flesh. My lips bled freely where I had bitten through to keep from screaming out my pain.

"My dear, this is really so unnecessary. You can stop it all with a word." Dennings was moving toward her as he spoke. He held a cup to her lips and she drank it obediently, never taking her eyes from my face. I shook my head and the movement caused me to begin to swing agonisingly. Her gasp reached my ears even through the blur of pain and I winked, or tried to.

In a vacuum, a pendulum will continue in perpetual motion. Thankfully, we were not in a vacuum. Eventually, so long as I remained completely still, my motion stopped.

They finished their tea and seemed to grow tired of this little game. I'd been hanging around for several hours by this time and Tary showed no signs of weakening. Casually, Mayfair yanked down hard, eliciting the first real scream I had yet uttered. Pain can reach sublime levels and this was close. He walked to Tarish as the tourniquet wires were adjusted yet again for maximum effect. Blood was starting to ooze from the lacerations and I heard myself whimpering pitifully.

"Are you familiar with the next phase, my dear? An interesting variation that usually causes dislocation of the shoulders, elbows, hips, knees, ankle and—well about everything. Sometimes there are severe internal injuries as well, as organs are torn loose. A victim will rarely survive more than two or three drops. It is called squassation. Please, permit me to have it demonstrated for you."

There is no way one can prepare to have every muscle, every joint wrenched beyond the breaking point. The two monks released the rope from the bracket and hoisted me all the way up to where the pulley was fixed in the ceiling. Then they tied off one end but continued to maintain the tension manually. I now hung suspended roughly twenty or so feet from the floor. Then, they released the rope. It caught and held when my feet were about 6 inches from the floor, jerking me to a halt. I'm sure my screams would have frightened the daylights out of anyone at that point. I was so far beyond anything but dealing with the excruciating pain of a separated left shoulder, that it was several minutes before my eyes cleared and I saw that Tary had fainted dead away.

"She is close, I think," said Mayfair as Dennings blotted her face with a pocket-handkerchief. He motioned to the two monks. "Get him ready. We shall do it again as soon as she regains consciousness."

I can tell you honestly, that my blood turned to ice water. My left shoulder had definitely been pulled out of joint entirely, but I couldn't tell for certain if anything else had been dislocated or broken. One thing was certain, however, another drop like that and I would be useless. My brain was still racing, the result of the amphetamine, no doubt. There was little hope that I could easily fall unconscious to escape whatever was next on their agenda. The robed assistants began to haul on the rope again. I was in agony, my shoulder feeling as though it would be literally pulled off my body as I whimpered and moaned. Suddenly there was a shout and the massive double doors at the entrance to the Temple began to splinter and crack. I thought I could hear tiny explosions, like gunshots. That was all I had time to observe as the rope went slack again and I dropped a few short feet. It was enough to send me into agony.

Dennings and Mayfair were busy. Tary had recovered from her faint and was struggling in their grip as they released her from the pillar and began dragging her somewhere off behind the altar stone. I shouted for them to stop, that there was no place they could run but predictably they ignored me. I glanced at the rope; the knot was slipping, but not fast enough. I gritted my teeth against indescribable agony and began swinging my legs, trying to hasten my descent. If they got away now, I might never find them.

The rope gave way and I fell, just at the moment that the doors buckled and men swarmed in. There were gunshots fired. I had the breath knocked out of me from the fall and I couldn't speak, but Fletcher had seen me go down. One monk had disappeared entirely, probably gone with Dennings to help with Tary. The other one was approaching me with a long knife. I closed my eyes helpless to move, expecting to feel the steel in my neck, but he never made it that far. He fell down dead, shot cleanly through the heart. I started to breathe again, wheezing in pain and shock as Fletcher came to kneel over me. He sliced the rope away from my wrists and carefully unwound the wires. The blood flowed freely as the tourniquets were removed.

"Looks like it were a near thing this time, Doc," he said unfastening the weights around my ankles. I sat on the floor trying to get a grip on the pain shooting through my arms and primarily my left shoulder.

"Yes. I wouldn't like to have gotten any nearer." I tried to stand and Fletcher caught me as I swayed, easing me back to the floor as I moaned.

He probed gently, then without warning he gave a swift yank and my shoulder settled back into its socket. I screamed and bit through my lip again.

"You just stay quiet there, Doc. Max'll be along any minute and we'll get you off to hospital and have you looked after properly."

I was gasping, though with the shoulder set the pain was beginning to settle into a dull throb.

"There isn't time! They took her, Fletch. They still have Tary." I pointed to the altar. "Over there, there must be a trap door or something."

"All right, I'll have a look. You sit and get your breath."

I nodded and he went taking two other men with him. They didn't find anything.

"No door that I could see, Doc. Are you certain that's where they went?"

I growled in very bad humour, "Well, they didn't pass you on the way in, did they? They must've gone somewhere!" This time I made it to my feet and managed to stay there. Maxwell came in and removed the brown robe from the dead man, helping me pull it over my head. The bullet hole was very small, and there was only a little blood. Hardly noticeable really. Well, I needed something and that was the closest thing to clothing to hand. It would do.

A close examination of the altar stone revealed there was a sort of a locked spring mechanism, probably to slide it over. There would be a crypt or passageway of some kind underneath. That's how Malcolm Dennings and Dr. Quentin Mayfair had escaped. They were finished; they must have realised that. Neither man could ever return to their old lives again. The raid had brought in enough evidence to convict each of them of a hundred different felonies, not the least of which was kidnapping, child cruelty and murder. I thought about it a moment, sitting on the edge of the altar. Both were rich and powerful, undoubtedly well prepared for this eventuality. They would have an escape route planned, with money hidden in a Swiss account. Enough money could

A Question of Balance

easily buy them new identities. There were thousands of places in the world where they could disappear to start up again. It would be like looking for the needle in the haystack.

I shuddered. They would be quite put out with me, I was sure, and they had my wife as well as the Grimoir. I winced at the light touch of a small hand on my shoulder. I turned. "Oh, Jenny. Thank you for saving my life."

She smiled. "They're taking me away now, with the others. Sir David said that what I did will be brought out at the trial. He doesn't think I'll get any prison time."

"Well, that's good." I couldn't look at her. I appreciated what she had done in the end, but I couldn't help remembering that it was she who'd betrayed us at the start.

"Look, I know it doesn't mean much, but I am sorry."

"Yes. That won't help Tary now, though, will it?" I spoke perhaps more harshly than I'd intended, but I'd been through a lot just recently.

"You mean they..."

"Yes. Dennings and your Master took her with them! They must have got out through a tunnel or something under the stone here." I kicked at it.

Jen leaned over and depressed one of the tiles that lined the trough. The bottom of the slab moved silently to one side, revealing a dark staircase leading down.

I jumped up. "Fletcher! Maxwell, here, down here!" Without waiting for them, I plunged into the darkness. The long robes got tangled around my legs and I stubbed my bare toe on the very first step. Trying to catch myself against the wall sent pain rushing through my abused arms and shoulders. So down I went. Actually, it was a very short fall. There were only four steps before the tunnel turned sharply. I was fortunate not to have hit my head or anything. For a minute I lay there panting, trying to ascertain whether I'd broken anything, like my fool neck. The beam of an electric torch lit the stairs as

Max offered me a hand up. "It seems to go on down. Probably runs all the way under the grounds and out to the road," he speculated

I looked at him. "Where exactly are we, anyway?"

"Oh yeah, that's right. You wouldn't know, would you? About sixty miles outside of London just east of Salisbury. The nearest village is called Wight's Glen-Cove" He grinned at me in the dark

"Wight's Glen-Cove? Never heard of it. What kind of place is this, eh?"

"Oh, big, huge, enormous, it's, well it's a gigantic..."

"I get the point. It's large. What's it like, though. I mean is it a house, a castle? A priory? What's the layout like? The grounds?"

"It's a castle like, but not an old one. One of them things they put up in Victoria's time; a folly. Got a moat and all." He grinned.

Fletcher was as stout-hearted as they come, cunning, crafty and very savvy, but he wasn't an intellectual.

"Perhaps we should follow it out, eh?" I suggested. "See where it leads?"

He nodded. "Right behind you, Doc." He stopped for a minute, and put a hand on my shoulder. I winced. "Just wanted to tell you, about the cock-up at the museum..."

"I know, Fletch. I didn't think they'd be so thorough either. It was a mistake; one that I only hope hasn't cost me too dearly. I've made enough of them myself on this job. Now, let's stop worrying about old errors and concentrate on seeing where this leads to."

After a very long trek through winding passageways and a number of blind alleys, it finally led us to a way out, apparently at the very edge of the castle grounds. There were signs that a car had been left for some time, and only recently driven off. We lost the tread once it hit the paved roadway. My heart sank, but there was no more we could do here.

"Let's get back to London. Maybe Sir David's turned something up." I said.

Chapter Twenty Two

Bryn Gwyddyn

I was disoriented, confused. Rough stone stairs, icy cold, tore at my bare feet. They were dragging me down... down deep into utter blackness. Perhaps they could see in the dark, but I couldn't and I was frightened. I struggled to pull free, to turn back.

"No! Arthur, Doctor..."

"He is well beyond your help now, Lady Tarish. The last jerk must have splintered his joints, torn his muscles to shreds. He is a broken, useless thing now. If he yet lives, it will not be for long. I left orders to kill him to cover our escape. For you, there is greatness in the future."

Malcolm barely slowed as he spoke, pulling me, dragging me as I stumbled on the stair, my bad leg holding me back. Mayfair was right behind, pushing at me as I tried to stop, to think. Arthur dead? It was inconceivable. Then the terrible echo of his screams reverberated in my mind. I tried to pull free, to put my hands over my ears to blot out that sound, that agonized sound of screaming. There had been a gunshot...

He yanked harder, trying to make me move faster. I couldn't. I couldn't move at all with Arthur's death cries ringing through my brain. I stumbled and fell taking him down with me. When we finally stopped falling I couldn't get back up. My legs refused to bear my weight. Through my tears I saw Mayfair bending over me. There was a dim light coming from somewhere behind him.

"She'll not get up on that leg now, Dennings. Have Peter carry her."

I was lifted and thrown over the shoulder of the acolyte he'd called Peter. He was one of the two who'd tormented my poor husband to his death; the one with the stun gun. I beat ineffectually on his back with my fists, but he ignored me. Malcolm held my arm out steady while Dr. Mayfair stuck a needle into a vein.

"It'll put her out for a few hours, long enough to get her on the plane."

"No," I tried to form the word, but suddenly it didn't matter anymore; nothing did. Arthur was dead. They no longer had anything with which to threaten me. Gratefully I succumbed.

When I woke, I was in a luxury car, my head cradled on Malcolm's lap.

"She's coming around," I heard him say.

Mayfair was sitting across from us. He leaned over and lifted my lid, examining the pupil and grunted.

"She'll be fine. I don't know about that leg, though. What was wrong with it before, do you know?"

Apparently, Dennings shook his head no, then Mayfair continued. "I wish we'd thought to X-ray it while we had her at the clinic. Then I'd have an idea what we were working with."

"Just do whatever you can, Quentin. It doesn't have to be perfect. She won't be expected to do much walking." I could hear the irony in his voice. "In fact, she won't be on her feet very much at all."

I struggled to get my sluggish brain to function. Slapping at his hand, which lay familiarly across my chest, I fought my dizziness and tried to sit up.

"Where are we? Where are you taking me now?"

Mayfair handed him a glass. He pressed it to my lips. I turned my head.

"Come Tary, drink. You must keep up your strength."

"Don't you call me that! Don't you ever call me that!" This time I was able to tear myself away from him and slide across the seat as far away from him as I could get. For a few moments I huddled in the corner, staring out the deeply tinted windows as beautiful green countryside rolled past. I didn't recognize any of it. Finally he reached across and pulled me to him with a not so gentle arm around my shoulders.

"I shall call you what I like, my dear." He touched a place just above my left breast. My heart seemed to stop at his command. It didn't flutter, merely froze in mid-beat. Gasping in pain and horror I put my hand to my throat, thinking somehow that if I could breath fast enough my heart would start again.

He merely laughed at me and removed his hand. My heart began to beat as though nothing had happened.

"You see, Tary, you are truly mine now. Perhaps you remain mistress of your soul for the moment, but for how long? Eventually, when you realize that it is upon my sufferance that you exist at all, I expect you'll give in. Then my dear you'll beg to make a gift to me of the talismans you hold."

"I will die before that happens."

"Oh that's easy enough for you to say now, but you'll change your mind I think. Even if you do not, it makes little difference. You may control the Key of Enlightenment and the Crown of Fae, but I control you. It won't take me too long to find ways to use you. Ways to make you use them for me."

I said nothing. I honestly didn't know if what he said was true. All I knew was that Arthur was dead by now. He had died screaming in torment that I could have spared him.

"Why have we left the Temple, Mr. Dennings? Why the sudden change in plan?"

"For reasons I choose not to reveal to you, Tarish."

"Does that mean that my dedication to this dark god of yours is off?"

It was Mayfair who answered. Laying a hand on my thigh, he began rubbing me, caressing me. I thought I saw Malcolm start, a brief flicker of anger in those deathless eyes. It was gone, if it even had been there, too quickly to be sure. In any event, he held tightly to my hands so I could do nothing about Mayfair's advances.

"Not at all, Lady Tarish. It simply means that your Master and I have decided not to share you with the congregation. Your dedication will take place tonight, at the Dark of the Moon, but there will be only the three of us as participants. I have invited a few close friends to observe."

Shuddering against the touch of his hot fleshy hands, I closed my eyes and tried to relax, to distance myself from what was happening. At a disappointed clucking from Quentin, Malcolm touched his finger to my breast again, wrenching me back.

For a minute I was too shocked to think clearly about what he had just done. I sucked in huge lungfuls of air, trying to fade, retreat, but it was as though I was pinned to the moment, unable to tear myself free. Finally I realized this was what he meant when he said he controlled me. He'd done something to me, an enchantment of some kind binding me to his will.

He chuckled, reading what passed through my mind as easily as the Sunday newspaper.

"Yes, you are correct. I have placed my mark upon you. I'm afraid it is there rather permanently, my dear, Tary. So long as I live you are bound to my will on this Earth. I truly am your Master."

He grazed the place above my heart with a finger. "How are you to call me?" he asked.

"Master." The word was torn from my mind, forced through my lips as though it was someone else speaking.

"That's good, Tary. Very good." He patted my cheek wiping at the tears as they spilled over. My humiliation was now complete.

Dr. Mayfair continued with his clumsy groping and I could do nothing to either prevent him or escape the maddening sensation of being held so helplessly in the grip of such ruthless evil.

The remainder of the trip was torturous as I was forced to submit to their careless whims. I felt I would surely go mad. Unfortunately, madness is also in the realm of the mind, and even my very sanity it

A QUESTION OF BALANCE

seemed, was under the control of my Master, Malcolm Dennings.

When we finally reached our destination it was near full dark. The young acolyte who'd been driving came and opened the door. Mayfair got out and Malcolm pushed me to him as he grasped my arms. As my feet touched the ground, I fell, pain spiking up and down the length of my damaged leg.

Dr. Mayfair stood looking down at my pain in disgust. "This is what you want, my friend? A cripple? There are hundreds of young and beautiful women in the world who could be yours."

Malcolm was smiling as he stepped from the car. "Yet none so beauteous as the rose which conceals a thorn to prick the blood from me."

It sounded familiar, though I couldn't identify the verse.

"Also, my friend, she holds the Key to the Power and the Crown with which it may be ruled. A very unique woman."

He bent over me, offering me his hand.

"Lady Tarish?"

I tried to stand, but even with his help the leg wouldn't hold up. Once more I was subject to the indignity of being hauled over Peter's shoulder like so much laundry.

It seemed to be a fairly large country house. The night was moonless, and so it had been too dark for me to see what kind of country surrounded it, but I was nearly certain, from the feel, the smell, it was moor. Inside, Peter carried me up the long stairs, following behind Dennings until we came to an oaken door. Inside was a suite, a huge bedroom with a four poster bed and a smallish sitting room. Against one wall of each room was a large fireplace, with logs burning brightly. It was beautiful, very elegant and charming. I was deposited on the bed and Peter left quietly.

"I'm sorry I don't have the time to repeat the ablution, however, I shall be pleased to perform the anointing once more before the rite."

I sat up, my eyes flashing at the thought of him rubbing that sweet sick smell into my skin. "Don't touch me!" I warned.

He just smiled. "I could compel your co-operation, my dear, like so..."

He held out his hand and closed his fist tight, as though a small animal was capture within. My heart jumped, and compressed as though squeezed in a giant hand. Pain shot down my left side paralyzing me. He opened his hand, and the pain vanished, leaving me pale and shaken.

"But, I prefer the traditional ways. So much more entertaining.." He lunged across the bed and I rolled to the side, but not quickly enough.

Pain throbbed in my ankle as I tried to stand. He reached me as I fell and swept me up into his arms as if I was a rag doll. I was thrown to the bed, my head striking the silken bolster. He leaned his whole weight on me as I struggled. Suddenly, his hand disappeared beneath the pillows and returned clutching a golden collar attached to the bed with a long chain.

I raked my nails across his face, drawing blood, but it took him less than ten seconds to snap the thing around my neck and lock it. Breathing heavily, he sat back across my hips smiling. It felt like the life was being crushed out of me. Slowly he touched his face where I'd scratched him. His fingers came away blooded.

I was panting for breath, afraid to look away from him. Casually, he ripped down the front of the silk robe and parted it. Once more I brought up my arm to rake his face. He caught both my hands easily, in one of his and held them tightly. Touching his face again he brought the blood on his fingertips to my breasts and drew a simple crimson rune over each one. When he had done, he released my hands and stood.

"There is nothing better with which to anoint than one's own blood drawn in passion." Holding my hair so I couldn't turn away, he drew his bloody

A QUESTION OF BALANCE

fingers across my mouth. Then, he bent and kissed me, licking at my lips.

"I will return to take you to the Temple."

I was sick to my stomach as he left the room. Peter came in and stared until I covered myself, clutching the rags of the robe around me. Obviously disappointed he sat in a chair, apparently to guard me.

In a few short hours it would be midnight. Arthur was dead, and I was far beyond anybody's help. I curled up on my side and tried to sleep, but it would not come. This was my new life; to be forever chained to a man I loathed. No, not forever, only for the single span of years left me in this life time. I conjured up an image of my initiation in the New Forest and it brought me comfort. I had been dedicated to the light and now I would offered to the dark. There seemed a symmetry in that somehow and it brought me comfort. I could visualize Lady Trewlane's gentle warm face, and imagined I heard her voice comforting me.

"Tarish, you are never helpless when you have magic."

"But his magic is far stronger than mine. He will counter whatever I can do and punish me." I shuddered knowing that Dennings would torment me for the rest of my days regardless.

Slowly I let the power build in me. I thought of my friends, my family. How long would it be before they learned I wasn't coming home? Would Malcolm Dennings cover my disappearance somehow? A letter explaining how I'd decided to stay in England? No. My son would never believe that. He must already be half-sick with worry at not having heard from me in days.

I wondered too, if anyone would find Arthur's broken body or if the disciples of Dark had disposed of it somewhere it would never be found. It wasn't fair. It wasn't supposed to turn out this way. The good guys are supposed to win. Arthur and I were supposed to live happily forever after.

I sat bolt upright. I'd been dreaming. I touched the collar, felt along its smooth edges. Concentrating, I put my finger to the tiny padlock. The face of my son came into my mind. He needed me. I couldn't give up. I stroked the metal, seeing in my mind the lock springing open. I tried the Key around my neck, knowing that it was far too large to fit the tiny catch, but somehow it did. There was a very soft click and the tiny padlock came away in my hand.

I looked over to where Peter sat in the chair. He was snoring, sound asleep. I was free of the chains, but could I manage to get out of the room. And if I did that, could I escape the house? Then once on the open moor, would I be able to... One thing at a time, Tary, I told myself. First find something to wear, then get out of the room.

I got out of bed and found some old clothes in a closet. I dressed as quietly and quickly as I could. My ankle was swollen and painful, but I thought I could manage on it. I would have to. Slowly, I stepped to the door. I tried the knob and it turned. A quick glance at Peter assured me he was still deeply in the arms of Morpheus. I held my breath, opened the door and stepped into the hallway closing it behind me.

Silence clung heavily to everything as I found my way to the stairs and stood, listening. In the closet where I'd discovered the black trousers and sweater, there had been a pair of plastic flip-flops. They would offer some protection on the rough ground outside. I carried them now, not wanting the flip-flop to give me away. My ankle ached, throbbing each time I put weight on it. I gritted my teeth and started down the stairs, limping as silently as I could. I pushed at the pain, sending it into a back corner of my mind where it could stay until I was safely away.

I felt no sense of Dennings now, nothing to tell me he was close. Not knowing how far a range this enchantment had, I prayed that shielding myself and using a spell of cloaking wouldn't send up an alarm. It didn't seem to.

A Question of Balance

Although the house was huge, I didn't have any trouble finding my way to the front door. The trouble I did have was finding it locked. I played with the dead bolt for a few minutes before I realized that it had been locked with a key, and even from the inside would open only with the key. So much for the easy way out. There had to be another exit, probably several in a house this size. I figured my best bet would be to find the kitchen. There's always a back door from the kitchen.

A darkly paneled double sliding door led me to the dining room. Swell, the kitchen should be right through there somewhere. I poked my head through one door. It was a silver pantry. Keeping my ears cocked for any hint of sound I moved to another door. Success, it was the kitchen. I ducked inside. From somewhere came a murmur of voices. It sounded like a small group of people male and female. I couldn't tell where they were coming from, but I could tell they were getting closer, and one of them was Malcolm.

Without realizing it I'd crossed the kitchen and felt the round hardness of the doorknob pressed against my palm. They were closer now, Dennings' sibilant voice penetrating through the soft buzz of the others. Although my brain was screaming for me to turn the knob and flee to safety, my spirit told me something else. Malcolm still had the Book. As long as the Grimoir was in his possession there would be no safety for me anywhere in this life, or for anybody else. I had to at least try to get it back.

Reluctantly I slipped back through the kitchen and into the pantry to listen. If I could find out where It was kept, there was just a chance I might be able to get my hands on It long enough to destroy the damned thing, if It even could be destroyed. I closed the door and prayed.

In a few minutes the group entered the dining room and settled themselves around the table. From the snatches of conversation I was able to understand these people were to be guests at the ritual. I pressed back against the wall scarcely daring to breathe as their host entered and I recognized the voice of my Master.

"Ladies, Gentlemen, I am most happy to have you attend tonight's rite. Dr. Mayfair and I feel certain that this special event shall be a memorable one. As you know, the Order has recently been able to recover the Grimoir of Infinity. I am most pleased to announce that the other two talismans, the Crown of Fae and the Key of Enlightenment are also under my control."

There was a murmur then a brief spate of spontaneous applause as the guests greeted the news enthusiastically. Dennings continued his little speech, and I leaned closer to the door to hear every word.

"In spite of the recent set backs, the raid on Dr. Mayfair's clinic and the Temple of Dark, the future of our Order seems assured. With the acquisition of the Three, there is nothing that can prevent our dominion. Tonight, you shall witness the dedication of she who holds the Key and the Crown."

A cultured feminine voice was raised. "Mr. Dennings, from your announcement, I was led to believe that the Two were now held by you? Is this not the case? Who is this mystery woman who carries the Power?"

"Who she is, is unimportant, my Lady. What she is, is my slave. I have marked her and she has acknowledged me as her Master."

"But where has she come from? What is her background?" The voice was masculine, with a whining lisping quality. Even from in the pantry it grated on my nerves.

"Ah, I save the best for last, my friends. She is a priestess of the Light, dedicated to Cerridwyn. Her debasement and seduction is nearly complete. After he has taken her tonight, Dr. Mayfair and I will share her before you all. At that moment she shall become His. There is nothing to prevent it."

"What is this persistent rumor we keep hearing about Doctor Pendargroom? Has he truly been the cause of all the recent mayhem?" It was the woman again.

"He is unimportant, I promise you, Lady Furstale. A temporary inconvenience, nothing more. Although it seems he has escaped me for the moment, when I hold the Power I will see him destroyed; slowly, meticulously destroyed by the hand of the one he loves." He paused and I pictured him smiling cruelly. "I can say for certain that in his current condition, he is in no position to be a threat to anybody."

I had to cover my mouth to keep from gasping aloud. The bastard had lied to me, Arthur was alive, at least he had been. My heart jumped, this time in hope not fear. I clung to the thought that I wasn't alone.

Just then the little party was interrupted. I couldn't see what was happening, but I could guess that it wasn't good for me. Apparently, Peter had woken up and discovered me gone.

Through the wooden door I could hear Malcolm begin to intone words. I could feel them seeking me out where I hid. This time, instead of stopping, my heart speeded up sending blood pounding to my brain. Behind my eyes everything was turning red.

I clutched at the Key around my neck, invoking the Power consciously, just a little, as much as I thought I could handle. I tried to shield myself from his spell, to keep my heart from bursting under the pressure of the pounding, but I couldn't slow it down. Even with the talisman I couldn't break his hold on me completely, the enchantment was too strong. Arthur's face wavered in front of my eyes, changing, reforming into the predatory features of the man whom I despised. I tried to stifle my cry as I flinched from the vision.

The door was flung wide and he stood there grinning in the flesh. The key dropped from my fingers at a gesture and fell resting just below my breasts. I stared, feeling my tongue begin to swell in the back of my throat cutting off my air. My heart continued pounding wildly, beating frenziedly against my ribs. My legs gave way and I pitched forward into his arms. Almost tenderly he touched my face and my throat was clear, my heart beat back to normal. I opened my mouth to speak but the words wouldn't form themselves. My arms were too heavy to lift, to strike at him and my legs too weak to support me. Once more I was helpless in this madman's grip.

"I underestimated you again lovely Tary. It was careless, an error I assure you will not be repeated."

Peter came and lifted me, waiting for instructions.

"Take her downstairs. Dr. Mayfair is there. He knows what to do."

The young man nodded once then turned and carried me through the door to the kitchen. For a moment, he set me on my feet, leaning me against the wall as he opened the door to the cellar. Then, he hoisted me back over his shoulder and continued down the stairs.

Dr. Mayfair seemed surprised, but smiled as Peter explained what had happened. The heaviness was easing from my limbs, as I was set down. I tried to slap at Quentin; to keep his white hands from groping me as he bound my limbs. Young Peter merely held me tighter as Mayfair wound thin cold wire around my wrists behind me. It dug into my flesh and I bit my lip to keep from letting him see the pain in my face. When my hands were secured, he bound them up with ribbon.

"It is specially prepared and impervious to any counter enchantment, Lady Tarish," he explained, knotting it tighter than was necessary as I struggled weakly.

"Your Master will be rather less than pleased with you for making him appear the fool." Peter held me up so the same procedure could be used on my legs. The pain of my ankle was overwhelming as the wire was tightened, but Mayfair didn't appear concerned.

Peter let go and I fell to the floor. I didn't make a sound. Quentin stood over me. "I fear that you shall regret your resistance. We may not harm you, but tonight you shall belong to Him."

I concentrated on lying perfectly still. Finally, he turned away and continued with whatever task I had interrupted. When he was finished, he motioned for Peter to lift me again.

At the end of the ordinary cellar, was a very ordinary looking brick wall. Mayfair touched it and it swung in revealing a dark opening. The tunnel led through a series of natural caves, from what I could see. We went on, our way lit by torches set in the walls at intervals until we were in a huge cavern. Here the stone altar was part of the natural cave formation and very impressive. Peter laid me down on the cold hard surface roughly.

"It is here, my Lady, that He shall come to take you. When The Lord of Dark has finished with you, your Master and I will be given our turn."

I shivered in the cold as my hands and feet were unbound and shackled to chains set at the four corners.

"Do not struggle, my Lady. This place is part of Him. There is no escape from here. You are held now in His Hand." He touched my face and my breast. "Someone will be along shortly to prepare you further."

Peter settled himself to watch over me as Mayfair left. This time I knew he wouldn't sleep.

Chapter Twenty Three
As Above

I had a very quick, though blessedly hot shower, after which the doctor on call strapped my shoulder up tight, as well as my left wrist, which had been sprained pretty badly. I was able to borrow some clothes from one of the operatives still legitimately working for the Institute. I was supposedly retired to teach. I was beginning to suspect that everything had fallen very aptly exactly the way Sir had planned it. He was not above dangling Tary and me for bait. However that was, he was certainly trying his best to help me now,

"We sealed off the area immediately, Doctor, but there is no sign of them. I have alerted all our branches around the world, wired your wife's photograph as well as Dr. Mayfair's and Mr. Dennings'. Someone will catch a glimpse of them sooner or later. Men like that are not used to keeping a low profile. Their needs are excessive. Eventually, it will gall them and they'll slip up."

"Oh, I see. And in the meantime it's just too bad about poor Tary, is it? Who cares what she's being put through, eh? And, Sir, need I remind you that for all practical purposes, they have all three of the symbols." I was fast losing my temper. I knew he was doing everything he could, but it wasn't good enough. Tary was out there somewhere.

"I know what you're feeling, Doctor, and I'm sorry she had to get in the middle of this. But you were warned repeatedly, warned about..."

I jumped to my feet and leaned as far over the desk as I could. Pushing my face right into his I spoke very softly, but with a barely controlled rage I was certain he'd appreciate.

"Now you see here you son of a bitch, and don't give me that crap about knowing how I feel, because you don't! Tary means everything to me, and it's my fault and yours, that she's in this mess. I don't believe you have ever loved anyone or anything in your miserable life, Sir, so you couldn't possibly have any inkling about what is motivating me now. Whatever you are doing is not enough. I want you to do more; I want you to pull men from wherever they are. Tary can't afford to wait until they slip up. You don't know what these people are capable of Sir. I do. I was there. It's gotten personal."

He said nothing; just let me go on until I'd got it all out of my system. When I sat back down he looked at me. "Are you quite finished, Doctor?"

I nodded silently, feeling a little ashamed. In truth I was the guiltiest party here and I just needed someone to share that guilt with me. "I have to get her back, Sir David," I choked. I had never felt so helpless and miserable in my life.

He nodded. "We will, Arthur."

There was a knock at the door, and new assistant entered. "Sir? They have Jennifer Morris here as you ordered."

"Yes, bring her in," he replied gruffly.

She was handcuffed. Stripped of her veneer of sophistication; the fancy clothing and make-up, her hair hanging in thin wisps around her face, she looked so young, so vulnerable. I stood to give her my chair.

She couldn't meet my eyes. "You wanted to see me Sir?"

"Jen," I started, as gently as I could. "Is there someplace to start? Somewhere they would have gone to as a jumping off point?" Jenny is one of those women who can cry without their eyes getting all red and swollen, or their noses running. She was doing it now, quietly, prettily, silently sobbing. It really annoyed me.

"Will you cut out the blubbering and listen to me!" She turned her eyes to meet mine. "Is there anywhere at all, Jen? We have to start somewhere. You're Tary's only hope. Please, Jen, help me,"

She nodded. "Bring me a map, Yorkshire to Scotland."

Sir rang for a map.

"We have temples here and here," she was pointing. They'll want to get to the North Sea. From there they will have a boat waiting to take them to Geneva. There are safe houses all along the route as I've marked."

I shook my head. "It will be too risky to travel overland the entire length of Britain, and it will take them too long. They must realise that they can't go by Rail, and we have roadblocks set everywhere. Sir, is there a dowser available to go over the route?"

We'd been at it for nearly an hour. The injection Mayfair had administered was working for me now, keeping me on my feet long past any level of normal endurance. It couldn't last, though. Eventually it would wear off, and I'd be in for a nasty crash. That wouldn't be for hours yet, perhaps as long as twenty-four. For now I was ironically grateful.

"I will send it down to the lab and have someone go over it with a pendulum, Doctor." The phone rang. "Yes?" Sir answered. . Excellent! Have her brought as quickly as you can." He listened, nodding. "Bring everything along, then. We'll sort it all out here."

I looked at him expectantly as he hung up the receiver.

"They've got Marge Kelly. She was still at Mayfair's clinic when our people moved in. I'm having her transferred here for interrogation." He raised his eyebrows. "You will want to be involved?"

I had to bite down hard to try and keep my face calm as I remembered Miss Kelly's part in Tary's abduction and torment.

"Yes, Sir. I want to be involved."

"I thought you might, Doctor. There is just one detail."

"What is that?" I had to ask the question, already knowing the answer.

"Your resignation. You no longer have any official standing." He stared at me and I knew what he wanted. I sighed.

"All right, Sir, you've got me. I'll sign."

He pulled the contract from his top drawer and slid it across the desk to me. I glanced at it briefly. It was the standard form, outlining the Official Secrets Act etceteras and so forth. It was dated five days ago. The last time he had pushed it across this desk to me, I'd pushed it right back. This time, I signed it.

He handed me my new identification.

"You realise this is blackmail?" I commented, putting the new card away in my wallet.

"Not at all," he replied the corners of his mouth twitching. "I believe extortion would more closely describe it. Now, shall we get on with it?"

By the time Miss Kelly was brought, held in an interrogation room, we'd gone over every inch of the map, marked every temple and safe house, and every possible overland route available. Sir David issued orders to have them all covered and sent the map down to the psychometry lab.

The new assistant came in, carrying a small cardboard box as Jen was led away. "They said you'd want this," she said, placing it on the desk.

Sir nodded, "Thank you, Helen."

When she was gone, he glanced into the box and pushed it towards me. "I think you will want to return those to your wife, Doctor."

Inside were all her things. Her passport lay on top of the jewellery; rings and pendants; her earrings, a yo-yo. Even her pocket knife and mini-screw-driving set were there, all packed neatly in a cardboard box. I reached out my hand and touched them. I took her little pentacle on the delicate chain and slipped it into my pocket. It made me feel more connected to her somehow.

"Yes, Sir. Thank you." Helen returned and handed me Tary's walking stick and I had to choke back my tears. "Any chance of getting Brian O'Connell here?" I asked, knowing he was the best psychometrist the Institute had. Sir nodded.

A QUESTION OF BALANCE

"Helen, contact New York and see what can be arranged. In the meantime find out who we currently have available in London and get them here." Sir David stood.

"Come, we want to see Miss Kelly. You may leave her things here. No one will disturb them."

I got up silently and followed him out.

Marge Kelly didn't seem in the least cowed or intimidated by her present circumstance. She was sitting quite calmly at the table, her hands folded demurely. I could see nothing but a faint mockery in her eyes as I walked in behind Sir David.

"So nice to see you again Miss Kelly. I'm pleased to be able to offer you my hospitality in return for the kindness you showed to me and to my wife." I smiled as I took a seat opposite her.

She looked at Sir David, 'I'm sorry, am I supposed to know this man?"

"Come, come, now Miss Kelly, Marge. We're old friends you and I. May I present David Marshall?" I leaned over to whisper in her ear. "He's the boss around here, Marge."

Ignoring me, she continued to address herself to Sir. "I have no idea why I'm being held here against my will. As I told the gentlemen who brought me here I will say nothing until I've been permitted to contact the American Consulate."

"That's not very friendly, Marge," I said. I got up and walked around her putting my arm on the back of her chair. "And not very clever either. You see, no one knows you're here. We're not the official police or anything like that. No report. No telephone call. You don't even exist, do you Marge?" I saw an instant of doubt in her eyes, then it was gone. She sneered at me.

"I'm a citizen of the United States of America. You can't keep me here, not without charging me with something."

"Can't Marge? Can't you say? There's no such word as can't!" I looked at Sir. "Sir, would we illegally detain a foreign national? A citizen in good standing of the United States, for example?"

He snorted and sat down "Miss Kelly," he began. "We would not dream of detaining you against your will. All we need are answers to some very simple questions and you are free to go."

"I am not answering anything. I wish to call the consulate,"

Sir sighed. "I'm afraid you are making this very awkward for me. You see, we need answers quickly, and we cannot afford to wait until all the diplomatic protocols have been observed. I believe you can assist us in our inquiries. I will do whatever is necessary to secure your co-operation. If that entails requiring that a Marge Kelly be free to return to the U.S., we can arrange for that. But I assure you, Miss Kelly, it will not be you. Since you refuse to assist, I have no other alternative than to treat you as a threat to National Security. It is well within my power to do so. In order to preserve the diplomatic amenities, I will also arrange for Marge Kelly to appear to leave England unimpeded, then disappear quietly somewhere back in America."

For a few minutes she sat there, silently thinking it over.

"He really can you know, Miss Kelly," I added quietly. "And you won't enjoy my hospitality any more than I enjoyed yours."

"Is that a threat, Doctor?" Her eyes flashed.

"HA! So you do remember me! No, Miss Kelly, that is a promise." I returned to my seat opposite her.

"May I offer you something? Some tea before we get started?" Asked Sir solicitously.

I objected. "Oh, no! I'm certain Miss Kelly doesn't want anything to eat? Or to drink? Do you? Why, I've known her to go for days without so much as a drop of water or a crumb! Oh, now wait. I'm terribly sorry. That wasn't you, was it Marge. No, I remember, it was Tary, wasn't it! Well, as they say, tit for tat."

"You don't frighten me, Doctor. England is a civilised country. You won't be permitted to..."

"Marge, I'm not asking anybody's permission, am I?" I brought my face in close to her. "If something very bad happens to my wife while we're sitting here playing games, I can promise you that the very same thing will happen to you. You are not here in any official way. Your consulate doesn't know you're here, the police don't know you re here. And I promise you, I'm not feeling so very civilised just at the moment. A hard day of torture does that to me sometimes." I think I had her attention.

"Where would Dennings have taken her?"

"I don't know. Probably to Dr. Mayfair's residence." She was being coy.

"Uh, Marge, that was the very first place we checked. Where would be your next logical guess, eh?"

She looked at me, and then at Sir. "I'd look in Geneva."

I got up and went to the door, "Fletcher? Would you come in here a moment, please? And see if you can find Maxwell."

I sat down. "Now tell me, Miss Kelly? How do you think he'd get to Geneva?"

She shrugged. "How would I know?"

"Oh, but I think you do know. Wherever he's gone he's got my wife with him. Now tell me, how would he get to Geneva?"

Miss Kelly smiled coldly at me.

"Your wife, Doctor, is nothing more than Dennings' plaything. She's been taken and marked. There is no power on Earth that can break his hold on her now. The last time I spoke to her about it, she actually seemed quite pleased with the idea of being his slut!"

The only excuse I can offer is that I was under considerable strain as well as the influence of Mayfair's drugs. I was in pain, not thinking clearly or rationally and my emotions were running out of control. I reached over and slapped the smile from her face. I was just getting my hands around her throat when Fletcher rushed in with Maxwell. It wasn't a ploy; not a 'good cop—bad cop scenario', as they call it in American cinema. I simply lost it. It took the two of them to get me off her.

"Take him outside," growled Sir.

They did.

"Doctor. If you kill her, we'll never get any answers out of her." It was Max's voice, strangely soft and gentle from such a big man. I stopped struggling and leaned my head against the wall.

"I've got to get a grip on myself."

Fletcher nodded his head in full agreement, "Go with Max and get a cuppa. You'll feel better. That's what my mum always said." He nodded his head in the direction of the interrogation room. "I'll see what I can get out of her. Come back in an hour."

"All right." I pressed my hands to my eyes. For some reason they were watering. "Come on Maxwell."

Fletcher stood at the door to the room and gave me a thumbs up, then he went in, closing the door behind him. He was a good man; one of the best. I followed Max back to Sir David's office,

Helen brought in a pot of tea and some scones, but I wasn't hungry. It had been some time since I'd eaten though, so I forced myself to take a few bites. The telephone on the huge desk rang and was answered elsewhere, presumably by Sir's new assistant. She knocked softly at the door and entered.

"Doctor will you pick up two please? It's Mr. Rollison from the New York Office on the wire.

I grabbed the phone. "Rolly! Hello?"

"Yes, Doctor?"

"It's me Rolly."

He paused for a moment, then spoke. "Is there any word on Tarish yet?"

The connection was crystal clear and I could hear the real concern in his voice through the miracle of digital technology.

"No, Rolly. Nothing yet. We've got one of the ringleaders though, Marge Kelly. Sir's questioning her now."

"How are you?"

I knew what he meant. He wanted to know how I was holding up emotionally.

A Question of Balance

"Oh, I'm okay, I guess. Had a bit of a stretch, be stiff as the devil in the morning I dare say, but I'll live." I thought for a moment. "I don't know, Rolly. Confused, worried? No, Rolly, you know me better than that. I'm terrified old friend. Terrified that I've gotten the only..." My voice caught in my throat as I struggled to go on. "...that I got Tary into something I won't be able to get her out of in one piece."

"We've been all through this, Arthur. She was involved already, you know that. Remember, you didn't give her the Crown. It's what drew her to you. She could have said no."

He was trying to help, I knew that, but I don't think there was anything that could have helped me at that moment. Quickly I wiped my eyes and took a deep breath.

"So, anything on your end?"

"Possibly. Brian took a troll-doll that Tary had given you from your desk ."

My heart started beating faster. "What a good idea, Rolly! Did he get anything?"

"I'll let him tell you..." He handed the phone to Brian.

"Brian here, Doctor. I can't be very specific, unfortunately. Tary is being extensively shielded."

I nodded. "I would have expected something of the sort. Were you able to get anything Brian? Anything at all?"

"There was a sense of deep, heavy darkness. I'm pretty sure she's underground, a mine or a cave, somewhere cold and damp. I think she's okay physically at least." He hesitated, then pressed on. "Arthur, there is something else. Some thing has a hold on her that I can't break through..."

"I know Brian. " I said softly, understanding that he was sensing the mark Dennings' had placed upon my wife. "Thank you, my friend, this may help."

Rolly came back on the line.

"We were able to get the New York State police to co-operate with Interpol and our operatives. We made a surprise move on the Dennings estate. You can imagine what we found. It's going to be difficult to keep it quiet. You know how the press loves a sensational story, and this one has it all. Sex, drugs, black magic, child abuse, white slavery, BDS&M, everything for a good Sunday supplement."

"Yes." I could imagine very well. "Anything to link him to Tary and me?"

"Plenty, Arthur. He had a book filled with clippings of stuff she'd written for those magazines of hers and several of your published papers too."

"It's interesting, but not very incriminating. Anything else?"

"Yeah, some pictures. Mostly of her, but there were a couple of the two of you. Looked like they were taken with a powerful long distance lens. It proves he was having her watched anyway. Oh, and we also found a silk bag. There was a tiny scrap of cloth inside and a button, all tied with black thread. Know what that's all about?"

I smiled. "He was probably trying to do a binding. If that was it, it wasn't very successful. Of course, something personal of hers would have helped; a lock of her hair, or nail clipping. He wasn't likely to get those, though. She was always very careful about that. Never let anyone else cut her hair or give her a manicure. Did it herself, at home."

"As it turns out, it was very wise of her, Doctor."

"I always told her she was being silly." For a moment I was silent, then I thought of something. "Do me a favour and put somebody on her family for me. Her son Jason especially. You have the address?"

"Already done, my friend. Anything else?"

"Not that I can think of at the moment. Maybe a prayer or two? Call me if something turns up."

"Of course, Arthur. Give Tary my love, when you find her. Arthur, take care of yourself."

"Yeah, Rolly, I will. Thanks." I rang off. God, it was good to talk to him again. We were close; he was probably closest thing I had in the world to a best friend besides Tary. I stood up and stretched a bit, trying to loosen up. Then settled my left arm carefully in the sling Max had provided. Everything

A QUESTION OF BALANCE

was beginning to ache now, and that, I was sure, was just the beginning.

"Come on, Maxwell Let's go see how Fletcher is getting on with Miss Kelly."

I knocked on the door of the interrogation room and entered. I thought she was looking less smug. At the sight of me, though, she balked.

"Keep him away from me! Get him out of here, he's crazy, he'll kill me!" she actually sounded afraid, which set me to wondering what I must have looked like coming at her that way. I grinned in what I hoped was a threatening manner.

"Kill you? I wouldn't dream of killing you my dear Miss Kelly. You wouldn't be able to talk to me then, not without a medium anyway." Sir looked at me.

"Are you quite in control of yourself now, Doctor?"

I nodded.

"Good, Then let me bring you up to date." He rewound the tape on the machine and played it back.

As she listened, Marge Kelly paled. I didn't blame her. If Dennings or Mayfair ever found out how much she had spilled, her life wouldn't be worth the match they'd use to strike the pyre. I, on the other hand, took a moment to savour that picture in my mind. The tape stopped.

"That's it? Nothing else?" I said, disappointment sticking in my throat. She had spilled a lot about the Order, maybe enough to bring in another three or four of it's leaders operating in England and Western Europe and a half dozen or so in the U.S., but she'd told us nothing about where Dennings might be now with Tary.

"Sir, may I please have a few minutes with Miss Kelly... alone?"

He stood and nodded

"No! You're not going to leave me with him? He'll kill me, I say!" She was near panic. "I've told you all I know, everything. I have no idea where they are. He didn't tell me. I was to go with him, I was to be his consort. He was going to make me young again, restore my beauty. But then he became obsessed with that little tramp..." she stopped, suddenly realising what she was saying and to whom.

I kept my face calm, but I took her arm and squeezed with my good hand. "And who was that, the person he so taken with, Marge?"

She scarcely breathed.

"Answer me!" I gave her arm a twist.

"Stop, you're hurting me. You're breaking my arm!"

"I promise I'll break a good deal more than that if you don't tell me everything you know. Now, who was it he was so taken with that he was ready to replace you as Consort? Who was little tramp, Marge? Was it Tary, Marge? Is my wife the little tramp, Marge? Is she?"

Sir and Fletcher did nothing to interfere.

"What's the matter, Miss Kelly, no stomach for this sort of thing? Funny, I could have sworn you enjoyed pain. You certainly seemed to enjoy inflicting it on others. Now answer me!"

Her eyes filled with panic as she stared wildly around the room. "Aren't you going to stop him? Are you just going to stand there and watch?" She pleaded with Sir David. He looked at Max who gave him the OK sign. Then he looked at me.

"Miss Kelly is quite right, Doctor. I cannot stand here and watch." He nodded to Maxwell and Fletcher.

"Gentlemen?" The three of them left.

I was in complete control of myself now, at least complete enough. There was just the right amount of madness showing in my eyes, though, that she didn't know where I would finish. I tightened my grip on her arm and dragged her up from the chair, slamming her backward against the wall. All the breath went out of her in a hiss, and her eyes opened wide. I kept my hold on her as she slid down the wall to the floor, and yanked her back up again. I'd ever beat up anyone before and I didn't enjoy doing it now. I kept the image of Tary, choking with thirst, strapped helplessly in a chair, pawed at by

A Question of Balance

Thornhill while this bitch laughed and flirted with me in my mind. I wrapped the hatred around my heart and found the strength to carry on.

"Now, I shall try re-phrasing the question, Miss Kelly. Think carefully before you answer. Where would Dennings have taken you, if you were to made his Consort?"

Her pallor was corpse grey and her eyes almost retreated into her head. I slapped her and a trickle of blood oozed from her lip, but she said nothing. It smeared over my knuckles as I backhanded her again.

"Don't try to trance away on me Miss Kelly. I'm married to a witch, remember. Now answer me, where?"

"Bryn.." Her voice was a whisper. I pulled back my opened hand.

"I can't hear you, Marge. Where?"

"Bryn Gwyddyn, near Dan-Yr-Of, the caves." She flinched away from me, trying to shield her face with her arm. I let her go and she crumpled to the floor, whimpering.

For the first time in many days I felt my heart lighten a bit. That tracked with what Brian had sensed; caves. I knew she was telling me the truth.

"You are not fit to touch the ground she walks on, Miss Kelly. Thank you for the information. I'll be certain to give your regards to Mr. Dennings when I find him."

"Please no! You mustn't tell him. Please, you mustn't..." She was grappling for a hold on my leg hysterically.

"Oh? And why is that, Miss Kelly?"

"He'll torment me. He'll, he'll..."

"And why should I care what he does to you? You didn't seem to care much about Tarish or me for that matter. Why should I care what he may do to you?" I turned to the door.

"You care. I know you care. I know because I know your type, so kind, so moral, so insufferably good." Her voice had a hysterical quality and she made the word good sound like a slur. I looked down at her.

"Good? What do you mean, good?"

"You're not evil. You won't let him harm me. That is your weakness." She was sounding smug now. I stared at her, sadly. My hand was shaking, her blood drying in the creases of my knuckles.

"No, Miss Kelly, I am no better than you, I only try to be. I follow neither the dark, nor the light. I am a scientist; I merely seek the truth. Dennings may do with you as he pleases. I would not interfere." The sound of her terrified sobbing followed me as I walked down the corridor, wiping her blood on my handkerchief. She had told me what I needed to know.

"Well?" asked Sir, his eyes half closed as he reclined in his chair.

"Wales, Sir. That's where I believe they've taken her." I looked at my watch. "It's getting late. With your permission I'll take Maxwell and Fletcher. We can be there in a few hours."

"I'll arrange for a plane, Doctor. Time is of the essence." He picked up the telephone and made the arrangements. He nodded to me. "Maxwell and Fletcher are waiting for you with a car to get you to the airfield"

"Yes, Sir. Thank you Sir." I rose and walked to the door.

"I have you know... once a long time ago." His eyes were nearly closed as he lost himself in some memory.

"What, Sir?" With my hand on the knob, I turned back to stare at him.

"Have what once, Sir?"

"Loved."

I nodded and left for the airfield.

Chapter Twenty Four
So Below

It was cold in the cave, only around fifty. Even through the heavy sweater and trousers I shivered. My bare feet were like ice and I longed for a pair of woolen socks. The stone slab was rough and very hard. There were no furrows along this altar, no trough. Whatever was spilled upon its fell surface went directly to quench the thirst of the underworld.

Malcolm Dennings had not forgotten me this time. My mind was as fixed to this place and time as surely as my body, chained to the rock. There would be no escape, no refuge in fantasy. I was tied to whatever fate would befall me. Instead of feeling lost abandoned by my Gods or frightened of what was to come, I felt a kind of exultation. Where there's life, there's hope, and the Doctor yet lived. Although I realized that he'd been terribly hurt and was unlikely to be able to aid me, in the private recesses of my heart I knew that he would never abandon me. Simply knowing that Arthur was alive gave me strength. Regardless of what Dennings did, or permitted to be done, I would not give up the talismans of Power. Thinking of Arthur I began to formulate a nebulous plan. What I needed was an ally.

"Peter?" I tried to remember the exact nuances my husband used during hypnosis sessions. Peter glanced at me. He seemed very young dressed in blue jeans, with a sweat shirt and denim jacket. I thought he couldn't have been more than twenty, just a little older than my son.

"What makes someone want to follow such men as Dr. Mayfair or Mr. Dennings? You do not seem cruel by nature. I want to understand, please help me. Why have you chosen the left-hand path? What made you choose the Dark?"

I didn't think he would answer me, but he did.

"For love, Lady." He said it matter of factly.

"Love?" What was there to love, I wondered in this way of darkness.

"Yeah. My girl, Rose, she went to Dr. Mayfair's clinic when she was...I mean when I got her... He takes in girls what are in trouble see? Helps them out. Finds them homes for the babies and such. Anyway, he took her in and all. Gave her a home and love, even a job. Then, he took me too, so I could be with her. It was fine for a while, a good life. So if I have to pledge my soul for a chance to live now, I done it. He has Powers, Dr. Mayfair. I owe him everything. I pledged to him and to He Who Rules in Darkness. The world is going that way anyhow my Lady. It makes sense to be on the winning side for once in my life."

From his perspective, I supposed that it did. There were many young people, older people too for that matter, who might feel that way. People who, looking at the state of things in the world today, might want to be, as he had put it, on the winning side for once. I could see how they got hooked, and once hooked, they just got in too deep to think of leaving.

"Do you know what the Balance is, Peter? I don't mean to balance like on one foot. I'm talking about the universal Balance. The Balance between Good and Evil. Can you understand that..."

"Look, my Lady, I'm sorry. I never was very smart. Not clever, in school or nothing. I leave that to my betters. Muscle is what I'm good for." He looked away.

"Yes, like what you and your friend did to my husband in the Temple." I softened my voice to almost a whisper. "Do you enjoy that Peter? Hurting people, making them suffer? Did you enjoy hearing the Doctor scream while you tortured him?"

He answered thoughtfully. "Yeah, I do sometimes. Especially people like that Doctor. People

A Question of Balance

like that always telling a bloke he's no good. Can't learn, can't think, and never amount to anything. Well, Lady, I have amounted to something. Your husband respected me for what I done to him. I had the power over him. It was me not some stinking teacher or copper, just me. I guess I do like it sometimes, my Lady. Proves I am something, somebody."

He walked to me and I could see the gleam of fanaticism in his eyes. He was gone. "Now you, my Lady, I wouldn't want to hurt you."

Peter touched my face, then moved his hand under my sweater. This wasn't going the way I'd planned. "Peter, please don't."

"Don't worry Lady Tarish. I wouldn't hurt you. You belong to Mr. Dennings."

He groped for a few more seconds, then pulled the sweater up. I was freezing in the dampness of the cold air. Gently, he traced the mark Dennings had left. Then, he pulled the sweater back down covering me and took his seat.

"He doesn't you know." I tried to sound compelling.

"Doesn't what?"

"Find homes for the babies. Do you know what happens to them, Peter? What happened to your baby, the baby Rose bore you?" I closed my eyes and willed him to understand.

"Yes, Lady Tarish. I know. They be dedicated to the Dark One. They never have to live in this crummy world, like I do. They're lucky to be chosen." There was nothing more I could say. How many more were there like him? How many so full of despair and hopelessness that the death of new-born innocence seemed preferable to life? More than enough I guess. I'd never realized before that even in a so called enlightened society, people could be so burdened with the task of living that those sacrificed to a god of cruelty could seem the lucky ones.

I lay there in the flickering torch light for another hour in silence. Peter, it seemed had nothing more to say, and I couldn't think of anything. I wondered where Arthur was and prayed for his recovery. Anything Dennings said was suspect. He twisted truth with words to his own ends. In my mind, I replayed those last few minutes in the Temple, Arthur's agonized screams. I must have fainted. There were gaps in my memory. I could remember the screaming and then suddenly being rushed underground. I thought carefully. He'd been shouting after them as they dragged me away saying something about there being no place they could run. He'd been trying to stop them. That's right. I remembered there were gunshots, the sound of wood splintering as a door was smashed in. Someone had rescued Arthur! The memory made me laugh out loud. Even trussed like a Christmas goose in a butcher's window, the Doctor had been warning them not to try to escape.

My laughter didn't last long before Malcolm came to gloat over me. There was a young woman with him, dressed in a simple black wool tunic, with dagged sleeves that reached nearly to the floor.

"My Lady, in truth I didn't expect to find you in such good humor!" He reached for the straps around my wrists. "This is Lady Mountcalm. She is a skilled cosmetologist, and has kindly consented to assist in your preparation."

Peter came and held me as Malcolm pulled the sweater over my head. I was shivering uncontrollably, my breath forming steam in the air. Lady Mountcalm took a long red robe from the bag she'd carried in, and slipped it on me. It wrapped around fastening in the front with three large baroque buttons and tied with a sash. As each arm was inserted into a sleeve, the strap was once more buckled securely. Next, my legs were loosed, the trousers pulled off and the robe pulled down over me. Then my ankles too were again fastened tightly. I did nothing to resist as they worked. There was little point. I couldn't hope to outrun them on my bad leg, even if I did somehow manage to get loose.

When the robe had been arranged to everyone's satisfaction, Malcolm came and sat on the stone, supporting my head so Lady Mountcalm could work. She applied heavy make-up deftly, professionally, while Peter held a large electric lamp to light my features.

"She's pretty, Malcolm, though not the sort you usually favor," she commented as she worked. "What is she, thirty five at least?"

I bristled. In fact I was nearly forty, but I could pass for thirty-one or thirty-two easily enough. Sometimes people couldn't believe I had a son of nearly seventeen. I suddenly realized that on the verge of being raped by a fanatical and utterly ruthless man, I was vain enough to be insulted about looking my age.

Dennings chuckled. "What she is, my dear Marcia, is the holder of the Crown of Fae and the Key of Enlightenment. She is also mine."

"Yes," she said, running her fingers through the tangle of my hair. "I suppose that would be some compensation."

"Compensation?" I blurted. "Who the bloody hell do you think you are, you ignorant..." Dennings interrupted me.

"Shh, Tary. Lady Mountcalm is used to working in the high fashion industry. She doesn't mean anything personal my dear. These are merely her professional observations. Besides you have more important things to occupy your mind at the moment, don't you?"

I did.

He leaned over and kissed me when she was through. "You are quite pretty, Tary. Very presentable with the proper accents applied professionally."

Turning to Marcia he complimented her. "A splendid job, my dear. I can see your reputation is well earned. She is lovely."

Marcia smiled. "Thank you, Malcolm. Actually, she does have good bones. Nice facial structure."

I wondered how long my 'good bones' would last under the kind of punishment I expected to take tonight.

"You can find your own way out can't you my dear? I would like some time with Lady Tarish before the others arrive."

"Certainly, Malcolm. Peter can show me the way, can't he?" She was looking the young man over with undisguised lust.

"Oh yes take Peter by all means." Malcolm smiled expansively. "I have her well under my control. Come back and bring food and drink my boy, after you have shown our guest out."

Peter nodded and the two left. Dennings and I were alone. He looked down at me.

"You truly are lovely, Tarish." He bent to kiss me and I turned my face away. "I will have you just one time more before you are sullied by anyone else. The last time you weren't really with me you know. I didn't like to complain it being our first time, and besides, it made it so much easier to place my mark." He carefully undid the three buttons and released the sash, parting the robe.

My skin erupted in gooseflesh at his cold touch. I shivered, and tried to pull away from him. There was some slack in the chains, enough for me to get my arms a little in front of me and to bend my knees a bit. I struggled. This time there was no way for me to retreat to my private place.

Dennings knew it and was enjoying what meager resistance I was able to offer. In the end I was forced to endure him, but I hadn't made it easy. There were new scratches on his face alongside the old ones I'd given him earlier. Instead of making him angry, though, they only seemed to excite him. He made a point of 'anointing' me again with the freshly drawn blood.

When he was finished, he covered me and fastened the robe. Reaching into the pocket of his own garment, he pulled out a pack of cigarettes and lit one.

"I didn't know you smoked." I said.

He smiled. "I don't. This is for you, Tary. I am a civilized man, after all." He held it to my lips, and I inhaled the smoke gratefully. When it was done, he stubbed it out and placed the filter carefully in the pack.

"As you have no doubt heard me explain you are to be symbolically taken by Him tonight, although naturally I shall portray the God in the actual performance of the act. It will be a bit more violent than what just occurred, I'm afraid, but one must keep to the spirit of the thing. Then, of course, Quentin will take his turn.

I let my lips curl into a mocking smile. "You will be able to perform again? Really, Malcolm, I would have thought you were passed your prime."

His eyes narrowed at that and I was gratified. It was the first time anything I'd said seemed to disturb him in the least.

"I assure you, dear Tary," he said, lifting my chin, "that I am more than up to the task." He turned and walked away somewhere behind me. He came back carrying an oblong shape wrapped in silk cradled in his arms.

"As I had started to explain, my dear, you will become one of us this night, willing or not." He set the thing down on the altar and unwrapped it.

It was a long gold box, encrusted with gems, all of which looked real to me. With a tiny key, he unlocked the box. He lifted the lid and held it so I could see inside.

"Behold, Lady Tarish, our Holy Grail. After you have drunk of the innocence contained within the sacred vessel you shall be truly another of his brides. It will of course be blended with certain drugs to keep you quiescent. Then you will be entrusted into my surrogate care for the rest of your life."

I stared not believing what he said. The thing inside the box was obscene; a mocking parody of a sacred chalice made of gleaming solid gold. Like the box, it too was encrusted with fiery gems that glittered fiendishly in the torchlight like eyes. A gross animal stench rose from the interior. He tilted the case to let me see inside. By the flickering firelight I could make out dark, crusted stains left by the blood of innocents. The psychic shock stunned me to my bones. I pulled away as far as the chains would permit, from the horror that lay in the jeweled box. My chest was heaving convulsively and I was nauseated at the prospect of being forced to drink from it.

Dennings laughed. "I am told that it is an experience no one may ever forget, or willingly repeat. It is a very rare honor, my Lady."

"No, you can't do that to me. Please, Malcolm, you can't do that to me." I was ashamed to hear myself begging, but I was horrified at the thoughts of what it would do to me.

"Oh but I can, dear Tary. Dr. Mayfair and I will have you, however, the others will have to make do with a substitute. There is a rather pretty little thing being prepared. A young girl really, a virgin not yet fourteen. She will be used in your stead by our small and very select gathering. You will be permitted to watch, of course, as she shall watch your dedication. At the climax her throat will be cut. Not dramatically, but an adequate incision in the carotid artery. Her blood will be collected in the sacred cup I have shown you and mixed with various herbs, including a powerful psychotropic Dr. Mayfair has been experimenting with." His eyes were fever-bright.

"Then, Tary, this cup will be offered to you, and I assure you, you will drink. I warn you dear one, you will be mine one way or another. You must choose to come willingly or I shall break your mind as well as your spirit." He shrugged. "The girl's life will be spared if possible, and kept for other purposes. She is young and strong. I don't believe in unnecessary waste.

I spat in his face and sneered. "No kind of real power needs to resort to drugs, you sick bastard! Why must you ruin another innocent life? I would rather you give me to your rotten coven. I understand life! I have lived, been happy. What happiness can a young girl just on the threshold of womanhood expect from your lot? Or do you just enjoy watching people destroyed?"

A Question of Balance

He wiped his cheek with the sleeve of his robe, and stood back a step. Then, he clapped his hands together three times.

"Oh, well and nobly spoken, Tary. You would sacrifice yourself to save the destruction of another innocent soul. Is that it?"

I met his eyes realizing how corny it sounded. "Something like that."

He grinned. "This is going to be a true pleasure, my lady, even more so than I'd hoped. I do, you see, enjoy watching innocence destroyed, Tary. In my world, the one I shall create, there will be no room for innocence."

My face was trapped between his hands. "I do so enjoy a good self sacrifice, as well. Perhaps something can be arranged, my dear. Perhaps this sweet innocent child may be spared her part in your ordeal. We shall see, when the time comes, how far you are willing to bargain."

Peter entered bearing a tray. He had changed into long black robes for the ritual. Malcolm turned.

"Ah good. I see we are offered some sandwiches and tea." He gestured to the acolyte. "Put it here, please, Peter then go and sit. I shall call if I want you."

I am embarrassed to say that I was famished. In spite of everything, my emotional turmoil had stimulated my appetite. I couldn't remember the last time I'd eaten. Besides, I reasoned, starving myself would only work in Dennings favor. I had to keep up my strength so I would be ready if and when a chance to escape presented itself. I held on to that.

Dennings seemed surprised to see me eat everything he offered. But he said nothing, as he continued to place small bits of sandwich into my mouth.

The tea was weak but it was hot and I drank it all, grateful for the warmth. When everything was gone he replaced the cup on the tray.

"I will be back shortly, my love, with the rest of our guests. I am going now to get the Book." He patted my cheek. "You will wait for me? I won't be long."

I shrugged. "I don't know, Master. Perhaps Peter can be convinced to run away with me."

Malcolm chuckled. "Oh, I don't think so my dear. He knows that I can find you instantly. He understands the power of my mark even if you have not yet learned."

He picked up the tray and was gone.

For a few minutes I stared at the gold box left upon the altar near my feet. Then I closed my eyes. Yes, I was frightened, but not so frightened that I would let myself give in to the helplessness of unreasoning terror. I knew what I had to be afraid of, and it was very real. At the best, I would be raped and abused repeatedly by the two men, humiliated, forced to drink human blood, kept drugged. At the worst I would be the direct cause of a young girl's sacrifice, my mind shattered and my body used until I died. In the end Malcolm would have what he wanted and I knew I would not be allowed to die easily. Either way I would be subjected to a humiliation and degradation seldom imagined by normal people in day to day life.

Somehow, thinking this way helped me prepare to deal with my situation. My real fear was that Dennings would force me to place the price of a young girl's soul on the Power of the talismans. I realized also, that so long as I was held in the grip of his enchantment, I would not be permitted to use that Power again. I felt I stood at the edge of a precipice. Silently I prayed to Hecate, dark Goddess of crossroads, that my decisions would be the right ones.

Peter was quiet, though I caught him watching me curiously when he thought I wasn't looking.

"Are you and Rose still together?" I asked. I was partly curious, and partly just wanted to hear another human voice. The whole weight of the Earth seemed to be pressing down on me where I lay entombed.

A Question of Balance

"No. She's gone on to more important work in the Order."

"Oh, I see. Hear from her at all?"

For a moment, I thought he was going to say something, but he must have thought better of it. Instead, he turned away and stared at the uneven rocky wall of the cavern. That made me wonder exactly what kind of 'important work' his Rose was doing. Perhaps she was another of the sacrificed innocents. I pulled at the chains in frustration. How could I fight them alone? How could I save all the innocents when I couldn't even save myself?

There are very few groups like the Order, who outwardly follow the left-hand path. Far fewer than you might imagine from reading the tabloid press. Although devil worship has been bit of a fad in the U.S. and England, most of the teenagers caught up in it outgrow the fad as I had outgrown my hula-hoop. A very few commit suicide or murder, or both, in a misguided longing to be united with the Dark God of Hell. Those are the ones who make headlines. Only a small handful graduate into organizations such as the Order.

In our modern culture, such Evil as exists in the invisible realm has been relegated, along with magic, to the backwaters of superstition. As man slowly begins to understand in small measure the mechanics of the Universe around him through his science, he is robbing himself of the wonder and the awe. This works very well for those who practice the Black Arts. Who can warn against a threat that to any rational modern mind, cannot possibly exist? There lies the greatest danger of all, and I was caught up in it.

Peter stood and moved to the end of the cavern where I knew the entrance to the tunnel leading to the house was. From a distance, I could hear the sound of chanting echo through the lesser caves along the route to this one. It was hauntingly beautiful, but I knew it signaled the beginning of the ordeal.

I closed my eyes and tried to steady my breathing, to still my racing heart. They could do whatever they liked to my Earthly body, but I prayed with every fiber of my being that I would be able to remain master of my soul. Quietly I chanted, matching the cadence to the chant floating on the air currents, using their power to fuel my own incantation.

"Hecate, grant to me the power of the crone.
Maha Kali, protect me with your many swords,
Nut, grant that my words may hold true power.
Cerridwyn, keep me safe within the cauldron of Eternity."

Dr. Mayfair entered first, leading a small figure on a leash, like a dog. She was robed in white, heavily veiled, with her hands chained in front of her like a prisoner standing in the dock. He led her straight to the altar where I could see her and she could see me. Carefully, he lifted the veil. It was a tiny, frightened heart-shaped face that stared at me, terror standing stark in huge brown eyes. Her pupils were tiny dots, and I assumed she, like Arthur, had been drugged to remain conscious for every lurid detail of her torture and rape.

Her dark eyes locked on mine as she whispered, "Please, Miss, he said you could save me. Don't let them hurt me anymore, please. I want to go home Miss." The voice was high, terrified and came in dry sobs.

Peter came behind the girl and took the leash from Mayfair. He jerked her roughly to the head of the stone slab. She was forced to her knees, the end of the chain fastened into a bracket fixed into the stone near my head so she wouldn't miss a single aspect of my rape. I lifted myself up as far as I could, turning my head awkwardly to see. I watched mutely as her hands were released, then each wrist chained to the opposing ankle as she kneeled on the hard stone of the cavern floor. Her robe, like mine, was fastened in the front.

I turned back to Mayfair who was watching, a sick grin fixed to his face.

A Question of Balance

"Why this? Why her? What has this child ever done to deserve this horror?"

His grin widened as he touched me intimately. "You are quite right, my Lady. She is not deserving of so great an honor, however, one must make do."

I flinched away from his hand, but he just smiled cruelly and turned his attention momentarily to the girl.

A small group of robed and hooded people had quietly assembled around the cavern, forming a semi-circle in front of the altar. They stood chanting softly, the music floating ethereally upon the cool air. I pulled at the chains, as Mayfair turned and began to unfasten my robe.

"Stop, leave me alone! Where is Dennings? Where is Malcolm Dennings?" Though Dennings' touch was certainly not to my liking, he at least had not the streak of sadism I knew was hidden behind Dr. Mayfair's eyes.

"He is coming, Lady Tarish. He is preparing himself. I am merely to ready you." He worked the robe opened to my feet, and roughly parted my legs.

Naturally I struggled trying to clamp my knees together. There was no way I would willingly submit to what was coming. Everyone's attention was suddenly diverted from me and I turned my eyes to see.

It must have been Malcolm Dennings, but I couldn't tell. The man who approached was naked save for a soft leather cloth knotted around his loins. He wore an ornately jeweled and adorned mask, huge horns jutting out to either side. It looked Egyptian, sort of like a depiction of the jackal-headed Anubis, with Minoan horns. The outrageous figure approached and I struggled against my chains, panicked at the sight of the abomination moving toward me.

Mayfair was having trouble holding me in position, so he gestured and two of the hooded figures detached from the semi-circle and came to each side at the foot of the altar. My knees were pried apart and held down firmly. The rough stone lacerated my back through the thin robe as I thrashed uselessly. I watched Dennings in his guise as the Dark God, lift the golden box and open it. A collective sigh went through those assembled as he took the cup from it's case and held it aloft supporting it with two hands. The poor child chained behind my head gasped and moaned in terror as Peter groped at her.

"Behold", he intoned, walking around the circle so each could examine it closely. It was even more hideous than it had looked in the box, and my struggles became frenzied.

Mayfair's eyes had gone. He licked at his lips, playing with the sash of his robe. Some small part of me was thinking that he'd never make it to his part in this little ritual. Then my attention was all on Dennings again as he moved to place the chalice on the stone behind my head. He set it down and smoothed the hair from my face as the young girl struggled. Beneath the mask I could see his eyes, pale and passionless. He turned and took something from a disciple standing at his back, Peter, I think. It was the Grimoir of Infinity.

Holding it aloft in his hands he cried out. "Behold the Book of our fulfilment, the Infinite Grimoir, receptacle of such mystery as mortal man has never before been permitted to know!"

For a moment he held it opened in his hand. Then, he closed it and turned to me.

"Will you Lady Tarish, Priestess of Cerridwyn and Cernunnos, release to me the Two? The Key of Enlightenment and the Crown of Fae, that I may unlock and direct the Power?"

I stopped struggling for a moment, feeling the skin of my back broken and raw. Lifting my head as far as I could, I cried out, intoning and vibrating the words to lend them power.

"Never shall you wield the Power I hold. In the name of Cerridwyn and by all the ancient gods of Earth, this I do swear."

He nodded. It was no more than he'd expected. Once before we'd played out this scene, though at that time I wasn't aware of all the rules. Even then, that black cold night in New York, I'd refused to give them up. I hadn't changed my mind.

Slowly, he handed It back to the man behind him.

"Then we shall begin your dedication, my Lady."

I began my struggles again, screaming at him to stop. He lifted himself up to the foot of the stone altar positioning himself over me as I was held down. I heard the young girl shriek as Mayfair fumbled with her robes, tearing at the poor child's garments while Peter held her steady. A gleaming knife appeared in Dennings' hand and I felt a cold metallic shape under his loin cloth press urgently against my thighs.

"Malcolm, please, this won't do any good. You'll never have the Key and the Crown. Please, please don't do this thing. At least let the girl go. Oh Goddess, let her go!" I thrashed wildly as Malcolm's mouth came down suddenly over my own smothering me. The girl's terrified screams filled my ears.

Suddenly chaos erupted in the cavern as bright lights split the soft flickering of the torches. The two men holding my legs let go, and I clamped them together, pulling myself upward as far from Dennings as I could. My back was bloody by now, I could feel it soaking through the robe, but it was a small enough discomfort, all things considered.

Malcolm tore the mask off his head and turned toward the sound of booted feet on the stone floor. I picked up my head and cried out joyfully as I spied Arthur looking around the cavern, searching frantically for me.

"Here, I'm here!" I had meant to shout, but Dennings placed a finger upon my breast and the words died before leaving my lips. He whispered something as he stepped to the floor and I felt very heavy. I couldn't lift my head, or move any part of me at all. Arthur had spotted me though, and was running toward the altar. Dennings held up a hand.

"Stop there, Doctor Pendargroom. Tarish bears my mark. I control her now. If you touch her, I have commanded her heart to stop."

He stopped, his face torn with longing and desperation.

"Release her, Dennings. Remove the mark. Set her free, now!" he demanded.

Malcolm smiled. All around there was confusion; gun shots; men shouting as others chased down the members of the Order, but nothing touched the tableau at the altar.

"If that is what you wish, Doctor, it shall be done." He stepped to the altar and held the long knife over me. He placed the point just above my heart and a tiny drop of blood appeared against my skin.

"No, wait. Stop that! Stop it!" Arthur was rushing forward.

"Stand away, Doctor. If you touch her, she will die. The only way the mark can be removed is if I cut it from her flesh myself."

"But..." said Arthur, his voice a horrified whisper, "...that will kill her."

"Yes," said Dennings calmly. "It will kill her. Either way, Doctor, she will die. At your hand, or mine, which is it to be?"

I could say nothing lying paralyzed on the stone.

"There is another way, of course, Doctor." Dennings was moving now, to release my wrists.

"What is that?"

"You may let me go. I will take her with me, keep her safe. As long as she lives there is always the hope you may find her again someday. It is a chance, the only one I will offer."

My arms were free now, but heavy, so heavy. Malcolm was at my feet, busy unfastening the chains. While he was distracted I concentrated all my focus on getting my left hand to move. I whispered an invocation to Morrigu to give me the strength I needed. I felt Her touch as I struggled to bring my hand to my chest, one millimeter at a time.

A Question of Balance

Finally, my fingers contacted the Key and I invoked its Power once again.

It wasn't much, but it got his attention. He moved to reach my hand, to knock it away from the talisman, but Arthur lunged, diving over the altar and throwing himself on Dennings.

I watched, my heart scarcely beating at all as the two men struggled. Arthur was attempting to pry the gleaming knife from the High Priest's hands as Dennings tried to plunge it into my husband's chest.

Arthur is a tall man but he was past forty and the punishment of the past few days would have left even a much younger man in a weakened state. I could see he was injured, frail and losing ground fast. The point of the blade was coming down in spite of his attempts to hold Dennings' arm away. Unbidden, strange words formed in my mind as my fingers clutched the warm metal at my breast. Dennings turned to stare at me, his mouth opening in mute surprise as I felt control return to my body. Slowly I sat up chanting words I knew no meaning for. Suddenly, Malcolm's attention was all on Arthur again. Without understanding why, I turned my wrist up sharply, screaming as Arthur seemed to just give up, all the fight gone out of him. As the blade came down, it somehow twisted between them. Malcolm impaled himself on his own knife with the force of his momentum.

For a split second in time they lay there, the two of them staring into each other's eyes. Then, Arthur placed both hands on the hilt and pushed with all his strength twisting the blade deep into Malcolm's chest. Dennings' mouth worked as if he had something to say, then blood poured out in a spray. His eyes glazed over and I knew he was dead. Arthur closed his eyes and taking a deep, shuddering breath, let the body fall on him, the blood of his enemy soaking his shirt. He had no more strength left.

I released my hold on the Key feeling the power drain away. I wanted to go to my husband but a deep weariness settled over me. I gave in and let my consciousness, free of Dennings now, slip away.

Chapter Twenty Five
Robin Hood

I could feel the effects of the amphetamine ebbing from my system in the plane on the way to Wales. My hands shook as I washed down two aspirin with tepid water. I felt old, ancient and decrepit as my joints and muscles screamed in protest at the least little movement. Well, they'd had a bit of a shock recently. Quite a large one actually, stretched beyond their endurance with forty kilos dragging them down, then jerked and snapped. It was a wonder that I could still move at all, that everything hadn't been dislocated, torn to shreds. I did ache, but I had to keep going. For a moment I toyed with the idea of taking another stimulant, but I discarded that as too risky. I was able to eat some cheese and biscuits and even have a bit of a kip before we landed.

Sir had arranged ahead to have the local police assist since just the three of us wouldn't make a very effective threat. The local sergeant had a good knowledge of the caves and knew exactly where the ritual would more than likely be taking place.

"We've had a share of complaints about the devil worshipers using the caverns for their blood rites, but the property's held by one of the aristocracy so we weren't able to get the warrant."

"Yes," I smiled tightly. "Well that's all arranged now. Are you certain you can get us into the right place without tipping them off?"

"Oh, I used to play among them caverns as a boy, Doctor. I can get us there and not a soul to know until it's too late. There's not a nook or tunnel what I don't know about."

"Good. I'll leave it to you then. If they hear us coming, I'm afraid the leaders will escape again, like they did at Wights Glen-Cove." What I was really afraid of, was that Tary would disappear with them.

I winced and groaned as I bent to get into the car. I felt every second of seven hundred and sixty years old. Fletch sat in back with me, and Max got in front with the sergeant. There was a wagon and two other police cars behind us as we headed into the dark night. It was clear and moonless and getting very close to midnight. I prayed, offering my words to whatever god might be listening, that we would be in time to spare my wife further harm. I knew she had already been abused, raped and marked by the monster, Malcolm Dennings. The thought of her still in his clutches, subject to his every twisted whim, made me ill.

Fletcher placed a gentle hand on my back. "Don't worry, Doctor. We'll get the lot of them this time."

"I know, Fletch. Thanks. I just hope we're in time to stop the ritual... that they haven't already.. that Tary's still okay, that's all." My voice caught in my throat, and Fletcher looked away tactfully.

Max turned around. "What are you going to tell her, Doc? About re-signing another two years of your life away to the Institute?"

For some reason that struck me as funny and I giggled, actually giggled a bit hysterically. "I haven't really thought about that Max. I haven't thought about telling her anything. I suppose I'll have to though. If I ever have the chance."

He winked at me. "Oh you'll have the chance, Doctor, and I bet it's not going to be easy. How much does she know, anyway?"

"How much? How much about what, Max?"

He just shook his head. "Never mind."

It seemed that we were moving too slowly. I kept looking at my watch as the hands moved closer and closer toward midnight. "Can't we go any faster?" I complained.

The sergeant looked at me through the driving mirror. "What, on these roads at night with no lights? Are you mad? We're already moving faster

A Question of Balance

than I'd like. Don't worry, it'll be a near thing, but I'll get us there before the stroke of twelve."

"Look, sergeant, I know you're doing your best. I'm sorry, it's just that they have someone I care very much for. I..I.." What I did, was something I'd never done before. I started to blub. It was humiliating, although I suppose under the circumstances it was understandable enough. Fletch put an arm around my shoulder as Maxwell explained to the sergeant.

"He's been a guest of that lot for the last five days. We only just cut him down this morning. Don't know what all he's been through yet, maybe never will, but one thing's for sure certain, he wasn't kindly treated. And, Sergeant Hastings, it's his wife they got. The Doc officially retired when he got married. These devils just couldn't leave him be, though. I'm sure you'll understand if he's seems a bit daft over the whole thing. It's got a bit more personal than our usual operation."

"I see," said Hastings. "I didn't realise." The car seemed to pick up a bit more speed.

Hastings pulled up in a glade and got out. We were well equipped with enough portable lighting equipment to shoot an epic film. That made me think of Tary as Maid Marian.

I certainly wasn't feeling very Robin Hoodish, just at the moment. Of course, it had always been the fat friar, Tuck, who was the brain of the outfit. Robin added the dash, of course, but it was the rotund, tonsured cleric who actually led the merry men of Sherwood. I thought it a very appropriate analogy, especially with John Little's heavy hand resting companionably on my shoulder, and Will Scarlet up front making my life sound like a Harlequin Romance.

We waited in the car while the police constables unloaded the equipment. Just before starting off I used the sergeant's radio and patched into Sir's office in London.

"We're ready to move in, Sir." I looked at my watch. It was eleven fifty. I found I was sweating in the chilly air.

"Good, Doctor. How are you holding up?"

"Well enough, Sir. Don't worry about me, Fletch and Max'll see I keep out of harm's way."

He grunted. "See you bring your wife, Terry.."

"Uh, that was Tary, Sir. With an A."

"Yes. Well I shall expect you both for tea the day after tomorrow."

"I'll try and fit you in Sir. I've got to go."

"Doctor..."

"Yes Sir?"

"Good luck, damn it. Out."

I replaced the microphone, saying softly, under my breath, "thank you Sir."

Sergeant Hastings did indeed know his way around the caverns and led us unerringly to the right one. It was just midnight. We burst through, turning the lights on them to cause confusion. It did that, but it also had the effect of blinding me as well. I rushed past, ignoring Maxwell's cries for me to wait, never even stopping to consider for one moment that I was unarmed. It didn't matter, nothing mattered except that Tary was in there. I had to get to her.

People were shouting, running in every direction. I stood in the centre of it all, calling her name, searching each hooded face. When my eyes grew accustomed to the bright lights, I spied the altar stone. There was Tary with an unspeakable abomination leaning over her. I shouted and the horror lifted his head and removed the mask. It was Dennings. I could see what it was I had interrupted and I went a little mad. Without thinking of anything I rushed the altar. I have no idea what I was thought I was going to do alone and unarmed. I only knew I had to get him away from her. Then, he told me to stop and I did. He reminded me that he held Tary completely under his control. I remembered.

She looked so small, so fragile lying naked and helpless, a tiny crimson stain where his knife had broken the skin just above her left breast. There was another girl, very young, chained behind her, going into shock. Suddenly Dennings was releasing my wife. He was going to take her away again, away where I might never find her. I knew I couldn't touch Tarish, not so long as he lived. That limited my options. Somehow I would have to kill Malcolm Dennings. Foolishly I rushed him.

I had come to the end of my physical reserves, and he was fresh. As I struggled to hold his knife hand away, I felt my strength ebbing and knew with a certainty that it was me who was about to die. "Tary, I love you," I whispered as the curved blade plunged toward my heart. Then, something happened which I couldn't explain. In the last seconds he must have grown careless, tasting his victory prematurely. Just when I'd thought I could taste my own death his attention slipped. In that instant, my wrist turned sharply, almost as though it had a life of its own. It should never have worked, my balance was all wrong and there was no power in my grip, but somehow it did and he took the blade. I used the last of my flagging strength to finish him off, then collapsed under the weight his body. It was over, Malcolm Dennings was dead and Tary would be free of him.

It was Max who found me, drenched to the skin in blood. He dragged Dennings off and screamed for Fletcher.

"Here! Hey, over here! It's the Doc and I think he's got himself killed this time!"

I forced my eyes opened. "Not just yet, Will. But for the record, where were you and Little John when I needed you, huh?"

Max grinned down at me. "Not killed just mad, then. What, you get hit on the head or something?" He was examining me for injuries. "We coulda got him you know, Dennings. If you hadn't put yourself right in the line of fire we coulda got him."

"I know, Max, I don't know what I was thinking... but when I saw Tary...never mind. Don't worry, it's not my blood." I managed to sit up. "Where is she?" then I saw her. Someone had covered her with a blanket and folded something to put under her head like a pillow. I tried to stand, but Max held me down.

"You stay put, Doc. She's all right, I think. Just fainted. They didn't ... I mean, what they were going to do, they didn't. We got here in time for that, at least."

I nodded gratefully. "Let me go to her, Max. Help me, will you?"

Tary was starting to come around.

Max looked, and relented. "Okay, but now you lean on me. You look like you ought to be dead yourself."

I half grinned, "It's just all the blood." Still, I was grateful to have a good strong arm supporting me.

She was pale as death under a thick coat of make-up I knew she would never have approved of. I touched her cheek lightly but she flinched away from me. I wondered what horrors Dennings had put her through.

"Tary, it's me, Robin Hood come to save the fair Maid Marion."

She moaned a little putting up her hand. Then her eyes opened and she stared at me, not speaking.

"Tarish, are you.. I mean, I love you, will you marry me?" I don't know why I said it. It was just the first thing that popped into my mind! It seemed to work though. Her lips moved a little and I leaned over close to hear what she whispered.

"You were right," her voice was tiny, barely even a whisper.

"I was?" I said.

"You do make a lousy Errol Flynn." She smiled at me and I kissed her.

By the time Fletcher came to report, she was sitting up, drinking tea from a flask thoughtfully provided by Sergeant Hastings.

"Looks like we got the lot of them. The big guys any way. Dr. Mayfair won't be practising outside of Dartmoor Prison, I dare say. Dennings is dead, right enough." He looked at me. "I got a spare shirt in the bag. Why don't you change."

I nodded. "In a minute, thanks. What about the Book? Have you found it yet?"

A Question of Balance

He shook his head. "Not yet, but we will. Only a couple of them got away. It's here somewhere, don't you worry."

Tary turned huge eyes on me, "Oh god, Arthur, what if.."

I shushed her with a kiss. Max threw me his shirt and I changed.

"You never answered my question you know." I said, dropping the blood soaked rag on the floor.

"What was the question?" she said, her eyes dark blue, almost stormy.

"Will you marry me?"

She wrinkled her nose. "What! You mean again? Doctor, you are pushing your luck!"

I sighed. "Sir David expects us for tea, day after tomorrow."

Smiling, she put her head in my lap. "We'll see," then she was asleep. I fastened the chain with her pentacle around her neck as she slept and wrapped the blanket closer around her.

When they were finished in the cavern, they started on the house. Max came to where we sat.

"We don't need the two of you, why don't you go. Fletch can take you to the Inn for the night. Tomorrow, we'll head back to London. Do you think she needs a hospital?"

I shook my head. "I can look after her, thanks, if Fletch will help me get her to bed. Her back's pretty marked up. It'll be painful, but it's not serious."

She stirred. "Arthur? Did they find the Book yet?"

Maxwell shook his head.

"Not yet, but they will. Come on, Fletcher's going to take us to the Inn in the Village. I brought some of your things. How does a nice hot bath sound."

She didn't say anything, but I could feel a shudder go through her whole body. I squeezed her gently wondering what horrors Dennings had subjected her to. "I'll tell you what, forget the bath, let's just get you to bed."

She nodded.

The local Inn had two rooms en suite, one with a tub and one with a shower. We took the one with the shower. I didn't want Tary to put any weight on her leg, so Fletch carried her. I managed her awkwardly in the shower, but it was a good thing Fletcher hung around. He really did have to help me put her to bed. I'd dressed her in a shirt of mine which was fine for a night-shirt, and I'd given her a sedative.

"Come on Fletch, easy there. Put her on her stomach."

Gently, we eased her into the bed and I drew the blankets over her. "Thanks. I'll sit with her. Why don't you go back and give them a hand. Call me if they turn up any sign of the Book, will you?"

"Right, Doc. You sure you'll be okay. You're not looking so good yourself."

"I'll be fine so long as you find that Book."

He left quietly.

I dozed off and on, holding her, comforting her as she dreamed, drifting, it seemed, from one nightmare to the next. This time, they would be gone when she woke up. I halfway wanted to close my eyes and enter her dream, like I used to do, but thought better of it. When she was ready, she would talk about it. Until then, all I could do was hold her.

In the morning, she opened one blue eye and stared at me. "It's true? You're really here? I'm really here?"

I smiled, tousling her hair. "Yes, Tarish. We're really here."

"Dennings?"

"He's dead. I'm sorry, I had to kill him. There wasn't any other way."

She nodded, wincing as she turned over onto her back.

"Careful there, Tary. You don't want to ruin all my handiwork, do you?"

"What handiwork? You mean you actually treated me? You went and played doctor while I was helpless?"

I frowned. "What do you mean played doctor. I am a doctor! I don't have to play at it."

A Question of Balance

"You're not a real doctor, Doctor. You never qualified to practice." Her eyes were bright, her smile mocking.

"What do you mean, not qualified, eh? Of course I qualified. I qualified at London University in forensic anthropology so don't tell me I'm not qualified!" I pretended to pout.

"Yeah, I take that back. With credentials like that you're qualified to treat anyone who's been dead five hundred years or more!" Her smile had turned into an out and out grin.

"Well, you may have a point," I huffed. "From the look of you this morning, you can't have been dead more than a month or two, at the very most."

She got up and hobbled to the mirror, grimacing at her reflection. "Yuck, you're right." Then her eyes filled as she noticed the pentacle. "Arthur, you found it."

"Yes." I smiled.

Tary hugged me for a long time, letting the tears spill over. At last she looked at me and asked. "You said you brought some of my stuff, or was that a dream?"

"No dream. I packed you a small bag."

"Did you happen to include my make-up kit? Shampoo? Deodorant?"

I nodded and pointed. "I believe I got all the essentials, yes. You can check it out though and make sure there's nothing I missed. If there is, I'll just pop 'round to the village shop and buy it for you, how's that?"

With one more look at me, she vanished into the bathroom. I could hear the sound of water running for a long time. Finally, she emerged, looking much better.

"Your turn!"

I found it quite difficult, however, to get off the bed. "How's your leg?" I asked, struggling to sit.

"Not too bad. I put the soft brace on. I think I can manage with a stick."

"Come here, let me have a look." She did, and I felt along the ankle. Seemed solid enough, nothing broken at any rate.

"You're probably right. I left your walking stick in the car. They should be calling any moment now, and I'll have Fletcher or Maxwell bring it up."

Her eyes suddenly brimmed over again. "You found my stick, Arthur? My stick?"

I smiled as she sat, putting her head on my chest. "Yes, your stick, Tary. And all your other things as well. Even that silly yo-yo I sent you for Christmas. They were at Mayfair's clinic."

"I thought they were all lost. Lost forever," she murmured softly.

"I thought you were. I'm very glad we were both wrong."

Eventually, I did manage to get myself into the shower. I took a good long one, letting the hot water loosen the aches in my joints and muscles. When I finally emerged, towel wrapped around my waist, Max was sitting with Tary.

"Max! What's the word, eh? How many of them did we get?"

"Almost all of them, Doctor. But I have some bad news. The Book is missing."

"What!" I sank down on the edge of the bed.

"There's more. London contacted us this morning. The Kelly woman's gone too."

That explained Tary's pallor.

"Arthur, Marge Kelly's gone and the Book is gone! What are we going to do?"

I made myself take a deep breath, so I could speak calmly and rationally. "Do? Why nothing, Tary. You're out of it now. We're going to go down to breakfast, then hire a car to take us back to London. Tomorrow we're having tea with Sir David, and the day after that, you're flying home!"

"But the Book! If Marge has it she'll..."

"There's no reason to believe she has it, or even knows it's still out there. Don't worry, Tary. Marge Kelly, will have all she can do to get as far away from

England as she can. I'm afraid I rather frightened her last time we met."

She smiled tentatively and sighed. "I suppose you're right. We are out of it now. Let Sir David and the rest of the Merry Men take it from here, right?"

I winked at her, and shook my head a little to warn Max not to say anything. "That's right. Now, just let me get some trousers on, and we'll go eat."

Max followed me into the bathroom.

"I thought you were going to tell her."

"I am, Max. I am. Soon. Right now, we both need some time to adjust. Surely Sir will give me that much."

He sighed. "Be honest with her you fool. She's far better than you deserve."

"I know it, Max. I know it. I will, I promise. Just not right now."

When Tary and I were alone, I sat her down on the bed. "You know, there's something I want to talk to you about."

"Me first, Arthur."

I smiled, relieved that I was getting even a small reprieve. "All right then, ladies first."

She took a deep breath. "While I was... I mean, when Dennings had me all that time, I realised something. There is so much suffering, so many people who don't know, or who don't understand what life is really supposed to be. I know that things are getting better, but sometimes, even I have trouble seeing it."

"Tary, I.."

She put a small hand on my arm. "No, let me finish. I know there's not that much a single person can do to change things really. Even the two of us together, but maybe, if we were to approach Sir David the right way..."

I couldn't help myself. I reached over and, muscles protesting, took her into my arms.

"I think you're wonderful, you know," I gasped.

She smiled, a little confused.

"Let me explain..." I began.

Chapter Twenty Six
Tea

Helen, the new assistant, showed us into Sir David's office. My head was still reeling with what Arthur had told me about the Institute. So, my first impression hadn't been so far off after all. They weren't enlisting entire covens, though, just the occasional psychic, the odd witch, and a few dedicated scientists backed up by the likes of Maxwell and Fletcher. Arthur was smiling as he explained, still trying to make me grasp the underlying principle and scope of the operation.

"You see Tary, we understand, you and I that is, and a few other individuals, that what you call magic can be and is in fact a very powerful weapon. It's especially dangerous when you consider the inherent power of ancient symbols such as the talismans you hold. Originally the Institute was founded during the second World War to investigate the effectiveness of occult practices being used by the Third Reich. Hitler was himself a practitioner of the black arts and invested vast amounts of money and manpower in exploring and refining such exercises for practical applications."

"You mean he used magic during the War?" I shook my head.

Sir David took up the story. "Yes indeed; but more than that, the investigations initiated on behest of the British Government at the time showed that he was using it with an astonishingly high degree of success. His approach which combined science with magic, was chillingly effective."

I was stunned. Vaguely, I recalled reading somewhere that Hitler had used astrologers and the prophesies of Nostradamus in his propaganda, but I never realized just how far reaching his actions had been. Arthur patted my hand.

"I am a scientist, Tary. My job is to try and find irrefutable substantiation that magic can and does work. If I can qualify and quantify it, devise repeatable experiments, authenticate results, we should be able to understand why it works. If we can do that, we can use it more effectively, perhaps evolve a whole new technology."

I shook my head, bemused. "But Arthur, it doesn't work like that. Magic isn't something you can mix up in a test tube. Magic is an inexplicable part of the earth synergy; of nature itself."

"Yes, it is unexplained now, but nothing is inexplicable, Tary. In the future it may just well become a bonafide physical science. Remember, it was alchemy that laid the groundwork for modern chemistry. And without the study of astrology, we might never have developed astronomy. Since Einstein postulated his theories, quantum physics and mechanics have begun to create an overlap between science and what up until now had been considered fantasy." He poured me a cup of tea.

"The problem is, that we haven't been able to come up with that proof. We need that one bit of hard evidence that the paranormal isn't 'para' at all, but perfectly normal within a definition of the Universe that we simply have yet to fully comprehend. We seem to always come to a stumbling block. Then of course, there's continually something cropping up to take me away from the research end and land me smack in the middle of one of the field operations."

Sir David snorted, it might have been a chuckle, and helped himself to another slice of treacle bread, smeared liberally with clotted cream. "Yes. That is certainly true."

"So, Sir, what exactly happened with Marge Kelly?" I asked, trying to turn the conversation around to something I could understand. "Surely you were prepared for her attempted escape?"

A QUESTION OF BALANCE

The huge man merely lifted his shoulders. "I don't know, but be assured Mrs. Pendargroom, I will find out." He changed the subject. "That girl, the one with you in the caverns, has been returned to her family. She'd been listed as missing, probably a runaway for about a month now. We might never know how she became involved with Mayfair. With the proper care, they expect her to be fine. I anticipate she will be well enough to give testimony when the time comes."

"Will he be brought to trial?" I asked.

"Oh yes. He should be in the dock by late October. That will be sufficient time to prepare all the evidence." Sir sighed. "We've taken special measures to see that he doesn't escape the way Miss Kelly did."

I wondered what kind of measures you could take against an adept like him, but I trusted that they knew what they were doing.

"Just as well about the other one, Dennings. After evidence given by the local police sergeant, a Sergeant Hastings it says in my report, the Coroner ruled that he either fell on his knife by misadventure, or deliberately committed suicide rather than be exposed when the rite was interrupted by the authorities." He looked at Arthur, his eyebrows raised quizzically.

The Doctor cleared his throat. "Uh, yes Sir. Well, it was something like that, anyway. I know how you dislike having one of us involved locally." He smiled wanly and a squeezed my hand. "Much neater this way, don't you think?"

"Hurrumph! I suppose you had no options?" he questioned gruffly.

"No, Sir. None." His voice was a whisper and I knew how effected he was.

"So what now, Sir David? What would happen if I just destroyed the ring and the key? Wouldn't that make the Book less dangerous?" I fingered the key hanging from its chain.

"The truth is, Tary, that we just don't know what would happen." Arthur replied thoughtfully. "We do know the Grimoir is an ancient text. It has been rebound any number of times over the centuries, but the pages themselves are the originals, trimmed down from papyrus scrolls. We also know that the Key and the Crown are more recent additions to the equation in just the last few centuries. My research leads me to think that a 13th century alchemist by the name of René Framontage created the Key and the Crown for the express purpose of containing the magic. You see I believe that in a way the Book Itself is sentient. If you were to destroy the talismans it might release something far worse than what we are dealing with already; setting off a sort of Pandora effect. I am very much afraid Tary, that it is the Book which must be destroyed."

I shuddered. "Pandora effect? So you're telling me that I just go off on my merry way tomorrow, back to New Jersey and pick up where I left off?"

"Yes, that is exactly what you are to do," said Sir. "The Doctor has been reinstated, although for all outward appearances he will remain a simple Professor of Anthropology at Leeds. He will be given ample opportunity to travel in your direction." He was frowning. "As for your own involvement with the Institute..."

"Sir..." said Arthur, his voice very low.

"Yes, yes. What I mean to say is that you have no official standing at all with either the Institute or the British Government, Mrs. Pendargroom. As a foreign national you could never be cleared..."

"But Sir, that doesn't make any sense and you know it!" I interrupted.

Arthur laid a hand on my arm. "What he's trying to say, Tary, and making a mess of it, is that unofficially you will be called upon to help out occasionally. If you don't mind, that is? Tary, it was the only way I could get him to guarantee your protection. You will need it you know, at least until I can find and destroy the Book. Rolly will look after you when I'm not there."

"You can't do it without me, Arthur," I protested. "I'm the only one who can..."

A Question of Balance

"Well, we don't even know where to begin at this point though, do we?" He sounded so weary. "And I don't know about you, but I definitely need a break. Besides, you have Jason to think about. He may be almost a grown man, but there are still some things only a mother can do." He smiled sadly. "For the time being, you've got to go home and I've got to stay here."

I knew he was right.

We spent our last night in London at a very posh hotel in the West End, at the expense of the Institute. I had some last minute shopping to do, then we retired early. Neither of us was in great shape physically, but somehow we managed.

In the morning we went by limousine to Victoria Station.

"Are you sure you don't want me to come to the airport with you?" He was supervising the porter loading my bags into the first class compartment of the Gatwick Express.

"Positive. I always wanted to say good-bye on the platform at Victoria Station. Besides, you have a train to catch back to Yorkshire."

The train guard came down the platform and Arthur gave him the difference for my upgraded travel pass.

"Well, at least I can see you off in some style!" he said, adjusting his sling and snaking his good arm around me awkwardly. I winced a little as his hand brushed a tender spot on my back.

"Oh, sorry," he said.

I giggled. "What a team, eh? Watch out Nick and Nora Charles!" The train whistle blew mournfully; it was time to leave. I boarded and sat staring out the window. He stood alone on the platform looking wistful as I cried daintily into my hanky. I put up one hand to touch his through the window glass. It was a great scene, just like in the movies.

The adventure continues in *A Matter of Perspective: Book Two of The Doctor and the Witch*. For a preview of the next gripping installment in Trish Reynold's occult trilogy, read on...

We were standing on the pavement in front of the most famous courthouse in the world. Arthur took my hand in his and squeezed.
"You okay?"
My smile was forced, but I managed to nod.
"Yup."
As we moved toward the stair, my eyes fell on the glaring tabloid headline displayed in the newsagent's stand: "Old Nick at the Old Bailey! Did the Devil Make Him Do It?"
I stopped, staring at the words.
"Tary, what's wrong?" Then his gaze followed mine.
"Never mind that. Come on!" He tugged on my arm and pulled me up the steps and through the ancient portals.
Seated on the hard wooden bench at the rear of the gallery my head felt like it would burst. A combination of jet lag and nerves, I told myself, as I fumbled in my bag for the Advil. I took two dry and felt them stick in my throat. I whispered to Arthur.
"Please, can you find me a glass of water?"

His grey eyes filled with concern. "What's the matter?"

I smiled. "I tried to swallow some Advil and they're stuck in my throat" I smiled ruefully.

He gave me a pat on the hand and got up to find me some water.

He'd just walked out, when the proceedings began. The room was huge for a courtroom and I had elected to sit at the very back of the observation gallery, trying to remain as inconspicuous as possible. Way up at the front and below me, in the section where the judge and the judiciary would sit, the main players were just making their entrance. Robed barristers in their powdered white wigs entered and settled at their places. I suppressed a giggle as I craned my neck, looking for Rumpole. I noticed that Sir David was nowhere to be seen.

Any feeling of levity died as the man I'd come to see stand in the dock was brought in. Not surprisingly, Dr. Quentin Mayfair was impeccably dressed and seemed not one bit ruffled. I hadn't realised it, but somewhere along the line I'd gotten to my feet. I saw the grey-haired head turn slowly toward me. Impossibly, his dark eyes met mine crossing the distance between us as if he knew exactly where I would be, as if I'd been expected. I was transfixed by those eyes as he held me firmly in his gaze. It was inconceivable to look away. The moment seemed to stretch on into infinity as I struggled to move my hand. If I could just reach the brass key around my neck, I somehow knew that it would free me. I couldn't move; my own body refused to obey my mental commands. There was no time except right that second, where I was caught like a bug in amber.

Arthur had returned and was shaking me, though I was barely cognisant of anything but those dark, dead eyes. Vaguely some small part of my mind could hear his increasingly frantic whispers, but I was helpless to do anything but stare.

"Tary! Tary, he's nothing, do you hear? Nothing. Tary look at me. Listen to my voice."

A small, cruel smile touched Mayfair's lips and he lifted his eyes briefly to glance at Arthur, releasing me from his thrall. Then, he turned away and moved to take his appointed place as the accused.

If it hadn't been for my husband's strong arm holding me up, I would have fallen. I felt dizzy, nauseous as if I was becoming unravelled. As my knees buckled, Arthur eased me down into my seat. He brought the cone shaped paper cup to my lips and I sucked down the water gratefully.

"Easy, Tarish." His face was a mask of concern, "Better?"

I nodded. "I... I'm sorry. I don't know what it was. Is it warm in here?" I felt hot and faint.

"Come on, we're leaving." He pulled me gently to my feet, supporting me around the waist as he guided me to the door.

I paused for a moment to glance back. Mayfair was watching us through hooded eyes. Arthur turned me away and we were through the door.

In the corridor, the air seemed cooler, not so close and stifling. The Doctor led me to a bench and asked a guard to fetch some more water. I was trembling all over and felt an anxiety attack coming on.

"Medication, in my bag."

Arthur rummaged through, cursing under his breath. "I don't see how you find anything with all this junk."

"Here." I took the purse and stuck my hand in, feeling my fingers close around the familiar prescription bottle. I shook out a tablet.

The guard came back with my water and I swallowed the tranquiliser. Arthur dipped a corner of his handkerchief into the cup and dabbed at my forehead. My breath was coming easier and I was able to get his face into focus and smile wanly.

"I could do with a cup of tea, I think."

He grinned, relief standing in his sombre eyes like a beacon. "Yeah, me too. Can you stand?"

I nodded and stood.

By the time we reached the outside air, I felt much better, nearly normal again, and very foolish. I noticed a small knot of people milling about near the entrance.

"Press," stated Arthur, steering me carefully away while he kept his face averted, collar up.

Of course, I realised with a start, they might recognise him and put two and two together. A tiny spark of panic began in my stomach. I definitely wasn't up to anything like dealing with the press.

"Just walk on normally. They're not expecting anything this early on. We can just slip by them." He propelled me forward purposefully and we made it to the pavement without incident.

There was a nice tea-room nearby. He ordered tea for both of us, with some eggs and bacon over my protest of not being hungry.

"You may not feel hungry, but you really need something in your stomach, Tary. If nothing else, it will make me feel better if you eat, okay? Doctor's orders."

I agreed reluctantly, afraid that anything I put into my stomach was wont to come right back up. He turned out to be right, however, and I started feeling better for having eaten.

"Now, what happened in there? I don't mind telling you, when I came back and saw you like that... you scared half the life out of me, Tary"

I saw love and fear. in his eyes as I told him. "I'm not really sure, Arthur. Mayfair came in and... he looked right at me. He knew I was there... he knew exactly where I was sitting! It wasn't as if he had to look around, his eyes went directly to mine." I shuddered.

"There was nothing I could do. I couldn't blink or look away; it was as if I was paralysed. If you hadn't come..."

"If I hadn't come he would have had to release you anyway, Tarish. You're safe, he can't get to you."

"Am I?" I wondered quietly, almost to myself.

"I wouldn't have brought you otherwise." He looked at his watch. "I'll call Sir and cancel our meeting for this afternoon. We can…"

"No, don't do that. I'll be fine. You said yourself there's no way he can get to me, right?" I forced a tiny laugh. "Besides, I can do with a lie down. It was probably mostly my imagination anyway, you know what that's like." I grinned up at him. "Imagination and jet lag, mixed well with a generous dose of nerves; a lethal combination in my case."

He didn't return my grin, but sat looking thoughtful.

"As well it might have been, Tary. As well it might have been."

We finished up our second breakfast and headed for the flat.

Look for *A Matter of Perspective: Book Two of The Doctor and the Witch,* coming soon from Pagan World Press.